Also by Rebecca Bradley

LADY IN GIL

SCION'S LADY

Rebecca Bradley

ACE BOOKS, NEW YORK

SCION'S LADY

An Ace Book / published by arrangement with
Orion Publishing Group, Ltd.

PRINTING HISTORY
Victor Gollancz hardcover edition / 1997
Vista mass-market edition / 1998
Ace mass-market edition / December 2000

Check out the ACE Science Fiction & Fantasy newsletter
and much more on the Internet at Club PPI!

ISBN: 0-441-00788-0

ACE®
Ace Books are published by The Berkley Publishing Group,
a division of Penguin Putnam Inc.,
375 Hudson Street, New York, New York 10014.
ACE and the "A" design are trademarks
belonging to Penguin Putnam Inc.

PRINTED IN THE UNITED STATES OF AMERICA

10 9 8 7 6 5 4 3 2 1

1

THE MARKETPLACE WAS in ruins; lush green things pushed up through rifts in the tumbledown stalls, mantled the wormy wood, sprang thick and gross and unhealthy from the poisoned mud. The Lady stepped down from the pedestal in Oballef's Fountain, wiping the paint from her face with the back of her marble hand. She glanced at me incuriously and glided away.

Above me, the grid trembled. I looked up and saw eyes, one at each nexus, silver pupils irised with black iron—the spikes, foreshortened, just as they always looked. They watched me as I strained against the fetters and the band of leather around my chest. From somewhere, a hiss; the grid shook itself purposefully and began to slide downwards in its oiled grooves, its progress measured in thickness of a hair, the points glittering, the squares of sky beginning to swell.

Calla sat down beside me on the platform, holding the fairheaded boy in her lap. Her face overhung mine. "What did you expect, Tig?" she asked. "Gratitude?"

"Of course not."

"Power? Fame?"

"You know me better than that."

"Love?"

"Never again. Not since you died."

She raised her eyebrows. "What, then?"

While I thought about it, I looked beyond her at the points of the Pleasure. The spikes were perceptibly larger. Behind the bars of the grid, the sky was shot with fire. Seawater dripped from Calla's hair and rolled down my face like tears.

"I expected this, I suppose."

But Calla and the dreamchild always faded away at this point; and next, if the dream were allowed to go on, there would come the thunder, the roar of an almighty wave, the wails of the damned; and then the green foam-edged slab of water would be poised a thousand feet above me, and the wails would turn to screams, and the green slab would start to fall out of the sky, slowly at first, as slowly as the grid of the Pleasure, spiked with the whitened bones of ships, crushing the towers, drowning the screams—I knew it all by heart. I forced my eyes open and wiped the tears off my face with the corner of the blanket. After a moment, I swung my feet off the pallet.

Faintly, from the city far below my window, I heard early morning sounds: unoiled wagons creaking to market, criers of fresh milk and cooked gruel, the plaints of small armies of dogs and roosters. There was no sound from the other cubicles except for Angel's deep, regular snore. The dream's aftertaste began to fade. Still wiping my eyes, I stumbled to the writing room and set to work.

This was the pattern of my mornings for six years—the first six years after Gil was liberated, the first years after the Lady in Gil and I, between us, sank the continent of Sher into the ocean and upset the delicate balance of the world. It was part of the pattern I expected to follow for all the remaining mornings and days and nights and years of my life: pottering about in the archives until death claimed me, absorbed in my work, celibate, happy in my small way, disturbed only by my dreams. I should have known better.

The archives were tucked away in a corner of the Temple Palace, reached from the main royal quarters via a long corridor, a steep staircase and an anteroom choked with old packing crates and broken furniture. Apart from the chambers we had cleared and stocked with bookshelves and scroll-racks and writing tables, the rooms on that level were either empty or still littered with rubbish left over from the Sherkin occupation. Shree and Angel and I slept, along with our not very committed pupils, in a large, low-ceilinged room which the Sherank had cut into cubicles for the governor's personal bodyguard decades ago. We were grubby, ink-stained, probably malnourished, often smelly and fishbelly pale from too little sun, and it was rare that anybody else came near us. It was lovely.

That morning, the morning of the night on which my life changed again, I was reviewing a scroll that had arrived on the latest ship from Sathelforn. It had been commissioned and funded by the new Compact of Nations, and represented a full year's labour by the Lucian Clerisy, a collective of venerable scholars. The margins were expensively illustrated, the calligraphy incomparable, the paper thick and smooth as cream; the text, on the other hand, was unrelieved shull droppings. When Angel and Shree joined me in the writing room, I was gloomily calculating how many *real* books we could have acquired for the same outlay of cash.

Shree, still picking his teeth from breakfast, pulled the scroll towards him and read a few lines. After six years of warming a chair in the archives, he still looked and moved like a fighting man, but he could translate from the Lucian almost as fast as I could. He chortled and then laughed out loud and pushed the scroll back at me.

"I don't see the humour in this, Shree," I said crossly. "This compilation of lies cost us nearly a quarter of the year's allowance."

"It's not lies, Tig," he chuckled, "it's politics. Diplomacy. Fascinating. Listen to this preface, Angel." He picked up the scroll again, and started to translate out loud. *"But, lo, in the seventy-third year of the Sherkin Empire, the gods of all nations made a compact among themselves to destroy the pride and wickedness that was Sher, and sent a great wave that swallowed up Sher and the great cities of Sher, even Iklankish the Capital in the west and Krin in the north and Kishti in the south, and all the peoples that were in Sher, and sank them beneath the sea, destroying Sher by water as in ancient times they destroyed Fathan by fire. And everywhere, in all the nations and the islands, the peoples rose up and threw off the evil yoke, and slaughtered the Sherank in their strongholds, and scuttled their ships, and burned their engines of war, and swept all their foulness from the surface of the earth, for the Sherank were accursed, and their works were accursed. And so, by the grace of the gods of all nations, the new age of peace and plenty began."*

"Propaganda," I muttered. "Expensive propaganda."

"Oh, Tig, stop moaning about your precious budget. You're just upset because you and the Lady aren't mentioned."

I sniffed. "Not true. I'm happy to let the gods of all nations, and anybody else, take the credit for destroying Sher. But I strongly object to the other nonsense."

"Slaughtering the garrisons? Destroying the works of the accursed Sherank? Beginning a new age of peace and plenty?" Shree grinned.

I could not share his amusement. It was true that the surviving Sherkin garrisons had been given a rough time at first, but in the end there had been more deals struck than death-blows; many a kinglet owed his continued health to a regiment or two of well-paid Sherkin mercenaries. And far from destroying any traces of the accursed Sherank, the peoples of all the nations etc. had been more apt to salvage what materiel the bastards left behind, to use against each other. Naturally, the eminent Lucian scholars found it impolitic to mention any of this.

Shree was still chuckling over the scroll, pointing out the richer falsities to Angel with his inkstained forefinger. Angel was shaking his grizzled head; I thought maybe there was distress behind the hair on his face, but it was not easy to tell. "Shut up for a minute, will you, Shree?" I said. "Angel, what are you thinking?"

He took the scroll out of Shree's hands, treating it with all the deference that written matter always called out in him, but none of the usual affection. "Peace and plenty?" he said, as one might quote a mention of the sun rising in the west. "Do they believe that?"

"Of course they don't." Shree patted Angel's shoulder.

"Then why do they write it?"

Shree sighed. "It's politics, Angel, I'll explain it to you."

He tried. Angel knew all about cruelty, betrayal, torture, destruction and rape from a lifetime of watching the Sherank through vents in the castle walls, but he still found diplomacy a puzzle. While Shree tried to untangle the issues for him, I shut my ears and wandered to the window. The city lay spread out below me.

The years of reconstruction had made little difference that was visible from that angle. Foul tracts of hovels and smoking tips still sprawled along the old corniche and down to the outskirts of the city, although new villas in fastidiously walled gardens rose here and there. I could see that Lissula's grand new brothel, in a prime location near the harbour, was already barnacled with lean-tos. The Sherkin revetments, built of pillaged stones, had themselves been pulled apart for building material, leaving the city crossed with pale linear scars like the marks of an old beating.

I leaned out, suddenly interested. A massive wind-galley was just gliding into sight around the edge of the harbour, ablaze with yellow and crimson pennons that fluttered on every spar and line from bow to stern. As I watched, she slid through the gap in the breakwater and rolled majestically towards one of the quays. She dwarfed everything else in the harbour. I broke into Shree's seminar to call the others to the window.

"Miisheli colours, aren't they?" asked Shree after a few moments. He sounded surprised. "Why is Gil so honoured, a miserable little backwater like this?"

"Who knows?" A flash of colour by the harbour caught my eye. Even while the ship was mooring, a phalanx of tiny green figures was moving on to the quay, headed and footed by ranks of green banners. The Flamens, out in force, and so early in the day; only an important visitor would get them from their soft beds at this hour.

I turned to the others. "Have you heard anything about this?"

"Not a whisper." Shree shrugged. Angel looked blank. "What on earth would they want in Gil?"

"It's more likely the Primate wants something from them," said Shree. "I'll bet he spent the last week coaching Arkolef in how to grovel with the dignity befitting a Priest-King. That's another of the arts of diplomacy, Angel."

The gangplank was already being lowered from the Miisheli ship. Sunlight flashed on a forest of raised trumpets, but the fanfare was too distant to carry. "Don't be cruel about my brother," I said absently, intent on the scene at the harbour. "He can't help being stupid. And if the Primate is getting Gil some help from Miishel, then I wish him well for a change."

"You wish him well? That's a terrible precedent, Tig."

"Oh, perhaps. But he seems to be leaving me out of it this time."

"I'm not surprised, after the fiasco you made when the Bashee of Plav was here." Shree glanced at me, grinning. I had to grin back.

"It was an accident, Shree. That ridiculous ritual robe—"

"—and the time you took a book to the Tatakil envoy's feast—"

"I knew there'd be speeches."

"—not to mention the time you dropped a rock sample on your uncle the High Prince of Sathelforn's toe—"

"My uncle didn't mind. He thought it was funny."

"The Primate was furious."

"I remember." We chuckled together, even Angel. "Maybe he's realized at last that I'm unfitted for the duties of a prince. I hope so—there's more than enough to do in the archives. Which reminds me, Shree, we'll be going out tonight."

Shree's grin disappeared. He sighed. "Not another cult?"

"Another cult." I went to the table, dug around in the papers for my notebook.

"Who told you about it? That scruffy-looking scragger who came to see you in the middle of the night?"

"That's the one."

"I didn't like the looks of him, Tig."

"He's a good informant," I said, frowning, shuffling the papers aside. At last I unearthed my notebook and found the entry. "This one will be Cult Number Forty-three, the Fiery Hand. Founded about ten days ago, meets nightly on the Thread-of-Gold."

"Is it urgent?"

"Could be. My informant says it could fold at any moment."

"Oh, all right." Shree turned from the window with resignation and trudged over to his worktable. Then the pupils trooped into the room and my last normal day in the archives started in earnest.

2

"TOO MANY BLOODY temples in this town. Where's the bloody taverns?"

The man from Tata pushed past me out of the portal of the House of the Fiery Hand. It was true the name was deceptive, also true that Gil was oversupplied with dubious places of worship, but we weren't short of taverns either. I pointed the Tatakil further down Thread-of-Gold Street to the House of the Green Door, which really was a tavern. Still muttering, he wove away. The acolyte at the door, as shabby as the temple he guarded, watched reprovingly.

"We offered him deliverance from the wrath to come," he murmured, shaking his head.

"I think he wanted a drink." I motioned to Shree. We each placed a token in the acolyte's outstretched palm and bowed our way past him.

The portal led into a narrow, grimy corridor lit by one feeble torch. At the end was a plain door, beyond which a few chanting voices seemed to be searching for the same tune. The air was redolent of decaying vegetation: old cabbages, onions, pikcherries well past their prime, the too-sweet tang of citrus fuzzed with mould. Shree wrinkled his nose as we stumbled along on the warped floorboards. "Has your brother passed a law," he complained, "that says these places have to smell bad?"

"It is a consistent feature," I admitted. I took a deep breath, knowing the air would be worse inside the sanctuary, and pushed the door open.

The service was in progress. The noise was coming from four straggly priests in white caftans, who were dancing as they sang—that is, they were shuffling their feet in a slightly embarrassed fashion and waving their hands about in time to the chanting. Since they were all wearing oversized wooden gloves, flat-palmed, crudely carved and badly gilded, the effect was reminiscent of the Fan Dance then popular in the whorehouses.

We took our places in a halfmoon of devotees squatting on the floor. Discreetly, I pulled out my notebook and began to jot things down. My part was to describe the physical details of each gimcrack temple, the regalia and the celebrants, while Shree kept track of the ritual, the chants and the high points of the sermon. This self-inflicted study threatened to be endless, given the renewable supply of subjects; for whenever one ephemeral little faith was suppressed by the Flamens or died a natural death, two or three others sprouted in its place.

Recording them was a thankless task—nobody else was interested, the Flamens actually disapproved, and the most we could hope for in the end was a series of volumes that nobody would want to read, on a phase of Gillish history that everybody would want to forget. It was just the sort of enterprise we memorians love.

I still have my notes on the Fiery Hand, but they are not easy to read through the splatters of blood on the page. The temple was a converted tailoring establishment. Hook-rails were still nailed to the ceiling, wound about with desiccated flowers; a price list was legible through thin whitewash on one wall. The altar itself, with its smelly heap of rotting vegetable offerings, was an old six-legged cutting table masked with a cheap cloth. Affixed to the wall above it was the eponymous Fiery Hand, supposedly a miraculous object risen in flames from the sea, actually a large chunk of driftwood that looked vaguely like a hand if you squinted at it. Its gilt, illiberally applied, was peeling off in patches. Not counting us, there were seven devotees, the four priests and two acolytes. A severe woman hovering by the door with a rent-box in her hands was not, I think, part of the congregation.

The chanting quavered to a close. One of the priests sat down, and was hauled to his feet again by hissed imprecations from the others. Not very well rehearsed, I noted. Somebody prompted them from behind the door, which was open a crack; they jumped to stand in pairs on either side of it, forming a kind of archway with their big wooden gloves. The door opened. The high priest swept through.

Delighted, I set to scribbling. I did not recognize the priest, who was half-masked, but his vestments were familiar. I wrote myself a reminder to visit the second-hand regalia market. The full-skirted black gown was from the recently bankrupted Temple of the Stars Immortal, the foil crown from the defunct Eternal Circle, the cape from the Rescissionists, and the feathered half-mask from some phallic-stone cult whose name escaped me. Only the sceptre, a staff topped with a knobby wooden hand, was original.

The high priest glowered around the assembly and brandished the staff over his head. "The Fiery Hand!"

"The Fiery Hand!" The underpriests shouted it lustily. Audience response was more hesitant.

"The Fiery Hand!"

"The Fiery Hand!" After a few similar exchanges, the high priest lowered his staff and turned to prostrate himself before the altar. He remained like that for so long that the devotees, and even one of the priests, began to fidget, and I started to doodle on the edge of my page. I remember thinking that this cult would not last long; the ritual was badly scripted, the priesthood lacked a sense of theatre. Nothing exciting would ever happen here. In the event, I was both right and wrong.

Suddenly, the high priest leaped to his feet and twisted to face us. We all jumped. "The Fiery Hand!" he shrieked. We responded dutifully, "The Fiery Hand!" and he stomped from side to side of the room, spraying spittle with his words. "The Fiery Hand will reach into your souls," he screamed, "it will pluck out the evil within you! It will crush the wicked between its forefinger and its thumb! It will cleanse the world in the fires of its flaming palm!" The devotees started to perk up. "The harlots and usurers, the thieves and liars! The kings and princes and high priests of the unbelievers, the merchants who give short weight! The tax collectors who bleed the righteous dry! The proud, the merciless, the fornicators, the murderers—" He stopped short as his eyes fell upon Shree, who was taking down every word. In the silence, I nudged Shree. He looked up.

The priest gathered himself to his full height and flourished his staff at Shree. "The hottest flames in the Fiery Hand," he hissed, "will be reserved for *spies*."

Oh dear, I thought, not again. Fortunately, the most sensitive cults were often the slowest; the greatest danger we normally ran was losing our notebooks. In that first moment of passive surprise, Shree and I drew knives from under our cloaks, jumped to our feet and began, according to a well-rehearsed strategy, to slide back-to-back towards the door making menacing gestures.

This usually worked. Only once had a congregation seriously tried to stop us, a gaggle of redoubtable old ladies in the Palace of the Effulgent Fowl. This time started out to be no different. The high priest spluttered ineffectually; the under-priests dithered towards us and halted, eyeing the knives; the devotees, interested but not keen to take part, watched open-mouthed. Something bounced off my head—the woman by the door had thrown the rent-box at me. I snarled at her and she scrambled into the corner. Then we were at the door and I groped for the handle. The handle broke.

This was unfortunate. The few seconds it took for me to pry at the doorcrack with my knife were all the high priest needed to recover his nerve. He leaped for us, pushing the under-priests ahead of him. They were not armed, but one of them, falling towards me, accidentally fetched me a stinging blow on the side of the head with his heavy wooden glove. Through the whirling lights in my eyes, I wondered if we should tell them the truth, that we were recording them for posterity, one small tile in a fascinating cultural mosaic. Perhaps they'd be flattered. The high priest smacked me, also on the head, with the hard wooden finial of his staff.

"Reverend sir—" I began, but at that moment the door crashed straight into the back of my skull and sent me flying into the high priest's arms. He managed to hit my head again as we tumbled together into the circle of devotees. "Reverend sir—" I started over, but he scrabbled away from me on his hands and knees.

I sat up groggily and tried to focus. The first thing I saw was my notebook, lying open on the floor a few feet away. I crawled in that direction. A familiar voice was shouting, "Tig—the knife!" I shook my head, trying to clear it, looking around dreamily. Near the door, a picturesque cluster of three bodies was engaged in the Viper's Wedding, another popular dance from the whorehouses. Stopping to watch, I became aware, in order of discovery, that Shree was one of the dancers, that he was not dancing, and that the other two were not dancing either.

"Raksh take you, Tig—the knife! Give me the tupping knife!" Something of Shree's urgency broke through, also the fact that he was cursing ferociously in Sheranik when he was not yelling at me. His knife lay beside the notebook; I picked up both and held them out helpfully. By kneeing one of his assailants in the groin, Shree freed a hand and grabbed the knife; then it was a quick double thrust, one-two, Sherkin-style, into the unguarded breast of one enemy, and a lightning slice at the neck of the other. Both collapsed. Bright bloody flowers blossomed on the open book in my hand.

Shree lunged for me, but was tackled by one of the under-priests. They landed in a tangle almost in my lap; thoughtfully, I raised my fist and brought it down hard on the back of the priest's head. It seemed only fair. Seconds later, Shree was dragging me down the dark corridor and the door was closing behind us to cut off the shouts from the sanctuary. At the portal, we stumbled. Something like a wet sack was lying across the doorstep, a sack with limp arms and legs attached, and a head lying at a strange angle. Shree stooped and pulled the head into the light—the acolyte on door duty, still bubbling red where his throat had been sliced across. "Who—?" Shree began, puzzled, but inside the temple the door crashed open again.

Shree grabbed my arm and started to haul me up the Thread-of-Gold, then jerked to a stop. The shadows across the way were moving forwards, taking murky shape, silently closing in around us. Shree bellowed in Sheranik, trying to slash in all directions at once without dropping my arm, but there were at least four assailants and they fanned out beyond the range of his knife. Such a fuss over a grubby little cult, I thought dazedly, then hands seized me from behind and a rough-fibred, vile-smelling darkness came down over my face. I gasped for breath, lost Shree, stumbled backwards; only the arms pulling at me from behind kept me on my feet. Through the muffling obscurity, somebody clouted the back of my head.

It was one clout too many. I sat down, hard. The hands groped for better purchase on my shoulders, then jerked and fell away. A dead weight slumped on to my back and bore me down into the mud.

Lights shot across the darkness inside my lids. I couldn't breathe. I deduced hazily that I was smothering to death under the pole-axed body of one of my attackers, but any action seemed like too much effort. I lay there quietly, waiting for my life to flash in front of my eyes—most of it would be painful or perhaps dull, but I wouldn't have minded seeing Calla's phantasm one more time. Or would she be waiting for me in the afterworld? I hoped so. But the pictures did not come; instead, the blackness began to fill with tiny points of light, like a soft mist of gold dust, and I was reminded of something I had thought was long gone; I was on the edge of remembering when the weight lifted and the world ripped open with a noise like a knife slashing through heavy sack-cloth. So that, I told myself, is what death sounds like.

"Damn it, Tig, wake up!"

I opened my eyes. The afterworld, if that's where I was, was no brighter than the one I'd left behind. I sat up and took a deep, gagging breath. Nor did it smell any better. I looked up and focused on a presumed guardian spirit who bore a strong resemblance to Shree.

"Am I dead?"

"It seems not." Shree pulled me to my feet, examining the bashes on my head with clinical interest. "Not yet, anyway. But it's not for want of trying."

3

"I DON'T UNDERSTAND it." Shree took the first gulp of his second beer and slammed the beaker on the table. I winced. The tavern's flickering lamps and clatter of voices were touching off explosions in the hollow of my head, though stopping for a drink had been my own idea. We'd be safer in a crowd, I'd told Shree, and furthermore my legs seemed to have jellied from the hips down and he could hardly carry me all the way back to the Gilgard. I needed a drink, or imagined I did. Shree had agreed readily, folding his bloody cloak innocently over his arm as we came in. My cloak was almost clean, having been covered by that vile-smelling sack during the bloodiest moments of the brawl, not that blood on one's cloak was at all remarkable in this unreclaimed neighbourhood.

Still involved with exploring the lumps on my skull, I had barely touched my beer. The vision of the golden mist teased at my memory, but I pushed it aside.

"What don't you understand?" I asked.

Shree jabbed at the top of his beer, raising little white welts in the foam. "The attack at the Fiery Hand. It doesn't make sense."

"Never mind," I said, "nothing about those cults makes sense, almost by definition. And they're not the first to mistake us for the Primate's spies."

He glanced at me impatiently and took another deep swallow of beer. "Were we at the same fight, Tig? Forget the Fiery Hand. You noticed the other ones, didn't you? The two bullyboys inside the temple, with masks and daggers? The ones who battered the door in at the last moment? The ones I killed?"

"Oh, yes," I said after a moment's hard thought. "Those ones. Yes, of course I noticed them."

"And then the bunch outside? Four masked scraggers who pulled a grain-sack over you and started dragging you away, and were doing their pitiful best to chop me into butcher's meat? Remember them?"

I closed my eyes and concentrated. "I suppose so. What happened to them, anyway?"

"Well," he drained his beaker and waved for another, "that's when the other bunch came along."

"Other bunch?" I managed a queasy sip of beer.

"There were four of them, too, but I didn't see their faces. They jumped out of nowhere and attacked the first lot of scraggers—the survivors, that is; I'd already dealt with two."

"They saved us?"

"I don't know about that," he said testily. "I was just getting warmed up. And anyway, once they had driven off the first lot—" He stopped and drank deeply.

"Yes?"

"They went after you themselves." He gazed reflectively into his beer. "Fortunately, they were not very experienced."

I stared at him, barely comprehending. He grinned at me and added a proverb in Sheranik, something about green plants having red sap, which I didn't even try to understand. I cradled my head in my hands.

"Interesting, Shree, but not really unusual. These temples bash at each other all the time. Remember when the Serene Recovery League was feuding with the Ever Divines—or was it the Everlastings? They practically wiped each other out, and over a very minor theological point. We were bound to get caught up in something of the sort eventually. No, there's no mystery there, except that anyone would bother with such a scruffy little religion as the Fiery Hand."

He drained the beaker, signalled for yet another, brought his head close to mine and spoke slowly and clearly, as if to an idiot with a hearing problem. "You're not thinking straight, Tigrallef. This had nothing to do with the cult wars. Didn't you see what was happening?"

"Actually, I didn't get to see much at all. People kept hitting me on the head. The whole body to choose from," I added feelingly, "and everybody hit me on the head. And I couldn't see anything with the sack over my face—"

"The scraggers who slit the acolyte's throat and crashed through the sanctuary door," Shree interrupted, "were only there because *you* were. They only killed the lad because he got in their way. They paid no attention to the priests. They were not interested in the Fiery Hand. They didn't want me, Raksh knows. Likewise with the ones outside, all of them. It was you they were after." He raised his beaker in a toast. "To you, Tigrallef. At last, somebody's taking you seriously."

I gaped at him for a moment, then pushed my beer aside. My head cleared; the gibberish of the evening's events resolved into a clear, coherent message. Shree was right. Somebody had tried to abduct me, somebody else had tried to kill me. My stomach began to heave.

"The informant who told you about the Fiery Hand—I'd wager he was in on it too. Or else somebody bribed him to get you there on this specific night. What do you think?"

"Mmm."

"And there was another interesting thing," Shree went on. "The last lot were using triple-curved swords, like the ones they make in Miishel—"

He broke off as I lurched to my feet and made for the door. My need was urgent for fresh air and a friendly gutter to be sick into. Shree caught up as I stumbled into the street.

"I can't take you anywhere, can I," he sighed. "Really, Tig, if you can't hold your alcohol, you shouldn't be drinking." He took my arm. Under his cloak, I glimpsed the shimmer of a

naked iron blade. Shree took me from the tavern as far as the
Gilgard gate, then vanished back into the city on some mysterious errand, which I assumed meant a visit to Lissula's
brothel for news and possibly pleasure. The way he handed
me over into the guards' keeping was not very subtle.

"Lord Tigrallef has had," he winked at the gate officer, "a
very wet night—and I don't mean it was raining." He mimed
emptying a quick succession of beakers. The officer grinned.
It was true I was weaving from side to side like a shuttle on a
loom, but who wouldn't after such punishment to a sensitive
head? "See he gets to the archives all right, will you?" Shree
added, and disappeared back into the street.

"Come on now, my lord Scion," said the officer, still grinning. "Up to bed—you've had your fun for the night."

Fun, I fulminated, as I staggered the long route to the
archives between two offensively helpful guards. Fun. An
expedition to a shoddy little temple, attempted assassination
and/or kidnap, several blows to the head, and half a beaker of
putrid beer. Fun.

One of the guards nudged my shoulder as we started up the
final flight of stairs. "Practising, my lord?" he said. His partner snickered. "Don't worry, Lord Scion, nobody thinks the
less of you, especially if you've had no experience in that line.
They do like you to have a bit of practice beforetimes." He
patted my shoulder, a little too familiarly for a low-ranking
guardsman to a Scion of Oballef, the brother of the Priest-
King, and a peer of Sathelforn through my mother the Lady
Dazeene. I shrugged his hand off. Whatever twaddle they
were talking, I felt too awful to be interested. "As long as
you're careful, of course," he added enigmatically.

They parted from me in the antechamber, still with those silly
smirks on their faces. I paused in the darkness until the pounding eased in my head, then opened the door. I expected more
darkness on the other side and no further barriers between
myself and my pallet, but the room was brightly lit and
crowded with people.

Six guardsmen, two pages, holding between them a green
silk cushion with a scrolled paper on it, tied in green-and-gold
ribbon, four third-grade Flamens, the Second Flamen himself,

a goggling handful of my pupils, and Angel, firmly ensconced in the entrance to the stacks, clutching a book in one hand and his largest scroll-knife in the other. The atmosphere was tense.

The Second Flamen, not a bad soul as Flamens go, cleared his throat. "My lord Tigrallef," he said, "your servant—is he dangerous?"

"Good evening, Revered One. Angel's my colleague, not my servant. And no, he's not dangerous. Put the knife down, Angel."

Angel slammed the knife point-down into the nearest table with a violence that made the Flamens jump, slid on to his haunches on the floor and pointedly began to read. I groped my way to a chair beside the table and sat down with my aching head in my hands. "Was there something you wanted, Second Flamen?" I murmured.

The Second Flamen, pulling himself together, sketched in the air the ritual greeting of a Priest-King's messenger. I freed one hand for a perfunctory reply. The Flamen coughed again and began to speak, lowering his pitch an octave or so while almost doubling his volume. It was serious, then. "The Hereditary King of Gil and High Priest of the Cult of the Lady in Gil presents his compliments to Lord Tigrallef, Scion of Oballef and Prince Royal of the Island of Gil." He lifted the scroll reverently from the silk cushion and handed it to me with a flourish.

I unrolled it, scanned it, dropped it on the table and put my hands back where they were needed, supporting my poor abused head. "If Arko wants to see me," I said, "why doesn't he just drop in? He knows where I am. There's no need for a formal summons."

"But, my lord," protested the Second Flamen in his normal voice, "this is an important matter, as you must know."

"I know nothing about it."

"But a formal audience is required."

"Why?"

"Well—for one thing, the Primate needs to be present."

The Primate. I moaned softly to myself. "Tell my brother," I murmured, "that I will attend him in the morning, as he commands." I signed a polite dismissal with my fingers. The Second Flamen, however, continued to hover at the other end of the table, until I finally gave in and looked up at him.

He was smiling, now that his duty was done. "I would guess, my lord Tigrallef, if it's not too much of a liberty to say so, that you've been enjoying yourself."

I groaned out loud. "I suppose you could call it that. So?"

"It's good, my lord, very good. Naturally, we all understand. The loaf before the feast, as they say, to prime the palate! Anyway, a little knowledge will be useful on the night."

I stared at him hard until his smile faltered, and then glanced around the room. Only my pupils looked as puzzled as I felt. Angel was flipping through his book and ignoring the whole scene. The guardsmen and Flamens, even the pages, wore tolerant little smiles.

I suppose I should have guessed at that point, but I was not at my brightest. Tiny hammers were pounding on the inside of my skull. The puzzle could wait until morning. I gave no more thought to it then, nor to the assassins at the Fiery Hand; nor, when I managed at last to dismiss the Second Flamen and wobble off to my pallet, did any premonitory nightmares come to me in my sleep. Only the usual ones.

4

SOMETIME MID-MORNING, SIX imposing guardsmen trooped into the archives with orders to escort me to the audience hall. Surprised and rather impressed—I'd never rated more than two before—I changed into a cleaner tunic that was long enough to cover the inkstains on my britches and the patch on my bum where the cloth had worn thin and allowed myself to be swept downstairs.

As we marched along, I reflected on how things had changed. The honour guards of the old Gil had carried purely ceremonial weapons, beautiful useless *objets* that couldn't cut cheese and weighed not much more than the gems set into their handles. These men were armed to the eyebrows, and their weapons were real. A short businesslike dagger hung in a sheath on each upper arm, haft downwards so it could be drawn quickly; the swords were long, sharp and hungry, and the only gems in sight were the crumbs of lapis on each man's insignum. I noted that a new weapon had been added, a loop of small razor-edged throwing discs depending from the belt opposite the sword. More and more, it seemed to me, Arko was ruling by force of arms. I suppose it was not easy being the custodian of an empty temple.

I paused on the threshold of the audience hall, cursing myself for not changing my britches as well as the tunic. Most of the senior Flamens were there, and about twice the normal number of troopers were formed up in a double honour guard from the door to the dais, backed by bands of harpists and hornists in full cry. Arkolef himself was seated on the high throne of Gil, his wooden leg hidden by the gold-heavy green robe of state, and one of his hands was waving majestically in time to the music. His face lit up when he saw me. He snapped his hand and the music stopped.

"Here he is now! Tigrallef! My dear brother!"

I looked at him narrowly. Arko was dim and rather sweet, and always seemed glad to see me, but he was not usually so bubbly about it.

"I have wonderful news for you, little brother."

"Oh?" All I could figure was that he'd decided to increase my book budget. I thought it over and finally permitted myself a noncommittal smile. Arko beamed back.

"Tig," he said grandly, "it's time you were married."

I gulped. The smile froze on my face. For the first time, I noticed the Primate glowering at me from the smaller throne situated significantly behind and to the right of Arkolef's.

Arko met my eyes with a clear, innocent gaze. "You're what, twenty-nine?"

"So?"

"So—you can't spend your whole life buried in the archives."

"Why not?"

"It's no life for a man."

"That depends on the man."

"You need a wife."

"I need a reliable supply of paper. The last batch from Sathelforn—"

"My lord Tigrallef." The Primate's razor voice cut cleanly through my diversionary tactic, rot him. I leaned sideways to see more of him around the edge of Arko's robe.

"Did you say something, Revered Primate?" I asked, keeping my voice polite.

The Primate rose and paced solemnly to the edge of the dais, his brows drawn together. He had worn the same face on that far-off day in Exile when he first decided to send me to Gil as a hero. He said, "Lord Tigrallef, the Priest-King is not just offering you brotherly advice."

I sighed. "That's obvious, Most Revered One. Where's the hook?"

The Primate's chin lifted reprovingly. "The Priest-King considers—" he began, but Arko himself broke in.

"Tig, you should be pleased. She's beautiful." He beamed again. Ever so quietly, the Primate's teeth ground together.

Those tiny hammers in my head, peaceful all morning, began to tap again. "She?" I asked.

Arko swept his hand gracefully through the air. "Yes, of course. And the dowry is superb, also the lady's rank. You're a lucky man."

I glanced down at my permanently inky hands to gain a moment, then back at my brother. "Am I to understand, Lord King of Gil, that you've already chosen me a bride?"

Arko laughed. "Did I forget to say? How stupid of me."

The Primate shook his head minutely and turned back to his throne. I could almost pity him for the job of running Arko as a king. My brother motioned to one of the Flamens standing at the edge of the dais, who advanced on me bearing a portrait in a garish gold frame. I stepped back.

"I'm not interested."

"But Tigrallef, you haven't even seen her. Just look."

I gazed perforce at the painting. A small, perfect, slightly feline face on a flower-stem neck; dainty shoulders and a snowy swell of bosom pushed high and wide in what I recognized as Miisheli fashion, but almost hidden by a crateful or two of heavy golden gew-gaws. A sweet smile, perhaps too sweet, belied by a certain set to the pointed chin that the artist had not been able to soften. But lovely indeed, exceptionally so, and rich with it. Miishel, eh? I said to myself. That explained the wind-galley in the harbour.

"I'm not interested," I said again.

Poor Arko. He was not even disappointed at this stage, only baffled. "Tig—she's a princess of Miishel."

"So I gathered. The answer is no."

He gawped at me from the high throne of Gil. "But you can't refuse. It's all been agreed—all except the final settlement."

"Already? Without consulting me?"

"They wanted a quick reply."

"You mean, you were advised not to approach me until the deal was complete."

Arko's eyes drifted away from mine. His grounding in the Heroic Code made him too honest for effective kingship.

The Primate cleared his throat. "Lord Tigrallef," he said smoothly, "whatever you may think, the Priest-King's sole considerations in this match have been your happiness—"

"Good. I'm happy where I am."

"—and the welfare of the nation. The situation is this. Miishel seeks an alliance with the Archipelago; Sathelforn, out of respect for the Scions of Oballef and the Lady Dazeene, insists on including Gil in the treaty. As a Scion and a descendant of the Satheli royal line through your mother, the Lady Dazeene, you can cement this alliance by carrying out one small, joyous duty—marriage with the Princess Rinn of Miishel. Naturally, you will reside with your bride's people."

"I see. As a kind of hostage."

"As the consort of the Princess Rinn," he said primly. "Is this too much to ask?"

"Yes."

"You still refuse?"

"Yes."

He sighed, and Arko dutifully sighed with him. The room was hushed with fascination—it was a rare treat to see the Primate being openly defied. The Primate glanced around, as if realizing this, and motioned suddenly for the musicians to resume playing. Under cover of the music, he stepped close to me and smiled, not a nice smile, more the kind you'd expect from a man who dined regularly on human babies. He took up a scrolled paper tied with green and gold ribbon and put it into my hand.

I unrolled it and read the opening few lines. The first jolt of shock hit my belly. Breathing hard, I forced myself to finish reading—the text was not long—and then I read it again. And again. The words written there refused to change. Stubbornly, they continued to affirm that the Primate of the Flamens was now also the First Memorian and, by special royal appointment, the Custodian of the Archives in Gil. I scrolled the paper up again and handed it back to the Primate.

"Couldn't you just torture me?" I asked.

"I wouldn't dream of it." The Primate leaned closer and whispered, "I need you unmarked and in good health."

"How did you get Arko to sign the appointment? Put something in his wine?"

"I pointed out that you'd be leaving us, and it would be necessary to find a new First Memorian. The Priest-King was grateful when I offered to take over the archives myself. After all, we couldn't leave your tame Sherkin and that lunatic Angel in charge of Gil's most precious asset."

"You hypocrite," I said, "you never valued the books before. You'd have thrown them out with the other rubbish when the Gilgard was being cleared—just as you left the archives from Exile to moulder on the quay—just as you grudged Arko giving me the rooms to work in, the ink to write with—"

"Really, Scion, this is not seemly." He was purring, as a cat might to the mouse trapped between its paws. "Can you imagine how it would grieve me," he added, "to have to sell the archives?"

I stared at him, shocked beyond words. The Primate said something, but the sound was lost in a crescendo from the horns. I found my tongue again and hissed into his ear, "Tell me you didn't say that."

"But I did. And why not? The Lucian Clerisy has offered me a very handsome price."

"The Lucian Clerisy!" I shut my eyes and cursed the Primate by the new gods of Gil, all of them that I could think of, up to and including the Fiery Hand.

"I'll only sell if I have to," the Primate went on placidly. "Gil needs money, Tigrallef. If you marry the Princess Rinn, we'll get it from Miishel, by the shipful; if you refuse, which you're certainly free to do, even now, we'll sell the archives. I'd much rather sell you, of course, we'll get more for you. But you choose." His eyes were full of the confidence of victory. Behind him, Arko strained forward in the high throne, trying vainly to hear us over the clamour of the musicians.

I put my mouth close to the Primate's ear and breathed, "This is revenge. You're punishing me for destroying the Lady."

"It's economics, Tigrallef. Though I admit, none of these cults that you find so enthralling would have arisen if we still had the Lady. No political factions, no popular movements, no questioning of the Priest-King's right to rule. The Lady would have guaranteed his power."

Your power, Primate, I amended to myself; an excellent argument for having destroyed the pocketing thing. I stared into his pouched eyes.

"Here's the deal I'm offering you, Tigrallef. Accept this alliance and the archives will stay where they are, under a new First Memorian of your choice. Refuse, and the entire library will be on its way to the Lucian Clerisy within the week. Do you understand?"

I was silent. Not out of indecision; there was no doubt by now that I'd marry the princess. Whatever dismay I felt at being sold to Miishel paled beside the thought of my beautiful archives being lost to Gil—and going moreover to the Clerisy, mediocre fumbling fanatical pack of plagiarists that they were. I'd have married the Primate himself to stop that happening.

No, this time it was grief that tied my tongue, a sudden, terrible wash of grief that poured down on me out of nowhere while the priest was speaking and my alliance with that gold-weighted Miisheli female was becoming inevitable. I didn't want the Princess Rinn. I wanted Calla. I always would. A voice spoke in my head, reminding me: Calla's dead. And so she was, dead and picked clean by the fishes, a scatter of bones on the seabed somewhere between Gil and the drowned towers of Iklankish, but that did not stop me wanting her. I shivered with grief—and a dark hole began to open in my mind, a hole with lights like motes of gold dancing on its rim.

"So? Do you accept the offer?" the Primate demanded.

"What?" I looked at him, surprised. I'd forgotten he was there. "Of course I accept."

The hole yawned wider. I stared through it, oddly detached, watching the lights flicker around the Primate's head as he motioned for the music to stop. Arko leaned forward.

"Well, Tig?"

"Bless me, Lord King of Gil," I said flatly.

Arko relaxed, then shouted for wine for the obligatory blessing. Through that strange golden haze, I watched the pages approach with trays of beakers, saw the Primate put a beaker into my hand with a kind of hard-edged solicitude, heard without listening as Arko intoned the words of the blessing. The Primate lifted a beaker to his lips. Wistfully, I found myself picturing the Most Revered One choking on that mouthful of wine.

The Primate coughed violently. Fountains of wine sprayed out between his teeth, stinking of dead fruit. He was indeed choking. The coincidence did not strike me then, though I was interested to see that there seemed to be more wine down the front of the Primate's green vestment than he had actually drunk. When I blinked, the hole closed in my mind, the golden haze winked out. I looked around as if I'd just wakened from a deep sleep.

The hall was in chaos; distraught Flamens were crowding around the Primate and pounding his most revered back, Arkolef was issuing contradictory orders, the pages were running about in circles, the musicians scattering. I stayed long enough to see if the Primate would actually choke to death, and when it seemed that he wouldn't, I left.

5

THERE WAS NOWHERE to go but back to the archives. I trudged up the stairs in a black depression, lightened only around the edges by the image of the Primate's purple face. Angel and Shree greeted me as I came in, but there was something wrong with my powers of speech and I slipped past them into the reading room without a word. Then I found that being among the books was even more depressing, so I cast around for an escape that would not involve having to talk to anybody and ended up climbing a narrow spiral of stairs that led to one of the small round towers of the Temple Palace. At the top was a bare cell dominated by a large casement window.

I looked speculatively at the window, swung it open and leaned out. It was a good long drop to the ground and the first thing I'd hit on the way down would be a bank of decorative spikes along one ridge of the Middle Palace, which would finish me off nicely. And then, with the bridegroom tenderized like a chunk of tough steak—the books would go straight to the Lucian Clerisy. No, throwing myself out the window was not the answer.

The door creaked open behind me. I didn't turn around, hoping whoever it was would go away. After a short silence, a hand swatted me heavily on the shoulder.

"You'll need to be more careful of your back now," Shree's voice said in my ear.

I turned slowly to face him. There were purple shadows under his eyes and some spectacular bruises were developing on his jaw from our visit to the Fiery Hand, which now seemed an eternity ago.

"You look terrible," I said. "How's Lissula? Did she send me her love?"

"She sent you more than that." I waited for him to go on, but he leaned past me to look out of the casement. I followed his eyes. The ship from Miishel rode in the centre of the harbour, blazoned and beribboned like some barbarian queen—or some doxy. I said softly, "If I'd looked out the window more often, I might have seen trouble coming."

"The scholar's life," Shree said. "Tell me, Tig, how did you like the princess? Did the portrait make your loins quicken? I have it on the best authority that her bosoms—"

I stared at him so fiercely that he stopped and grinned. "How did you know?" I said through my teeth. "What have you heard?"

"Only what everyone else has heard. Rumour mostly, but I know the cloth has been ordered for your nuptial robes. Omelian silks—at Sathelforn's expense, of course; they say Gil couldn't afford homespun at the moment. Is it time to tell you where babies come from?"

"I know where babies come from," I said. "Damn it, Shree, if you'd heard something, why didn't you tell me sooner? I might have been able to talk Arko out of it."

He dropped the light manner. "I only heard last night, after I left you. Lissula told me."

"Lissula knew?"

"Of course she knew. I went to see if she could shed any light on our late friends at the Fiery Hand, and she greeted me with raptures on your forthcoming marriage."

I spluttered with indignation. "Why does the whorehouse know before the archives?"

"Come along, Tig. The shints know everything first. Fact of life. Actually, almost everyone outside the archives has known for days, ever since the ship from Sathelforn came in. The bookmakers are already taking bets on the size of the dowry."

I remembered the guardsmen sniggering, the Second Flamen and little pages being grotesquely paternal. Bits of the puzzle fell into place. Practise! Experience! The loaf before the feast! They thought I was a virgin. Shree waited patiently until I'd finished grinding my teeth, and then asked, "What are you going to do?"

"I've already accepted. I have no choice. The Primate's talked my brother into handing the archives over to his tender care, and he'll sell the library to the Lucian Clerisy if I refuse. I can just see him doing it, too. I can't let that happen."

Shree whistled. "Clever old Primate. I wondered how he'd bring you into line."

"You sound almost approving."

"You're a prince," he said bluntly, "of two royal lines."

"So?"

"So they were bound to marry you off someday. At least this one's rich and pretty."

I glared at him. "Did the Primate talk you into this?"

"The Primate couldn't talk me into breakfast. As your friend, I think you should accept this fate as gracefully as you can."

I turned back to the window, feeling betrayed. Shree put his hand on my shoulder. "Did the Primate offer you any terms?"

"Yes, if he can be trusted. I can choose my own successor in the archives—I suppose that will have to be you."

He shook his head. "No. Make it Angel."

"Angel! He'll be no match for the Primate."

"Nor were you, in the end. But it doesn't matter—the Primate won't bother with the archives, not once he has what he wants."

"But why not you?"

"Because," he explained, "I'll be going with you to Miishel."

I stared at him. A murderer, a barbarian, a traitor who had learned about treachery from experts; who better to have with me in a snakepit like the royal court of Miishel? However, I had not yet forgiven him for accepting my horrible fate so calmly. "I don't recall inviting you," I said.

"I'm coming anyway. It's for your own protection, Tig—"

"Protection!"

He shook my shoulder gently. "Yes. Do you think what happened at the Fiery Hand was a coincidence? If you're not careful, you won't live long enough to claim your bride."

"Well, then," I exclaimed, "so be it. Let me be killed! Let me die in the archives with a book in my hand! Die happy!"

"Who are you trying to fool? You're not happy. You're the most miserable soul in Gil. You might as well be married."

I cooled my cheek on the cold stones that framed the window and shook his hand off my shoulder.

"Go away," I said.

He walked to the door, where he paused. I didn't look at

him. Then, softly, he said the thing I had been thinking, waiting for and most dreading to hear. "Tigrallef—Calla's dead."

"I know that," I said bitterly. "I killed her."

"Not by intention. But if you're still trying to punish yourself, Miishel's as good a place as Gil. Probably better." Then he was gone.

I stayed in the tower for a long, long time, watching the Miishel ship flaunting itself at anchor. When I came downstairs, Angel and Shree were debating some subtleties in a new work on Plavipern ethics, and the subject of my marriage was not raised.

To my relief, the Princess Rinn was not on board the ship from Miishel. The display of Gillish splendour turned out to be for her cousin, the Frath Major, who had come to Gil to negotiate hard cash terms. I waited for another official summons from Arko and the Primate, but they seemed to be bartering for me sight unseen. This hardly surprised me. It was in the Primate's interest, also in his character, to keep me invisible for as long as he decently could.

I waited. All evening I waited and continued obsessively to argue Plavipern ethics with Angel and Shree. Shree claimed to grow tired of the debate and went out early in the evening. Angel was prepared to carry on unstoppably until sun-up, or possibly the sun-up after that, and so we carried on. I doubt if Plavipern ethics have ever been more thoroughly dissected, even in Plav.

And all the while, one part of my brain was busily writing scripts for the benefit of the Miisheli Frath Major. The alliance was not yet final; if the Frath didn't like me, I reasoned, Miishel could well withdraw, even at this stage, and then I'd have a fighting chance of saving the archives.

Maybe I could make him not like me. An offhanded reference to unspeakable diseases; a mournful mention of tainted blood. Or I could play on my reputation for oddness. I could feign feeblemindedness. Or froth at the mouth. Or bark like a dog. Or pick my nose. Or play with my privates. Or all of the above. What, I asked myself, would be likely to impress him the least?

"Angel, you've missed the whole point of the tortoise

metaphor," I said testily. "The shell is not the reason for the soft parts—it's the complement. Likewise with the Will Simple and the Will Immanent, the shell and soft parts of the Will Absolute."

At the same time, I was thinking: I could show up naked and daubed with woad, like one of those religious fanatics from Calloon. Or turn up in a harlot's nightgown and flirt with the Frath Major. (But he might like that.) "You see my point?" I added.

Behind the beard, Angel was grinning. I realized there was a hole in my argument as big as a wain-wheel, and there was no chance that Angel would miss it. Tongue-bound though he usually was, he was a carnivore in debate. He drew a long breath. I knew what he was going to say, and also that I had no valid counter-argument. He opened his mouth. There was a knock at the door.

I jumped to my feet. "Sorry, Angel, we'll have to leave it at that," I said quickly. But halfway to the door, I realized that my hands were shaking and my knees were unsteady.

It could not be Shree behind the door, since he wouldn't bother knocking. The pupils were playing fingersticks in the reading room. My mother was in Malvi for the summer. The water had been delivered. I'd forgotten (again) to send the laundry out. As for casual visitors, few ever bothered with the archives if they could help it. Was this the dreaded summons? Was I about to be called for inspection? Informed of my fate? Sent off to the tailors to be measured for my nuptial robes?

At that moment, something in me revolted. I squared my shoulders. Forget the games, I told myself. Forget the play-acting. Miishel might own me for the rest of my life, but at this moment I was still my own man. And, short of being dragged down to the council chamber unconscious and in chains, I would not leave the archives that night, not even if it meant reopening the debate with Angel, which I was losing. Trembling again, but this time with determination, I flung open the door.

There was nobody there.

I stared stupidly into the darkness of the antechamber. The lamp that usually burned on the staircase had gone out—but I remembered sending one of the pupils to fill it just after supper. Among the shadowy hulks of broken chairs and crates, there was a faint whisper of sound, like rough cloth brushing along a dusty surface. Not a shull, I knew by long experience what shulls sounded like. "Who's there?" I called.

Angel stirred behind me. "There's something at your feet."

I looked down. A small brown sack, apparently empty. The twine that had been used to tie it had dropped in a coil beside the mouth. Another stirring in the darkness beyond, and I looked up, aware of the fine target I made, outlined against the lamplight. A rustle, at my feet this time; when I looked down again, the twine had moved.

I froze. It was not twine. The death-diamond pattern was visible down the length of the tiny body. I could see the head now, too, a jewelled arrow-point no larger than the nail of my little finger, twisting back and forth, questing towards my sandalled foot. Minutely forked, fine as a filament of silk, the tongue flickered out to kiss the leather sole. Not a twitch, I told myself, not so much as a muscle. I held my breath, pleaded with my eyelids not to blink. Sparks began to shoot across the insides of my eyes. Golden sparks. *Go away*. The snake hesitated and then slid over my foot, over the crossed straps of the sandal, into the room behind. Almost at my heels, there was a thud.

"You can move now," said Angel.

I didn't for some seconds; then, a quivering lump of raw nerves, I turned. Behind me on the floor was the *Ethics of Plav*, a weighty work in both senses, given its heavy wooden covers bound in iron. There was no sign of the snake until Angel squatted down and lifted the book. "Parth-asp," he said conversationally.

"Bless you, Angel." I tottered to the nearest chair, weak with gratitude that the Plaviset didn't write on scrolls. I could taste the overcooked fish we'd had for supper. Suddenly I remembered. I leaped up, grabbed a lamp, vaulted over the spot where Angel was scraping the snake off the floor and skidded to a halt in the open doorway. The antechamber was silent. The light played over broken tables, upturned chairs, splintered crates, giving them strangely architectural shapes in the shadows, like a ruined city by moonlight. Nobody was there. I prodded at the bag with my sandal, and then picked it up. A paper crackled within. Thoughtfully, I closed the door.

Angel dangled the little corpse in front of my eyes. "Shall I put it with the natural history specimens?"

"Don't bother. Just throw it away. Please."

He disappeared into the kitchen. While he was gone, I withdrew a folded paper from the bag and spread it open on the table. The message was in black ink, in Gillish, in a sprawling, inexpert hand: IF YOU LIVE TO READ THIS, STICK TO YOUR BOOKS. I stared at it for a few moments, then refolded it and tucked it into the top of my britches.

Angel returned, minus the snake. He sat down at the table and leaned forward eagerly. The killer light was back in his eyes. "Now as to your interpretation of the Will Absolute—" he began.

I sat down, stood up again, walked a few paces back and forth. Angel broke off and watched me. The floor seemed to be shifting treacherously under my feet, the solid walls thinning to a shell that a breath could crack wide open. The archives, my sanctuary for six years, could not protect me any longer.

"The Will Absolute—?" Angel prompted hopefully.

I stared at him. Oddly enough, I wanted nothing more at that moment than to sit down and be demolished by Angel on a point of pure logic. Who could tell? It might be for the last time. I sat down.

"All right, Angel," I said. "What about the Will Absolute?"

6

DREAMING AGAIN. THE *green slab of ocean hung above me, the towers trembled on their foundations, the chorus of the damned echoed around the Pleasure. Calla said: really, Tig, must we go through this every night? I gaped at her—she'd never stayed for the finale before—and when I lifted my hand to touch her, the chains shattered like glass, my arm broke free*

*and grew golden, like mist, like a pillar of shining smoke, as
high as the sky; and I found I could push back the ocean, halt
the winds in mid-fury, bounce the flaming balls of lightning off
the palm of my great fiery hand, and Calla said: now you
know. I said: now I know what? Either the silence swallowed
her reply, or she had already vanished. Wondering where on
earth she had got to now, I swung my legs off the Pleasure . . .*

. . . and on to the cold, hard flagstones of my sleeping cubicle. Feet first, I started to wake up. Sunlight was streaming
through the window at an acute mid-morning angle. I slumped
on the pallet and rubbed my eyes.

"There's a message for you," said Shree.

Too bleary to be startled, I opened one eye while continuing
to massage the other. Shree was squatting, fully dressed, by
the cubicle door. It took a moment or two for his words to
penetrate.

"I said, there's a message for you."

"I heard you."

He had another of those damned scrolls on his lap. I
splashed my face from the jug beside the pallet, letting the icy
water disperse the last trailing shreds of the dream, and then
held out my hand. Shree tossed the scroll over. Green ribbon
only, no gold this time; this love-note was from the Primate.
I yawned, admired the green ribbon, assayed the paper as I
unrolled it, swept a critical eye over the calligraphy.

"I've always suspected the Primate of weak scholarship,"
I said. "Two dubious case-endings here, and one spelling mistake. Who taught this man to write?"

"What does it say?"

"Say? If I read it correctly, it says I'm banned from the
archives. I'll be moved to new quarters this morning."

"What? When did you say?"

"This morning." I yawned again, elaborately. "Don't look
so shocked. It had to come some time."

"I know that. But so soon!"

"Why not? A quick, clean break—I'd rather be chopped in
half than sawn in half, and this is similar in principle." I
stretched and stood up, looking around the familiar cell,
knowing that I'd never sleep there again, telling myself that it
didn't matter, knowing that I was lying to myself.

"I don't like it," said Shree.

"You don't? I thought you approved of the Primate marrying me off."

"Not exactly approved—I just said it was bound to happen some time. But there's something very much stranger than your marriage going on, Tig. Angel told me about the snake—"

"Yes, our little visitor." I reached down to the floor and fumbled in my discarded britches for the note. STICK TO YOUR BOOKS. "This came with it. Good advice, if only I could follow it."

He read it with a grave face and tossed it back. "Outside the archives you'll be even more exposed."

"It makes no difference. Anyway, I have no choice. I'm surprised that the Primate's little helpers aren't already here."

"They are here, the vultures." Shree looked up, suddenly fierce. "They're waiting for you in the reading room. But never mind them, I have to talk to you."

"Of course. Talk as long as you like. Talk all day." I lay back on the pallet and grinned. It hurt my mouth muscles.

At that moment, heavy boots clumped along the passageway towards my cubicle. Shree shifted until he was sitting with his back braced against the door. "I heard something last night."

There was a firm tapping on my door.

"You'll have to tell me quickly."

He took a deep breath. "The Fiery Hand no longer exists."

"Is that all?" I asked, surprised at his portentous tone. "I didn't give it long anyway. That priest had no idea how to stage a service—"

"They were all murdered."

I looked at him sharply, the grin fading. The tapping became louder and more insistent. I called out vaguely and beckoned for Shree to continue.

"The bodies weren't discovered until yesterday, battered to death, the whole lot of them, priests and all. There were many dark whispers around the old quarter last night—the general feeling is that the high priest raised a demon he couldn't control."

"Not a chance," I said grimly. "That one couldn't have raised chickens. They were killed because of me."

"Probably. I imagine that the friends of whoever attacked us wanted to leave no witnesses—even though they failed to get you."

I lay back and stared at the ceiling. "So. More deaths on my conscience."

Shree snorted. "Stop it, Tig. You didn't bludgeon those people to death, somebody else did. You weren't even the instrument this time."

"I was the cause."

"That doesn't mean—"

"If I hadn't gone to the Fiery Hand that night, those people would still be alive."

"Oh, go ahead then," said Shree. "Flog yourself if it makes you feel better. The point is, somebody is playing a very deadly game—deadly enough to massacre fourteen or fifteen innocent bystanders simply to discourage them from gossiping."

I pondered. "Tata? Grisot? They can't be happy about the alliance. They may have chosen this somewhat direct method to scuttle the negotiations."

"The only swords I saw were triple-curved, like they make in Miishel."

"Miishel!" At that, I had to laugh. "But the Miishelu already own me! They can poison me at leisure after the wedding, if they feel like it. Why would they go to such trouble to kill me beforetimes?" I bellowed with laughter, which created a momentary silence on the far side of the door. Then the tapping became pounding. Shree leaned his shoulder against the door to hold it shut.

"Before you start picking at the bedcovers," he said acidly, "there's one more thing."

I rolled myself off the pallet, drew my night-tunic over my head and picked my britches and yesterday's wrinkled tunic off the floor. "Better hurry."

Shree took a deep breath. "Have you been feeling normal lately?"

"No more so than usual."

He didn't smile. "Nothing strange?"

"Under the circumstances, nothing to mention."

"No visions, no strange feelings—?"

"No."

(But then a flash of memory: sparks across my eyelids, the silent command, the snake gliding over my sandal-strap . . .)

"Well, perhaps," I said.

(The Primate choking at the end of the golden tunnel . . .)

"Maybe one or two coincidences," I added thoughtfully. "Why do you ask?"

I think he almost told me then, not that it would have made a grain's-weight of difference in the end. But as he opened his mouth, the door crashed open and the impact shoved him halfway across the cell. He recovered instantly and snapped around in a classic Sherkin fighting crouch, his hand already at the knife tucked into his waistband—so I clamped my hand on his arm and yanked him towards me.

"If you carve up that nice trooper," I whispered into his ear, "I won't take you with me to Miishel."

Shree subsided. The trooper, a smooth-cheeked young officer, showed no awareness of the fact that I'd just saved his perfect skin. He greeted me with all the correct gestures, far too courteously for a man who had just broken my door down. He had yet another of those damned beribboned message scrolls in his hand. No wonder there was a paper shortage in Gil. "Lord Tigrallef, the Priest-King commands you—"

"Save your breath, I'm coming."

"So am I," said Shree.

The officer coughed gently. Three armed troopers appeared at the door. Others were audible behind them.

"I think not, Shree," I said. I paused to shoot a meaningful look at him: *behave yourself; we'll continue this later*. A final glance around the cell, and then I was on my way down the corridor, the officer ahead of me, two troopers on each side of me, four more behind. Thus, even before we left the archives, I was a prisoner.

Angel did not glance up as we trooped past his open door. He was reabsorbed in the *Ethics of Plav*, probably working out a few more unanswerable arguments to devastate me with. I knew he'd never get the chance.

In the reading room, I kept my eyes straight ahead. The

books were all around me and if I dared to look at them, the soap-bubble standing in for my head would certainly burst. The pupils were whispering in a corner, waiting for a lesson I'd never teach. On my worktable, beside the appalling Lucian scroll, was the critical review I'd never finish. Books were piled high beside it—books I would never read.

This is just like death, I thought.

And so, for the last time, without ceremony or farewell, wearing a rictus that tried to pass itself off as a brave smile, I walked through the reading room and out of the archives door. All I remember thinking, as they marched me down the stairs, was how badly the walls needed a new coat of plaster.

I expected to be taken to the audience hall for inspection, but my escorts swept me right past it. They led me deeper into the Temple Palace, past the antechambers of the Priest-King and the other Scions of Oballef, past the court hall and the vestibule of the sanctuary, to a quarter where the ceilings were low and the plaster on the walls covered living rock. The gloom, both mine and the castle's, deepened as we went. This quarter was windowless, buried in the mountain, theoretically receiving daylight via a cunning maze of lightwells and horizontal shafts fitted with bronze reflectors at every angle, which the Sherank, it must be said, had kept scrupulously clean and polished. Arko's regime had other priorities and no slave labour. Therefore, although it was a bright spring morning in Gil, our way was lit by lanterns set at intervals along the passage floors. For every lantern, there was at least one guard.

"The Most Revered One is taking no chances," I commented. "Not counting the dungeons, this must be the closest thing to a prison in the Gilgard. Is this to protect me, or keep me from running away?"

"Is there any chance you'll try it, my lord Scion?"

"Really, trooper. Why would I want to run away? I should be on my knees," I went on bitterly, "thanking my dear brother and the Revered Primate for finding me such a lovely bride."

"That bad, is it?" The officer looked sideways at me with a flash of compassion.

"I don't know what you mean." This was the man who, not

ten minutes before, had smashed my door down and been ready to drag me bodily out of the archives. He could keep his compassion. I walked on in frosty silence until he stopped in front of an open door and ushered me inside.

The décor was obviously designed to reflect my new status. I hated the room on sight. Green hangings threaded with gold crowded the walls; the floor was lost under a carpet as lush as a fallow field in springtime, which was lost in turn under a forest of carven and freshly oiled furniture. The Second Flamen beamed at me as we came through the door.

"My lord Tigrallef, welcome! As you see, we finished just in time. I was afraid we wouldn't be ready for you."

I looked around. "Your work, Second Flamen? Very nice."

He flushed, pleased. "We gathered the best for you, my lord."

"So I see. The hangings are from the Priest-King's own chambers, aren't they? And aren't those chairs from my mother's parlour? What is the Lady Dazeene going to sit on when she comes back from Malvi?"

"It's only temporary, my lord," said the Second Flamen. His smile slipped. "When you go, we'll put everything back again."

"When I go. Yes, I suppose my mother can make do for a few days. Thank you, Second Flamen. Please leave now."

He moved closer. "My lord Scion, is there something here that doesn't please you? Just tell me. The Primate ordered that you should have anything you ask for, within reason."

"How very thoughtful of him. Well, for one thing, I'd like the archives back. And I'd like my own life back." And I'd like Calla back. Far behind my eyes, gold lights flickered. I roused myself and refocused on the Second Flamen. Relenting, I patted his shoulder. "Never mind, Second Flamen. I know there are matters you can't arrange. But I haven't had breakfast yet; and I wouldn't mind having some paper and ink and pens, and some books and scrolls. Perhaps the Primate would be good enough to lend me a few from the archives. I'll make you a list."

His face cleared. "I'll present your request to the Primate."

"You do that."

I watched him go. The officer closed the door behind him—from the inside. I glared at the man with rising hostility.

"There's no need to stay. I promise you, I'm not going anywhere."

"I have my orders, lord Scion." He stood imperturbably beside the door.

"And what if I order you to leave? Doesn't a Scion of Oballef outrank a Flamen?"

"My orders have the stamp of the Priest-King, my lord Scion. I've been permanently assigned to your service."

"Permanently? Does that mean you'll be going with me to Miishel?"

"Yes, my lord Scion."

"Whether I want you or not, which I don't?"

His eyes didn't even flicker. "Yes, my lord Scion."

I turned from him with disgust and idly catalogued the room's scraped-together splendours, hating the man for his serenity, his impermeable courtesy, and most of all for the Primate's green band on his arm. There was no doubt in my mind that the Primate had planted him in my retinue as his personal spy.

"Tell me, trooper," I said without turning around, "do people like you have names?"

"Chasco. Captain, Third Guardtroop, Second Company," he answered smartly. After a pause, he added in an undertone, "of the House of Clanseri."

"A Clanseri! Well, well." I twisted my head to look at him, up and down, coldly. "One of the great old families. Some prime poets in your ancestry, though I don't suppose that means anything to you. They were great friends to the Scions before the invasion—I believe a Clanseri or two died beside the Priest-King in Malvi, may their bones bring forth flowers. I wonder what they'd make of you."

"Times change, my lord Scion."

I shrugged and crossed the room to lie down on the pallet, a gorgeous pile of furs and soft blankets that must have been levied from half the best bedrooms in the Gilgard. I cursed the pallet, silently but in detail, then settled down to the serious business of not thinking.

Three days ago, my greatest problems in life had been low-quality paper and some creeping mould in one corner of the scroll room. I had two friends, a few pupils, eleven-thousand-plus archival items to love and care for, and enough work to keep the nightmares at bay.

Now I had nothing.

7

I WAS NOT permitted to leave those quarters for nearly six weeks, during which period I was bored, overfed, and never once left alone. A box was sent down from the archives containing my own notebooks and writing materials, but no other books; nor, until the very end, were there any sinister visitors, assassination parties, threatening notes, or special deliveries of a potentially lethal nature, any of which would at least have enlivened the monotony. There was a small army of Miishelu, Gillish and Satheli bodyguards encamped in the hallway outside my quarters, also a taster who comprehensively sampled every dish sent up from the kitchens. Whoever it was (besides myself) who disapproved of this alliance, the forces promoting it seemed to be well in control.

True to his word for once, the Primate installed Angel as the new First Memorian; but I had to go on hunger strike before Shree was allowed to join me. Four days without food did me no harm; indeed I was glad of the fast, since the sudden rich diet was destroying me. The Primate, however, was gratifyingly reduced to a nervous wreck by the third evening, my health being dear to him for the first time in our long and troubled coexistence. Though I could happily have gone on for days, I was relieved when he surrendered. I wanted Shree with me, not so much for my protection as for his; and the taster began to get even fatter on double portions, for I made sure he tasted Shree's dishes as well as mine.

Only two incidents in those six weeks stand out in my

memory, the first involving my mother. Earlier in the spring, Arko had suddenly sent my parents to stay in a villa near Malvi, for the sake, so he claimed, of my poor father's health. It was true that my father was not strong, but he was not sick either. In retrospect, I realized that the Primate had simply wanted my mother out of the way while he arranged the sale of her son.

It was about a month after the formal settlement, and I still had not been presented to the Frath Major. My mother, back from Malvi, was keeping me company while the imported Omelian tailors swarmed about me in a kind of measuring frenzy, brandishing great swathes of imported Omelian silk. She said, "You decided well, Tig."

I flinched as a pin grazed my thigh. "I decided nothing. The Satheli envoy chose the cloth. And why not? The Archipelago's paying for it."

"I don't mean the cloth, my darling son, I mean the marriage."

"Oh. That. Mother, I didn't exactly agree to the match, you know, I just stopped disagreeing."

"It comes to the same thing."

"Not to me, it doesn't," I said darkly. I had to stop talking while a billow of gold silk descended on me and wrapped itself around my head, and when it whisked away again, the session seemed to be over. The whole crew packed up and disappeared in a flutter of rolled-up bolts, debating the cut of the sleeves. My mother and I were alone.

Almost alone. Shree was asleep on his pallet beside the fire. Two alert, well-armed troopers were stationed by the door. Chasco the Clanseri was seated on what had become his usual chair in the far corner, politely pretending to be deaf and blind. I poured out two beakers of wine and put one on the table beside my mother, who was knitting long woolen underbritches for both Shree and me against the icy Miisheli winters.

"Don't look so worried, Tig," she murmured.

"Do I look worried?"

"Yes, you do." She glanced at me placidly over the underbritches. "Worried and unhappy. There's no reason for it."

"I'm fine, Mother, really," I lied.

"Of course you're fine," she said, "and you're going to be very happy." She smiled fondly at me, looking about ten years younger than her actual age. I smiled back and leaned across the knitting to kiss her cheek.

"You don't believe me," she stated tranquilly.

"Not really."

"You should believe me. Remember back in Exile, when the Primate chose you to go to Gil? Didn't I tell you that you'd find the Lady? Didn't I know your father would still be alive?"

"Where is my father, anyway?"

"He's sleeping. Don't try to change the subject. I was right, wasn't I?"

"Yes, you were," I admitted grudgingly, "but this is different."

She shook her head, her flying fingers never pausing in their work. "Not as different as you might think."

Thoughtfully, I sat and watched her. My mother did have an uncanny way of being right, almost as if little gods whispered the future into her ear, as they were said to have whispered to the prophets of ancient Fathan. Maybe Rinn would not be the distaff version of the Primate I was expecting, maybe I'd misread those signs of obstinacy and ill temper in her portrait. Strength of character in a woman could be a very desirable trait—just look at Calla. But at the thought of Calla, my spirits slumped again. Whatever paragon Rinn might turn out to be, she would still not be Calla.

"You're thinking about that Sherkin girl again, aren't you?"

I jumped. "Mother, I wish you'd stop reading my mind. Anyway, she was only half a Sherkint, and she was the best on earth until—"

"Until she betrayed you to Lord Kekashr. Poor thing."

"Me or her?"

"Both of you." My mother laid her knitting down and picked up the beaker of wine, but she didn't drink from it. Instead, she peered into the beaker for so long that I leaned over to peer into it myself, to see if any prophetic pictures were dancing on the surface of the wine. I saw nothing except our own reflections, but my mother carried on gazing. I felt a chill run down my spine.

"Mother?"

She looked up dreamily, sipped the wine, smiled at me. "You will be happy, Tig. I know you will."

"Of course, Mother." I drained my own beaker in one gulp. It had just occurred to me that, in two dialects of Satheli, "happy" was a euphemism for "dead."

The other—and more sinister—incident occurred some time before dawn on the last morning of my imprisonment. I had still not been presented to the Frath Major, Arkolef had not once visited me, and nobody was telling me anything. As far as I knew, I'd be spending the rest of my life in that hateful jewel-box of a prison cell, sunless, workless, hopeless, and assaulted daily by squadrons of wild-eyed Omelian tailors. The only distraction was a tutor who had come a few times that week to instruct me in the Miisheli segment of the wedding ritual, but for once it was a lesson I was not eager to learn.

That last morning, as always, I was not properly asleep, but dozing, floating in and out of my standard nightmare—the damned pallet was too soft, the fire too warm, and two of the four troopers who slept in my chamber were chronic snorers. I was thus finely balanced between sleeping and waking, and what happened had, at first, the ineffable quality of a dream.

The door opened softly and two men crept in. Both were muffled in dark cloaks, which they retained although the room felt stifling. Unsurprised, I drifted halfway back into the dream as they approached the pallet. Their whispers seemed to come from a great distance, beyond the grid of the Pleasure, beyond the great sloping ceiling of water just starting to break in the sky.

"He looks younger than twenty-nine."

"Never mind, it's the right man. Just do it."

Calla came and sat down beside me, looking skywards with mild interest on her face. We watched together as the hovering ocean contracted to one glittering focus of light, still rising, infinitely slow and far away. A galaxy of minute golden stars winked into existence around it, but I could tell they were inside my own head, and the one true light was gradually taking on the semblance of a knifepoint flashing in a gloved hand and beginning to descend, with equal leisure. In the dream, the chains exploded from my wrists in a shower of golden shrapnel; my dream-hands rose to command the water. The water stopped.

"Do it!" A frantic whisper.

"I can't."

"Fool! Give me the knife!"

"I can't move!"

Otherwise, the doomed city was wrapped in silence. Calla smiled at me and nodded approvingly and began to fade. I reached out to grasp her, but she was already no more substantial than the shadow of a wisp of smoke and my dream-hands closed around other things, things that were hard, hostile and ruthless, and my dream-fingers convulsed around them with the shock, which is when the wave broke at last—red, not green this time, warm, like blood, not the salty cold tide of other nights, other nightmares. Through the deluge, I heard Shree's voice.

"Great Raksh! Tigrallef!"

I rolled over on to my side. The furs were sodden and smelled metallic.

"Tig!"

"What is it, Shree? I am trying to get some sleep." I sat up and yawned. There were three figures bending over me. Shree was one of them, dressed in his normal night attire, which was nothing. The other two were fountain statues, spouting dark water from their mouths. One of them held a knife in his upraised hand, but made no move to use it. He made no move at all. On the far side of the room, the guards muttered and stirred. Shree glanced wildly at them over his shoulder.

"What is it, Shree? What's going on?"

He lunged for the knife and prised it out of the unresisting hand. Then, to my horror, he slashed at the stone-still figures in what looked like a curiously methodical fury, choosing his angles carefully, biting his lip all the while as if solving a difficult problem in logic. "That should do it," he whispered, and toppled the bodies over on to the floor, dropping the knife at the same time. He had struck like a snake, quickly and quietly; the guards were just rising in confusion from their bedrolls.

A panic of shouts: "The Scion!" "Murder!" "Bring a light!" The door crashed open. More troopers, greater panic, louder shouting. I slid off the pallet, which was unpleasantly wet. By the time a lamp was located and lighted, I was fully awake, and had identified the metallic tang in the air as the sharp copper of fresh blood.

Shree had wrapped himself in a blanket by then, and was ranting at a tousled officer by the door. "You call yourself bodyguards? Ten of you lumped along the corridor like a string of tupping pack-asses, and you let them walk right past you without so much as a pat-you-down? Four of your imbeciles on chamber duty, and not one of them heard a tupping thing? If I hadn't wakened in time, the Scion would be dead now!"

The officer was Chasco. He gave Shree a long, calculating look, then bent over the two bodies on the floor and flipped one of them on to its back with the toe of his boot. He called for a trooper to hold a lamp above the dead face. The trooper took one look and stumbled back, retching. Chasco took the lamp from him with a steady hand and knelt for a closer examination.

A glance was enough for me. It brought to mind a half-grown hare I'd once found on the edge of a field in Exile, a luckless little beast which had first been stepped on by one of the great Satheli plough-horses, and then, quite unnecessarily, been run over by the harrows of the plough. The dead assassin had a similar look: eyes pushed out into startled, bloodshot protuberances, mouth gaping around the engorged tongue, red tear-tracks down the cheeks and into the hair where the ears and nostrils and eyes had wept blood—the harrow-slashes from Shree's knife were an obvious redundancy. When Chasco, with admirable nerve, reached down to close the eyes, he could not make the lids meet over the eyeballs. He gave up on this and sat back on his heels.

"Do you know this man, my lord?"

I forced myself to take another look and a slow trickle of shock began to course down my backbone. Chasco was watching my face, so I kept it blank, but I prayed that he wouldn't look down at my shaking hands. I said, very firmly, "I doubt if his own mistress would recognize him now." I had no intention of telling that Clanseri bastard everything I knew, nor of letting his masters know how much I guessed. The face may not have been familiar, but the medallion which had slipped free of the tunic was unmistakable.

The dead man was a Frath Minor of Miishel.

The next hour belonged to the cleanup detail. Shree and I were shunted off to sit on cushions near the fire, but we had little chance to talk, since two or more of the troopers seemed always to be virtually sitting in our laps. We sat quietly and obediently sipped the beakers of warmed wine that had been prescribed for my valued nerves, and at the first opportunity I put my head close to Shree's and whispered, "They were bleeding before you slashed them."

"Nicely observed, Tig."

"I think they were already dead."

"Do you, now?"

"Shree—" I broke off as a trooper in Satheli colours crawled past our cushions, nose to the floor, ignoring our bare feet. Heaven knows what he was searching for. When he was well past us, I leaned close to Shree again.

"Shree—you didn't kill those men."

He gave me a long, tired look. "All right, I didn't kill them."

"So why did you slash them, if they were already dead?"

"Obviously, Tig, they had to be seen to die of something."

I digested that for a moment. "But who killed them? One of them was a Frath Minor of Miishel. Who would dare to assassinate a Frath Minor? And how? They looked like they were *squeezed*. It's not that I mind, of course, Shree, it's just that there was nobody near enough except you and me, and yet—"

"Perhaps you killed them."

"That's ridiculous. I was asleep."

"That needn't have stopped you."

Which was so absurd that no further argument was required. All I said in the end was, "Pass the flagon, Shree."

He passed the flagon.

8

THOUGH I DID not know until later, my bride's windcatcher was breasting the breakwater of Gil harbour at about the same time as the Frath Minor was being carried out of my bed-chamber in a somewhat compressed condition. Nor were those the only events taking place at that moment. The Gilgard was on the boil.

In the stables, carpenters were working through the night to finish renovating one of the old pre-invasion carriages, to convey the princess from the harbour to the castle in a suitably imperial style. In the kitchens, the final touches were being put to a dazzling feast, more intricate and sumptuous and indigestible than any feast Gil had seen since before the Sherkin invasion. Miishel, of course, was paying for it. Three dozen deer and half a hundred lambs were already turning on iron spits borrowed from Sathelforn; three stuffed whales had been roasting for days in a firepit outside the North Gate. Over the previous week, two bakers had died of heat exhaustion and an underchef had drowned horribly in a vat of lentil hotty; the fate of one sausage mincer was unknown.

In the city, the warning had been issued—rather, the happy tidings had been published. The streets were to be lined with smiling, cheering, dancing crowds—or else. There was to be no trouble. There was to be lots of enthusiasm. To encourage the populace in the correct attitude, Arkolef had caused barrels of beer and provender to be stationed close to every cross-roads on the entourage's route from the harbour, along with hordes of troopers "to keep order" and a large complement of paid cheermongers. By dawn, the crowds were already gathering. Free food was a powerful incentive.

Meanwhile, up in the Temple Palace, all unaware, I continued to drink beaker after beaker of wine on the reasonable assumption that I could sleep through the day. So what if two men had been wrung out on top of me like bundles of wet laundry? So what if the Fraths of Miishel couldn't decide whether to buy me or slit my throat? This was just what a man in my position should expect. It was even reassuring to be caught in a vortex of treachery, machination, thuggery and deceit; it showed things were normal. All that bothered me was *how* the Frath Minor had died, and I was getting drunk in order to forget about that. Nobody thought to mention that it was my wedding day.

The first sign that the great millwheel of events was starting to grind was a trolley trundling through my door, bearing three covered platters. I sat up unsteadily on my cushion and nudged Shree, who had long since gone back to sleep. The taster, a round and red-nosed little Satheli, set to work with his spoon while Chasco the Clanseri watched impassively from the doorway. All the other troopers had gone. I didn't want any breakfast and the noise of the taster doing his duty made me feel, deep down, that most of the wine had been a terrible mistake.

"My lord Scion?" the taster said at last. He belched.

"Mm?"

"Some unusual dishes this morning."

"Oh?"

He belched again, inscrutably, on the way out. Shree roused himself, moved to the table and lifted the lid off one of the platters. From my vantage point, the dish looked like cubes of goat's cheese floating in a thick green sauce. Shree bent down and sniffed it, and recognition dawned on his face. He beckoned me over.

"I know what this is," he said. "Diced whales' balls cooked in kelp. I've eaten it at Lissula's." He lifted the second lid with more confidence, revealing long, narrow slices of pinkish meat arranged artistically on a bed of parsley. Nodding, he picked up one of the slices and dangled it in front of my eyes. "Braised bull pizzle."

"Oh lord," I said, instantly sober.

"They're aphrodisiacs, aren't they?"

"They are."

He lifted the last lid.

"This doesn't look so exciting. Little white cakes." He picked one up and bit into it. "Almond."

I said dully, "They're called love-cakes. Powdered mazselhorn with almond flour and honey. A very potent aphrodisiac."

"Oh." Thoughtfully, Shree swallowed his mouthful and put the rest of the cake back on the platter. "You eat them, Tig. You need to keep up your strength."

"Indeed." The Primate's voice. Shree whirled to face the door. So did I, but a few degrees at a time, with little rests in between.

The Primate was not alone. My uncle was beside him, the High Prince of Sathelforn. Just stepping into the room was a barrel-chested roughneck in light armour whose waist-length grizzled hair was held in place by a fine Miisheli courtcap. From the medallion clanking against his chest, I knew him to be the Frath Major. Close on his heels was a sober old nonentity in a grey tunic, hooded and unadorned; his face was hidden partly by the hood and partly by a wispy growth of white beard that straggled as far down as his plain rope belt. I greeted the Primate formally, my Satheli uncle fondly, and the Miishelu not at all. The first courtesies were theirs to make.

The Frath Major stepped forward and cleared his throat. "Scion of Oballef," he recited woodenly, "it is my great joy to welcome you this day into the Royal House of Miishel."

He did not look joyous. There were lines of strain around his hard blue eyes and he held his impressive military frame as tensely as if we were embarking on a duel instead of a cousinly relationship. His club-sized hand kept straying to the pommel of his sword. He was wary of me. I could not understand this at all. Feeling an absurd compulsion to put him at ease, I saluted him respectfully in the Gillish manner. He inclined his head in response and stood there for a moment, watchful and uneasy, then turned on his heel and withdrew from the room. The old shadow-man in grey followed him.

I looked at my uncle the High Prince, bemused. "What's wrong with him? I thought I was the one entitled to be nervous."

My uncle laughed and came forward with his arms wide to embrace me. "Never mind. The Miishelu are not like us—I doubt if we'll ever understand them."

"Who was the other man, the one who looked like a grey mouse?"

"He's no mouse, Tig. That's Ardin, the Bequiin, the Miisheli counterpart of the First Memorian. You've probably heard of him."

"More than that," I said, brightening, "I even corresponded with him a few years ago, on a point of Fathidiic history. He was very helpful then—but why didn't he introduce himself? Why hasn't he come to see me? There are things I'd like to discuss with him."

"Perhaps later," my uncle said vaguely, "when his official duties have been discharged. He's here as an adviser to the Frath Major."

"But—"

"Not now, Tig." Keeping his arm around my shoulders, my uncle turned to the Primate and said, "A few words alone with the Scion, if you don't mind."

The Primate frowned. "It is the Priest-King's wish that Lord Tigrallef—"

"Oh, I'll make the peace with Arko," interrupted the High Prince lightly. "You run along, Mycri, and make yourself magnificent. Remember you have a part to play this afternoon."

I chortled quietly to myself. Mycri! I'd forgotten the Primate had a name, and that anyone remained in this world who could call him by it and live. He stood his ground, stiffening like a slowly inflating bladder, his face blanching with indignation except for red blotches near the cheekbones. My uncle brightened his smile and raised one eyebrow. The Primate glared back. My uncle lifted his chin a fraction and drew a long breath in through his nostrils, still smiling. It was a subtle battle, and I cursed myself for not learning my uncle's technique ages ago, particularly because he won. The Primate chuffed a bit, but he retreated. My uncle then turned his smile on Chasco, who followed the Primate through the door—his face was flushed too, but I could swear it was with enjoyment. That left only Shree, who also started to follow, but the High Prince put out a hand to stop him.

"Shut the door—from this side," my uncle said.

"You honour me."

The High Prince, making no answer, waved us over to the

table and set himself down. He smiled at both of us. "Who would have thought, even eighty years ago," he reflected, "that a Sherkin warlord would be sitting at the same board as a Scion of Oballef and a High Prince of Sathelforn, with a Frath Major of Miishel just outside the door?"

"Forget the historical ironies, Uncle," I said. "What's going on?"

"Well, for one thing, your bride arrived this morning. She'll be brought ashore at midday."

"I guessed she was here, from the interesting breakfast. What else?"

He looked me in the eye. "You'll be married today."

"Today." My stomach did a slow roll, but I struggled to put a look of polite anticipation on my face. Casually, I dipped a finger in the kelp sauce and poked at a cube of whale's ball. "Why so soon?"

My uncle smiled. "Officially, the young couple, by which I mean you and the princess, are panting to be in each other's arms."

"Quite right," I said drily. I picked up a morsel of whale's ball and began to chew it. With my mouth full, I said, "What about unofficially?"

His smile faded. "Unofficially? Ah, well. No doubt Miishel has its reasons. I suspect the Frath Major is worried about intrigues at home while he's away from court, and we've also picked up rumours that Tata and Grisot are arming for war and could start making trouble for the alliance some time soon. You were scheduled to make a state visit to Sathelforn on the way back, but the Frath insisted you should sail directly to Cansh Miishel."

"What's the hurry? Why would a week make such a difference?"

"Who knows? Listen, Tig. When a treaty as favourable as this comes up, we don't ask too many questions. We don't even know why Miishel insisted on having you in the first place."

He sat back with the air of not having thrown a firebomb into a hayrick. I went on masticating slowly, staring at him, and swallowed with difficulty.

"Wait a moment, Uncle. Did you say *Miishel* insisted? I thought that tying me into the package was Sathelforn's bright idea."

"That's what you're meant to think." He tented his hands on the table. "But the truth is that when Miishel first approached us about the treaty, Gil was already a condition. To be more specific, your marriage with Rinn was already a condition. They were not to be shaken on it. No Tig, no treaty."

Shree said quietly, "Why didn't you tell him this before?" His face was white and watchful.

"No one in Gil is meant to know. Even the Primate believes the initiative came from Sathelforn."

"So why are you telling Tigrallef?"

"Because, Warlord, he's my sister's son, and I'm really quite fond of him. Also because I don't entirely trust our new partners, and I think the knowledge may be useful to him someday, which can only be in Sathelforn's best interests. And Gil's, of course," he added, a little too obviously as an afterthought.

I prodded at another morsel of whale's ball, and put it in my mouth. "What about my best interests, Uncle?"

"You're a Prince Royal, Tig, and a Scion. You have no best interests that are separate from the nation's."

Gloomily, I picked at the love-cakes, which were cloying and textured like wall-plaster and were having no perceptible effect on my loins. I had no answer for my uncle; a resignation from the post of Scion was not likely to impress him, and there were also the best interests of the archives to consider. When the silence had gone on long enough to become awkward, my uncle put his hand on my arm. It weighed on me like a hand made of stone.

"Listen, Tig."

I looked at him politely.

"I'm sorry, Tig, but Miishel's offer was too good to turn down. We needed this alliance, and you were the price."

"A price you were willing to pay."

"Yes."

"Even though you don't trust them."

"Exactly."

"And without consulting me."

"You're a Prince Royal," he repeated.

I let it pass. "And you don't know why they want me?"

"I honestly can't imagine. No insult intended, of course."

"And you never tried to find out?"

"We wondered—but too many questions might have endangered the treaty."

His face was too composed, his answers too ready. It was hard to believe he was the same man who, twenty-five years before, had sneaked illicit honey-cakes to me and taught me the Satheli names for the constellations. I could think of nothing further to say to this man who used to be my uncle.

It was Shree who broke the silence. "What about me?" he asked, leaning forward. "Did they agree to let me go with Tig?"

"Yes, Warlord, they did. A little too easily, I'm afraid."

"What does that mean?"

"It means, Lord Shree, that if I were you, I'd try to grow eyes between my shoulderblades."

Shree grinned slowly. "They think I'll be easy to remove if I get in their way."

"I get that feeling, yes. It was one of the few points they didn't haggle over. A bad sign. But I've been watching you for some time, Warlord, and I think we can trust you to surprise them."

"You want me to watch over Tigrallef?"

"I think it would be a good idea, yes. And there's one more thing." He reached under his cloak and pulled out a heavy leather bag about the size of my two fists together, which clinked as he set it down on the table. "This is for you, Tig. Two hundred gold palots. Officially some of the marriage portion is for your personal use, but of course I doubt you'll see any of it."

I looked at the bag without touching it. "Is this a bribe, Uncle? Something to salve your conscience?"

"Not a bribe, and my conscience is fine, thank you. Call it emergency funds—just in case."

"In case of what?"

"In case someday you need cash, and it is—inconvenient—to ask the Miishelu for it. You understand me."

"I understand, Uncle," I said softly, while Shree picked up

the bag and hefted it in his hand and then hid it in the one box of books I'd be taking with me to Miishel. "It seems that you're not very hopeful about my chances of a long and happy marriage."

He laughed, a great booming laugh. "I hope you have a long and fruitful life, and as many children as the waves on the ocean—but for your sake and ours, keep Lord Shree close to you, and watch your back."

"Certainly, Uncle," I said. I even managed to smile at him. But when he rose to leave, parting from me with an affectionate embrace and a large dose of avuncular wisdom, I was not overly sorry to see him go.

Of course, If I'd known he'd be dead within the fortnight, I'd have been much sorrier.

9

FORTUNATELY FOR ME, Omelian silk was the lightest material in the known world. Cut from any ordinary cloth, the nuptial robes would have outweighed me; in Omelian silk, they only smothered and stewed me. There were three layers of ceremonial undergarments and three of outer robes, their gold embroideries wasted under a cape with a nine-foot train. I looked like a tent.

"It would be nice to sit down," I said hopefully.

Chasco the Clanseri signed *no* with his fingers, which surprised me. I wasn't aware until then that he knew the finger-speech. "The tailors are very insistent on that, my lord Scion," he added out loud.

"The tailors aren't here to see, are they?" I grumbled. "Anyway, what's the delay? We've been here for hours."

"As I understand, lord Scion, you're not to appear before the people until the bride's carriage has arrived at the gate."

I swayed on my aching feet. We'd been put into one of the small state receiving parlours off the great entrance hall, Chasco and I, and then left alone except for the occasional tailor looking in to check I wasn't rumpling the silks. I hadn't bothered to ask Chasco why he was so honoured. He was resplendent in dress uniform, his weapons polished until they gleamed in the chinks of light from the curtained window, his leather breastplate laid aside for a gold-chased confection that looked like a genuine Gillish antique.

The door opened. It was not a tailor this time, but the Primate, magnificent and heavily perfumed, robed in state like one of Tallislef Second's own lieutenants in the heyday of Gil's glorious Bright Ages. I bet myself that Miishel had paid for that, too.

"Mycri," I said brightly, "how very nice you look."

He gave me a murderous glance, turned his back on me and swept out through the door again. Chasco prodded me gently and said, "You're supposed to follow him."

Knowing what was ahead, it was only the thought of the archives that could make me leave the relative haven of the receiving parlour. Reluctantly, I followed the Primate out on to the sparkling flagstones of the great entrance hall, where a long and colourful procession was forming up: dancers, harpists, hornists, drummers, scatterers of rose petals, sprinklers of lily water, bearers of smoking braziers and unmanageable banners, and the inevitable herd of green-gowned Flamens with their retinue of acolytes and pages. Chasco and the Primate and I stood in a strained little group off to one side while the massive doors swung open and the procession began, not without chaos, to move out. A mighty cheer greeted them from the forecourt.

"Quite a spectacle, Mycri," I commented. "It's a good thing Gil is rich now."

He turned his imposing head in my direction. It had never struck me before, but he looked like a fish from the eyes up, and a goat from the nose down. I chuckled.

"This is a solemn moment, Tigrallef, not a time for levity."

"This is a farce, Mycri. Why shouldn't I laugh?"

"Laugh, then. We'll be rid of you soon enough, thank the Lady. You always were trouble, Scion, trouble as a child, trouble as a youth, trouble as a man. We'll see how the Miishelu deal with you."

"You're hoping I'll be killed in one of their famous court intrigues, aren't you?"

"I'm hoping never to see you again, Scion," he snapped, "and I don't care how it happens." Then he seemed to recollect that Chasco was there, for he turned his back on us both until the call came for us to join the procession.

Our turn came at last. Per Satheli custom, the Primate tied a silken blindfold over my eyes, not very tenderly, and led me by the hand through the great doors. The contact was not welcome to either of us, but those were the parts we had to play. I felt the heat strike my face as we stepped into the sunlight and heard the roar of a vast crowd. Behind me, I could hear Chasco's iron-heeled boots clicking on the pavement. A few faltering steps, towed behind the Primate like a barge in a heavy sea, then I stubbed my foot on the bottom of a flight of stairs. When I had stumbled my way to the top, there was a tremendous blast of noise from the herd of musicians and the Primate whipped my blindfold off. The crowd roared again. All eyes, mine included, turned towards the gate.

What was supposed to happen then was the princess and her attendants stepping gracefully out of the grand carriage which was pulled up inside the forecourt gate. There should have been rose petals floating down to carpet the pavement for her dainty feet, lily water fountaining into the air to sweeten it for her delicate nose (indeed, given the heat, the stench rolling off the assembled multitudes was enough to make a pig faint), and the bride should have been led along a processional way lined with writhing dancers and puffing, plucking or pounding musicians to a bridegroom made breathless with this first revelation of her veiled form—

In practice, nothing happened. The carriage door remained closed. A few rose petals landed half-heartedly on the pavement, the crowd carried on cheering and the musicians continued bravely to play, but no princess emerged. By twos and threes, the musicians fell silent. The cheering grew ragged. People started to look at each other and shrug. Nobody knew what to do.

We waited. We were on the great curved portico overlooking the main forecourt, on a circular dais at the head of the grand gilded staircase. On one side of me were the collected nobilities of Gil and Sathelforn, with my parents in the position of honour. I could see my mother had kept her promise to keep Shree and Angel close to her, although Angel was barely recognizable at first, shaven, long hair neatly tied back, even the First Memorian's chain of office around his throat. Silently and fervently I blessed my mother.

We waited. On my other side was the Miisheli delegation, including nine Fraths Minor and several dozen lesser peers, also the Bequiin Ardin, who was conspicuously sombre in his plain grey robe. I was interested to observe no gaps in the ranks of the Fraths Minor. Beside them were the envoys from Storica, Calloon, Luc, Plav and a dozen other nations of the new Compact; but significantly, I could see no representatives from Tata and Grisot. The High Prince of Sathelforn, the Frath Major and Arkolef occupied gaudy high-backed thrones on platforms behind the dais. The Frath Major had his hand over his eyes.

We waited. I looked across the crowded forecourt of the Gilgard, where a thousand banners in the colours of the three nations were rapidly fading in the hot sun. Beneath them was a sweating multitude of the humbler people of Gil, most of whom were looking sorry they'd come. The burst of enthusiasm, or relief, that greeted my appearance had given way to abject puzzlement in the heat.

We waited. Eight minutes, nine minutes, ten minutes. There was plenty of time for reflection. Layer after layer of silk joined the sodden mass plastered to my skin; an intolerable itch migrated around my body and finally took up residence in the small of my back. Beside me, the Primate shifted from foot to foot. Unfortunately, it would not have been thinkable for anyone to approach the carriage—according to immemorial Miisheli custom, it would have obliged the bride's kinsmen to go berserk in defence of her honour, which would have run foul of the ageless Satheli law making violence at a religious ceremony punishable by death, which would have clashed in turn with Oballef's ancient statute against capital punishment. We were at an impasse.

We waited. Finally, the door of the carriage swung open. The forecourt susurrated with the sound of thousands of lungs drawing in a deep breath. A shining silver waterfall poured itself out of the carriage—and then there she was, my princess, my bride, Rinn of Miishel. The silver waterfall was her nuptial gown, which didn't actually seem to be on her, although my eyes were too bad at that range to tell for sure until she stepped over and past it. The crowd drew another breath, and then erupted into sound: whatever she was or was not wearing, they loved it. They also seemed to love her. Unattended, she strolled along the lane left clear for her, ignoring the crowd, looking neither to the right nor the left. Rather belatedly, the rose-petal and lily-water brigades remembered themselves, after which she seemed to be floating towards me through a cloud of pink and silver spray. I squinted, cursing my weak eyes.

"Chasco?"

"Yes, lord Scion?"

"What's she wearing?"

After a pause, he said, "She's wearing a great deal of gold, lord Scion."

"Anything else?"

"Not that I can see, my lord."

I threw a glance at the thrones behind me. Arkolef looked politely diplomatic, no doubt under the impression that Rinn was following another of those quaint Miisheli wedding customs. The High Prince of Sathelforn looked frankly appreciative. Only the Frath Major was grim, and there was a suggestion of habit there, as if this were not the first time his beautiful cousin had enlivened some boring old ritual by taking all her clothes off.

Rinn reached the foot of the gilded staircase and climbed to just above the heads of the crowd. She stopped there and turned around, hands on hips, chin high, and surveyed the multitude in the forecourt. Though her back was to me, I could tell: this was no gracious acknowledgement of the citizens' adulation. There was languid contempt in the curve of her elegant back: *Who are these unattractive people?* that posture seemed to be saying; *and what is that awful stench?* The look was still on her face when she turned and continued up the stairs.

Oh, there was no doubt she was beautiful, though the closer she got, the less she looked like her portrait. In the portrait, she'd been blonde; but her hair, which was gathered tightly on top of her head in a golden clasp and cascaded from there over her shoulders and halfway down her back, had been dyed in a score of rainbow colours, lock by separate lock. The effect was striking, except it reminded me of my mother's knitting basket. Her face was like a cat's, triangular, with wide winged cheekbones slanting down to a dangerously pointed chin; enormous cat-eyes, green-irised, with a thick fringe of gold lashes. Fangs and whiskers would not have seemed out of place.

As for the rest of her, she actually was wearing more than jewellery; that is, there was a thin loincloth of some shimmery material tied around her milky haunches, and she had sandals on her feet. Beyond that, she was carrying about as much metalwork as in the portrait, including that interesting gold contraption that pushed her breasts up and out in the Miisheli style but otherwise left them bare, under enough spiked chains and studded necklets to have achieved modesty if only they'd stopped shifting about. The way she moved made that impossible. I'd wager every man there was wishing he could change places with me for just one night—except the Frath Major.

Rinn suffered herself to be led on to the dais and placed beside me. The Primate, as shaken as ever I'd seen him, linked our hands and then hesitated. The script called for him to lift the outermost of Rinn's veils at that point, but she wasn't wearing any, and he was not good at improvising.

Rinn yawned, again like a cat. "Hurry up, goatface," she said to him in charmingly accented Gillish. At that moment, I came as close as I ever would to genuinely liking her. But when the Primate turned away from us to call on the gods of the three nations, she playfully dug several of her knife-pointed nails into the palm of my hand and giggled when I jumped.

"They tried to make me wear ugly, stupid clothes like yours," she whispered, "but I would not wear them."

"No, really?" I murmured.

"No! I tore them in the carriage—like so!" The nails ripped across the back of my hand.

"That would do it, I suppose." I gritted my teeth. "Didn't the attendants try to stop you?"

"Yes! But I slashed at their faces—like so!" Again the

damned nails. I caught her hands and held them firmly in both
of mine, not caring what the crowd thought. In that overheated
atmosphere, they probably saw it as a sign of ungovernable
passion.

Rinn may have thought so, too. She seemed pleased.
"Tonight," she whispered, pushing her thigh against mine, "I
will make your back into ribbons. Like so!"

I sighed. And resolved, on the souls of my ancestors, that
my first private act as a husband would be to trim my wife's
nails.

10

IF I HADN'T been watching through the jaundiced eyes of a
participant, I'd have enjoyed myself. Somebody, and I suspected it was the Bequiin Ardin, that great Miisheli scholar,
had crafted a very clever ceremony from bits and pieces of the
three different traditions, enough of each to satisfy everybody,
nothing that would offend or nauseate anybody. All the important deities were mentioned at least once, the interminable
Satheli confessions were boiled down to a few crucial sentences and human sacrifices were omitted altogether out of
deference to tender Gillish and Satheli sensibilities.

Speaking as a critic and connoisseur of cult practices, I
think the only mistake was to include the Miisheli rite of
entrail-divination. Six bulls' bellies were sliced open, and,
although the priests foresaw wonderful things in the resulting
carnage, the forecourt stank like an abbatoir in the hot sun
long after the blood had been swilled away.

Other than that, the weaving of traditions was a master-
piece. I had to admire the artistry of it, even as the net of oaths
and solemn undertakings to a daunting number of gods tightened around me, binding me for ever to that clinking cat-
clawed Miisheli slut. I kept thinking that this ceremony would
make a fine appendix to our compendium of cults; then I
would remember that the book would never be written now,

that the little cults of Gil would have to blossom and die without me, and I would sink back into misery until distracted by the next rolling phrase or entrancing morsel of folklore, and the cycle would begin again.

In the end, it was the soporific music of the Satheli eeldance that put me to sleep on my feet. The forecourt swam in and out of focus; the monotonous wailing of the reed-pipes rose and fell, rose and fell, accompanied by a drum like a mother's heartbeat as an unborn child might hear it in the womb. The slender line that tied me to the waking world slipped its knot.

Suddenly it was not Rinn beside me, but Calla; the music was the voice of despair singing out from the doomed city of Iklankish, the drum was my own heartbeat as the points of the Pleasure fell towards my chest. The great wave rose up out of the western horizon, tipped with dead ships and foam the colour of milk. Higher it rose, blotting out the bloody sky. The music whimpered into silence. A man's firm, familiar voice began speaking, but the words were puzzling: *now the two are one*. That made sense in a way, but not, I told myself, the way the speaker seemed to intend it, and the true meaning was just beyond my grasp. Then the wave came.

I let Calla's hand drop and lifted my arms to hold back the water—but it broke around me, clamour upon clamour of it, battering my ears like the thunder of thousands of lost voices. I opened my eyes and looked around, and then slowly lowered my arms. It *was* the sound of voices. The people were cheering. The ceremony was over.

I was married.

My bride and I were separated after that, she to be bathed in maszel oils and prepared for the marriage bed, me to be fed to bursting point at the grand nuptial feast. They didn't even give me time to change my silks. It was straight down to the Hall of Harps, staggering with exhaustion the whole way, to be ceremoniously dumped at the apex of a great horseshoe of eating benches, between Arko and the Frath Major. There were no women present, but maybe half a thousand men, including all the foreign delegations and the cream of the Gillish and Satheli nobility, plus all those high Miisheli peers who had accompanied Rinn and the Frath Major to Gil. I could not see the Bequiin Ardin, which surprised me, however, Shree and Angel were sitting together about a third of the way around one arm of the horseshoe. I envied them for the animated discussion they were locked into. My own dinner partners were not very strong on conversation.

Arkolef, poor stupid soul, was so radiant that you would have thought he was the bridegroom. In graceful, vapid phrases, he went on and on congratulating himself, myself, the Frath Major, the High Prince of Sathelforn (who had the misfortune to be seated on his other side), the Primate, the Flamens in general, and the entire populations of all three new allies. It was almost enough to put me to sleep again, but I rather wanted to stay awake. I felt the Frath Major would bear watching.

He was being noticeably watchful himself—it was partly that he still seemed to be nervous of me, but there was a curiously possessive element as well. *We own you now.* He might as well have said it out loud. He was watching me as I've seen a horsetrainer watch a valuable animal that needs to be tamed—wary of the iron hoofs, but eager to be in control, waiting for just the right moment to teach the meaning of the spurs. The High Prince's words came back to me: no Tig, no treaty. I was certain of one thing: whatever the purpose for which Miishel had bought me, I was going to be as difficult as possible.

Course after course flowed in an unending river from the kitchens. The Frath Major and I swapped a few courteous nothings now and then, but mainly we observed each other from the corners of our eyes. Both of us drank sparingly and ate little of each course—although, with fifteen or sixteen courses, that still amounted to far too much. It was as if both of us wanted to keep clear heads for an approaching battle of wills. Not until the short breathing space between the ninth and tenth courses did we exchange any significant words.

He leaned towards me and said in his rather precise Gillish, keeping his lips tight against his teeth, "We shall be seeing the Kaana soon. You have heard of the Kaana, I think."

"The Kaana! Yes, yes, of course I've heard of it." I stared at him with the beginnings of pleasure. "You mean it's going to be performed here? Tonight?"

He gave me a reproving look. "Naturally. You could not go to your bride before seeing the Kaana. It is our custom."

"Oh, I'm not objecting—I'm delighted. The Bequiin Ardin wrote a monograph on it, years ago; I can remember reading it in the archives in Exile. But I never thought I'd see it performed with my own eyes, especially not in the Gilgard."

"It is our custom," he repeated warily. He seemed confused by my reaction, which added to my pleasure. The Kaana! For me, this was the only good thing to happen all day. I sat up straight, rummaging in the ragbag of my brain for the details of the Bequiin's monograph.

"Let me see—if I remember correctly, the Kaana incorporates a number of survivals from the ancient Fathidiic tradition, isn't that right? Fascinating."

"Yes." He took a rare gulp of wine from his beaker.

"In degenerate forms, of course," I added thoughtfully. "Only to be expected, since it's more than a thousand years since Fathan fell."

"Yes," he said again. His eyes were suspicious, and something else. Nervous, perhaps. My attack of enthusiasm was unwelcome. I slapped him on the shoulder, feeling almost friendly, and looked around with high anticipation.

I was not the only one. When the Kaana was announced, all the Miishelu who were not too drunk or too torpid with food or already unconscious sat up and began to take notice. What barbarians they were! One could always tell by the formal getup: the more horns and spikes and other sharp objects a nation had poking out of its finery, the more likely it was to be bloodhungry, battle-happy and given to burning things—and the Miishelu were in almost the same sartorial class as the unlovely Sherank. Watching them, I wondered if the princess's metalwear would render her totally unapproachable, not that it mattered much to me. Anyway, the Omelian tailors had sewn me into my own silks, and I had no idea how I was going to get them off when the time came, assuming I survived the culinary onslaughts of the feast.

But I would worry about that later. Already the area inside

the horseshoe was being swept clean for the Kaana (the previous entertainment had involved some old and rather incontinent rippercats) and the drums were being carried out and set into position—big broad drums like laundry vats, little squat drums with bells tied to the rims, drums like tree trunks and pancakes and cooking pots, a whole shipload of drums; and in the centre, a round platform about thirty feet across and three or four feet tall, its sides chased with brass writings that were pure old Fathidiic. I glanced over at Shree and Angel, seeing with satisfaction that Angel was busy with a notebook where his trencher used to be. Then the drummers came and I forgot my friends, forgot that I was married to a woman I didn't know and was reasonably sure I wouldn't like, and lost myself in the ancient magic of the Kaana.

It was a pageant, but more than a pageant; a ritual, but more than a ritual; a historical document, written in drum-beats and intricate bodily movements whose meanings had not changed for nearly fifteen centuries. The drums began, muffled at first, low and expectant. The hall was hushed. I held my breath.

Out of the shadows at the end of the room came a fantastic figure, twelve feet or more tall, proportionately broad, swathed from shoulders to floor in a goldcloth cape. Its head was enormous, a great flat gold-foil face frozen in a lofty smile, stylized eyebrows upswept to signify cruelty—the mask of Fathan. The giant stepped on to the platform and began to sway back and forth with an oddly stilted grace. I knew that this represented the Fathidiic Empire in the years of its greatest power and pride, not to mention its spiralling corruption and viciousness, when it ruled more than half the known world and unwisely declared itself to be more glorious than the empire of the gods.

Other figures, masked but of normal stature, began to emerge from the shadows and dance among the drummers, mounting one by one on to the platform: Fathan's subject nations. The masks were white, etched with exaggerated lines of pain and hunger; the cloaks were sewn in artful rags. I thought the symbolism was not very subtle. When all the nations had taken their places on the platform, cringing around the towering figure of Fathan, the Dance of Tyranny began.

It was good theatre. No, it was great theatre. Twelve pairs of feet thudded in perfect synchrony, beating out a complex rhythm that echoed in my bones and made the little hairs bristle on my neck—for the platform was itself a great drum, the masterdrum, and its brazen voice engulfed the rhythm from the others. The dance dramatized the episodes of Fathan's wickedness—the giant swayed among his victims, swinging a battleclub in one hand and a triple-curved sword in the other, and the nations fled and fell and writhed and died in orchestrated chaos, never missing a beat. It was beautiful, and unspeakably violent. All that was missing was real blood.

Around me, the Miishelu were being caught up in the visceral throbbing of the drums, eyes glassing over, bodies twitching in time to the music, a chorus of wild cries ringing out whenever the giant scored a coup. I'd swear one of the Fraths Minor was having a brain seizure, but his companions simply shovelled him under the bench and carried on watching. I found the audience almost as fascinating as the dancers, and somehow more disturbing: the vignettes of mayhem on the masterdrum were play-acting, the frenzy building up around the horseshoe was real. But the room froze into breathless silence when smoke began to rise from the hem of the giant's cape.

I have always wondered how they did that. The Bequiin's monograph made a vague reference to secret magical arts, but I suspect the cloak was treated with some substance that made it burn vividly enough for a good dramatic effect without actually roasting the actors inside it. However they worked it, the cloak seemed to flare up in a blinding flash of red fire as all the drums crashed in concert; the giant fell apart—rather, he was revealed as one man on the shoulders of two others. The top man, he who was wearing the mask of Fathan, was seized and carried offstage by the lesser nations. That left only two: Grisot and Miishel.

Miishel and Grisot, the sibling states, for ever at each other's throats. In ancient times they had been two of the three heartland provinces of the Fathidiic Empire, bowing only to the hegemony of Fathan; after the earthquake, or volcano, or great fire sent by vengeful gods—or whatever it was that left Fathan a wilderness of blackened ruins, charcoal forests, smoking mountains, contorted corpses—Grisot and Miishel began their long and bloody debate as to which of them, exactly, was the heir to the vanished Fathidiic glories. Fortunately this kept them busy with each other for nearly a millennium, sopping up all the resources and belligerence that might otherwise have been turned against the rest of us.

Thus, the second movement of the dance was a coded history of that fraternal struggle, and I would really have needed the Bequiin's monograph in order to follow the action in detail. The two dancers grappled and posed and bashed and generally threw each other around, sometimes Grisot triumphing, sometimes Miishel, but it was clear throughout who had justice on his side. That is, Grisot (in the ugly mask) would win by fighting dirty, Miishel (in the noble mask) would win by fighting better. It was brilliant but predictable, and after a while it became repetitive. I leaned over out of sheer mischief and tapped the Frath Major on the knee.

"I'm sure you know," I whispered, "that Grisot has a ritual dance called the Binn-Al which is very similar to this, except that Grisot gets to wear the nice mask."

He looked at me without expression. "Just watch."

I shrugged and looked back at the masterdrum. Suddenly I sat up straight. Something was happening that did not feature in the Bequiin's monograph. Two additional figures had joined Grisot and Miishel; the drummers, already gleaming with sweat, doubled their efforts until they seemed to be trying to batter their drums to tinderwood. I glanced at the Frath—he was watching me—and then back at the dancers, just in time to see Miishel leap on to the shoulders of the newcomers and throw his arms wide. A long glittering cloak rolled magically down from his shoulders as far as the floor, and the audience gasped: the giant had been reborn.

At its feet, Grisot writhed in spectacular death-throes, but I was more interested in the nature of the giant's cloak. The Miisheli spectators went wild, bellowing and frothing at the mouth and stamping their iron-heeled boots on the floor, and I turned again to the Frath Major under cover of the noise.

"That was a statement of intent, wasn't it? I must say, it's a bit premature to dress the giant in the Fathidiic Cloak of Empire."

"What do you mean?"

"Well, cousin, it's clear that the two dancers on the bottom are meant to be Sathelforn and Gil, and that you're intending not only to stomp all over Grisot and its allies, but also to recreate the Fathidiic Empire, with Miishel at the top this time. Right?"

"So?"

"So nobody wants the Fathids back. They were worse than the Sherank. Anyway, large oppressive empires have gone out of fashion."

He did not answer. He sipped from his beaker and rose to signal the end of the Kaana and to permit the performers to withdraw. Then, while Arkolef rose to thank the Miishelu for showing us their very interesting folkdance, the Frath Major smiled at me tightly and took another sip of his wine. We exchanged no more words that evening.

11

IT HAD BEEN six years since I last awakened beside a woman. I lay open-eyed on the edge of the pallet, stiff and cold in the gloom of the nuptial chamber, remembering how Calla's body and mine had fit together like the halves of a broken coin. Rinn was sprawled beside me, having commandeered about five-sixths of the pallet and most of the bedcovers. Now and then she whipped an arm across my face or kicked out with one sharp little heel, and I had to keep brushing her damned hair out of my face. When I could bear it no longer, I quietly disentangled a blanket to wrap myself in and curled up in a chair to watch her sleep. Every morning so far had started out this way.

By a terrible effort of will, I had managed to consummate our marriage on the night of the Kaana. Rinn had fought like a rippercat, laughing, when I tied her up to cut her nails, and then seemed strangely disappointed when I untied her and tried to fight me again, but I was too worn out to oblige. She had just begun to be scornful about that when, unaccountably, she stopped and became thoughtful for a few seconds, then just as inexplicably melted into tender acquiescence. It rang false, just as false as the sweetness of her face in the portrait, but it was blessedly convenient at that moment; ten minutes later, having sealed our union and ensured the future of the archives, I was permitted to fall asleep.

I wondered as I watched her. Not about Rinn herself: all through the five action-filled days and nights of our marriage she had swung like a pendulum between those two extremes of behaviour, but I was in no doubt as to which was the real Rinn. I was only wondering what they could have promised her that made her keep reining herself in. Gold? Jewels? She routinely wore enough for ten women, and rarely repeated her ensemble. Sexual favours? I wasn't deaf and blind. It had taken me about two days to discover that she numbered half the Miisheli court among her ex-lovers, and the other half among her current ones. Perhaps I exaggerate slightly, but there was no word for chastity in the Miisheli lexicon, and no expectation of fidelity in the Miisheli concept of marriage, and somehow I didn't think she would need to be sexually bribed. Power? Now, that seemed like a good enough incentive. I could imagine my bride enjoying the feel of whip and rein in her pretty hand.

And how did I feel about her? That was also something to wonder about. I would never love her, nor even like her much, but I was surprised to find a tolerant, head-shaking kind of half-fondness growing up for her, if only because she was so thoroughly, transparently and unaffectedly a monster, despite her rather touching efforts at disguise. In her own way, and without meaning to be, she was quite entertaining. Hell knows, I was otherwise short on entertainment. The five days had been taken up mostly by ritual felicitations, ritual leave-takings, ritual this and ritual that, and over it all had hung the terrible prospect that I was only now permitting myself to think about, since it was just about to happen. This awakening was fated to be my last in Gil.

The black arch of the window began to lighten; I pulled the blanket up around my shoulders and went to stand looking over the still-sleeping city, watching a few lights glide along the dim streets as the wains began to come in from the countryside. Outside the harbour, a small fleet rode at anchor. Miisheli ships, mostly, along with three grand Satheli wind-galleys and one rather tawdry Gillish longship, which was all Arkolef could spare from his so-called navy. In the dusky dawn they all looked the same, a winter forest of masts, black on the grey water. Only the *Tasiil*, the great Miisheli wind-catcher, bulked larger than the rest. That was the ship that Rinn and I would sail on.

"Tigrallef? My love?"

Rinn's voice from the pallet. I turned from the window to find her stretching sinuously on top of the bedcovers, naked and golden, quite delectable if you happen to fancy the type. She covered a yawn with one hand, and beckoned to me with the other.

"Come here, my love, I feel cold."

"You could get back under the blankets," I said reasonably.

"Do not tease me, my love, I want you to warm me up."

"Not now, Rinn." I turned back to the window. The dawn was progressing too fast—already I could make out the gay flags and bunting strung from the rigging of the ships. That was bad. I did not want this day to begin.

A touch on my back. Rinn had padded up behind me, and was pouting prettily over my shoulder. She's smaller than Calla, I thought; Calla was just about my height. I forced a smile. "Not now, Rinn," I repeated gently.

The genuine hellfire-and-thunderclap personality took over her face for a moment, then vanished behind a mask of hon-eyed complaint. She slid her arms around me and tried to look hurt. "But Tigrallef, beloved—why did you leave me alone?"

"Because you stole all the blankets. Please, Rinn. We're sailing today. I may never see Gil again. All I want is to watch one last sunrise from the Gilgard."

She humphed, suddenly and completely herself. "Have it your way, then. But you should be happy to leave Gil. Dirty little hole! I shall be happy to get out of here." When the real Rinn surfaced, the accent thickened. She stood beside me and gazed down with contempt at the distant streets. "Ugly, dirty, stupid little hole," she repeated.

"They used to call Gil the pearl of the world," I said softly.

"It was more beautiful than you could imagine—but it couldn't last. It was built on the wrong foundations."

"Ugly, dirty, stupid hole," she said again, all spite and vinegar, but then she caught herself. She frowned, perhaps searching for something positive to say; finding nothing, she kissed me rather wetly in the hollow of my throat and tried to change the subject by dragging me towards the pallet.

"Not now, Rinn." I patted her lightly on that delectable bottom and turned back to the window. After a moment, I heard her stomp to the pallet and slide under the blankets. Then I put her out of my mind. The sunlight was just beginning to strike the ridges of the Lower Palace and the old grey stonework was gleaming like gold.

Sunset of the same day. Rinn was down in our wildly opulent suite of cabins, bathing the dust of Gil off her perfect body. Chasco the Clanseri had disappeared below deck soon after we sailed and I had not seen him since. Shree and I stood alone on the afterdeck of the *Tasiil*, gazing back in the direction of Gil. All that we could see now was the Gilgard, a blunt, lonely finger of rock on the western horizon, silhouetted against a sun as red as fresh blood, as red as Rinn's lips.

"I hate the sea," I said.

"I know. You told me."

"Did I tell you how seasick I got, sailing from Exile to Gil? Half the time I was afraid I'd die, the other half I was afraid I'd live."

"You seem fine right now."

"Give me time," I said darkly. "It wasn't just that journey, either. Even short hops from one island to another in the Archipelago, even stepping into a rowboat sometimes, and I'd start puking before we even left the beach."

"You don't look sick."

"I will be, later. Right now I'm distracted by my emotions." Sourly, I turned my back on Gil and leaned against the rail. It wasn't true, if anything I was numb, feeling nothing, not even at the memory of Angel's stricken face as he fought to follow me on to the tender, nor of my mother's parting smile—*I know you're going to be happy. I know I'll see you again.*

Happy! She might as well have predicted I'd be handsome. I shifted my weight as the *Tasiil* rolled to one side.

"Tigrallef?"

"Yes, Shree?"

He gulped. "How do you feel now?"

"Still healthy." I swung back to the rail, struck by a sudden realization. "We're about two hours out from Gil, aren't we?"

"About that."

"Then we must be about where Calla was when—" I stopped, unwilling to say it out loud. In my mind, I was standing again on the barren summit of the Gilgard, the Lady coruscating in my hands, the terrible deed not yet done, Calla still alive, her ship a far-off silver gleam on an ocean as smooth as a silken counterpane. She would have been somewhere around here when the sea started to boil around her; if I looked down, I thought, deep into the water, I might find the very spot where her bones were busy bringing forth flowers—or crabs, or jelly-devils, or whatever bones bring forth on the seabed. I peered down into the turbid water, knowing how absurd the idea was. The ship yawed again and I had to catch the taffrail to keep my balance.

"Merciless Raksh," mumbled Shree, and vomited over the side.

I looked at him incredulously. "You're green, Shree. Are you sick?"

"What does it look like?" He sank down on the deck and hung his head between his knees.

I looked back at the water. The wind had freshened and the sea, calm before, was building up into a series of low, rolling dunes that were moving towards us at just the wrong angle. All around us, the other ships were pitching and tilting on their sides and performing slow rolls that should have been nauseating just to watch, but my stomach remained the most cheerful part of me. The wind-galleys were pulling in their oars, sails were being shortened, the Gillish longship was wallowing far behind in the hazardous swell. Shree vomited again, this time on the deck.

"Are you all right, Shree?"

"No, I am not."

"I'm fine."

"Tup you, Tig."

"No, listen. The point is—"

"Go away."

One of the minor Miisheli nobles came towards us at that point, gazed thoughtfully at the puddle of puke on the deckboards, added to it, and wandered off. Sighing, I helped Shree to his feet and got him down the companionway and into his tiny cabin, the ship's powerful rolling motion tossing us from side to side all the way. I had never seen Shree so helpless. I took off his sandals and cleaned him up a bit, then tucked him into his pallet with the pisspot handy by his side. All the while, I was waiting almost impatiently to get sick myself; there was something unnatural about not throwing up when other people were, especially with my terrible history on the water. I wanted to discuss this with Shree, but he didn't seem to be in the mood. When I left him, he was vomiting again into the pisspot.

His cabin was one of a maze of cubicles given to lesser members of the court; a young Frath Minor whom I knew to be one of my wife's recent lovers was next to Shree, and I'd earlier seen the Han-Frath in charge of the Miisheli troopers on board the *Tasiil* going into the cabin on the other side. The corridor was empty now, but I could hear retching noises behind the Frath Minor's door. Shaking my head sympathetically (Rinn's lover or not, he seemed a pleasant and earnest young man), I climbed back up the companionway leading to the afterdeck.

The rollers were high and wild; spray and rain spattered across the deck in a wet grey curtain. Above me I could hear sailors calling back and forth in the rigging, and realized we were tacking to take the waves at a better angle. Already, the *Tasiil* seemed steadier in the water. I waited for a rainsquall to pass over, then headed for the taffrail to see what was happening to the Gillish longship. I heard a step behind me.

"My lord Scion!"

"Yes?" I started to turn. A heavy weight hit my legs below the knees, knocking me against the taffrail—my feet slipped from under me on the slick deckboards and shot straight over the low lip of the deck, but I caught at the taffrail and clung to it, praying it would hold, feeling empty space under my dangling feet, then water to the knees as the ship canted and the

swell rose to meet me. Out of the corner of my eye I saw
something long and white wash past me under the taffrail and
teeter on the edge of the deck for a second before plunging
overboard. I hung on grimly until the deck tilted back the
other way, then let go of the rail and scrambled downslope
towards the elegant portal that sheltered the companionway.
Chasco the Clanseri met me halfway.

He grabbed my arm and dragged me through the door,
slamming it shut behind him. His face was white and he was
panting. He took hold of me again and pulled me down the
companionway and through the labyrinth of little doors to one
with his name marked on it in Miisheli script and pitched me
inside. He shut that door more softly and leaned against it, still
panting, still looking like someone had put a nail into him.

His cubicle was identical to Shree's. I sat down on the pallet and gazed at him. He was too breathless to speak.

"I'm dripping all over your floor," I said.

He waved his fingers—*don't mention it*.

"I should thank you for helping me, Clanseri. Did you see
what happened? I nearly got much wetter than this."

He sat down beside me on the pallet. "It's not safe up there,
my lord Scion," he said. His face and breathing were returning
to normal. "I thought we'd lost you."

"Well, the sea is rough," I admitted, "but there was no danger until something knocked me over from behind. What was
that, anyway? I think I saw it go overboard."

"I didn't get a good look at him—"

"Him?" I sat up straight.

"Yes, my lord Scion; that is, I'm not altogether sure, but it
didn't look like a woman."

My jaw dropped with horror. "But it was someone rather
than something?"

"Yes, my lord, in a sailor's white cape. That's why I
couldn't tell for sure—"

"Chasco!" I shot to my feet. "Why didn't you tell me? We
might have been able to rescue him! By the Lady! We'll have
to tell someone, find the captain, find a rope, maybe the poor
bastard can still be saved—"

Chasco, sitting quietly on the pallet throughout this outburst, put his hand on my shoulder and shook me—respect-

fully—until I shut up. Then he said, "Quietly, my lord Scion. And don't worry about the poor bastard in the water, he won't drown."

"What do you mean, he won't drown? He's a fish, is he? You saw those waves, trooper, he won't last ten minutes—"

"My lord Scion."

"What?"

"He was dead before he hit the sea. I shot him with a dart-tube."

I gulped. "You did what?"

"I shot him with a dart-tube, my lord Scion."

"Why did you do that?"

"Because he was about to put a knife into your back."

"Oh," I said.

There he sat, the descendant of great poets, looking up at me politely, as if he'd just announced that my bath was ready. I dropped back beside him and stared at the wall of the cubicle. It was painted bright yellow, and there was a pattern of red interlocking spirals running around the base. Miisheli colours. Ghastly combination. Ghastly people.

"I called out to warn you, my lord, then shot him. I had no choice—he was too close to you. But it's a pity the body went overboard; I wanted to see who it was."

"Oh yes," I agreed, "a great pity. I wouldn't mind knowing who wants me dead so badly. This is at least the fourth attempt."

"Four? I knew of only two," Chasco said thoughtfully. "The matter of the Frath Minor in the Gilgard has not yet been explained. The Miishelu said they'd investigate."

"Did they?"

"I don't know, lord Scion. The Satheli captain and I were not welcome at their deliberations." He frowned. "Tell me, my lord, who would gain by your death? And why?"

I thought it over. Having lost both Calla and the archives, I had nothing much to live for; but the puzzle had some intrinsic worth. "I would guess that since the Frath Major seems to want me alive for the moment, his enemies naturally want me dead. Which would put most of the Miisheli court under suspicion. In fact, there could be any number of unrelated factions trying to kill me, all for different reasons—that would be interesting. How did you happen to be on deck at just the right time?"

He accepted the abrupt change of subject. "It was my business to be there, lord Scion. I've had you in sight ever since we embarked."

"I didn't spot you."

"I learned how to stay out of sight," he announced calmly, "when I served in the Web."

"Oh." I drew a deep breath. Of course he had been in the Web. I should have guessed. All the signs were there, the fingerspeech, the reserve, the inaudible feet, the invisible watchfulness. Mentally, I smeared a layer of professional grime on his very clean face, substituted filthy rags for his spotless uniform, then I knew he was telling the truth. I had seen a hundred like him in the old days, quiet rebels, shadows, risking their skins daily under the sharp eyes of the Sherkin garrison. I hesitated, then asked, "Why didn't you tell me this before?"

"Is it important?"

"It's important to me. I owe a great deal to the Web. But after the liberation, I could find very few of you to thank."

He shrugged. "Many of us were wiped out in the last days of the Sherkin Empire. The rest of us disbanded shortly after. The Web wasn't needed any more, and we had new lives to build."

I drew another deep breath. "Did you know a woman called Calla?"

"I knew her. Everybody knew Calla."

"Yes," I said sadly. "Yes, I suppose everybody would." The grief swept over me again, undiminished by the passage of years. I stared hard at the hateful yellow wall, followed the hideous red spirals with my eyes. Chasco sat quietly beside me. After a while, he touched my arm.

"My lord Scion? I think that was the mess-bell. The Frath Major will be expecting you."

"I suppose he will." I stirred myself, wondering if the Clanseri would notice the moisture at the corners of my eyes, but not wanting to make it obvious by brushing it away. If he noticed, he gave no sign. I made what was probably a pathetic attempt to be businesslike.

"One more thing, Chasco. Did anyone see you use the dart-tube?"

"I don't think so, my lord Scion."

"Because there are bound to be questions—"

"I doubt it, my lord, with respect. The man's accomplices, if he had any, won't want to draw attention to themselves. Everyone else will assume he was washed overboard in the squall."

I sighed. "I hope you're right. And if so, that will be the end of it." We sat awkwardly for a few moments, not speaking. Then I said, "I suppose I should get these wet britches off before dinner."

"Yes, my lord Scion."

"I might catch my death otherwise. That would save somebody the trouble of killing me."

"Yes, my lord Scion."

"I don't want to make things easy for them."

"No, my lord Scion."

"Goodbye, then."

"Goodbye, my lord."

"Though I suppose you'll still be following me."

"I'll be following you, my lord."

I nodded, and got up to leave; but paused at the door and looked back at him, noticing something for the first time.

"Chasco?"

"Yes, my lord Scion?"

"Where's your green armband?"

He looked at me steadily. "I discarded it when we left Gil, my lord. I'm in your service now."

"I see. Chasco?"

"Yes, my lord Scion?"

"I wish you'd start calling me Tig."

12

ONLY FOUR AND a half of us appeared in the eating salon that night: myself, the Frath Major, two of the lesser Fraths, and the Satheli envoy to Miishel, who dashed out with his hand over his mouth when the fermented chicken innards were brought in. I ate enormously, although the ship was rolling and bucking and the platters slopped about disgustingly on the eating benches. Some Of the Miisheli delicacies should have turned my belly even on dry land.

The Frath Major watched me narrowly. "I see you enjoy Miisheli cooking," he said, as if the idea didn't quite please him.

"Actually," I said with my mouth full, "I don't like it much. These snails are repulsive. What are they cooked in?"

"Garlic-root."

I popped another one in my mouth to confirm that they were as awful as I first thought, and swallowed it without chewing. The Frath was still watching me with embarrassing concentration and it dawned on me that I may have been ever so slightly tactless, so I ate another snail while casting around for something other than food to talk about.

"Tell me, cousin," I said at last, "where is the Bequiin? I'm anxious to talk with him."

"Why?" the Frath asked sharply.

I looked up at him, surprised at his tone. "For one thing, I'd like to borrow something to read. Presumably he brought some books along."

"No." Again, the sharp tone. Then he recovered himself, and said more affably, "Poor old Ardin is indisposed. He suffered badly from seasickness on the voyage to Gil, and I expect he will keep to his cabin until we reach Cansh Miishel. You will have all the books you want then."

"I will? That's cheerful news." I wiped the snail juice from my chin and beamed at him. But somehow I felt, looking at his hard, clever face, that I was being offered either a poisoned sweetmeat or one attached to a hook and line. Like Rinn, the original weathervane, the Frath seemed to be playing a rather devious game called Keep the Scion Happy, which suited me for the moment; but I'd have given my back teeth to know what the prize was going to be.

Rinn herself, poor little doxy, was in a bad state when I returned to our suite for the night. The serving maid who was holding the silver puke-bowl for her was not much healthier, so I sent her off to bed and took over the bowl-holding duties myself, also freshening the damp cloth that covered Rinn's forehead and eyes. She stirred miserably.

"Niil, darling, is that you?" she whimpered in Miisheli. Niil was a Frath Minor, not very young but undeniably good-looking in a tired and dissolute way. I gathered he was on Rinn's current roster.

I patted her hand. "It's Tigrallef, Rinn. Your husband."

She pushed the cloth off her forehead and stared up at me with dull eyes. I think she was too sick to remember who I was, and wouldn't have cared anyhow. She rolled on to her side and proceeded to fill the silver bowl, and then was fast asleep before I even finished mopping up her face. For the rest of the night I sat by the pallet, dozing, holding the bowl as required, occasionally sponging the sweat off Rinn's forehead, feeling the *Tasiil* strain and creak around us as she rode the energetic sea. Sometime around dawn, the storm subsided and Rinn stopped throwing up at regular intervals, and I was able to fall into an uneasy sleep.

In the morning, when I went to Shree's cubicle, he was up and dressed in fresh clothes and feeling well enough to be harrying a steward to do something about the stench of sick in his room. I dragged him up on deck with me, telling him in a low voice about the cold swim I almost took, and the knife I almost had between my shoulderblades, and the timely intervention of Chasco the Clanseri, ex-member of the Web and new faithful retainer. He listened without comment or expression until I said, not mincing words, that I no longer numbered Chasco among the enemy and expected Shree to follow my example. Shree put his head on one side and frowned at me—mutinously, I thought.

"Chasco's the bastard who dragged you out of the archives."

"He didn't drag me. I walked."

"The one who was in command when the assassins broke into your bedchamber and might have killed you."

"Yes, but—"

"The one who hogged the second-most comfortable chair in the room all the time the Primate had you locked up in the Temple Palace."

"Yes, Shree, all right, but—"

"The one with the Primate's green band around his arm."

"Not any more. Trust my instincts on this, Shree, I don't think he's the Primate's man now, if he ever really was."

"All right."

"He—what did you say?"

"I said, all right, I'll trust your instincts."

"Oh." I had expected more resistance, somehow. This was like a tug-of-war where one man suddenly lets go of the rope. I was flustered. "Why?"

"I've seen his kind before, in the Sherkin army. Too intelligent to be good spear-fodder, too much initiative to be trusted in the ordinary way. Very dangerous in the ranks."

"So what did you do with them?"

"We promoted them. It wasn't just viciousness that made us a good army, you know. No, I should think your instincts are right. Your friend Chasco doesn't look stupid enough to give his loyalty to a grubbing old puppetmaster like the Primate. Or to a puppet like your esteemed brother Arkolef."

I hesitated. It seemed even less believable that he'd give it to a fumbling, nearsighted, unprincely and apolitical grubber in old books like me, but I didn't like to disturb the accord by asking Shree what he thought; he'd probably have told me.

I had to leave him then while I took breakfast with the upper aristocracy, a meal which was only slightly better attended than dinner on the night before. The Frath Major hardly spoke to me; the Satheli envoy managed to last out the entire meal this time, though he paled dramatically when exposed to the frogspawn in aspic. As soon as I decently could, I took my leave and went to find Shree again. He was not on deck; he was not in his cabin, which now stank worse of incense than it had of vomit. I tried the small salon reserved for junior courtiers, one deck down from my quarters, and found it was deserted. The only other place I could think of was Chasco's cubicle, so I started up the broad midship companionway that would take me into one end of the maze of cabins. I remember thinking it was not wise to be wandering alone like that in the dark ways of the ship, though my uneasiness could hardly be classed as a premonition. I had no warning of what was about to happen.

Stop!

A woman's voice, with the persuasive force of a hammer-blow to the head. I stopped dead.

"Who's there?"

No answer. No stirrings on the deck below; no stirrings on the deck above, where three dark corridors branched from the top of the companionway. I shook my head, certain I was imagining things, and went up another step or two.

BEWARE!

It was so persuasive this time that it knocked me right to my knees, my hands over my ears, halfway up the flight. At almost the same moment, something whirred over me at about the level where my throat had just been.

Puzzled, I looked up the stairs. A large Miisheli with a *very* large triple-curved sword poised over his head was just beginning to topple towards me. He also seemed puzzled, probably because of the throwing disc half-buried in his belly.

I stepped out of his way and looked down the stairs. Another large Miisheli was crouched at the bottom, aiming a second throwing disc in my direction. Before he could let fly however, the first Miisheli finished tumbling past me and crashed into him sword-first, skewering him as neatly as a sausage on a toasting fork.

I did not wait to check their health. In two leaps I was at the top of the stairs; I threw myself into the right-hand corridor at full gallop, skidded to a halt at the sight of a cloaked figure running ahead of me, saw it glance back at me before vanishing at the next turning. A moment later, a door slammed. I wavered for a few seconds; then, since no one seemed to be pursuing me, I ran cat-footed to the turning and poked my head around the corner.

Eight closed doors stood between me and the end of the passage, four to a side. Eight eminent name-plates: two Han-Fraths, four Fraths Minor, the Bequiin Ardin and the Satheli envoy. The shadowy oval of a face I had glimpsed could be any one of them. Behind the doors there was only silence.

As I thought, my two protectors were in Chasco's cabin having a cosy chat. They seemed to be getting on very well together. They sat me down and told me what they had decided: that they thought I might still be in danger, and from now on, one or both of them would be guarding me at all times. After all, they said weightily, there could be other assassins on board besides the one Chasco killed.

It gave me the best laugh I'd had in ages.

Eventually I became coherent enough to tell them about my adventure in the companionway, and took them with me to see if the assassins were still there, alive or dead. We were not very surprised to find the foot of the stairway deserted and quite damp, as if the floorboards had been hastily swabbed. Nor did we hear subsequently that any members of the crew were missing. None of this was reassuring, smelling as it did of conspiracy and concealment. The related question of the figure in the corridor was thoroughly turned over; for future reference, we discreetly noted down the names of the two Han-Fraths and four Fraths Minor. The Bequiin and the Satheli envoy we considered unlikely candidates.

What I did not tell Shree and Chasco about was the *voice*. As far as they were concerned, I had been saved by tripping over my own feet, according to the luck the gods frequently bestow upon the innocent and clumsy. I did not tell them about the voice because I only half-believed in it myself, and even so it frightened me. Although it had probably saved my life, the memory of it was repellent.

Of course this was not the first time I'd been on board a ship, but it was the first time I'd been able to sit up and take notice. The *Tasiil* was a lovely vessel, clean-lined and massive, built to transport members of the Miisheli royal clans around the oceans. As far as I knew, she was the largest manmade object on the face of the Great Known Sea. She was a four-masted windcatcher, not a galley, and her lower foredeck was broad enough for forty men to stand shoulder to shoulder across its width, and long enough to use for foot-races. The upper foredeck was smaller, graced with a number of little ornamental deckhouses and a whole garden in pots and a tiny temple with a built-in altar so that the priests could burn their offerings without setting fire to the ship.

Below, the space saved by not having oarbanks was taken up by a honeycomb of cabins and galleys and opulent staterooms, while two positively sinful royal suites were sited under the afterdeck. Rinn and I were in one of these, the Frath Major in the other. Both suites opened on to a large pleasure salon that outdid anything else on the ship in terms of sheer eye-punching ostentation, all marble tables and heavy brocade hangings and silk-slipped settees in alarming colour combinations, more vulgar even than anything Arko dreamed up when he refitted the Temple Palace two years back, and vastly more expensive.

I spent as little time as possible below deck. This was partly because Rinn decided she would pass the rest of the voyage on her pallet with a wet towel on her head, and my presence was an unwelcome distraction. I suspected she was occasionally doing more on that pallet than resting, judging by the number of Fraths Minor and lesser courtiers that I never saw above deck, but I honestly didn't care.

Anyway, I liked being outside. I liked watching the companion ships of the convoy lolloping through the waves on all sides of us, and set myself to learning what the flag language meant. I liked the fresh tang of the air, laced with salty spray, especially after the sinus-stopping cocktail of incense and heavy floral perfumes in the state quarters below. I liked the parade of empty islets and atolls and navigation points and low barren hills rearing out of the sea. I liked the schools of silver finnyfish that streaked along beside us just under the surface, and the whales that investigated us and prudently swam away. I liked not being seasick. I liked being in the sunshine and the open air. We'd never had much of those commodities in the archives.

It was fortunate Shree and Chasco liked all those things too, because they stuck to me like lint for the next three days. I was not left unguarded for a moment—by day they flanked me, by night they took turns sleeping in the salon outside my quarters. Chasco developed a disconcerting habit of practising his knife-throws as we sat at leisure on the upper foredeck. Shree spent a lot of time conspicuously honing his sword. This seemed to deter any would-be assassins for the time being, though we often had the feeling we were being watched or followed.

And so those three days of the voyage passed, so pleasantly

that I forgot from time to time that I didn't want to be there; that someone had been trying to kill me; that a bride I didn't love was already cuckolding me regularly in a stateroom I regarded as a bad joke; and that in something over a week, we'd be making landfall in Cansh Miishel.

We sighted the first ships far to the north on our fifth morning out of Gil. There were maybe four of them, maybe five, certainly no match for the seven fighting wind-galleys and three rammers in our own escort. My eyes were too short-sighted to see them at all, but Chasco and Shree, strolling beside me along the rail of the lower foredeck, could make them out well enough to disagree on the exact number.

"It doesn't matter how many we outnumber them by," I said wearily, "as long as we outnumber them. Anyway, they could just as well be traders or fishermen—there's no evidence that they're hostile."

"It's safer to be suspicious," said Shree, exchanging a meaningful glance with Chasco.

I squinted at the northern horizon. "I still can't see them, you know. Are you sure they're still there?"

"They've changed course," said Chasco, peering keenly towards the north. "They're moving parallel with us now. Checking our strength, maybe. What do you think, Lord Shree?" He didn't bother to ask what I thought.

"Perhaps," I said evenly, "they're innocent traders who think that we're dangerous, and they're sensibly keeping out of our way."

"Perhaps," said Shree.

"Perhaps," echoed Chasco. This time, I got the feeling they were avoiding giving each other significant glances. They were humouring me.

"What's going on?" I demanded. "Are you two holding something back?"

"No, Tig," said Shree.

"No, Lord Tigrallef," said Chasco. It was as close as he could bring himself so far to calling me by name. I sat up, all primed and bursting with difficult questions, when I was interrupted by shouts from the rigging. Looking overhead, we saw that a dozen or so sailors had climbed the shrouds and were doing complicated and probably useful things in the webbing of lines strung high on the upper masts.

Chasco peered up thoughtfully. "That's interesting. They're preparing to put on more sail. I'd have thought we were carrying enough for this sea."

"How do you know so much about it?"

"I used to be a sailor, Lord Tigrallef."

"Did you, now? I'd never have taken you for the sailor type. When was that?"

"After the Web disbanded, before I joined the Guard. I sailed for two years on a windcatcher like this one, only smaller, one of the first trading vessels out of Malvi after the liberation."

"So that's when you gained your sea-belly."

"Yes, Lord Tigrallef."

More shouts from above; but this time when we looked up, we saw they were not from the sailors playing catch-me in the rigging, but from the lookout in his cage at the top of the mid-foremast. He was shaking the bars of the cage, stabbing his arm towards the north again, and bawling out a number. Seventeen.

We scrambled to our feet and ran to the rail. "There!" Shree exclaimed, pointing. I still couldn't see anything but a grey blur, but Chasco nodded and made a smooth, unconscious gesture towards the knife in his belt-sheath.

"What is it? What does he mean, seventeen?"

"Seventeen ships," murmured Shree, "just on the horizon. I make it only fifteen, but I bet he's right. He can see further up there."

"Pirates?"

"Not likely," said Chasco. "Pirates never travel in such large packs, and they feed mostly on lone sheep. How many are we?"

"Twelve, if you count that limping old longship that Tig's brother sent along; ten good fighting ships, anyway. No pirate would attack a convoy this big even if they outnumbered it."

"Then they're not pirates." Chasco nodded as if his darkest

suspicions were being confirmed. "What do you think? Grisot? Tata? We'll see the colours when they come closer."

I was feeling left out again. "Why Grisot? We're not at war with them—yet—and it's too late for them to scuttle the alliance. If anything, an attack on us would only make the alliance stronger, give the three nations a common cause. The Grisotin may be barbarians, but they're not stupid."

Shree put his back to the rail and gazed at me grimly. His eyes were narrow, hard and shiny, and he'd never looked more like an archetypal Sherkin maniac. "Certainly, Tig, it's too late for them to prevent the alliance. Certainly, attacking the nuptial ship would invite the vengeance of Miishel and Sathelforn and Gil. So what? Maybe the Grisotin are more worried about something else. Maybe their spies tell them there's something on this ship that's worth the risk."

I didn't like the way they were looking at me. "What did you have in mind?"

They glanced at each other.

Chasco raised his eyebrows a hair's-width at Shree. Shree shook his head at Chasco by the fraction of a hair's-width.

But they both jumped a foot when I pounded my fist on the rail.

"Will you two stop that? I'm not blind at this range, you know. I can see you're hiding something."

In the awkward pause that followed, the lookout on the mast bellowed a name that temporarily froze every Miisheli in sight. "Grisot! Grisoti colours!" A second later, the *Tasiil* was resounding with warcries, echoed lustily across the water by every Miisheli ship in the fleet. The deck shook with the pounding of feet below and moments later a horde of troopers swarmed up the companionway from the barracks in the depths of the ship, some of them still belting on their battle-skins. Every face was shining with the pleasant anticipation of mayhem.

Raising his voice over the din, Chasco said calmly, "I think you'd better tell him what you told me."

"Perhaps it is time," Shree answered, his face thoughtful. "He should be prepared. Let's get off this deck, Tig, we'll only be trampled if we stay here."

13

WE SAT IN a row against the wall of the little temple, me in the middle, our feet straight out in front of us. We had a good view from there of the approaching Grisoti fleet, which even I could discern now as individual grey blobs tossing on the swell about halfway to the horizon. Below us on the lower foredeck, bright-eyed Miisheli troopers were setting up rows of gaunt flame-slings and lethal metal-sprung spear-chuckers and draping anti-boarding nets, inwoven with thousands of glittering hooks, over the rail.

"They're enjoying themselves," I said with disgust.

"Of course they are. There was a time I'd have felt the same." Shree pulled out his silver flask and offered it around. "I think you'd better have some," he said when I waved it away. "You're not going to like what I have to tell you."

"Just tell me."

He sat up poker-straight, nursing his flask in both hands. "You're going to hate it."

"Go on, tell me. I'll love it, I promise." I grinned at him to show how much I'd love it.

He looked gravely back at me. "It has to do with the Lady in Gil."

"The Lady in Gil?" I laughed. "The Lady is gone, Shree, I destroyed her myself, six years ago, and threw the fragments into the sea. You watched me do it."

"I saw you break a piece of glass."

I took a moment to absorb this, then grabbed his shoulder so suddenly that he flinched. His flask tilted, spilling a few drops of fith-liquor on to his tunic. "What are you saying, you fishbrain? That so-called piece of glass *was* the Lady."

Very deliberately, he rubbed the spilled liquor into his tunic, in the full knowledge that it would eat little holes in the fabric. "I saw you catch fire and not burn."

"That's—"

"Shut up, Tig. Let me speak. I saw you break a piece of glass. I saw you catch fire and not burn."

"You said that already."

He ignored me. "I saw the fire sucked in through your pores. I saw your bones outlined like your body was an alabaster pot with a light shining through it, and I also saw your heart beating. It looked like a fist clenching and unclenching."

"This is a joke, right?"

"It's no joke. Like it or not, that's what happened. And then the light faded, and you were still breathing and looking reasonably human, so I woke you up."

I held out my hand for the flask, and took a long swallow. "So the Lady's destruction was accompanied by some interesting and unexplained magico-physical phenomena. So what?" I took a defiant pull at the flask and erupted into coughs as the liquor burned down the wrong passage. Shree pounded me on the back.

"I'll tell you what. I wasn't sure what it meant at the time, so I said nothing about it. I didn't know if it meant anything. But I've lived with you for six years since then, and all that time I've been watching you and wondering about it, even though you never seemed anything but human, sometimes too tupping human. But after what I've seen in the last couple of months, I'd bet you six Calloonic tablets against a Lucian scroll that you didn't destroy the Lady at all."

"You saw me do it," I said patiently.

"I saw you break a piece of glass," he said, less patiently. "I saw you catch fire and not burn. You destroyed the vessel the Lady was lodged in, Tig, that's as sure as breath and death—but as for the power that was known as the Lady in Gil—"

"Stop, Shree. Don't say it."

"—maybe she couldn't be destroyed—maybe she went into something else—another vessel—"

"She went to the bottom of the sea," I said, but not very firmly. As he was talking, something peculiar had started happening inside my head. I was remembering the shock that went up my arm when the Lady cracked, the pit of darkness that opened under me; the horror at the magnitude of my crime, so many deaths, the innocent along with the guilty, so much blood. More blood today, I thought with a stab of revulsion, listening to the click-clack of the spears being slotted into the spearchuckers.

Shree was staring at me with fiery intensity. "Listen to what I'm saying, Tig. Think of the Frath Minor, the one who was squeezed out on top of you like a sponge full of blood. What were you dreaming about when that happened?"

"The usual," I said, increasingly distracted by events inside my brain. Golden dust-motes were gathering at the edges of my vision.

"The attack at the Fiery Hand—you took some blows to the head that should have crushed your skull like a rotten pikcherry, but you didn't even bleed, you walked away with no more than a headache."

"A terrible headache," I amended absently. I could hardly see him now for the haze of gold in front of his face. I squinted past him at the far-off Grisoti fleet, found I could see them perfectly, detailed miniature war-galleys and rammers, trailing battle-flags, at the end of an infinitely long golden tube.

"And another thing—the taster died."

"Hmmm? Who died?"

"The taster, Tig. In agony, on your nuptial day. A slow-acting poison—where was the poison, Chasco?"

"The diced whale balls."

"That's right—of which the taster ate one, and you ate two or three."

"Four, I think," I corrected him. Nothing he was saying seemed very important.

"Four of them! Great Raksh! That should have killed you four times over! And while we're on the subject, you haven't had so much as a day's illness in six years, not even when the selti plagues came and Angel and I were squitting blood for a week; and why didn't you get seasick the other night, when the rest of us drylanders were laid out flat on our arses? It's not natural, Tig!"

A small part of me was listening tolerantly to Shree's spate. The larger part was watching the Grisoti fleet and the exultant preparations on the lower foredeck, and thinking, more blood; so much spilled already, and these spike-happy barbarian louts were panting to spill more. Somebody should stop them. The gold was rippling now, like molten metal in a jeweller's pan.

"But the clincher is how valuable you are suddenly—valuable enough for Miishel to pay a double dowry to have you, and for Raksh knows how many attempts on your life to stop them having you; and now, suddenly, the Grisoti fleet coming down on us like a pack of wolves, for no reason I can see except maybe that you're on board. They know, Tig. Somehow they *know*."

"Know what?" I got up and strolled towards the rail. Silence behind me, then the sound of four knees cracking as their owners leapt after me. I stood at the rail watching the spears being primed in the spearchuckers, the sulphur-pitch for the flame bolts being heated in a massive bronze cauldron over a portable fire. More blood. I shut my eyes.

Shree was yammering at me again, Chasco was clutching my arm as if he thought I intended leaping overboard with my boots on, but I ignored them. I opened my eyes and looked back at the western horizon and was not surprised to see a great cloud forming there, growing massive, piling itself up, the colour of cold iron with a dull red glow at its heart, roiling and billowing as it began to sweep towards us on a front broad enough to engulf both fleets, driving the sea before it, lightning standing out against the grey like swollen veins under a giant's skin. Shree was still babbling. He hadn't seen it yet.

"I think we should go below," I said to him, cutting into some nonsense about the Lady and the Lady's new receptacle. "There's a nasty blow heading our way." My body tingled; the golden motes danced in front of my eyes.

Shree looked beyond me and saw the storm. His face blanched. "Raksh! Where did that come from? The sky was clear a moment ago."

The troopers had seen it, too. There was a groan from the foredeck. Orders were given. Somebody stomped out the fire under the cauldron. Others, looking bitter, hurried to dismantle the spearchuckers.

"Can't play games in a storm, eh? Not good for the toys, I imagine." I chuckled. Chasco and Shree looked at me soberly, and then at each other, and then turned to gaze with disbelief at the moving mountain of cloud. It was coming up fast—already the sea was rising around us in angry peaks and the sailors were rushing about in the rigging like demented monkeys, securing the sails.

Shree turned and faced me squarely and threw his words at me like punches. "Is this your doing?"

"How could it be? I'm only a man like you, only not as strong." I laughed softly. "What were we talking about? Never mind, tell me later, I should go down to see that my lovely Rinn is well wedged into her pallet."

I left them frozen at the railing, and hummed softly to myself as I trotted aft towards the royal suite. More blood? Not today, there wouldn't be. I grinned as the *Tasiil* rolled sickeningly under the first assault of the winds. No blood today.

The salon was empty but showed signs of hasty abandonment, gambling sticks scattered over the floor, a smashed beaker, a decanter on its side rolling back and forth across the table trailing a dark stream of wine behind it. A cloak I recognized as the Frath Major's was getting thoroughly wet. I laughed out loud.

But as I reached the door that led to Rinn's boudoir, the last of the golden haze vanished as suddenly as a candle snuffed in a bucket, taking my elation with it. All at once I was myself again, drained and shaken, with the door handle in my hand and nothing much in my head but an ache of doom and the echo of Shree's ridiculous revelation.

I saw you break a piece of glass. I saw you catch fire and not burn.

I shook myself. It was nonsense. I started to turn the handle.

Very sudden, this storm. Odd how it came just when you wanted it.

My hand dropped from the handle. That was a voice I'd heard at least once before.

Not the first time that golden fog's showed up, either. Remember on the mountaintop—

Voices far off down the corridor, approaching the salon: Shree and Chasco. I didn't want to see them. I sprinted back through the salon and into the transverse corridor just before they turned the corner and made for the companionway to the afterdeck. They passed by without seeing me and vanished into the salon.

The afterdeck was empty, battered by the wind, drenched by

fountains of spray crashing over the taffrail. These were only the advance squalls; the main body of the storm reared out of the sea maybe ten minutes behind us. I lashed myself to a stanchion in the shelter of the deckhouse and settled down to think.

I had destroyed the Lady. I had destroyed her, and then I had thrown her damnable sherds over the side of the Gilgard, into the sea. As for what Shree thought he saw that fateful morning, he had simply partaken too freely of the contents of his little silver flask, or had hallucinated in the thin air on the Gilgard summit, or both. That was what I told myself. There was nothing in the Secrets of the Ancients about the Lady having an immanence separate from her crystal housing, no historical precedent for her taking up residence in a living human body.

The rain lanced against my face; the words came clearly inside my head. *There wouldn't be a precedent, would there? Nobody ever broke the glass before.*

True, I retorted, *but why would the Lady then spend six years stowing away in my head, without so much as a whisper of her presence?*

Perhaps there was no need before now.

What do you mean, no need? I can think of plenty of times I could have used a bit of power, and where was she then? Anyway, wouldn't I have felt her presence, like a lump in my brain, or a hollow place, or—?

The Harashil, the answer came back coldly, *is neither a lump nor a hollow place.*

The who?

Silence for a few seconds, then a silvery chuckle, not in my ears but between them, mixed with the keening of the wind. I shut my eyes and found the golden motes already there, with a figure behind them, silver-maned and shimmering, all too familiar, that pulsed and flickered and receded, and then seemed to vanish teasingly into some secret chamber in the back of my brain.

Come back! Come back here and show yourself!

Silence.

Come back!

A sudden gust snapped the shrouds over my head like so many harp-strings. A great flap of sailcloth collapsed on to the deck and twitched there for a few seconds like a living thing, a dying thing, before the wind picked it up and whirled it out of sight. The edge of the storm was a dark curtain pulled across the sea only a few boat-lengths away.

"I'm going mad." I said that out loud, but the reply was inside my head.

No, you're not.

14

I CLUNG TO the stanchion for perhaps an hour, taking no notice of the rain that soaked me to the skin and the waves that washed over the afterdeck. Towards the end of the hour something happened that was too grievous to watch, but I forced myself to watch anyway, and tried every way I could think of to influence the outcome; and when it was all over, I howled some useless and totally unheeded threats at the murdering stormbitch and went below deck.

I could hear the Frath's voice in the salon, so I bypassed that door and headed for Shree's cabin. It was empty, so I tried Chasco's cabin. Shree's voice was audible inside it. I threw open the door.

Chasco saw me first. "By the Lady—!"

Shree whirled around and lurched towards me, only partly because the ship pitched at that moment. He looked divided between wanting to strangle me and wanting to throw his arms around me, and compromised by half-throttling me in a fierce embrace. "Damn you, Scion!" he hissed. "Where were you? We went mad searching every corner of this tupping tub for you—"

"I was on the afterdeck."

"What? In this weather?"

"Of course in this weather. There's no other weather available. Calm yourself, Warlord."

That made him too apoplectic to speak for a bit. I took advantage of the lull to ferret the flask out of his pocket and treat myself to a good long drink. He grabbed the flask out of my hand and had another. Chasco took it from him and drained it dry. Then they stood on either side of me, feet planted squarely against the tossing of the ship, glaring at me like two irate aunties at an unrepentant nephew. I spoiled the tableau by sitting down on the pallet.

"What were you worried about? Nothing could have happened to me."

"Tell that to the wave that might have swept you overboard!"

"No such luck. Anyway, the next wave after it would have swept me right back." I shut my eyes and quoted, flat-voiced, from the Secrets of the Ancients, "—and it is woven into the fabric of her power that she can bring no harm to Oballef, nor to the Scions of Oballef—" Shrugging, I broke off.

Chasco looked puzzled, but Shree's righteous anger faded out of his eyes, to be replaced by something that dangerously resembled pity. "So that's what you were doing up there? Testing the truthfulness of the Ancients?"

"Certainly not," I said. "The Ancients never lied. I was watching the storm. And why shouldn't I? Can't the artist admire his own work? Can't the cook savour his own dishes?"

Chasco, still lost, frowned from my face to Shree's. "Cooks? Dishes? What's he babbling about?"

Shree's shoulders slumped. "He means, why shouldn't he sit out there and watch the storm? It's his storm."

Silence; rather, a long few moments when the only voices in the cabin belonged to the ship itself and to the tempest, the hunting cries of wind and water mingling with the wails of wood and metal. The *Tasiil* was having a rough time. She bucked suddenly, breaking the spell. Shree dropped to the floor and wedged himself with his back against the wall and his feet braced against the pallet. Chasco remained where the pitching had thrown him, on the pallet beside me.

"You were right," I said to Shree.

"What?"

"It seems I broke a piece of glass six years ago. It seems I caught fire and didn't burn."

Chasco had caught on by then. "Lord Shree was right—you raised the storm."

"Of course I did. Inadvertently, of course; all I had in mind was that I didn't want those martial idiots to start chopping each other up, and the Lady must have taken over from there . . ."

"The Lady in Gil," Chasco affirmed softly.

"In person. In my head, rather. Not that I can feel her there just now, she likes hiding in the dark corners." I began to rub my temples, gently at first to soothe the ache in them, then harder, wishing bitterly that enough pressure could force the stowaway out through the pores of my scalp.

The *Tasiil* lurched mightily, as if some monstrous hand were shaking her keel from below. This was followed by a resounding crash somewhere above us, then a series of smaller crashes, then a hideous grating noise that prickled the hair on the backs of our necks. The ship heeled to what felt like a fatal angle, hung there for a few moments, sluggishly righted herself.

Chasco, in his most composed fashion, said, "That would be one of the masts."

"Thank you, sailor," said Shree crossly. "Tig? For the sake of Eshkarat!"

"Yes, Shree?"

"Don't you think your storm has served its purpose?"

"Oh, admirably."

"Both the fleets should be well scattered, they'll be too busy keeping afloat to think of chopping each other up."

"Quite right. What's your point, Shree?"

He gazed at me with the beginnings of impatience under his sudden interesting pallor. "Stop your storm. No ship is built to take this kind of punishment for long."

I threw back my head and howled again—laughter, this time, but of the bitter variety. After I'd been laughing for some time with no sign of stopping, Chasco slapped me soundly across both cheeks.

I stopped laughing.

"Better watch yourself, Clanseri. The Lady might take umbrage."

He looked at my face and took a step backwards.

"No, Chasco, I'm not threatening you. But I can't answer for the Lady."

"Aren't you in control?" That was Shree, sitting to attention.

"Not exactly."

"You can't command the Lady?"

"I don't think it's quite that simple—"

"Tig! You called up this tupping great tempest; can't you send it away?"

I smiled gently. "I spent the last half-hour on deck trying to send it away. I invoked the Lesser Will—I tried to remember the Greater Will—I recited the Caveat, in case it meant anything useful, which it didn't—I ordered, I argued, I reasoned, I begged—"

"And?"

"And nothing. It happened anyway."

"What happened?"

"More deaths. Ironic, isn't it—all I wanted was to stop the bloodshed, prevent a few deaths, but—"

"What happened?"

"—the power is so unpredictable, Shree, it's as if once you slip the knot of the flame-sling, there's no way of stopping the bolt—"

"What happened?"

"—and my part is simply to slip the knot, and then stand back and watch the fires break out—"

"*What happened?*"

I finally consented to hear him. "What happened? The Gillish longship sank, that's what happened. One wave turned her turtle, the next smashed her to tinderlengths. No survivors. Oh, a few of our countrymen lasted long enough to cling to the wreckage for a while, pleading for help, a stone's throw away, but there was nothing anyone could have done."

They looked at me blankly.

"Rather like last time," I added; and then started pounding the piss-yellow wall of Chasco's cell with my fist until my knuckles left bloody smears that blended nicely with the Miisheli colour scheme, which was also when the two of them managed to catch my hands and hold me down on the pallet until I stopped struggling and started to curse instead.

The tempest lasted three full days and nights, and the *Tasiil* rode it out like the sturdy unsinkable matron she really was under all her extravagant fripperies. Two of the four masts were lost overboard, and all the rigging, and the garden, and most of the elegant ornamentation that had sparkled on her decks when we sailed away from Gil harbour; but below deck, with the hatches secured and all loose objects tied down, the damage was confined mostly to shins, bellies, heads and tempers.

I don't know if we were ever in serious danger, nor what the Lady would have done if the *Tasiil* had started to break up under the smashing, grinding assault of the waves. I do know, however, that in a strange and terrible fashion, we were safer on the high seas than we'd have been almost anywhere on dry land at that lamentable moment in history. The worst casualty on the *Tasiil* was a broken shoulder, sustained when one of the sailors fell off his sleeping shelf on to the edge of a wooden table; but ashore, the people were already dying in their thousands.

It was called at first by many names, the pesh, the Khalingi fever, the dancing plague, the greenshakes; but one name came to be used in the end, an innocuous name, a name that was not entirely descriptive of the associated sorrow and suffering, and yet was oddly appropriate: the Last Dance.

It started in Storica, as so many plagues seem to, at about the same time as the Primate banned me from the archives; spread to Maalas and Canzitar by the overland routes and Calloon and Kuttumm by sea within the next month; appeared in Luc only days after the first pustules broke in Kuttumm, leapt the sea-lanes to Plav and Glishor, and set its first victims dancing in the Archipelago three days after my marriage to the Princess Rinn. We heard nothing about it before embarking on our journey to Miishel; indeed, it seemed that the same ships that carried tidings of the plague often carried the plague as well—and its progress was speeded by ships and caravans of refugees, who carried the contagion with them as they fled the stinking death-traps of the port cities.

The sickness took only five days to make the jump from Sathelforn to Gil. By the time the Lady and I raised our tempest, the people were dancing again in the streets of Gil, but not, this time, in celebration. At this point the captains in Gil harbour, panicking, repelled the tender-loads of frantic citizens that pulled towards them from the quays and hastily put to sea; and a few weeks later, therefore, there was dancing in the streets of Tata and Grisot and Cansh Miishel and Zaine.

We knew nothing about this. It was only later that I could work out dates and places and chart the progress of the disaster as it rippled outwards from its centre in Storica. The *Tasiil* moved in her own little world, its borders lost in the sheeting rain just beyond the railings of her decks, its inhabitants convinced that nobody on earth was as miserable as they.

Most of the passengers kept to their beds, afflicted to varying degrees by seasickness and fear of a watery death. Shree and Chasco and I spent much of the storm wedged into uncomfortable positions in Chasco's cabin, debating in hushed voices whether the Miishelu and the Grisotin really did know about the Lady, and if so, how? When our speculations became a bore, we played fingersticks. When fingersticks became a bore, I went to visit my wife.

This was on the third and last evening of the storm. I had looked in on her a few times before that—the dutiful husband—but she'd been asleep, probably drugged, and at least once she hadn't been sleeping alone. This time she was both awake and alone, and she turned fearful eyes towards me as I came through the door. She was huddled under a blanket in one corner of the pallet, feverishly pushing the beads back and forth on a gold Miisheli prayer-frame.

"Raalis? Is that you?"

"It's Tigrallef, Rinn," I told her cheerfully. As I sat down on the pallet beside her, the ship canted to a drunken angle and Rinn shrieked and dropped the prayer-frame and covered her head with the bedclothes. I patted the mound of blankets. "Don't worry, wife of my heart, we're not going to sink."

Silence under the bedclothes. Then one eye and a rainbow tangle of hair appeared. "You say so?"

"Yes, I say so."

Dubiously, she withdrew the blankets from the rest of her face and stared at me. She was raddled with fear, almost delirious with it, eyes enormous, mouth pinched, more catlike than ever. When the ship heeled again, she caught her breath sharply and her eyes rolled in her head. She cried out in Miisheli, "I'm afraid! Hold my hand, Raalis!"

"It's Tigrallef," I repeated; but I took her hand anyway and gripped it soothingly while she curled herself up into a tight ball under the bedclothes and proceeded to cry herself to sleep. It was only when she was breathing quietly and I was able to disengage my hand, that I noticed the knuckles I had damaged on Chasco's wall two days before were whole again, the bloody abrasions invisible, the skin healthy.

I stared at my hand for a few moments, then slid under the covers with my clothes on and lay pensively on the edge of the pallet. I didn't close my eyes for a long time. I was trying to remember the last time I had picked at a scab.

15

BACK IN THE dark, forgotten First Age when the world as we know it was created—probably by a committee—it was decreed that the land should be divided into a few very large chunks and a great many small ones, and that salt ocean should compose the remainder of the earth's surface. Conveniently, the creators also arranged that almost no point in the sea should be far out of sight of some bit of land, whether it were the massed hills of a continent, the smoking peaks of an island group, or a miserable scrap of rock just big enough for the deepsea turtles and the legendary fishmen to sun themselves on.

This was a useful provision. It allowed our ancestors, seafarers by necessity from the earliest recorded days, to navigate by sightlines in the daytime and by the stars at night. Any experienced sailor, dropped in a bumboat anywhere in the Great Known Sea that stretched from Storica on the west to Fathan and Zaine on the east, could determine where he was with more accuracy than, say, a Storican dropped in the continental wilderness of Storica, and he could probably also make it to the nearest landfall unless the seabeasts, pirates or fishmen got to him first. In theory, it was difficult to get lost.

"So where are we?" Shree said to Chasco.

Chasco looked down at him unhappily. "I'm not sure."

"You're a sailor, aren't you?"

"Ex-sailor," said Chasco. He rotated slowly, scanning what looked to me like a perfectly featureless horizon under the hard brazen bowl of the sky. His feet were on one of the highest surviving points of the upper foredeck, the remains of a bijou observation gazebo; the two remaining masts towered nakedly over us. Gangs of Miisheli sailors were already picking through the rubble for salvageable wood, sounding the masts and deckboards for damage, bringing great coils of rope and swathes of sailcloth up from the hold.

Further along the deck, a trio whom I knew to be the Miisheli navigators were doing the same thing as Chasco was, with roughly the same expression on their faces. Uncertainty, confusion, puzzlement, and an additional element of wounded professional pride—navigators consider themselves an élite among sailors, which is quite unjustified, given that any ordinary seaman could do the same job just as well. All they're called upon to do is recognize some distinctive excrescence in the sea and counsel a course that will go past it without actually hitting it, towards some other easily identified point of land—I have had harder times finding my own sandals.

That day, there was no land to recognize.

Chasco jumped down, shrugging. "Nothing. Not even a rock. I have no idea where we are."

A dispute broke out among the Miisheli navigators, involving much arm-waving and shouting and the magical appearance of knives from under the dandified sea-cloaks. We moved discreetly down the deck while a knot of troopers moved in to break up the debate before it got bloody.

"Those idiots don't know where we are, either," said Chasco, sniffing. "If the storm had ended sooner, they could have taken star-sightings—but your Lady waited until just after dawn."

"No doubt she did it on purpose," I said sourly.

Shree was walking beside me with his head bent and his

forehead creased. "By Raksh, Tig, I've never seen a storm stop so suddenly, between one moment and the next. How did you persuade her?"

"I didn't do anything. I was asleep."

"We've already established," he said, with a measure of sarcasm, "that you do remarkable things in your sleep. Don't forget the Frath Minor. Were you dreaming at the time?"

"I don't remember." Then I stopped short and laid a hand on his shoulder. It was a flash of that morning's dream—I was back on the podium in the Gilgard, a woman beside me, her face hidden by a straight fall of silver hair, her unnaturally thin hand gripping my elbow; she started to turn, but I guessed what was coming and shut my eyes before they could catch more than a grey gleam or jawbone through the peels of desiccated skin, a shifting luminescence like a cloud of shining blowflies pouring out where the eyes should have been—and in the background, a voice like the Primate's at his most sonorous, echoing over a forecourt where the people were dancing and dropping, dancing and dropping: *now the two are one*.

"Come to think of it, yes, I was dreaming, but nothing I'd consider relevant."

Shree looked at me narrowly. "The usual nightmare? Calla, the child, the Pleasure—?"

"No," I admitted, "a different nightmare, though I wouldn't call it a change for the better." Between my ears, the voice of the Lady softly demurred. I was hearing her quite frequently these days. I told her to shut up. "Never mind how suddenly the storm ended. The point is, we've lost the rest of the fleet, there's no wind to catch and no sails to catch it in anyway, we're drifting in an uncharted current and we won't know where we are until tonight, when the stars come out. Is that a fair summary, Chasco?"

Chasco nodded. "The sun's been up for a couple of hours at least. No position that I know of is more than half an hour out of landsight at the speed we're making in this current. You can draw your own conclusion, my lords."

"What about the current?" Shree asked. "Where would you find a current like this one? You can't tell me that something this powerful hasn't been noticed before."

I sat down with my back against the stump of a mast. Some time back, I'd read an immensely long scroll entitled *The Royal Satheli Commission on Currents, Whorls and Storm-bowls in the Great Known Sea (Subtitle: To Forewarn Merchant Argosies of the Archipelago and Safeguard Satheli Shipping in the Further Reaches of the GKS)*, a work that was just as detailed and yawn-inducing as its title would suggest. I knew the answer to Shree's question. For some reason, the knowledge didn't bother me. There was something oddly attractive in the notion of being lost for ever.

Chasco, however, hesitated and glanced at the position of the sun before speaking. "There is a current," he said finally, "along the southern edge of the Great Known Sea, and it's never been fully charged because it's—" he coughed apologetically, "it's—too dangerous to risk getting caught by it if the wind drops. It's the only one I can think of, Lord Shree, though I believe we're too far north."

Shree flopped down beside me and frowned up at Chasco. "Just suppose it is the southern current. Where does it go?"

Chasco joined us on the deck. "Nobody knows."

"Then guess."

Chasco hesitated, reluctantly to answer. I said cheerily, "It sweeps past the southernmost point of Zaine."

"And after that?"

"That's what nobody knows. Zaine is the limit of the known world. Of course there are those," I said, settling back happily, grinning up at the merciless sky, "specifically the Lucians, who believe the sea on the far side of Zaine pours down the side of an immense boiling cauldron, where the spirits of the wicked drown endlessly inside little wooden cages—surely you've read the Lucian Maledicta, Shree?"

"I remember avoiding it," he said drily.

"Very wise. Horrible minds, the Lucians. The gentle Plaviset, on the other hand, believe the earth to be a great pottery bowl of water covered by a tortoise-shell, the inner surface of which forms the sky—in which case there would be nothing much beyond Zaine but the line where the shell meets the rim of the bowl, and our fate would depend entirely on how hard we smashed into it. Whereas the Storican theory involves a great ring of fire encircling—"

"Tig?"

"Yes, Shree?"

"What do you think is beyond Zaine?"

"My own opinion?"

"Your own opinion."

"More sea." I smiled at him. "And more land, maybe. The unknown world."

Shree sighed, after which we all sat quietly in the sun watching one of the navigators being hoisted up the forward mast to get a wider view, which was mildly entertaining because navigators tend to be overfed as well as arrogant. When that began to pall, Shree grunted and produced a long flat box out of his tunic pocket—the fingersticks. He looked at me questioningly.

"Why not? There's nothing useful we can do, and nothing's going to be known for sure until the stars come out."

So Shree dealt the sticks and we began the first of many games. As it happened, however, we did not have to wait for the stars to appear.

The Frath Major came on deck not long after the sun reached the zenith. I was winning for once and Shree and Chasco between them owed me just under seventeen million gold Calloonic palots, or roughly six times the pre-storm value of the *Tasiil* and contents, including Rinn's jewellery. Since we didn't have any actual gold, we were using smashed tiles from the ruined gazebo as markers, at fifty thousand palots per fragment, and betting big. I waved genially at the Frath Major, but the stakes were too high for me to interrupt the game. He stood alone by the remains of the railing, looking over the ominously empty sea, until the captain and one of the navigators came up to him with humble salutes and engaged him in conversation.

Suddenly, a cry from the bowsprit echoed the length of the ship. "Landsight!" We leapt to our feet, scattering fingersticks and chunks of tile over the deck, and ran towards the bow. We weren't the only ones, the Frath Major being just ahead of me in leaping down to the lower foredeck and the navigator just behind me. A little cluster of sailors on the forward point of the deck parted respectfully to let us through. Some of the faces were puzzled—others were distinctly fearful.

The so-called landsight wasn't much to my weak eyes, nothing more than a distant disturbance in the water. Beside me, the Frath Major said softly in Miisheli, "Well, navigator?"

The navigator was silent for a few moments, then said, "Wait a little, Great Frath, until we get closer."

"Don't you recognize it?" Softly. Not well pleased.

The navigator shot a despairing glance at the Frath Major; I got the feeling that more than his pride might be about to suffer, in that high Miisheli lords are unforgiving of incompetence in their underlings. But, looking around the faces of the other sailors as the current carried us on towards that insignificant pimple on the ocean's great green bum, I realized that not one of these experienced men of the sea had ever set eyes on this pimple before. I raised my eyebrows at Chasco. He answered in the fingerspeech: *unknown.*

Better and better, I told myself. The known world would be a safer place if the Lady and I weren't in it. Rinn would be disappointed—she'd left half her jewels in Cansh Miishel. The Frath would be disappointed—whatever game he was playing was finished now, the gameboard upset, the pieces scattered. We were lost in the unknown.

Or so I hoped.

The landsight was close enough now so that even I could make out the shape. It was maybe the length of the *Tasiil*, a barren double-peaked chunk of rock rising almost sheer out of the water, no beach, no reef, no visible landing place, no trace of vegetation except for some dark patches near the waterline that might have been a scum of seaweed. The only sign that other beings had passed this way was a conical cairn of white boulders, which I judged to be about twelve feet tall, on the summit of the higher peak. That should have been diagnostic, if this were the known world. My hopes soared.

I glanced around again at the sailors' faces, finding a selection of furrowed brows, pursed lips, puzzled eyes, until I came to one, the most unexpected of all, the last man on the ship (except myself) whom you'd expect to identify an oceanic landsight, and found the face tight with shock, the eyes wide with recognition. Discreetly, I poked him in the side.

"Shree," I hissed into his ear, "what's the matter with you? You look like you've seen a ghost."

"I have." He made no attempt to keep his voice down. The Frath Major turned to him, frowning.

"Do you know this place, Warlord?"

Shree, his eyes still fixed on the island, nodded.

"Then tell us." The Frath scowled at his navigator, who cowered, probably foreseeing himself swabbing decks by sunset.

Shree pushed forward, his eyes not leaving the island. His hands were clenched into fists. When he reached the bowrail, he leaned over it to peer intently down into the calm, clear water.

"Well, then?" demanded the Frath Major, in the voice of a man who resents having to ask more than once. "Tell us where we are, Warlord."

And still Shree gazed into the water, then back to the island as if calculating its distance from the ship, then back to the water.

"Don't blame the navigator, Great Frath," he said. "There's no reason for a sailor to know this place."

"Then how do you know it?" The Frath was reaching the limit of his patience, but Shree only smiled.

"I grew up under its shadow," he said.

The words seemed to echo in the hush. The Frath's frown deepened. As for me, I could feel ice starting to form along my backbone and spread through the surrounding tissues.

"I was taken to that cairn to make sacrifice, on the day I became a man," Shree went on calmly. "He was a prisoner of war—Glishoran, I think. The first blood I ever spilled, may the gods of Glishor forgive me, but that's how things were in the warcourt of Sher."

At the mention of Sher, the sailors around us began to mutter restlessly. The Frath, his face pale, gazed at the island with dread in his eyes. Shree seemed not to notice; he carried on in the same quiet, nostalgic tones.

"If you asked the protection of Raksh," he said, "you first had to give him something, and blood was the only thing he had any use for. Speaking as a memorian, I'm sure that accounts for much of the history of Sher." He narrowed his eyes, peering not at the island but at the smooth water around its base. "The temple might be visible if the sea's clear enough—it wasn't far below the summit."

I forced myself to move, to swing Shree around and take him by the shoulders.

"Where are we?"

He shook himself free, a touch of colour returning to his face. "Come now, Tig, you must have figured it out by now. It's the Tooth of Raksh, Sher's holy mountain; and, I suppose, all that's left of Sher—above water, anyway." He took me in turn by the shoulders, swung me to face the island, the holy mountaintop, and pointed down into the clear, sunlit waters. "Take a good look, Scion of Oballef. Iklankish should be directly below us."

16

THE SAILORS WERE mumbling charms against danger, against the dead, against the dark hosts of vengeful spirits said to inhabit the water that covered lost Iklankish, but I barely heard them. My eyes were following the shafts of sunlight down into the water, through the green-tinted clarity of the upper layers, deep into the murkier bands where the light began to spread itself, mote by golden mote, among the suspended particles and the little moving shadows.

"Careful, Tig." Shree was still holding my shoulders, but I pulled free to bend far over the rail, straining my eyes to follow the sunshafts—hardly noticing when one kind of gold merged with another, and the two rose together to draw me down. Their combined pull was irresistible.

"Tigrallef?"

"Scion!"

The voices faded. The water felt warm on my skin, and not particularly wet—I found myself wondering if a fish is any more conscious of the water surrounding it than a bird is conscious of the air. I also wondered what would happen when I needed to breathe, but the impulse never came.

I fell slowly, arms and legs spread, pinwheeling through the water like a starfish in a smooth downwards spiral. The seabed was dim below me, obscured by grey clouds of ooze, or silver clouds of fish, but now and then when the clouds parted I caught a glimpse of concentric circles and intersecting lines, a suggestion of pattern and symmetry blurred by the bottom sediments. Then I broke through the clouds and the drowned city of Iklankish was spread out below me like a faded map of itself.

It was built on what used to be a coastal plain between the mountain and the sea—it was rather like a small mountain itself, a kind of artificial volcanic cone, a series of massive circular walls centred on and rising towards a great round citadel bristling with towers. I looked around for the satellite city of the warcourt, but it was lost in the turbid shadows of the Tooth of Raksh.

And still I fell. This was so clearly a dream, and such a painfully interesting one, that I had no fear of being pulped when I hit bottom. The towers spun towards me, closer and closer; I could see now that they were topless, crumbling, and that sea-vines with long sinuous leaves were twined lushly around them as ivy might smother the stones of a ruin on land.

And still I fell. In moments I was among the towers glancing into empty window-holes as I dropped past them, brushed by the waving fronds of the sea-vines, glimpsing murals inside more fantastic than any human hand had ever painted—murals of seagrowths and coiled shells and anemones in soft luminous colours; saw the street approaching, twisted in the water like a cat, and landed with a gentle thump on my two feet, ankle-deep in ooze.

I looked around in the green twilight. I was on a street of tall cheek-by-cheek houses, actually shells of houses, all the roofs gone and the wooden doors and shutters eaten to nothing, the stones suspended perilously over gaps left by vanished wooden beams, balanced as though a touch might send the whole fragile construction tumbling into the ooze. Over the seaweed-ridden tops of the houses, I could see one of the great city walls rising, so thickly shrouded in seawrack that it looked like the world's most overgrown garden hedge.

"Anybody here?" I called out. There was no reply except a current wafting windlike past my face and stirring the sediment into little whorl-devils at my feet; also, perhaps, a few curious fish, but I saw them only at the corners of my vision, and they were gone before I could turn.

A metal nameplate was set into the wall beside a door down the street; I skated across to it, raising a knee-high carpet of ooze, and found the inscription was still legible although the plate itself had corroded into a film of metal on the stone: Kasakr, Apothecary. At last, one of my victims had a name. I scratched at the metal with my fingernail and watched as it flaked off and floated downwards in a lazy shower.

"Hoy! Kasakr? Anyone?" No one. That annoyed me—it was *my* dream, a product of my own guilty conscience, and if I wanted to be harrowed by hosts of reproachful phantoms, that was my right. It was the only reason I could think of for being there. "Come out, you poor murdered sons of shulls!" I shouted. "I'm here! Come and get me!"

There was a clatter behind me; I whirled hopefully, but it was only a loose stone giving up the struggle to stay in balance. No accusing faces appeared at the windows, no fleshless hands reached for me out of the yawning doorways. I was getting frustrated.

"Come on now," I called. "I'm the one who did it. I murdered you. You've been haunting me for six years, damn it—why stop now?"

A spangled fish nosed out of a gaping window to see what the row was about and gave me a long, cold stare. That was all the response I got. In a sudden fury, I kicked at a mossgrown stone lying beside the doorway; realized too late it was a skull, banged my own forehead against the jamb in remorse, picked up the skull and tenderly dusted the silt off it. Kasakr the Apothecary? I thought not. The skull was too small, more likely a relic of one of my younger victims. I held it for a moment, then replaced it gently where I had found it, turned and trudged away.

The street curved around to meet one of the radial avenues, broad and perfectly straight, that cut Iklankish into four equal quadrants. I paused on the intersection, convinced for a moment that I was not alone. The illusion was short-lived. Down the centre of the avenue stood a long queue of green man-monsters with misshapen heads, goitred throats and great humps on their backs, their grand conquering postures bloated by seamoss and colonies of limpets. These, I supposed, were the statues of the Hammers of Iklankish; Shree had described them to me as being of dubious decorative value to begin with, and they hadn't aged well. Their still, swollen faces glared at me as I passed.

I turned inwards on the avenue, towards the centre of the city, following the swathe of the road to a grand, high-jambed gateway with massive green copper gates hanging askew from their hinges. It was not easy going. Dream or not, I had to wade through waist-high beds of sea grass, clamber over slippery pillars, menacing hillocks of seamoss that might once have been chariots or horses or humans, spongy tussocks that grabbed at my feet and had *things* in them, nasty unsavoury things, sharp things, gelid things, things that popped under pressure; I tried to swim over them, but that apparently contravened the logic of the dream, and I was obliged to do it the hard way. It seemed to take hours to reach the gate.

At last the remains of the lintel hung precariously far above me. The rest of it was on the ground, partially blocking the gate, overlying something that looked like a riding-litter, very fancy under a coating of mud and slime. As I scrambled across it, I saw that the passenger was still lolling inside it on great mouldy puffballs of cushions, but he was not the accuser I was searching for. Only the sea vines twined around him were keeping his bones together, and he moved only in response to the current. I stepped inside the gate.

Before me was the citadel, the Hub of Iklankish, sometime residence of the Princes of Sher. A broad compound separated the gate from what appeared to be a grand entrance to the inner citadel, but the destruction was more dramatic here and the enclosure was impassably choked. I gave up immediately and started to turn away—there was a whole city to wander about and reproach myself in—but then a flicker of light inside the cavernous ruin of the keep caught my eye.

It was the Lady. I should have known she'd be somewhere about. She floated out through the shattered doorway of the citadel, and I noted with interest and some envy that her feet, unlike mine, were keeping well above the top of the debris. Her features were indistinct through the drifting silver hair, but I thought she had a look of Rinn this time. She glanced around as she approached me and made a deprecating gesture at the drowned courtyard, the rubble, the tottering towers of the citadel.

I said, "Why do you get to swim, when I have to walk?"

She gazed at me through her cloud of hair and started to drift away inside the enclosure, along the inner edge of the great city wall. She was beckoning to me to follow. I thought it over and concluded I should. Perhaps this very detailed hallucination wasn't the work of my guilty conscience after all; perhaps the Lady had brought me here for a purpose of my own, in which case I was partly curious and partly eager to get it over with. With a sigh, I set off, clambering and picking my way after her through the rubble.

The debris formed a treacherous slope up the inner face of the great wall, partly stabilized in places by seamoss and creepers, but still as awkward to climb as a gravel scree on a mountainside. As I toiled upwards I caught glimpses of what composed the mound—a motley jumble of bones and skulls and smashed furniture, distinctively Sherkin tableware (I'd washed a few in my time), beakers and krishank and broken pots and fragments of masonry, all softly blanketed with a layer of slit. The Lady was hovering about halfway up the slope, meditating on something at her feet.

I managed the last few feet on my hands and knees and examined the spot without being impressed. It looked like the same pathetic mix of rubbish as the rest of the slope. I glared up at the Lady.

"So what?" I demanded.

She didn't reply, just continued staring at the same spot, so I muttered a bit and followed her example. This time, a little current riffled the surface of the silt, exposing something that glittered in the dim light with the true and incorruptible gleam of gold. I reached down and uprooted a patch of waterclover, flicked away an indignant crab and cleared away the silt.

• • •

He was buried to the neck in the rubble and his head was flung back as if he'd been trying to catch a last glimpse of the sky before he died. The lower jaw was pushed to one side, giving the skull a sneer rather than the death-grin I had seen too many times. A gold hoop was lying in about the right position to have been hanging from his vanished earlobe, but it was not the object that had gleamed at me through the silt.

Around the vault of the skull, pinning down a few wisps of hair that might once have been red, was a gold circlet—heavy and ostentatious and not at all to my taste, spiked with great gaudy chunks of crystal and jade. A princely diadem, Sherkin-style. Carefully, I uncrowned the Prince of Sher, admired the bauble for a moment, then tossed it away and watched it tumble downslope until it was lost among the other rubbish.

"Empires always fall, Scion."

Startled, I looked up. "Not usually into the water, Lady."

"But empires always fall," she repeated.

"I know. Twitches in the eyelid of eternity, that sort of thing. Did you bring me down here just to tell me that?"

She appeared to be looking through me, though I could not quite make out her face. "I'm telling you something of great significance, twig of the great tree," she said. *"Empires always fall."*

I settled back on my haunches. "Go on, then. I'll bet you've seen a few."

She seemed to be growing taller. "I have seen them all, seed of the Excommunicant. Before Sher, Fathan; before Fathan, Vizzath; before Vizzath, Myr; before Myr, Itsant; before Itsant, Khamanthana; before Khamanthana, Baul; before Baul, Nkalvi and the Great Nameless First."

"Should I be taking notes?" I asked. "What's your point?"

"Empires fall like apples when the wind shakes the tree; and the Naar is the tree, and the Harashil is the wind, and—this is what you must remember, Scion—the wind and the tree are one."

"Are you being intentionally obscure?" I frowned up at her—something was different. I had to tilt my head far back to see where her face was hidden by the nimbus of shining hair. She really was getting taller. Already she appeared at least twice my height, and when she bent over to stretch her hand out to me, she looked like a tree toppling. I skittered back a few paces, loosing a small landslip of potsherds and bones.

"The Caveat," she said severely, "has never been considered obscure."

"Then it's a pity nobody can read it these days."

She tutted with disapproval. "Listen, Scion: If you fulfil a prophecy, you live with the consequences."

"What pocketing prophecy?" I had to shout—her head had risen as high as the shattered capitals of the great columns, and my head, when I scrambled to my feet on the slippery slope, reached to about the middle of her calf. She scooped me on to the palm of her hand, still growing, breadth in proportion to height, and lifted me level with her face. I stamped experimentally on her palm, finding it solid.

"What prophecy?" I repeated. She didn't reply.

I looked down. The citadel forecourt was dwindling, the redheaded prince's skull diminishing to just another nondescript bit of rubbish in a heap of nondescript rubbish. A moment later I could see down into the roofless maze of the citadel on one side, and over the great ring wall to the frozen procession of the Hammers of Iklankish on the other, then over the next ring wall, and the next, and the next, to the tangle of mean streets in the city's outer circuit. Then the tops of the towers were sliding past me, the details of the city shrinking as the view expanded, the middle slopes of the Tooth of Raksh rising like a black curtain behind the Lady's face, which was the size of a cornfield by this time. When I glanced up, I saw the dark fish-shape of the *Tasiil* dropping towards me so fast that I instinctively crooked my arms over my head.

The Lady said, "Remember, twig of the great Naar—the wind and the tree are one."

"Is that supposed to mean something?" I cried, furious, but then I looked up again and the ship seemed to be just on the point of crushing me, so I shut my eyes; and when no pain came, I opened my eyes again, and saw only blue sky overhead. I looked down—over the bow-rail—and saw shafts of sunlight plunging deep into the green water. Shree had me by one shoulder, the Frath Major by the other.

"Tig?" Shree's voice was anxious.

I shook myself like a wet dog and found that my clothes were already dry. The island was closer, but still ahead of us. I asked, "How long have we been standing here?"

"A couple of minutes. You were dizzy, remember? You almost fell overboard."

I let him lead me away from the rail into the shelter of the ruined deckhouse. The Frath trailed us—I suppose he was worried about the health of his investment. The sailors remained on the point of the bow, muttering as they watched the island approach.

"Shree?"

"Shut up, Tig. Drink some of this."

"No—I need to ask you something. It's important."

"What?"

"Did either of the Princes have red hair?"

He frowned at me, still holding the flask to my lips. "Yes. Prince Ksher did, the bastard. Why?"

"Never mind." I let the liquor burn down my throat. "But tell the sailors not to worry—there's nothing left to fear in Iklankish."

17

YOU MAY AS well tell the wind not to blow as tell a sailor not to worry. Everybody knew we were sailing in haunted waters, and it would have taken more than my pronouncement on the foredeck to convince anyone otherwise. Fear hung over the ship like an invisible fog; long after the Tooth of Raksh had vanished over the horizon behind us, you could hardly walk six steps along the deck without falling over some supplicant fiddling with a prayer-frame, or pouring a libation on to the long-suffering deckboards.

However, we now knew where we were—a place, granted, where no ships had sailed voluntarily since Sher plunged under the ocean, a great blank hole on the most recent sea-charts, but at least a place that was part of the known world.

The navigators, using Iklankish as a fixing point, quickly ascertained that we were passing over the drowned central desert of Sher, and that Cansh Miishel was no more than seven or eight days' sail to the northeast.

This was good news to most, bad news to me; but as that day wore to a close and the night came on, the others began to feel worse and I began to feel better. The current was still sweeping us steadily south and away from Miishel, and I seriously began to hope that it would flow into the great southern current, which in turn would carry us past Zaine and on to the unknown world. I wasn't the only one to think so. The crew was pushed mightily to have the new sails rigged by nightfall, in case enough wind arose to let the *Tasiil* break free of the current; and, at the captain's urgent request, the Bequiin Ardin was carried up from his cabin to perform a wind-summoning spell on the foredeck, which had no discernible effect on the weather, nor on my opinion of Miisheli magic. In the end, he was carried below again before I had a chance to get near him.

That night, however, as I slept on the pallet beside Rinn, I dreamed of a wind blowing through the streets of the drowned city. Silt swirled around the heads of the Hammers of Iklankish. Houses tottered and fell, the fish and sea-beasts fled in silver clouds, the towers tumbled, the great ring walls were forcibly stripped of their greenery. I woke with a start and heard the whistle of a real wind outside the ship, accompanied by a tortured creaking from the masts and the jury-rigged sails. Tight-lipped, I slipped out of the cabin, tiptoed through the salon where Shree was sleeping and bounded up to the afterdeck three steps at a time.

It was a warm wind, warm as Rinn's breath, though not so fragrant. The sails were full of it—the ship was skating along under the spangled sky as if she'd suddenly remembered an appointment. I sat down on the deckboards, full of despair. It seemed I was fated to go to Miishel after all.

Look at the stars, you twig of the great tree.

Startled, I looked overhead. The sky was clear, but it took me a moment to adjust to its uninterrupted breadth and to find familiar constellations; we were much farther south than I'd ever been before. Suddenly I caught my breath. I was facing aft, and I'd found an old friend. The Crown was upside-down directly in front of me; the King's Eye, the fixed northern star around which the other constellations appear to revolve, was only a few fingers above the horizon, in line with a stump of the vanished taffrail at the corner of the deck—behind us. I scrambled to my feet. "We're heading southeast," I breathed.

"Indeed, Scion."

I spun around, bracing for an attack—but the shadowy figure stepping from the head of the companionway raised its hand in greeting. It was the Frath Major.

"Easy, Scion," he said. He sounded weary. "I have just been conferring with the captain. Yes, we are heading southeast, but that is better than due south, and we have nothing to worry about now."

"What do you mean, cousin, nothing to worry about?"

"It is a strong wind. It has blown us out of that damned current, right enough, although we cannot tack and we cannot head north for Miishel. For the time being, we shall have to go where it blows us. I am sorry to tell you," he clapped his hand on my shoulder, "that our arrival in Cansh Miishel will be delayed—perhaps by as much as six weeks."

"Ah." I tried to sound disappointed.

He released me and stood with his arms folded, gazing at the sky. I could just distinguish the harsh outline of his profile against the spatter of stars. "Food is not short, fortunately," he went on. "The fresh water is low but will do for a few days, and we can eke it out with wine if we have to. There is no shortage of wine, Scion."

"I suppose not," I said, trying to imagine the fine vintages in the wine-cabin being dispensed to anybody under the rank of Han-Frath, no matter how thirsty they were.

"Anyway, we hope to make landfall in a day or two," the Frath Major added.

I squinted at his profile. "Landfall? Where? From what I remember of the charts, the southern waters are the emptiest in the Great Known Sea. Lots of barren little atolls, but not many that would be of use to us."

He turned towards me so that I could see the dark glitter of his eyes. "The navigators have found a place—some islands that were part of the Sherkin empire and may have survived the deluge. He mentioned the name, but I did not know of it."

I searched my memory for something in the right area. Southeast of Sher—west of Zaine—a fellow-sufferer under the Sherkin yoke. "Vassashinay, perhaps?" I asked.

"Vassashinay! The very name. You know it?"

"No more than the name."

"Ah, well. The captain thinks we can make landfall there before this damnable wind blows us all the way to the Great Southern Current. I hope so. I have no desire to visit the unknown world."

I have, I said to myself. To the Frath, I said, "You realize, of course, that Vassashinay's practically in the unknown world anyway."

"True, Scion, but it is still on the right side of Zaine. We can lay up there for repairs and supplies, and catch the autumn southerlies when they start to blow in a month or so. That is what the captain assures me."

"Excellent," I said, grimacing into the night.

"Never fear, Scion, you shall see the fine towers of Cansh Miishel yet." He clapped his hand on my shoulder again, in an ownerlike way. My overgrown sense of tact kept me from shrugging it off. "I would not have planned it this way, though," he went on sourly. "Who knows what those Grisoti *fliis* will be getting up to—who knows what state we will find Miishel in when we arrive?"

"I'm sure," I said cheerfully, "that the alliance will manage very nicely without us for a while. I can't see Miishel getting into real trouble in the next few months, even though it's temporarily deprived of your generalship." I bowed in his direction, comfortably aware that any irony would be lost in the darkness.

"I was not thinking of my generalship," he muttered in Miisheli, in a voice so low that I don't think I was intended to hear. But I did hear and as it set my mind working, an obvious piece of the puzzle slotted itself into place. I could no longer deny that Shree was right; the Frath Major knew about the Lady. How did he know? It didn't matter how, though it probably involved the Bequiin Ardin's meticulous scholarship. What mattered was that I was being cast as the Frath's secret weapon—rather, the Lady was the secret weapon and I was her self-propelled carrying case, and he planned to use us to win the Cloak of Empire for the Miisheli giant.

I grinned into a gust of sultry wind. His hopes and plans were so transparent. Rinn, of course, was supposed to enslave my spirit with her matchless body—how else would the Frath think he could control me? And Rinn, poor poppet, was doing her best.

My way was clear now. Up to a point, I had to give the Frath exactly what he wanted. He wanted Rinn to bewitch me, so I was going to be well and truly bewitched, starting tomorrow. The Frath couldn't know that I was not only resistant to Rinn's charms, but that my spirit was already enslaved, and by a woman who was dead; and there was another thing the Frath didn't know, that Rinn didn't know either, that only Shree and Chasco and I knew at that time.

I had to resist an impulse to laugh out loud. How would the Frath feel about his bargain when he discovered that, even if Rinn were able to control me, I couldn't control the Lady?

Vassashinay. The kind of dot on the sea-charts that one assumes at first is a squashed fly or a speck of dirt or a slip of the cartographer's pen; the kind of name that gets accidentally omitted from even very careful catalogues, and is generally misspelled when it does appear. A nothing place, a backwater, a gutter. The kind of place where no man in his right mind would think of going, even if he'd heard of it, which most people hadn't.

This was partly due to blind geographical mischance—Vassashinay's extraordinary bad luck in being Sher's close neighbour, and the first to be conquered whenever Sher felt an imperialistic itch. That was about all I could remember about the place, but I knew where I could find out more. After a few minutes of desultory chat, the Frath went back to confer with the captain and I dashed below to waken Shree.

He was stretched out, dressed right down to his boots, on one of the amazing silk settees in the great salon. I sat down at the table and chucked an ivory gaming piece on to his chest.

He awoke instantly, soldier-style, and was crouched in the Sherkin fighting stance with his sword out before his eyes were even focused. When he saw there was no danger, he gave me a filthy look and collapsed back on to the settee. "Beard of Raksh, Tig, what is it?"

"Vassashinay," I said.

He yawned mightily. "Oh, gods. What about it?"

"Tell me everything you know."

"About Vassashinay? Is that why you woke me up?" Another jaw-breaking yawn.

"We're going there."

"That's fools' talk," he mumbled, "nobody goes to Vassashinay." Then he opened his eyes wide and sat upright, suddenly alert. The voice of the wind had finally penetrated his ears. "We're going there?" He said. "Who told you?"

"The Frath Major, up on deck just now."

He looked disapproving. "What were you doing on deck without me or Chasco?"

"The Lady was with me," I said wryly, "so I was safe enough. Now tell me what you can."

"Oh, gods. All right. Vassashinay, is it?" He leaned back with his eyes closed and after a moment he started to chuckle.

"What's funny?"

"The place was a joke. When I was a child, our nurses used to say things like, be good, you little shrikkhead, or I'll send you straight to Vassashinay where the other shrikkheads live."

"Was that supposed to frighten you?"

"No. It was like being told we'd be dipped in cowshit if we didn't behave, or sent to live in the Fourth Circuit. Frightened, indeed! Nothing was supposed to frighten little Sherkin warlords."

I said thoughtfully, "So being sent to Vassashinay was equivalent to being dipped in cowshit."

"Roughly speaking, yes."

"Did you ever go there."

"Certainly not!" He looked offended.

"So you know nothing about the place."

He frowned. "Only a little. We, I mean Sher, conquered it so regularly that it should rightly have been considered part of Sher, except that there was no colonization and precious little interbreeding. There was a garrison there, of course, mainly badheads sent out on punitive duty, and it was a staging port for trade with Zaine. Other than that . . ." his voice faded.

"Nothing else?"

"There was something else—I'm trying to remember, if you'd only shut up. Ah, yes." He peered reflectively through me. "Something about magicians—fortune tellers, diviners. I know. There was an oracle on one of the Vassashin islands, strictly small-time of course, but a few of their priestesses were sent to Iklankish now and then to serve in the temple brothel. I vaguely remember having one of them once."

"And?"

He shrugged. "She was a temple shint, that's all. But she told my fortune afterwards."

I didn't ask. I didn't have to. His face changed as the memory filtered back.

"She said—and I think I remember clouting her for the impertinence—she said I was two men in one body, and one of them would die by the other's hand." He paused, fiddling with his sword. "I suppose that's just what happened, in a way. Maybe I shouldn't have clouted her."

"Quite right," I said severely. "Anything else?"

"One other thing." He passed his sword thoughtfully from hand to hand, back and forth, making it flash in the lamplight. "She said we'd meet again someday, she and I."

"Where? In Sher?"

"No." He had picked up the edge of one of the priceless brocade sofa-throws and was using it to polish his sword.

"Come on. *Where* did she say you'd meet again?"

A minute speck on the blade caught his eye and he rubbed at it vigorously before looking up. "In Vassashinay," he said.

18

In the end, there was no need to use the wine to eke out the water supply. The wind, strong and steady, blew us across the sunken south coast of Sher and on to the Kalish Shallows, where the first landsight since the Tooth of Raksh was greeted with a roar of relief. It was a sad little bump of rock thrusting up from the shallow seabed, spattered with birdlime and stinking intolerably of kelp even at a distance, but you'd have thought the crew was catching a glimpse of heaven—the Miisheli heaven, which sounds rather like an everlasting orgy, as opposed to the Lucian heaven, which sounds exclusive and very dull. It was an identifiable sad little bump, that was the thing. It signified we had left the newborn wastes of the Sherkin Sea behind us and re-entered the old shipping lanes that once led along the south coast of Sher towards Zaine; and whatever ghosts did or did not haunt the tomb of Iklankish, we were back again on the sea-charts of the living.

There was still a chance that the wind would blow us right past Vassashinay, but the captain proved to be a wily and experienced old seabelly who took advantage of every brief slackwind to tack us on to a better course. And thus my hopes of the Great Southern Current grew dimmer as that day wore on, and I began to build my hopes on the other foundation. Surely, I said to myself, it was better to be going to Vassashinay than to Cansh Miishel. In six weeks, anything could happen—a small boat might be left unguarded, a few tuns of water and cheese acquired by stealth, a quiet and unannounced departure taken one dark, moonless night. Six weeks left plenty of scope for escape. I started to lay my plans.

"We could steal a boat in Vassashinay, and make for the southern current." I was speaking in a low voice, with one eye on the top of the companionway.

Shree tossed a fingerstick with a practised flick of the wrist.

We had rigged up an awning on the afterdeck, because the sun in these southern climes was too strong to be borne for long, and the air below deck was even worse. I felt a little guilty about ordering Chasco to stay below, but I needed him there. The stick fell to Shree's profit, so he picked up another to continue his turn.

"It may be harder to get away than you think." He paused, then asked quietly, "Is there any chance you can use the Lady?"

I snorted. "I wouldn't depend on her. She works her own will these days, or hadn't you noticed? No, I think we'll leave the Lady out of our plans, and hope to heaven that she stays out."

"Then I don't think it's going to be easy. If the Frath does know about the Lady, he's going to sew you up as tightly as the Primate did to keep you from getting away. You'll be guarded all the time—I doubt if you'll be allowed to stir off the ship all the time we're in Vassashinay."

"I'm working on that, Shree." I surveyed the sticks gloomily. Shree had won back all that he owed me, and now I was sliding into his debt. He threw again, and this time lost the turn.

"My throw." I tossed a stick, cursed mildly when it fell on the dark side. "Listen. All I've got to do is convince the Frath that I have no intention of getting away."

"How are you going to do that?"

I paused with the next stick in my hand. "I'm going to snap up the bait he's offered me."

"The bait?"

I tossed the stick, disastrously. "Damn it. Your throw. Keep playing in case we're being watched. I mean Rinn."

Shree tossed the stick into a brilliant placement on the pile and looked at me with the beginnings of irritation. "What about Rinn?"

"She's the bait. She's obviously been told to captivate me— so I'll tupping well be captivated. From now on, I'll be paying her more attention. Flattering her, mooning after her. I've been far too honest so far. They're going to think I don't care about her."

"You don't."

I snorted. "That doesn't matter. She doesn't care about me,

either. But all I've got to do is convince the Frath that I'm wet clay in her hands. It's what he desperately wants to believe, so it should be easy."

Shree passed his hand over his eyes. "Easy, eh? It might be easier if you jumped overboard and swam. She's trouble, Tig."

"Oh, I'm counting on that. And I'm counting on you as well."

"What for?"

"Keep playing, and I'll tell you." As we threw the sticks, I laid out for Shree the workings of the Frath's mind as I understood them, the illusion he laboured under regarding the Lady's biddability, the advantages to be gained by being Rinn's abject slave. And I told him what he had to say. By the end, he was grinning.

"I like it, Tig. You don't have to do much but play the fool, and you're good at that. What are you waiting for?"

"Chasco."

"Where is he?"

"Watching to see when one of Rinn's lovers joins her."

But Chasco was, in fact, striding up the companionway at that very moment. He stepped quietly on to the deck and beckoned to me. "It's time, Lord Tigrallef. Somebody just went in."

"Good." I started to gather up the fingersticks to shove them into their box. That's when the first wave of stage-fright hit. A few sticks fell out of my hand and clattered on to the deck. I said, "Perhaps I should give them some time to get started first."

Shree and Chasco looked at each other with complete understanding. "Come on, Tig," said Shree, "this is your own idea."

"I think I need to perfect it a bit first."

"It's fine as it is. What's wrong? You're not afraid of her, are you?"

"Not since I cut her nails."

Shree leered at me. "Well, then, are you worried you'll really fall in love with her?"

"Not a chance," I said grimly. That was true, and would have been true even if my heart had not been rotting on the seabed along with Calla's beloved bones. Likewise, I reck-

oned that Rinn's affections, if she had any, were more than
safe from me. The sudden revulsion I felt was partly a matter
of honesty—it was one thing to do my marital duty, it was
another thing to pretend to worship the little harlot. And all
the time, the Lady would be observing the comedy through
my own eyes, which was downright embarrassing. As I
thought of the Lady, I felt a ripple of her amusement spread-
ing through my head.

Do you need any help, Scion?

"No. Don't bother."

"What?" said Shree.

"Nothing." I picked up a fingerstick that he'd missed, and
handed it to him. Of course, he was right. It was a good strategy. The sooner I got started, the better. "All right, let's go."

I preceded the two of them down the stairs, resisting an
impulse, now that the moment for action was approaching, to
make a break for the foredeck. A couple of Fraths Minor
passed us in the corridor, but the salon was empty when we
reached it, possibly emptied by the sounds of passion being
generated on the other side of Rinn's door. I stopped at the
threshold.

"I don't know how to start."

Just then, we heard the footsteps of several men approaching the salon; the Frath's deep distinctive voice rumbled, at
least two other men laughed with him.

Shree snapped, "Hurry, Tig. This is ideal. You can throw the
bastard out in front of the Frath Major himself."

"But how do I begin—?"

"Go! You'll think of something."

"Is that supposed to be helpful?" I turned sourly back to the
door and took a deep breath. At that moment, seconds before
the Frath Major entered the salon, inspiration burst like a
flame-bolt in my head. Acting on this inspiration, I flung open
the door and slammed it shut behind me.

"Wife!" My very best bellow.

Abrupt cessation of noises from the pallet; the appearance
of two pairs of startled eyes amid an improbable tangle of
body parts. I strode to the pallet, chose one of the hairy legs,
grabbed a handful of flesh, and pulled. Rinn's lover squawked

and tumbled on to the floor. It was Zimin, the downy-faced Han-Frath who commanded the guardtroops on board the *Tasiil*, not Rinn's usual type at all; I was surprised, and a little shocked, that she'd sleep with any rank lower than a Frath Minor.

"Out!" I said, using a special low and dangerous voice that I'd learned from listening to the Primate. Zimin hastily started to gather up his clothes, and I forgot my role for a moment and actually bent over to help before I caught myself.

"Out."

He took another look at me, abandoned the rest of his clothing and went—with all possible haste, naked as a newborn, dropping bits and pieces of gear all the way to the door. I smiled to myself. This was not hard at all. Then I turned to face Rinn.

She was going to be more difficult.

Imagine a kitten the size of a rippercat, with teeth and claws in proportion; a rippercat, moreover, whose most recent kill has been rudely dragged from between its paws. I very nearly turned and followed Zimin out the door.

"How dare you?" she breathed. I gulped, but remembering my lines just in time, advanced a pace towards the pallet and struck a pose of passionate suffering.

"My life is not worth living if you continue travelling this road," I intoned fervently, by memory. "You must choose, wife—renounce all others, or watch me die for love."

She obviously wasn't familiar with the script: *The Tragedy of the Faithless Wife*, a classic farce-of-passion by the great Calloonic poet Ervard n' Ilthon, which I knew well because I had translated it as an exercise when I was studying Calloonic. I was glad she didn't know it, since the plot ended in a suicide pact after many misadventures, but the first confrontation between wronged husband and errant wife contained some nicely relevant lines. She was now supposed to throw herself at my feet weeping great waterfalls of remorseful tears. Instead, she threw her prayer-frame at my head.

I ducked. Under the circumstances, Ervard n' Ilthon's next line didn't apply, so I improvised. "Rinn, my angel, I'd do anything for you!" The flagon came next—I ducked that too. "I'm the slave of my passion!" I added hastily, noting that she was now hefting the heavy silver flagon-tray in her hand. "Your slave," I amended.

She paused with the flagon-tray cocked above her head, that familiar calculating look returning to her eyes.

"My slave?" she said thoughtfully. She lowered the tray.

I could almost see the simple chain of consequences being forged in her mind: the Scion swears he is my slave, therefore I have achieved what the Frath Major asked me to do, therefore the Frath Major *owes* me. The tray clattered to the floor. Rather belatedly, she began to follow Ervard n' Ilthon's script.

19

ACCORDING TO SHREE, Zimin's hasty exit from Rinn's love-life coincided beautifully with the Frath Major's arrival in the salon, and most of our improvised enactment of *The Faithless Wife* was audible through the door. The Frath appeared sceptical at first—after all, this was a very sudden turnabout—but Shree humbly took him aside and told him in whispers, as instructed, about my hidden heart-burnings of the last few days, my growing obsession with Rinn's sensual charms, my sudden uncontrollable explosion of passion and jealousy. When Shree lies, he tends to overdo it, but this tripe fitted in so well with what the Frath wanted to hear that Shree could have been a much more florid liar and still have been convincing. By the time Rinn and I emerged from the cabin two hours later, myself staggering with exhaustion, the princess hanging triumphantly on my arm, the Frath was well on the way to believing in my conversion to the cult of Rinn-worship.

We went up on deck, lover-like, to watch the sunset. From a discreet distance, the Frath Major watched us with a smug look on his face. Shree and Chasco sat a little apart from him, also looking smug, but for different reasons. As for me, I was starting to realize one of the drawbacks of my brilliant strategy—from now on, I would have to pass a large proportion of my time with the Princess Rinn, not all of which could be spent in bed.

We strolled hand-in-hand in the fading dusk as the stars emerged one by one and the moon slowly undertook to paint the sea with silver. It was a perfect night for lovers—the wind had dropped to a gentle breeze, the water was lapping musically against the hull, somewhere on the forepart of the ship someone was plinking a sweet, melancholy tune on a wooden thumb-harp. Now and then a firestar flashed across the heavens.

None of this stage-dressing helped me as much as one might expect. I could not, to save my life, think of anything romantic to say, although Rinn rapidly made it clear what she wanted to hear. It seemed this did not include speculations on the crystalline nature of the stellar sphere, nor on the mysterious aethers which might fill the hollow globe of the universe; she was not interested in the constellations, nor in the messenger-stars that roamed more freely among their fixed brethren, nor in the Zelfic protocol for predicting eclipses of the moon. The stars were there purely as a counterpoint to her own magnificence. My brief was to assure her that she outshone them all.

I tried. Unlike Shree, I'm a woeful liar. My imagination will sometimes freeze under pressure. I could sense Rinn's mounting impatience as I struggled to think up passionate avowals and lush, steamy tributes to her charms, coming up instead with what sounded like lectures on female anatomy. At last I abandoned my own words and fell back gratefully into the arms of erotic literature, after which Rinn seemed satisfied and I felt even more like a fool and a charlatan. Bit by bit I worked my way through all I could remember of the *Gillish Odes to Love*, the *Seduction of Cul the Golden*, the *Passionale* and the *Maiden's Silken Purse*, and was just starting on the *Erotic Mistifalia* when Rinn turned her glorious face to mine and hushed me with a slender finger on my lips.

"Shut up for a moment, Scion," she said. "What is that red light over there?"

I looked where she indicated. A spot on the horizon was glowing, faintly and diffusely, as I remembered seeing

Sathelforn glow in the distance on a clear night, from a hill in Exile; but this glow was red and fitful, and after a few minutes a bright hard ruby of light slid above the edge of the sea, the glow forming a soft halo around it. The lookout's cry, "Land-sight!," broke the evening quiet.

There was a footfall behind us. "Landsight—that would be Vassashinay," said the Frath Major. His voice was relieved.

Rinn lost interest immediately. She twined herself around me and looked up into my eyes. "Tell me more," she purred, "about how much you worship me. Tell me how you will do anything to make me happy." This was probably to impress the Frath Major; the unspoken message was *See, cousin, how well I've got him in the bag.*

"You have enslaved my soul," I said dutifully, "I would do anything to make you happy. You are the sun in my heaven, the moon that shines in my heart, the stars that whisper to me in the night. If you asked me to, I would tear out my liver with my own hands and give it to you in a golden box." As if she'd have a use for it. And so on and so forth in the same sludgy vein, praying that Shree couldn't hear any of this twaddle, or I'd never live it down.

Meanwhile, over Rinn's head, I watched the burning red eye of Vassashinay as the wind pushed us slowly towards it through the sultry southern night. The Lady stirred now and then—but whether it was due to the sentimental garbage I was talking, or to the fact that we were approaching Vassashinay, she gave me no hint.

Distances can be deceptive at night. The red beacon of Vas-sashinay looked close enough to spit at, but it stubbornly appeared to remain at that distance for a very long time. The wind had dropped so that it barely filled our sails, which meant the *Tasiil* was only creeping along, but that could not completely account for it. Gradually, however, that small clear-cut gem of light suspended in the sky was seen to be bal-anced on the apex of a looming dark triangle, silhouetted against the dense field of stars; and then a rumble, like thun-der, came to us across the water and bright arcs of fire launched themselves from the centre of the glowing jewel. What I had thought was a beacon or a light-tower was a reasonably lively volcano. Never having seen an active one before, I was fascinated.

Rinn was not.

I wanted to stay and watch, but she dragged me below for food and wine and more plagiarism and another practical demonstration of my humble worshipfulness, and my commitment to my own damned strategy made me helpless to refuse. And so it was that I missed the final approach to Vassashinay and slept the sleep of utter exhaustion throughout our arrival and the moonlit dropping of anchors in the peaceful harbour of Vass, and the ensuing frenzy of activity on the upper decks; and I also missed any words the Lady might have whispered about the fate, and something else, that was lying in wait for me on those silent shores.

Contrary to expectation, Vassashinay was luxuriantly, rampantly beautiful. It was not one main island but four, three of them being low green hummocks huddled in the shelter of the majestic fourth, the volcano. The surrounding sea was dotted with little whalebacks of coral, some of which were large enough to have collected tiny beaches and scrubby vegetation and permanent populations of seabirds, crabs, turtles, even wild dogs. More corals grew among and around the main islands, in places forming causeways and coralfields that were high and dry at low tide and could be used to cross from one island to another if you were careful about timing.

The main town, Vass, was on the largest of the three low islands, to the west of the volcano. Its harbour was a broad lagoon demarcated by a natural breakwater of coral that had been banked up with chunks of shiny dark stone, which I later found to be volcanic basalt. That same mix, coral from the sea and rough-quarried rock from the flanks of the great cone, was a dominant theme in Vassashin architecture.

Not that much architecture was visible at first. When, that first morning, I woke at dawn and removed Rinn's hair from my mouth and her heavy little skull from my windpipe and padded quietly to the open porthole, all I could see was a fine curve of white sand being lapped by the wavelets on one edge and running up to a lush fringe of jungle on the other. Numerous canoes and fishing boats were pulled up on the beach, and

a few more were moored to a well-built jetty thrusting far out
into the lagoon. At the edge of the line of trees, small knots of
people were gathering and looking out towards the *Tasiil*. I
could just make out the pale ovals of their faces.

Some of the knots came together, and I could see that a
kind of ceremonial procession was forming up. The sound of
drums and whistles floated thinly across the lagoon. I heard
the splashing of oars as well, and craning out of the porthole,
I was able to see one of the *Tasiil*'s smallboats moving
smoothly across the water towards the jetty. The Frath Major
was seated in the bow, along with a handful of lesser nobles
and a surprisingly small number of troopers.

The smallboat reached one end of the jetty just as the procession reached the other. I had a wild, brief moment of hope
that the Vassashin were going to fall on the Frath immediately
and do something barbaric to him, but they waited patiently
on the sand, banging their drums and tootling their whistles,
while he and his retinue clambered out of the smallboat and
proceeded along the jetty. When they reached the sand, the
Miishelu were engulfed at once—but still there was no violence. I cursed quietly to myself.

A large roll of carpeting was carried through a gap in the
treeline and spread out on the sand. The Frath Major was
escorted to it by a tall man in a peculiar cone-shaped headdress, followed by the entire population of the beach, Miisheli
and Vassashin. I was amazed that the Frath was so trusting.

Quietly, I gathered up my scattered clothes and escaped to the
salon, where Chasco and Shree were waiting for me. Rinn
didn't stir when I left, which was just as well, because I really
felt I couldn't face worshipping her before breakfast. We took
refuge in Shree's cabin, where Chasco and I shaved as usual,
and Shree did not—he hadn't shaved the day before, either,
and was already looking villainous—and then raided the galley for some breakfast to eat on deck.

Emerging from the companionway into the bright morning
sunshine, we all stopped short in amazement. Early as it was,
we were not the only people up and about. While we slept, the
flame-slings and spearchuckers had been set up in a row on
the lower foredeck, all of them targeted on the beach. And

every trooper on board was not only present but in a full set of battleskins, and their formation was designed to present any observer on the beach with a thought-provoking array of fighting power, a veritable lawn of javelins and helmet-plumes and battlestaffs held stiffly at attention. Now I understood why the Frath was being so trusting.

I shrugged and led the way to the bow, weaving through the dense ranks and files of troopers. If that was how they chose to spend a beautiful morning, it was nothing to do with me. There was a clear space near the bow rail big enough for us to sit down and spread out our picnic breakfast, well placed to watch the parley on the beach while we ate.

There was a tap on my shoulder. I looked up with my mouth full of bread and swallowed with slight embarrassment. It was my wife's most recent ex-lover.

"Good morning, Han-Frath Zimin," I said cheerfully in Miisheli. "What are you all doing here?"

The Han-Frath of the guardtroops surveyed me courteously. If he were also embarrassed by the memory of our last meeting, he didn't show it. "You should not be so exposed, Lord Scion. We do not know yet how the Vassashin are going to receive us."

"Oh?" I said, passing a chunk of bread to Chasco. "So that's what this is all about. A show of force. What comes next—setting fire to the forest?"

"No, Lord Scion. Not if the parley goes well. But if it goes badly," he touched the hilt of his sword, "we will slaughter them."

"I so admire Miisheli diplomacy," I said. "Cheese, Han-Frath Zimin?"

"No, Lord Scion." He shifted from foot to foot, ill at ease. "Lord Scion, the Frath Major's orders were quite clear as to whom should be seen on deck. You must return to your quarters."

I bit into a pikcherry and spat the stone overboard. "It's a lovely morning, Han-Frath."

Zimin sighed. Behind him, rank upon rank of troopers sweated in the sun in their heavy battleskins. I was prepared to be carried away bodily by any number of them, and waited for Zimin to give the order. He didn't. He gave up and hovered over me, looking watchful, as though he'd personally take it on himself to defend me if the Vassashin turned ugly. I chewed thoughtfully for a few moments and then reached up to tap him on the shoulder.

"Han-Frath Zimin, about last evening—"

He looked down at me with dignity, in striking contrast to his bare-bottomed retreat from the bridal cabin, and said stiffly, "I most humbly beg the Lord Scion's pardon."

"Oh, no need for that," I began, when Shree elbowed me viciously in the side. "I mean," I said hastily, "that I quite understand the intoxication of my wife's charms, and I bear no ill will to any man who has drunk from them in the past. I forgive you, Han-Frath."

"You are very generous, Lord Scion," said Zimin woodenly, and I was certain for a few moments that I had made an implacable enemy when I threw him out of my wife's bed. Then I saw his eyes. I can recognize relief when it's staring me in the face. I began to wonder how many of my lovely wife's lovers had been volunteers.

It was well over an hour before the Frath Major returned from the parley. In the meantime, in response to signals from the beach, the second smallboat was sent ashore loaded with an assortment of costly gifts: gold, both as jewellery and ingots, fine wine from the Frath's private stock, a great bale of white furs, and two rolls of Omelian silk which I recognized as coming from my personal endowment.

Not long after the second smallboat landed, a wild chorus of cries rang out on the beach. The Han-Frath stiffened and motioned the flame-sling and spearchucker crews forwards; but a moment later he dropped his hand and nodded them back. The drums and whistles started up again, the crowd of Vassashin that had increasingly obscured our view moved aside, leaving the Frath Major and his parley partner visible on the carpet surrounded by heaps of valuables from the smallboat. The Frath was then escorted in state to the jetty, to return to the *Tasiil*. His face was too far away to see clearly, but I read self-satisfaction in the way he held himself in the bow of the smallboat. It was obvious that a deal had been struck.

Behind me, Han-Frath Zimin sighed with disappointment. No blood today.

20

SO THERE WE were, safe in Vassashinay, and Vassashinay had welcomed us with outstretched palms. Several days passed before I was able to set foot ashore however, and much of that time was necessarily spent in attentions to my lovely and insatiable bride. This put some strain on my body and my powers of invention, and also on poor Rinn, who normally went through lovers like the Tatakil eat hog-nuts and was not used to being amused by the same person for more than two days at a stretch. But she played her part creditably and put up with me playing mine—when she yawned, it was behind her hand.

The Lady herself seemed to sleep through this period. I heard no inner voices, saw no golden mists, experienced no impromptu exhibitions of magical power. Likewise, I had no hope that she had gone away. I was learning to recognize the taste of her presence, like the faintest of fragrances or a ghostly feeling of being watched.

When I could excuse myself from Rinn, entertainment was provided by the progress of Shree's beard—which goes to show how starved of entertainment we were. Excitement was limited to the volcano's frequent bursts of activity, mainly splutters of lava and billows of black cloud, or occasional spectacular volleys of sparks and thunder. It was interesting that, however harrowing we found these displays at first, the Vassashin we could see on shore paid them no attention, going about their business without even glancing up.

I was careful not to seem too eager to get ashore, since the chance was bound to come sooner or later. Although the *Tasiil* had been seaworthy enough to get us to Vassashinay, there were slow but increasingly serious leaks in the hold and some problems with the forward caulking, and the ship really needed to be beached for a few days. Somehow, I could not see Rinn putting up with the noise and smells of a ship under structural repair—and where Rinn went, I would surely go.

• • •

Three days after our arrival, while Rinn was mercifully busy with her afternoon nap, the Frath Major sought me out on the upper foredeck where I was lounging with my companions, going over what Chasco had gleaned about security arrangements on board the *Tasiil*. Shree saw the Frath coming and coughed discreetly, a signal to start discussing the nature and history of volcanoes.

"Of course," I was saying when the Frath came up to us, "I can't prove there's no deity involved—and if you want to believe that what we're hearing is the rumbling of some enormous divine belly, I can't stop you. But I've heard of volcanoes that erupted even when they were being regularly fed—how does the hungry-god theory explain that?"

"It's obvious," said Shree. "They were being given the wrong diet. For instance, they say that Mount Zza, before it blew itself up into bits of flaming gravel, was fed only on virgins. Virgins, by Raksh! Everyone knows it's useless to sacrifice virgins."

"Why?" Chasco asked dutifully.

"Well, apparently, they don't taste of anything—"

"To some gods, that is," I broke in. "It appears to be a matter of preference. Some gods actually seem to prefer virgin sacrifices, others prefer chickens, or apples, or—"

"Tigrallef."

I pretended to jump with startlement. "Cousin! I didn't hear you come up. Perhaps you can settle something for us."

He looked stern. "Tigrallef, there is a matter we must discuss."

"Yes, indeed, cousin. By the way, what can you tell us about the volcano?"

The mountain chose that moment to tremble, and a thin slow dribble of molten rock spilled over the crater's lip. The Frath regarded it thoughtfully.

"Does it worry you, Tigrallef?"

"No, it interests me."

"There is nothing to worry about," he said, watching the lava delicately finger its way down the bald crest of the mountain. "I have been told that it does this always. The fire-spirits who inhabit the great cone are given weekly offerings of fruit, fish and goats."

"No virgins, notice," Shree said with apparent satisfaction. I shot a glance at him, which the Frath followed.

"No, Warlord, no virgins. But perhaps you should know that many of the surviving Sherkin garrison were either thrown into the crater or sealed into the killing-caves not long after Sher fell."

Shree became watchful. I hastened to fill what was threatening to become an awkward silence.

"You'd think," I said, "that a whole garrison should be enough to keep the fire-spirits happy for a decade or so, however greedy they are."

But the Frath was watching Shree's face. "I tell you this story for a reason. It shows how little love the Vassashin had for the Sherank."

"So? Nobody had any reason to love the Sherank, least of all the Vassashin—"

"Tigrallef. I would speak with you alone," he broke in firmly, with a pointed glance at Shree and Chasco. Taking the hint, they moved down the deck, out of earshot, and stood talking quietly by the rail.

The Frath fixed me with a gimlet eye. "Your companion is a Sherkin warlord."

I was taken aback by his bluntness. "He was once, cousin. He's a Gillish memorian now. And his mother was a Gilwoman."

"If the Vassashin learn of his origins, it will not matter what his mother was, nor will it matter that he can read and write. He was a warlord of Sher, and I will not be able to protect him."

I stared at the Frath for a moment, thinking fast. There was no unspoken threat here. He had nothing to gain as yet from betraying Shree, and he must have known we didn't need the warning: what was Shree growing his beard for, if not to disguise his history? The upper-caste Sherank had always gone clean-shaven.

No, my rapid calculations were about something else. I had been waiting patiently for an opportunity to sound out how much the Frath knew of the last moments of Sher. It was obliging of him to provide one. I said, "But the Vassashin should be thankful to Lord Shree. After all, he played a part in destroying Sher—" And then I bit my lip, and tried to look as if I feared I'd said too much.

"What do you mean, Scion?" A glint of interest shone in the Frath's eyes. "Sher was destroyed by the combined vengeance of the gods of all the nations when its cruelty and greed became an offence to their nostrils. What part could this Sherkin halfblood have played in that?" He watched me narrowly.

"The same part as we all played, cousin," I said in my most pious tones. "He prayed fervently for the downfall of the wicked when their sins became too great for him to bear, even though he had been nurtured in the same wickedness. What else could I mean?"

"One hears stories," he said vaguely, but his eyes were alert.

"What stories, cousin?"

"Absurd stories, Scion, myths, legends in the making. You know what the world is like. I have even heard it said," and his eyes bored into mine, "that it was you yourself, Tigrallef, who destroyed Sher before you destroyed the Lady in Gil. Absurd, of course."

Time to reassure the man. I let my eyes drop, and fiddled with the catch on my belt. "Absurd," I agreed. A touch of furtiveness in the voice; a tremble in the hand picking at the polished leather.

"No kernel of truth in it, I suppose," he prompted softly.

I avoided meeting his eyes. "No. Well, yes, I suppose the part about breaking the Lady is true. I am a little clumsy."

"Clumsy?" He was bending close to me, almost whispering now. "One of the four Great Magics of the world, and you broke her by being clumsy? I wonder. I would hate to think so little of my beloved cousin's bridegroom."

I wriggled. I glanced up at him guiltily, and let my eyes drop again. I coughed a couple of times as if searching for something to say and signalled discomfort in every way I could think of, short of writing it down for him. Finally he put his hand on my shoulder.

"Never mind for now, Tigrallef," he said, and his voice

oozed satisfaction. "We shall talk of this matter again, for it would please me to hear the legends of our new brothers in Gil. For now, I came only to say to you—Lord Shree is safe for the moment. The Burgher of Vass asked me if any Sherkin survivors were on board; as Lord Shree is only half a Sherkin, I told only half a lie. As far as the Vassashin are concerned, he is a full Gilman and a member of your personal staff. You must warn him, though, to be careful of what he does and says, and you must find him a new name."

"I am most grateful to you, cousin," I said in a subdued voice.

"I shall remind you of that someday." Ownership was back in his eyes. He hesitated. "Tomorrow, we go ashore. Be ready, cousin." Another searching look, and then he nodded graciously, and moved away. I grinned at his back.

"What was that about?" Shree asked as I rejoined him and Chasco at the rail.

"My august cousin is trying to score points for kindness. He has obliged me by not turning you over to the Vassashin as volcano fodder."

"How very good of him. Were you properly grateful?"

"Of course. But I think you're safe only so long as I continue to play the game."

"That's to be expected. Anything else?"

I smiled dreamily up at the dribbling volcano. "He came quite close to asking me about the Lady—about what happened after I destroyed Sher and broke the glass. I had to bring it up myself, though. He's being very cautious."

"Are you being cautious enough?"

"I think so. Anyway, we're being allowed ashore tomorrow. Shree, you need a name that won't get you killed, something harmless and Gillish. Tasolef?"

"Thank you, but I'll do without the Scions' suffix. Look at the trouble it got you into."

"Would you take Selki, Lord Shree?" offered Chasco. "It's a good name for a scholar."

I whistled. "Your four-times-great grandfather, one of the greatest Clanseri poets. Chasco is honouring you, Shree."

"Then I am honoured," Shree said. "Selki it is."

The mountain rumbled again and both Shree and Chasco

glanced up at its coronet of sparks. I kept my eyes on Shree.
With the hair burgeoning on his jaw and cheeks, he looked
like almost anything from a Lucian eremite to a Miisheli trog,
but nothing in particular like a Sherkin warlord. The beard
masked the hungry lines of his face and filled in the hollows
of his cheeks, appearing to drop his high sharp cheekbones by
an inch or so. The Vassashin shint, if she'd actually managed
to return to Vassashinay before the Sherkin débâcle, was
going to have a hard job recognizing the Gillish scholar Selki.

The next afternoon, our fourth in the harbour of Vass, I sat in
the bow of the smallboat with Rinn and my watchdogs, the
Satheli envoy and a few highborn Miishelu, watching the jetty
approach. The Frath Major, the Bequiin Ardin and an assortment of other luminaries were ahead of us in the other smallboat. We were to be the honoured guests of Lillifer himself,
the Burgher of Vass, who was the closest thing to a kinglet in
the islands of Vassashinay.

   He was waiting for us on the beach, a tall solid man in late
middle age, whose height was exaggerated by the conical
headgear he wore as his symbol of office. By that, I recognized him as the man who had parleyed with the Frath Major.
He stood at the head of a wedge of obvious local dignitaries,
all of them men; but standing by his left hand was a tiny figure
in a long flame-coloured hooded gown, whom I thought at
first glance was a child.

   A large crowd was on hand to watch us disembark; I ran my
eyes over the faces as I handed Rinn tenderly on to the shore.
The Vassashin were a handsome race, well-built, almost as
dark-skinned as the Storicans, with long ropes of reddish-
brown hair hanging down their backs and ornaments of shell,
coral and shiny stone jingling on their scanty costumes. Multitudes of healthy naked children swarmed around the edges
of the crowd and I saw somebody doing a brisk business in
spit-broiled fishes up near the treeline. There was a feeling of
festival in the air. None of this was what I expected in a nation
that had spent most of its history being raped and looted by
the appalling Sherank. Where was the bitterness that festered
on in Gil and Tata, Glishor and Kuttumm? Where were the
hard haunted faces you saw on the streets of Gil City?

Burgher Lillifer stepped forward to greet us formally. I bowed to his bow, put my hands palm to palm with his, since that seemed to be expected, and as I did so, my eyes fell on the child beside him. She was no child. Thick white streaks ran through the plait coiled on top of her head, half-hidden by the scarlet hood; her sharp brown eyes were set in a web of wrinkles. She watched me intently as I stepped back from greeting the Burgher.

This was the odd thing: I felt I recognized her. Not the face, not the half-size body, not the surprisingly strong voice she raised a few moments later in a prayer to the fire-gods—all those were strange to me, but *she* teased at my memory. I glanced at her again and saw she was still gazing at me with an intensity that made me very uneasy.

She looked away from me at last when the ongoing ritual of welcoming demanded her attention. Obviously she was a personage of importance among the Vassashin. Her last act in the ritual, after the forementioned prayer, was a fairly provincial bit of conjuring—a handful of black powder thrown to the ground at the Frath's feet, a flash of white light, a sparkling cloud that hovered around the Frath's head and shoulders for a few moments before its particles winked out and fell to the sand. A kind of trashy Zainoi firework from the looks of it, but the Miishelu managed not to snicker or sneer, while the Vassashin spectators were breathlessly impressed. In dead silence they listened to the little woman's final blessing, then parted respectfully to let her depart. Still puzzled, I watched her join a phalanx of red-robed figures at the edge of the crowd and vanish into the trees.

Suddenly: *Scion—that one is more than she seems.*

Those were the Lady's first words to me in days, and for a change they cleared something up for me. I had a flash of understanding.

It was you that knew her, I said to the Lady, *it was* your *recognition I was feeling, not mine . . .*

The two are one, Scion. The wind and tree are one. And she is more than she seems.

Typically cryptic, and it was all she would say. After a while I gave up on her and returned my attention to the real world.

• • •

Meantime, the Burgher Lillifer had begun a speech of formal welcome. I could understand most of what he said, even without the interpreter, a young Vassashin named Coll. The language of Vassashinay turned out to be a dialect of Sheranik, with slight differences in vocabulary and case endings, and an accent that was far more melodious than the rasping Sheranik growl. I caught Shree's eye. He was doing a good job of looking blank while Lillifer was speaking, pretending to understand only Coll's rendering into Miisheli.

The speech went on and on. Vassashinay was honoured. More than honoured—awed by our grandeur, grateful for the privilege of serving us, shamed by the humble hospitality that was the poor best they could offer. Vassashinay was enchanted. More than enchanted—for the esteemed visitors were more than beautiful, more than noble, more than wise and puissant; Vassashinay covered its dazzled eyes, fearing to look upon such brilliance. And so forth.

At last, after a series of especially florid and bejewelled metaphors, greeted by the crowd with roars of appreciation, Lillifer appeared to be finished. My party heaved deep sighs almost in unison, and gratefully prepared to move. Lillifer, however, turned to one of the worthies behind him and motioned him forwards. In a low, monotonous and unstoppable voice, the wretched man began to speak.

Inwardly, I groaned. I counted the eminent citizens in the wedge behind Lillifer: there were thirteen, not counting the one who was currently in full drone. Some hot and tired corner of me knew by instinct that every one of those good men was going to welcome us with a speech. I was right, too.

21

BY SUNSET WE had been well and truly welcomed. Every one of us, from the Frath Major right down to the Satheli envoy's page, was cross-eyed with boredom and aching in muscle and gut from standing so long in one place. At least one of the

Fraths Minor was desperate to relieve himself, and the old Bequiin Ardin was swaying on his feet. Rinn, in spite of her marked talent for disrupting ceremonies, behaved herself with such impeccable apathy that I began to fear I was having a good influence on her.

The people of Vassashinay, in contrast, seemed to be having a wonderful time, their enthusiasm never waning, the cheers that rewarded each speaker never diminishing in fervour. I began to realize that the Vassashin *liked* speeches.

Just when I was starting to think it would take the Han-Frath Zimin and his battery of spearchuckers to get us off the beach, it was over. Drums and whistles and chanting started up; the sudden flaming of scores of torches pushed back the gathering shadows of dusk. We were swept along in a body with Lillifer and the Frath in the lead, towards that opening in the treeline. I could still see nothing that resembled a town.

Nevertheless, the town was there. The gap turned out to be the mouth of a long basalt-paved avenue that curved gently towards a distant square, beyond which loomed the dim beehive shape of a large building. It was the only structure in sight at first, and the forest seemed to press threateningly up against both edges of the avenue; but a minute or so later, I realized that the squat, black shadows of many little houses were hidden among the trees, already showing the pale circles of lighted windows. I got a clear impression that they were small and tightly clustered together, and that the jungle was trying earnestly to cram itself into every remaining pinhole of space. Looking ahead, I saw that the beehive building had blossomed with four tiers of glowing windows, and was both larger and somewhat further away than it had seemed at first.

All around us, the trees rustled in the evening breeze; birds disturbed by the procession's noisy approach leapt into flight with odd screeching cries. The town was otherwise so empty and peaceful ahead of us that I realized most of the population must be in the chanting, foot-stomping, drum-banging mob behind us. The air was heavy with unfamiliar flower scents, but I could also detect the lingering traces of cooking smells, fish and woodsmoke, and the inevitable subtle underlay of sewage and decay.

We reached the square in front of the beehive building and

halted before a broad flight of stairs leading to a great pillared porch, where Lillifer delivered a surprisingly short speech of welcome to his humble dwelling. I tried to catch Shree's eye, but found that he was staring fixedly at the edge of the square, to one side of the building. I followed his eyes.

There were three great posts planted in the ground there, thick and solid as old tree-trunks, perhaps nine feet tall; on top of each was a cage, not quite high enough for a man to stand in, and in each cage a dark figure was slumped. The silhouettes were strangely familiar. I was still trying to puzzle out why when the moon came out and struck full into the square, illuminating the cages. Snouty helmets; high black boots; Sherkin armour that might have been empty, except that something white and knobby caught the moonlight where the sleeves ended. It appeared that at least three of the Sherkin garrison had not been fed to the volcano.

The chambers assigned to us were small but comfortable and looked down on the main square of Vass from the third tier of the building, as I discovered when I awoke not long after sunrise. A hummocky carpet of green treetops spread beyond the square, broken here and there by the dull black humps of beehive buildings. There were a few small clearings jammed with earth-coloured awnings that suggested market stalls, but no discernible streets except the broad paved avenue we had traversed the night before. I could not see any houses. Beyond the trees stretched the polished expanse of the Sherkin Sea, with only the mast-tops of the *Tasiil* marking where the harbour lay.

It was a drowsy, golden morning; even the volcano's rumble was somehow slumbrous. Although I could not see anyone from that angle, a soft murmur of voices drifted up from the square below my window.

I lay down on the pallet again, quietly, so as not to disturb Rinn. Contrary as always, she awoke at once. She sat up and stretched, then propped her cheek on one hand and looked at me inquisitorially from under her long curling lashes.

"What were you dreaming, Tigrallef? You were talking in your sleep."

"Was I? I'm sorry." I laid my arm over my eyes.

She poked me. "What were you dreaming?"

"I don't remember." A lie. All night, the people had been dancing in my dreams, dancing and dropping in the main square of Vass, under the grisly guard of the Sherkin corpses in the cages. Blood had glistened in pools on the dark basalt pavement. Calla had been watching with me, with tears on her cheeks and the fair-headed child in her arms. I remembered that she had buried his face in her black-silk shoulder to hide his eyes from the carnage . . .

"Tigrallef?" Rinn shook my elbow.

"What is it, Rinn?"

She edged closer, until I could feel her warm breath fanning my cheek. I opened my eyes to see her face suspended confidently over mine. "You were dreaming about me."

"No. Not about you."

She looked surprised—and offended. I reached up and patted her cheek, and tucked some stray wisps of hair behind her ear.

"It wasn't a pleasant dream, Rinn. You wouldn't have liked being in it."

That only halfway mollified her; it seemed I was being self-indulgent in having a nightmare when I should have been dreaming about her. She moved a few inches away, pouting, apparently forgetting for the moment that she was supposed to be nice to me. I remembered at that point that I was also supposed to be nice to her.

"I'm only joking, my darling Rinn, of course I was dreaming about you."

She cocked her head at me coolly. I was not yet forgiven. "A bad dream?"

"A wonderful dream."

"Tell me about it."

I thought quickly. "I dreamed we were in Cansh Miishel at last, and the people were dancing in the streets to celebrate our safe return. You were covered in gold. I think you had a circlet in your hair."

"A circlet?" For some reason, her interest sharpened. She sat up straight and stared avidly down at me. "What kind of circlet?"

"Oh, just a circlet," I said. I was getting tired of feeding

Rinn's vanity, and I was not feeling creative. I put my arm back over my eyes.

She pulled it away. "Blue brilliants?"

"Could be."

"Set in gold, on a silver fillet? Tell me, Tigrallef."

"Maybe. I didn't notice, really. I was too wonderstruck by your beauty—"

"Never mind that. Were there little gold vipers along the bottom edge of the fillet?"

"I suppose there could have been."

"Ah." Her smile was calculating. "You were dreaming about the crown of Miishel!"

"What?"

"The crown of Miishel. It rests now on the brow of my uncle the King, the ugly old fool. He has warts and bad breath and a cast in one eye, and the crown does not suit him at all." Her lips turned down at the corners. "My cousin the Frath Major wants that crown for himself, Scion. How strange that you dreamed it was resting on my brow." Her voice vibrated on the last two words. Her eyes were snapping with excitement.

"Now, wait just a minute!" I sat up, horrified. It was already as clear as Crosthic crystal that the Frath had personal designs on both the crown of Miishel and the Fathidiic Cloak of Empire; and the various attempts on my life showed that others knew and disapproved of his plans. Life was complicated enough without Rinn getting ambitious on her own account.

Or was it?

I looked thoughtfully at my bride, who was all but rubbing her hands with unholy glee. Perhaps it would not be such a bad thing to set one cousin intriguing against the other. At least it would be entertaining.

"You know, now I think about it, you've described the circlet in my dream exactly, right down to the last detail. Rinn—do you think perhaps we've been given an omen?"

Rinn didn't reply in words. She turned to me with the smile of a cablesnake about to swallow a chick, and proceeded to be very, very nice to me indeed.

As near as I can reckon, it was that same morning on which my uncle the High Prince of Sathelforn died. Later that afternoon, my poor father followed him. The gods alone know where he found the strength to dance. The Primate was still pacing the floor of the great audience chamber, issuing useless edicts through my brother's lips. In Gil, the Last Dance was in mid-measure.

The Gilgard gates had been sealed on the third day after the plague first broke in the streets of the city. This was a prudent if somewhat heartless move on the part of the Primate—but in any event it was too late. Not more than two nights after the gates were barred against the wretched multitudes who were battering to get in, a young Flamen danced pus-faced out of the Contemplation Hall of the Novices and dropped at the Primate's feet. Before long, there was another; and then a third and a fourth and a fifth; and soon after, too many to count. Death had leapt the ramparts of the Gilgard as easily as a child might jump a line drawn in the dirt. A few days later, because it no longer mattered, the gates of the Gilgard were thrown open; but by that time nobody wanted to come in.

I have heard how the citizens of Gil and Malvi fled to the villages; and finding the village streets alive with dancers, they fled to the countryside; and there, many of them ended by dancing among the cornfields and fruit groves, and others gave up and went home to the cities, where at least they had the dubious comfort of the priests, shrivers and doomsayers.

Indeed, it was a grand time for the cults. The prophets of doom stood on the street corners and in the squares and ranted over the wickedness that had brought this terror upon mankind. Naturally, they could not agree upon which brand of wickedness bore most of the blame, nor which of a wide range of deities might most fruitfully be invoked. It is said that more than one priest cheated the plague by getting himself murdered in the course of some theological wrangle. In that respect only, life was almost normal.

I have calculated that as many as six in ten danced themselves to death in Calloon, Canzitar and the Storican ports, and five in ten in Glishor, Luc and Plav. Gil and Sathelforn escaped more lightly, losing no more than four in every ten, but this was quite enough to overburden the wains hauling the dead to a hasty charnel-ground in the Great Garden. I can see this in my mind's eye: the statue of the Lady smiling vacantly across the long silent stinking rows; a doomsayer preaching to the dead from the fountain's foot until he stops and looks thoughtful and then slowly starts to dance; a deathly quiet in the streets.

22

I PEERED OUT through the portal of Lillifer's residence at the dusty, shimmering heat of the square. Inside, the main hall was as cool and dim as a cave; the few windows were no more than narrow slits and great puddles of shadow lay behind the columns that supported the high ceiling.

Coll, the Vassashin interpreter, noticed my hesitation. "We only have to cross the square," he said comfortingly in Miisheli, "and then we will be among the trees. It will be cooler there."

Chasco shrugged. Shree pushed past me and surveyed the empty square carefully before crossing the threshold. I noticed that his eyes narrowed as they reached the corner where the Sherkin dead were continuing their long hot bake in the sun. I nudged Coll's shoulder and pointed to the cages as we hurried across the burning basalt pavement.

"Who were they?" I asked.

Coll had a long, cheerful face, handsome as all the Vassashin were. He grinned and stooped to pick a pebble off the pavement, and hurled it towards one of the cages. It pinged off the side of the Sherkin helmet.

"They were our overlords, Gilman. The Sherkin commandant and his brothers. The rest, we fed to the volcano or killed in other interesting ways. Did you know we were once part of the Sherkin Empire?"

"Yes, I'd heard something about that. But the wrack of Sher was more than six years ago. Why have you kept these dismal reminders up all that time? A sort of monument?"

"In a way. But mostly," he picked up another pebble, "we keep them to throw things at." This pebble missed its mark, but Coll only made a rude gesture at the dead Sherkin and laughed again.

I noticed a certain stiffness in Shree's back, which was just in front of me. It occurred to me that the commandant and his brothers might just have been relations of Shree's, given the tangled web of kinship in the warcourt of Iklankish.

We were inside the shade of the forest by this time, and at last I could see the houses plainly. It was obvious at once that Vass was like no other town I'd ever seen or read about. For one thing, it did not look as if any trees had been cleared. The houses sprouted at random out of the undergrowth, haphazard little drystone hovels thrown together out of slabs of volcanic rock and chunks of coral, thatched with broad-flanged leaves. Very few were free-standing—they seemed to have grown up in clumps and colonies, or bubbled out of the ground like yeast. Scores of narrow paths wandered mazily through this architectural jumble, but there was nothing that could be called a street. Overhead, sunlight filtered dimly through the unbroken canopy of the treetops; creepers and mosses seemed to flow down the trunks from the upper branches and wash up the sides of the houses, and heavy-scented blossoms were everywhere.

Coll led us through the labyrinth along a bewildering series of pathways. Not many adults were about—it was mid-morning, and I suppose that most of them were either fishing or at the market—but it took something under two minutes to gather a long and ever-lengthening tail of children. They trailed silently after us, stopping whenever we stopped, watching in hushed fascination when Chasco knelt to tighten his sandal-strap, cooing when I took my notebook out of my tunic and jotted down a few observations. If we stopped for any length of time, we'd find them creeping forwards to finger the cloth of our tunics or our strangely coloured hair, scattering when Coll barked at them, only to gather again when his back was turned.

"You must forgive them," Coll told us. "Your ship is the first to land in Vassashinay in nearly two years. Some of these little ones never saw an outlander before."

I nodded. We were coming to the first clearing we'd seen since leaving the square, and the black curve of one of those massive beehive structures was just becoming visible through the foliage. Another few steps and we were in the open, gawking up at a small mountain of beautifully fitted black masonry. The structure was neither as large nor as impressive as Lillifer's residence, but it was still a respectable pile of stone. It looked deserted. Green branches leaned like anxious maidens out of the upper window-holes, and the undergrowth was rampant in the clearing, almost waist-deep in places. Nobody had cut it back for some time.

"Coll?" I asked. "Doesn't anyone live here?"

"In this one? Nobody."

"Why not? It seems solid enough."

Coll whacked the flank of the building, almost affectionately. "Of course it is solid. It was built to last. But nobody has used it since the Sherank were overthrown—too many terrible things happened here. This one, they used as a prison."

"But the Burgher's house—?"

"It was the main Sherkin barracks. The only bad thing that happened there happened to the Sherank. But it was Vassashin blood that was spilt on these stones." He paused and shivered, although the sun was beating down on our unprotected heads. "There are strange noises here at night, Gilmen. No man, woman or child comes here after dark."

I tried to visualize the view from my high window. "But there must be eight or nine of these structures. Is Lillifer's the only one that you've reclaimed."

"No, there are two others—the Sherank used them as a storehouse and a granary, and there is no Vassashin blood on the stones. But we leave the rest of them alone."

Shree had been staring thoughtfully up at the perfect parabola of the building against the deep blue sky, running his finger along the tight joints between the courses. Now he turned to Coll, scowling. "Who built them? It wasn't your lot, considering what the rest of your architecture is like."

"Indeed, Gilman, I do not know who built them. I can tell you only that they are very old. As far as we know, they have been here from the foundation of the world." Coll was puzzled by the question, as if Shree had asked who built the volcano, or put the salt into seawater.

Empires always fall.

Startled, I looked around to see who had spoken. Nobody was there except we four and about one hundred rapt children.

Did you hear me, Scion? Empires always fall.

I sighed and leaned my forehead against the smooth stone wall.

Yes, Lady, I heard you. You're being just as informative as ever.

There are things you must find out for yourself, seed of the Excommunicant. Go to Valsoria.

Go where?

Not where, who. Go to Valsoria. There are matters that will be lightened for you in Valsoria's house.

What matters?

No reply; but the wall against my forehead grew very hot, and the air also, hotter and drier and stinking of sulphur, and the sun felt like a steady flow of molten metal on my face. I cried out and whirled around; Shree was gone, likewise Coll and Chasco and the children. The wall was still beside me, but it was surrounded by wooden scaffolding, and it ended only a few courses above my head.

There were no trees and nothing was growing on the ground, not so much as a blade of grass—only a bleak black landscape of hardened lava flows and smoking fissures, bubbling mud pools, drifts of ash that hissed quietly in the wind and crept over the barren ground at my feet. The volcano was not there either, although I should have been able to see it from that point; instead, a squat black cone no higher than a hill rose at the far edge of this island, with a thin dark column of smoke issuing from its summit. Another beehive structure, also shrouded with scaffolding but nearly complete, reared out of the ground a few hundred feet to my left. There were workmen around me, but they did not look like the Vassashin. Their skins were smooth and black, darker even than the Storicans', and they wore long kilts and headcloths secured with ornate copper clasps. I could hear them talking, dim lost voices like the whispers of a distant sea, but I could not catch the words.

Watch, Scion.

A man was walking alone across the scorching plain. He was too far away to see clearly, but he wore a kilt and a long white cloak hung off his shoulders. There was a blinding light in his hands, or perhaps a mirror that flashed in the sun. Where he walked, the hard lava surface seemed to shift and shimmer behind him. He raised the light above his head—

"Lord Tigrallef?"

That was a corporeal voice, coming from outside my head. I blinked open my eyes and stared into Chasco's concerned face. It blurred around the edges and then snapped back into focus.

"Lord Tigrallef? What's wrong with you?"

There were no bones in my legs and the stems of flesh I was balanced on were bending under the weight of my body. I put my back against the masonry and slid gently into the long grasses at the foot of the wall. Three faces wavered in front of mine: Shree, Chasco, Coll. I flung out one boneless, apparently water-filled arm and managed to snare Coll by the shells around his neck.

"Who is Valsoria?"

"What's he saying?"

"What is it, Tig?"

The golden mist was coming down in front of my eyes. I dug my teeth into my lip for a moment to help myself cling to consciousness. "Who is Valsoria?"

"Did he say Valsoria? She's the Divinatrix, of course. You saw her at the ritual of welcoming."

The Divinatrix. The mist faded. So did everything else.

"It is very serious, Princess. I think he is dying. You must send for the Frath Major at once."

A hand lifted my head; something was held to my lips. A large quantity of bittersweet liquid was poured down my throat before I sputtered and opened my eyes. The Bequiin Ardin dropped my head and sprang back with a shocked cry, clutching his chest.

I sat up on the pallet, feeling fine. "Bequiin Ardin!" I cried, delighted to see him at last. I was back in our quarters in Lillifer's house, and the room had been dimmed by a tapestry hung over the window. Rinn pouted across my pallet at the Bequiin.

"You are well now, husband?" she said. "Boring old

Bequiin! He always exaggerates." She kissed the air beside my cheek and crossed the room to the table where her flagons of scent and pots of unguents and powders were laid out. Lids clattered.

That left only me and the Bequiin, whose face was very grey, even to the lips. After a moment he quavered, "How— how are you, Lord Tigrallef?"

"Much better," I said heartily. "I'm sorry I startled you."

He sniffed the open vial in his hand, looked at me oddly, stoppered it and tucked it away. Then he started to back towards the door, murmuring excuses, but I shot my hand out to catch the edge of his mouse-grey cloak. This was the first time he had been allowed near me, a rare opportunity. If any man other than the Frath Major knew about the Lady, it had to be the Bequiin, which put him high on the list of people I wanted to talk to.

"Please don't go, Honoured Bequiin," I said. "Why have you never visited me before? Don't you remember that we corresponded a few years ago?"

He examined my face warily and moved a step nearer. A little colour was returning to his cheeks above the wisps of white beard. "I remember," he said. Another tentative step. "I remember very well." And in a slightly peculiar voice, "How are you now?"

"Much better," I repeated. "It must be that draught you gave me."

"Yes," he said flatly. He still looked like he was poised to jump for the door, but after he had studied me for a few moments longer and I had grinned at him and invitingly patted the edge of the pallet, he relaxed and smiled a little ruefully and sat himself down. "I can stay only a short while, Lord Tigrallef. Yes, I remember your letters. You wrote to ask me about Lakshi Cor Cahn's treatise on the last days of the Fathidiic Empire."

"That's right. I found his account unconvincing and wanted to know if such an eminent scholar as yourself, Honoured Bequiin, thought the same. You didn't, though."

"I approved of your arguments, but I could not agree with you." The Bequiin, relaxing further, settled himself more comfortably.

I said, "You agreed that Cor Cahn was too glib, his story was too pat. To me, it seemed like he was trying to conceal something about the end of the Fathids—as if it mattered. Fathan was already in ashes by then, the dynasts couldn't touch him because they were all dead. I thought he was writing lies, but I wanted to know why he would bother."

"Really, Lord Tigrallef. Your arguments were intriguing—you're a clever young man—but Cor Cahn was writing not long after the fall of Fathan, and we have no choice but to accept his account."

The very opening I wanted. "I wonder if that will be said a thousand years hence regarding the Lucian Clerisy's account of the wrack of Sher. Which you and I both know is nonsense," I added casually.

His eyes became wary again. "Is it?"

"Of course it is. A weaving of diplomatic lies, carefully designed to spread the credit around. The truth serves nobody in particular—but it remains the truth. Isn't it the task of a memorian to serve the truth?"

"High-minded words, Lord Tigrallef. But then, you're still a young man." His face had gone almost as grey as before. His eyes flicked across the room to Rinn, who was not listening, and her inattention seemed to help him towards a decision. He leaned forwards and murmured, "What is the truth, Lord Tigrallef? How would you say the ruin of Sher was accomplished?"

I lowered my voice to match his. "You know very well, Bequiin. And you know that I destroyed the object after. I suspect you also know what happened after that."

The Bequiin asked so quietly that I could barely hear him, "What did happen, Scion?"

Just as quietly: "I caught fire and didn't burn. But I think you already know something about that, you and the Frath Major."

He jumped to his feet. "I must go now," he said loudly.

"No, don't go. Talk to me, Bequiin Ardin."

He wavered and then slowly sat down again with a cautious eye on Rinn. I glanced at her myself. She was humming to herself among her little golden pots.

"How did you know, Honoured Bequiin?" I whispered. "What is the Frath hoping for? What other secrets have you found?"

Again, he seemed to be waging an internal struggle; he leaned forwards, leaned back, glanced fearfully at Rinn, drew closer to me. His breathing was unsteady. "Lord Tigrallef," he murmured at last, bending so close that his lips were almost at my ear, "the Frath Major—"

—was suddenly audible just outside the door, in conversation with Shree. The Bequiin gasped.

"Quickly, Ardin. What about the Frath Major?"

But he was already backing away. "I can tell you nothing, Scion, nothing," he said, fast and low; and then even lower, "nothing except this: I like you, and I dearly wish I did not. Whatever happens, remember that we should have been friends." Then he moved away from me and I had to admire how rapidly he composed himself in the seconds before the door swung open and the Frath Major marched in. I could see Shree and Chasco were on guard in the hallway.

"Welcome, cousin," I said brightly. "Don't worry; it was just a touch of sunstroke. The Bequiin has been kind enough to minister to me. We must talk again, Bequiin Ardin," I said, turning to him. "I'm eager to hear your views on the great bard Karforth of Miishel. Is it true he was born a troglodyte?"

A smile, apparently genuine, spread over the Bequiin's face. "There are three schools of thought on that, Lord Tigrallef. I have some notes on Karforth somewhere—I shall bring them with me next time, and we shall decide the matter between us."

The Frath looked keenly from Ardin to me to Rinn and back again. He was not pleased, but he did not seem overly suspicious. After wishing me good health and speedy recovery, he bore the Bequiin away, leaving me to my thoughts.

So the Bequiin liked me, and wished he didn't. His words had been far from what I expected to hear. Trivial they sounded, too, but the desperate sincerity in his voice had given them the weight of an omen. They had also given me a strong sense that Ardin was not a willing player in the Frath's game.

23

"YOU WERE TAKING a terrible chance, talking to the Bequiin like that," Shree said. He was angry, pacing back and forth across the little chamber he shared with Chasco. I had been booted out of my own quarters, sunstroke and all, while Rinn prepared herself for a great feast in our honour that evening.

"What chance?" I said. "I'm sure the Bequiin already knew that I knew; I was just letting him know that I knew that, and it's immaterial whether or not he lets the Frath know that I know. Anyway, I suspect the Frath knows already."

Shree and Chasco frowned at each other. They looked confused. "Knows what?" said Shree.

I sighed. "Let's go through it again, nice and slow—"

"Let's not," said Shree. "I get the general idea. You and the Frath are circling around each other like a pair of dogs or diplomats, and he knows about the Lady, probably from the Bequiin, although Raksh knows how the Bequiin knew, but the Frath doesn't know how much you know, so you're gradually letting him know that you already know everything—"

"Don't you start, Lord Shree," Chasco broke in.

"I'm glad you understand now," I said. "The point is not what the Frath knows but what he doesn't know: he doesn't know that I am not besotted with Rinn, that he therefore has no hold over me, that I have no intention of helping him win the Fathidiic Cloak of Empire, and that I have no control over the Lady's powers. As long as he's ignorant of those inconvenient facts, we're safe."

"From the Frath, perhaps," said Chasco.

"True enough," I said cheerfully, "but nobody's tried to kill me for some time, and perhaps we can assume that the Frath's critics have all been silenced by now. And if Rinn starts to intrigue on her own behalf, it's not in her interest to have me assassinated, quite the reverse. No, my friends, I think we're safe. For the moment."

Chasco paced to the window, frowned down at the square and turned to face me again. "Lord Tigrallef—" he began, and paused, looking significantly at Shree.

"Yes, Chasco?"

"Lord Shree and I have been thinking."

"And?"

"Lord Shree will tell you."

Shree spoke reluctantly. "You're right, Chasco, I'm the one who should say it. Tig, this is too risky a game you're playing with the Frath—it's also complicated and inefficient, and that makes me uneasy. We didn't like inefficiency in the Sherkin army."

"This isn't the Sherkin army. Have you got any better ideas?"

He hesitated. "You have the Lady. You don't need to play games with the Frath Major."

Softly: "What are you suggesting?"

He was worried by my tone, but he ploughed on anyway, more firmly. "That you come to terms with the power, perhaps even use it—you've got to parley with the Lady, Tig, discover how to control her, and if you can't control her, come to some arrangement with her—"

The golden mist tempted me with its shimmer. A whisper: *the two are one.* I pushed both aside and bit fiercely on the heel of my own hand; I was finding that a little pain helped to drown her voice. "I don't think so, Shree."

"But, Tig—"

"Not a good idea. In fact, even if I could use the Lady, I wouldn't."

"Tig—"

"No. We've been through this before. To put it bluntly, I would rather play games with the Frath Major from now until the sun burns out than to make terms with the Lady. Better that we die by our own efforts."

"But—"

"Look at what's already happened, Shree. She's a knife with two edges—evil follows from any good that she does. How many continents do I have to sink into the ocean to show you that? One was enough to convince me."

You cannot deny me for ever, twig of the Great Naar. Go to Valsoria.

I gritted my teeth. *I will—but for my sake, not yours.*

The two are one, Scion.

The two are two, Lady.

She faded into the back of my skull. I found I was breathing heavily, there was sweat rolling down my face and my fists as well as my teeth were clenched. Shree and Chasco were watching me with grave concern. I wiped my sleeve across my soaking forehead.

"Why are you looking at me like that?"

"Was the Lady—with you just now?"

"How could you tell?" Bitterly.

"What did she say to you?"

"She's on your side. The three of you should get together."

"Tup that, Tig!" Shree bashed his fist on the table so hard that the wine flagon danced. "There's no question of siding against you. I'm afraid for you! And not only because of the Miishelu—I'm afraid the Lady will destroy you in the end if you won't make terms with her!"

"She couldn't do that," I murmured. "She can't harm a Scion of Oballef, it's one of the rules that bind her. I don't know why it should be so, but I'll probably regret it in the end."

There was a long silence. Then Shree said, so off-handedly that I could tell how anxious he was, "Is there any rule to stop her from driving you mad?"

"I wouldn't know. Anyway, it's a little late for that."

"No," said Shree darkly. "You're unusually sane. I'd say that's always been your problem."

I laughed alone. At that moment, down in the square below the window, the inevitable drums and whistles sounded to call the invited guests to the feast. I rose to go.

"I suppose Rinn will be dazzling enough by now. I'll see you at the feast, my friends."

Chasco caught my arm. "At least think about what Lord Shree has said."

"I'll think about it—and you two think about the sinking of the Gillish longship—think about the wrack of Sher. Think about how Calla died."

I turned and left them and trudged down the torch-lit corridor. The end where Rinn and I had our quarters was already marked out like a he-dog's territory by Rinn's distinctive mixture of smells: best-quality incense, flowery perfumes, musky powders. I tapped at the door of our bedchamber and went in.

Only three dressing-maids were with her—Rinn was rough-ing it. They had just finished threading her hair through the holes of a Miisheli court-fashion skullcap, so that it swept in a great high-standing crest from forehead to nape and thence halfway down her back. The close-fitting sides of the cap were jewelled in an intricate pattern that close inspection revealed to be dozens of tiny interlocking vipers on a back-ground of blue brilliants.

"That skullcap is not subtle, my darling Rinn," I said, pok-ing around in my one box of clothing for a fresh tunic.

"Whatever do you mean?"

"Vipers and blue brilliants? You might as well tell the Frath straight out that you're after the Crown of Miishel. Perhaps he'd lend you his Fathidiic Cloak of Empire."

Her lips tightened and she shot me a venomous look via the polished bronze mirror; she waited while one of the dressing-maids added a few strings of faceted gemstones to those already clinking against the massive golden bosomspreader, and another bent to fasten golden sandals on to her small golden feet. Then she dismissed them all with an abrupt ges-ture and turned to me. This time there was no mirror to reveal her true face; she was smiling sweetly.

"Tigrallef, darling, it is my best courtcap and I want to do honour to the Vassashin by wearing it. That is the only reason."

"Of course it is, my dearest love. Just my little joke. Any-way," and here I bent close enough to whisper into her ear, "I think the Crown of Miishel would suit you very well; we'll have to see what we can do."

Rinn was pleased by this, but she put her hand playfully over my mouth. "Hush, my darling—you know it is the gods who must choose the brow the crown rests upon."

"Yes, my petal—but the gods can take a hint. Or give one. Don't forget my dream."

Rinn pushed past me to survey herself in the mirror. Her face was radiantly self-satisfied. I think she was already see-ing herself reflected, not in the courtcap, but in the viper crown. "We shall talk of this again, husband," she said. "Surely we must try to discover what the gods will for me—for us."

"Yes indeed. Oddly enough, my love, I've heard there is someone in Vassashinay who can tell fortunes. Perhaps we should go to her."

Rinn made that expressive Miisheli gesture with two fingers and one thumb that signifies utter contempt. "*That* for any fortune-teller in this dirty little hole. We need a real soothsayer."

I smiled. "Quite right. In fact, I wasn't impressed with her yesterday. She's the one who produced that pathetic fireflash on the beach."

"That was a woman? That little ape?"

"Her name is Valsoria; they call her the Divinatrix. But you're probably right, my darling, we don't need some provincial bone-tosser, so we'll just forget about her. Anyway, we've got too much to do."

My wife frowned into the mirror. "What do you mean? There is nothing to do in this boring stinkpit."

"You're quite wrong, darling Rinn. This is our chance to get to know each other better. I have it all planned out. We'll go for long walks on the beach, and I'm sure Lillifer would lend us a boat to go fishing. And I'll read to you, of course—I've got quite an interesting scroll on Calloonic philosophy in my box, and a well-argued work on geometry by the great mathematician Mosphor of Zelf—"

She shuddered. "Enough, Tigrallef. It might be amusing to see this—this Divinatrix."

"A waste of time, sweetness."

Thunderclouds gathered. "But amusing. I think it would please me to consult this Divinatrix. Yes, we shall go. Perhaps tomorrow."

"Certainly, my flower, if it pleases you." I suppressed a smile, unnecessarily. She was absorbed again in her own reflection.

"That's settled then," she said absently. Then, with a quickening of interest, "Look at me, Tigrallef. So beautiful, like an empress. Do you see how beautiful I am?"

"Of course. You look—stunning." This was true. I was stunned, anyway. It stunned me to think that anyone would voluntarily look like that, much less spend three hours in achieving the effect. But Rinn was pleased with my reply.

• • •

Lillifer's idea of a feast involved a great many speeches, endless barrels of what tasted like innocuous fizzy fruit juice, and vast copper trays mounded with a porridge-like substance profusely larded with sharp little bones. The taste suggested chicken, though there was also a nuance of fermented fish, and I gathered from the lumps that the dish was based on some kind of coarsely ground root vegetable. Following the example of our hosts, we ate this directly from the trays, with our fingers, except for Rinn, who would not touch it at all.

The great hall where we were feasting occupied most of the ground floor of Lillifer's ancient beehive—exactly how ancient, I hardly dared to think. Rush matting and circles of cushions had been laid over much of the floor except in the centre, the place of honour, where the biggest and fattest cushions reposed on a very grand carpet that looked like it came from the best of the Tatakil looms. Inherited from the Sherank, I supposed, like the gold Calloonic candlesticks, the stemmed beakers from Kuttumm, the Gillish flagons carved from alabaster. Given that the building itself was inherited from some distant, long-forgotten precursor, I began to wonder if the Vassashin made anything themselves, other than speeches.

Lillifer himself led the Frath, the Bequiin, Rinn and myself to the grand carpet in the centre of the square, which was the signal for the other circles to fill, free-for-all. Chasco and Shree managed to shove their way into a circle that adjoined mine, so that Shree was directly behind me. Rinn was on my left, with a Vassashin notable on her other side. On my right were Lillifer, the Frath Major, and a very pretty young Vassashin woman who turned out to be Moscala, Lillifer's primary wife—he had seven, and this one was not the oldest, but she seemed to take precedence over the others. I could guess why. The Bequiin Ardin was seated on the far side of the circle between a couple of venerable Vassashin, and the interpreter Coll hovered behind our backs waiting for any opportunity to be of use.

The food was brought in with no ceremony—the great trays were simply slapped down in the centre of each circle, the beakers were filled with juice, and everybody proceeded to get uproariously drunk. This was because the fizzy fruit drink was nowhere near as innocuous as it tasted. Rinn, who was eating nothing, got very drunk, very quickly. I drank as much as anybody but remained depressingly sober and after a while, bored with the speeches and drunken antics around me, I lapsed into my own thoughts.

Gradually, I began to notice that no orator had risen for some time and the uproar had died down to a muted babble. I looked around. The mood of the feast had changed. Moscala was weeping softly on the Frath Major's bosom while Lillifer snored; Rinn was alternately giggling and hiccoughing; the Bequiin's eyes were dramatically crossed and one of his neighbours was making an earnest effort to grab the flame of the nearest candle. When I crawled over to move it out of his reach, he smiled and fell asleep with his head on the Bequiin's shoulder. Ardin uncrossed his eyes for a moment, but gave no other sign of noticing. All over the great hall, the servers were quietly moving among the supine diners, shifting candles and beakers out of harm's way, propping heads on cushions, wiping chins, removing trays. Behind me, Shree was lying flat on his back and dreamily counting and recounting his fingers. The interesting thing was, he kept getting the answer wrong. Chasco was fast asleep. I shrugged and pushed my beaker away.

A movement on the far edge of the hall caught my eye. It was at the very midpoint of the curved wall, opposite the great portal, about sixty feet away. A shadowy figure was sitting on a dark chair atop a dais at least six feet high—that's what it looked like, but I was puzzled, since I did not remember seeing a dais there earlier. I sat up, squinting.

There were other shadows lined up in a double row in front of it, holding in their hands candles that burned with dull points of flame. Their forms glimmered grey in the deep shadow; the shadow-man on the dais stood up and paced slowly down stairs I did not remember seeing, stopping at a dark translucent altar, placing on it a box of utter darkness, so black that my eyes seemed to fall into it as into a deep dry well and I had trouble looking away. Other figures appeared in front of me then, swaying along in a slow procession from the direction of the portal—grey cloaks that might have been white, faces that were ovals of darkness enveloped by the grey hoods, grey-flaming candles in their hands.

I watched with fascination. This was no ordinary procession. I began to doubt that it was even real. The men in grey robes paced through the snoring, babbling, giggling litter of the feast as if the floor were quite bare; I could see through them to the yellow flames of the candles beyond, only slightly dimmed, and the servers went unheeding about their business in the very path of the procession.

When the grey figures stretched in an unbroken line from altar to portal, the shadow-man from the dais stepped forward again. Slowly, he reached for the box of darkness and lifted the lid. Light burst from it, pure light like the livid thread down the core of a lightning flash, and the sordid jumble of the feast vanished as shadows do when a lamp is lit. Gone were the carpets and rush mats, the feasters, the unrelieved black stone of walls, ceiling and floor; the ceiling was plastered a blinding white, the floor tiled with white polished stone, the walls and columns blazing with a coat of silver leaf. The man at the altar, silver threads flashing from his white robe, raised a familiar shining cylinder in his hands—

Stop it.

The light winked out. The feast came back. I glowered at the featureless curve of wall opposite the portal: no dais, no altar.

Lady, I'm getting sick of this.

The past is your business, memorian. I thought you'd like to see.

Just leave me alone.

Long ago, the great tree was rooted in this place.

I'd gathered that. I'm not stupid. Next you're going to tell me that empires always fall.

Empires always fall, Scion.

Oh, be quiet.

Surprisingly, she obeyed. I curled up on a cushion and waited gloomily for the feast to finish. After a while, like almost everyone else, I fell asleep. I dreamed of—nothing.

24

THE DAY AFTER the feast was a quiet one in Lillifer's house. The Vassashin had headaches and spoke in whispers and winced frequently; the party from the *Tasiil* was virtually comatose. Since I wasn't affected myself, courtesy of the Lady, I passed the morning as a kind of angel of mercy. I spooned water into Rinn's mouth and flattered her on how ethereal she looked; swabbed the foreheads of Shree and Chasco; checked that the Bequiin Ardin was still breathing and found that he was not quite as dead as he looked; and paid a visit to the Frath Major, during which I was careful to make a great noise about his comfort. I also prevented a massacre when Han-Frath Zimin came ashore to ask why he was getting no signals from the Frath Major, and concluded on reasonably powerful evidence that we'd all been poisoned.

When the Han-Frath had been safely packed back to the *Tasiil* and Lillifer had returned unscathed to his bed, I found myself alone and free. I stole into the room where Rinn was groaning in her sleep and fetched a notebook from my bookbox, meaning to pass the afternoon quietly mapping escape routes and hiding places in the centre of Vass. Nobody was stirring on the stairs or in the great hall and I trod lightly out of the front portal without seeing a soul, although I heard children playing in the trees across the deserted square. My first objective was a gate in the beehive's enclosure wall, just beside the grisly monument to Sher.

It was a stone archway, almost certainly of the same age as the beehive itself, and tantalizing chasings on the jambs suggested they might once have been covered with inscriptions, long since weathered away. I traced them regretfully with my fingertips and peered through the gate. Beyond it was a garden, a curving strip of greenery bounded by the black flank of the beehive on one side and the enclosure wall on the other. Gardeners had been at work here; the grass must have been scythed in the last few days, the encroaching creepers had recently been cleared from a fine blackstone pavement and were just starting to blur its edges again. The air was cool and green and altogether tempting. I hesitated, balancing my duty against the leaden, oppressive heat of the afternoon; then I stepped off the pavement on to the silken lawn and propped myself against a tree-trunk with my notebook tossed down beside me.

Sandals spanked along the pavement. I looked up, startled. It occurred to me that this was the first time in days I had been left unguarded.

"Ha, there you are. I thought I saw you come into the garden." Coll the interpreter, carrying a leather-bound pottery flask and two beakers, beamed at me as he plunged off the path. He looked heavy-eyed but cheerful. He set the flask and beakers down beside me and stretched himself out in the grass.

Rescued from my own sloth, I thought, not ill-pleased to see him. This way, I could sit quietly in the shade and still gather useful information. I picked up the notebook and opened it on my lap. Coll sat up and poured two beakers-full from the flask and handed one to me. I sniffed at it cautiously. It smelled like goat's milk seasoned with fish.

"What's this?"

Coll swallowed his in one gulp and poured out another. "We drink it after a feast. It flushes away the masollar, and makes you feel better. Drink up, Gilman."

"I feel fine already." I put the beaker down on the grass. "What is masollar?"

"Masollar! The wine of the fire-gods, may they be exalted. Did you not know what you were drinking last night, Gilman?"

"That fizzy fruit juice, is it? Yes, I thought there must be more to it than its taste. It's a good strong brew."

Shocked, he opened his eyes wide. "Not brewed. The gods give it to the Daughters at the Sacellum, and they distribute it among the people of Vass so that all might hear the echo of the gods' voices."

"Sorry."

He swigged another beaker from the flask. "How could you taste masollar from the Daughters and not know it for what it was? Did you not hear the echo of the fire-gods (may they feed for ever) talking to you?"

"Not that I noticed. Whose daughters are you talking about?"

He choked on his drink. "Whose Daughters? Gilman, do you not know anything? The Daughters of Fire, indeed! At the Sacellum, up on the mountain of the blessed living fire-gods. Their fame is everywhere—why, even the accursed Sherank honoured the oracle of the fire-gods! They took the Daughters to Iklankish sometimes, to bear the wisdom of the blessed fire-gods to the ears of the Princes. How can you not have heard of the Daughters of Fire?"

I heaved a sigh. It was not my place to tell him how broad the known world was, and how insignificant Vassashinay, nor why exactly a selection of the Daughters had been carried off to Iklankish. Anyway, I wanted to hear more. There's nothing I liked better than a good old cult.

"You must pardon my ignorance," I said humbly. "Tell me more about the Daughters. Did any of them ever come back from Iklankish to Vassashinay?"

"Aye, Gilman, heaped with honours."

"Oh." Oh gods, I thought. Shree had better hurry with his beard. "And the oracle? Is that where the Divinatrix comes in?"

"Not just that! The Divinatrix rules the whole Sacellum!"

Shaking his head at my ignorance, sipping from his vile goat/fish restorative as he talked, Coll launched into a long, confused exposition on the Daughters of Fire. As a cult, it sounded fairly typical of the volcano-feeding class—bringing to mind, say, the Flames of Zza and certain aspects of the Fathidiic tradition—but it had a few interesting twists; and sacrificing to appease the fire-gods of the volcano was only a small part of the Daughterhood's duties. I gathered that most of the Daughterly income derived from the sale of masollar and the profits from the oracle, plus offerings given in trust for an inmate of the Sacellum called the Kalkissann, which meant the Great Saviour. This modestly named personage, from Coll's account, sounded much like the Holy Fool of Zza—a puppet with few duties or functions except to swell the cult's treasury. I began to think the Divinatrix must be quite the wily old businesswoman.

"How does the Oracle work?" I asked Coll. "Do the gods speak directly to the Divinatrix?"

"No, no, no. No, the gods, may they be blessed, speak to one of the Daughters in the Oracle chamber, and then the Daughter comes out, and the Divinatrix interprets what she says."

"Why is that? Is it dangerous, speaking with the gods?"

Coll looked surprised, as if he'd never thought of it that way. "Dangerous? Maybe so. Some Daughters stay too long in the Oracle chamber—I've heard they bleed with the words then, and the words are more powerful than at other times, and the Daughter often dies in the next few days. Yes, I suppose you could say there is danger."

"It sounds hard on the Daughters."

"Ah." His face became wistful. "But it is a great honour to hear the gods—an honour that men are denied. They say we can hear the echo of the gods when we drink masollar, and it is true I have heard wonderful things after only seven or eight cups—but the Daughters hear them as clearly as I hear you, and you hear me."

"But it takes the Divinatrix to understand what they say?"

"Indeed so."

I leaned back on the grass to gaze at the bright flowers nodding on the branches, and beyond them to the dark column of smoke, shot with sparks, which was all I could see of the volcano. It seemed to me that Valsoria was on to a good thing—all the benefits of a direct connection with the gods (bless and feed them), with none of the risks. I reckoned she could well be the major power in Vassashinay, standing in the same relationship to Lillifer and his cronies as the Primate stood to Arkolef.

"How long has Valsoria been the Divinatrix?" I asked.

"Oh, many years. From the time of my grandfather."

"So she was there under the Sherank?"

"Of course."

"I see." The next question had to be tactful. "When the Sherank invaded my country," I said carefully, "they wiped out the priesthood almost to a man. Our temples were taken over or destroyed, our sanctuary desecrated, and anyone who spoke of the Lady in Gil was in the Pleasure or under the Claws by the end of the same day." Coll clicked his tongue with sympathy. "And after Gil was liberated, anyone who had

collaborated with the Sherank was given a very hard time
indeed. Many of them were killed along with the survivors of
the Sherkin garrison. Therefore, it seems strange to me that
Valsoria was able to be the Divinatrix both before and after
the downfall of Sher."

My tact was wasted. Coll looked quite uncomprehending.
He glanced behind him. Over the enclosure wall, we could
just see the top of the cage where the late Sherkin commandant adorned the edge of the square. Coll gathered a handful
of little brown tree-nuts that had fallen into the grass and
tossed them over the wall; we heard them plink down among
the armoured Sherkin bones. He said, "It is not strange at all,
Gilman. The Sherank had great faith in the Oracle. Valsoria,
and Hassana the Divinatrix before her, always predicted great
things for them, conquest and riches and empire."

"I see. They knew which pot their fish came out of—"

"No, no! All the words the gods gave to them were true.
Sher did win a great empire, did it not? The gods did not lie,
and neither did the Divinatrix."

I shrugged, taking the point. "And did the Divinatrix foresee the wrack of Sher?"

"Foresee it? Gilman, she and the fire-gods brought it
about!"

"Oh?"

"Yes! Did you not know? Does not the whole world know
that Sher was destroyed by the blessed fire-gods of Vassashinay?"

Coughing gently, I avoided his eyes. "Yes, well, actually,
there have been a number of different stories going about
since Sher sank into the sea, and a fair amount of controversy
about who can claim the credit—"

"All lies." Coll dismissed the rest of the world with a wave
of his hand. "Who better to know what happened, then we of
Vassashinay?"

"How do you know?"

"The Divinatrix told us."

"Ah, yes. Now I see." Sighing, I turned to a fresh page in
my notebook. "Tell me about it."

Coll had already shown himself to be an unsatisfactory
informant, confused, rambling and apt to misplace the point

of one story until he was well into another, but this time the fault was in the subject matter. It seemed that, without being at all conscious of any inconsistencies, the Vassashin were able to believe: (1) that the fire-gods had told Valsoria what they intended to do about Sher; and/or (2) that Valsoria had told the fire-gods what they really must do about Sher; and/or (3) that Valsoria and the fire-gods, between them, had decided what they were going to do about Sher; also that the fire-gods had channelled their powers through Valsoria, and/or that Valsoria's own considerable powers, drawn from her connections with unspecified old ones, had been channelled through the fire-gods. Coll didn't put it that clearly.

In fact, the only clear and consistent conclusion I could draw from Coll's account was that Valsoria had not made her prediction public before the event. This, Coll said when I pressed him, was because she had not wanted the Sherank to hear of it accidentally and take warning—well and good, but the truth was that upwards of eight hundred Vassashin had drowned when the waves from Sher's passing deluged the islands. Surely, I thought, someone should have wondered why the Divinatrix didn't circulate a gentle hint among the populace beforehand, a discreet intimation that high ground would be healthier than low on that fateful morning. However, Valsoria's powers of prophecy were unquestioned.

In all Vassashinay, in fact, it was only the Sherkin garrison which had been displeased by the lack of advance warning. Soon after the wrack of Sher, Commandant Skran had sent thirty troopers to fetch Valsoria to the Pleasure of Vass—it had not yet dawned on him that Sher's downfall was also his own. None of that party returned alive to the barracks.

"They thought we had gone mad, Gilman. They rode through the crowds trying to herd us back with swords and horses, but we ran roughshod over them, and pulled them off their horses, and some of them we trampled to death, and some of them we killed with boathooks and mattocks, and oh Gilman! How surprised they looked!" Coll laughed so hard at the memory that he fell over into the grass.

"Ho ho," I said. "And the others? The ones left in the barracks?"

"We took them alive." Still chuckling, he sat up. "That was

on Valsoria's orders—the rest of us would have killed them all on the spot, which would have been a great waste. It was so much better to kill them later." He broke off, beaming, and slit himself from throat to navel with an imaginary knife, hissing suggestively through his teeth.

I sighed and laid my pen down. "You didn't like the Sherank very much, did you?"

"Oh, we liked them very much. Never have we seen such deaths!"

"Never mind, I can imagine."

But he told me anyway, with an impressive amount of fiendish technical information. And the Vassashin had seemed like such nice, gentle people! I was inclined to be shocked until I remembered some of the imaginative deaths meted out to Sherkin survivors in Gil—and we had only seven decades of bloody occupation to avenge, whereas the Vassashin had suffered more like seven bloody occupations.

I tried to change the subject several times.

"The islands' chief agricultural exports? We have none. But I was telling you about the tapestry of eyeballs—do you know how much skill it takes to tan an eyeball—?"

I learned more than I wanted to about the pre- and post-mortem preservation of bodily parts and in the end Coll succeeded where masollar had failed. He made me feel ill.

Far out on the Sherkin Sea on the night of that same day, two Vassashin fisherman, a father and son whose names I never learned, were drawing a fine catch up in their nets. Of all the known world's mariners, only the seamen of Vassashinay never feared the ocean that rolled over lost Iklankish; in fact the fishes that battened on the bones of Sher were held to be particularly plump and flavourful. The moon was high and the sea was calm enough to mirror the stars, even though a gentle breeze was blowing.

When the bottom of their boat was full and they were thinking of turning home, a sound came to their ears from somewhere close at hand. They looked up and saw a vision—a great white three-headed dragon, its three necks proudly curved and its six eyes glowing, bearing down on them across the placid water. The son whooped with terror and dropped the net he was holding; the father retrieved it with a boathook, and clouted his son about the earhole in a fatherly fashion.

"It's got masts, you snivelling git, it's a ship," he explained, not unkindly. (The story, complete with dialogue and all its homely detail, spread throughout Vassashinay over the next few days.) He hallooed to warn the ship of their presence—it would run them down on its present course—and when no reply came, he made some comments about the captains of large ships and instructed his son to row them out of danger.

It was already almost on top of them, the water sliding noiselessly around its bows and smooth sides: a mid-sized windgalley, two-masted, well-conditioned, with the three dragons' heads rising from the figurehead and catching the moon in their blue-glass eyes; a Calloonic trader from the description, like those that used to bring cloth and carpets to the harbour of Gil. A ship that size should have carried a crew of at least thirty to forty including the oarsmen, but the fishermen saw nobody on deck, and the sails were drooping on the ropes as if set for quite a different wind. The father shouted again and then, the ship drifting very close to them, he snagged the tailrope with his boathook and pulled his craft alongside the other.

The silence was broken only by the creaking of the sails on their slack ropes as the fisherman hauled himself up to the rail and surveyed the deserted deck. It was remarkably tidy for a derelict, with the spare ropes still neatly coiled and the deck-freight lashed down; all that seemed out of place was an open strongbox lying on its side at the foot of the foremast, spilling golden palots almost as far as the scuppers—enough gold, it seemed to that simple fisherman, to buy all of Vassashinay and have enough left over to pay for lunch. He advanced on the treasure with such wonder that he failed to notice the body in the shadows until he tripped over it.

The son was not far behind his father; they looked at each other wonderingly across the contorted corpse. The silence seemed heavier, the stars remoter and less friendly, and the breeze was not quite fresh enough to disperse a whiff of corruption that hung over the ship. Without speaking, they pulled the body into the moonlight and stared for a long moment at its face. Another very short moment after that and they were already casting themselves over the side of the doomed windgalley into their own boat, and pulling for Vassashinay as if all the demons of a Lucian hell were panting after them.

Having seen the dead man's face, they wisely counted the gold well lost; if others had done the same, the lives of many people, including my own, would have taken very different courses. However, there were some thoughtful frowns at daylight on the beach at Vass, where the two fishermen first told their story—and a few days later, many small pieces of gold began to circulate in the market, some of them in the form of shapeless chunks still warm from the crucible. And a few days after that, a fish broker rose pensively from his stool in the central market of Vass and began to dance on a carpet of dried fish.

25

THE CORALFIELD BETWEEN Vass and the volcano was crossed by a narrow low-tide road that meandered along the exposed spines of atolls and around deepwater pools filled with seablooms and bizarre bright fishes. The road, a crazy pavement of rough blackstone slabs, was obviously a Vassashin construction, nothing to do with the master masons of my vision. We laboured along it under the blinding afternoon sun, slipping frequently on the scummy paves, choking on the stench that steamed from the hillocks of stranded seaweed.

Not Rinn, though. She had flatly refused to walk. Her voice issued fretfully from behind the draperies of a closed litter, complaining of the jolts, the heat and especially the smell, although I knew she was holding a towel soaked in powerful perfume under her nose. The four stolid Vassashin carrying the litter paid no attention to her complaints.

We were finally on our way to see the Divinatrix Valsoria. Not counting the bearers, there were seventeen of us in the party: Rinn and myself, Coll the interpreter, Shree and Chasco, two of Rinn's serving-women, four lightly mailed but heavily armed Miisheli guards and a half-dozen Vassashin

notables who were also going to consult the Oracle. I had
hoped that the Bequiin Ardin would be allowed to come, but
the Frath Major decided the old man was too frail for the journey. We had been given no more chances to speak with each
other.

As we reached the midway mark of the coralfield, I
squinted up through the glare at the volcano glowering above
us: velvety green on its lower slopes, a dull dark-grey cone
from treeline to smoking peak, the harsh surface fissured with
black shadows. The only sign of habitation was a straggle of
white buildings along the treeline, just coming into view.
When I was sure this was not a trick of the sunlight, I caught
up with Coll and asked him about it.

He glanced up at the mountain without breaking stride.
"Yes, Gilman, we can see the Sacellum from here. Not long
now, and we will be there."

I scanned the apparently unbroken greenery below the
Sacellum. "How will we get there?"

"There is a road up from Villim. You will see it soon
enough."

I decided any road would have to be a viciously steep one,
and wondered if Rinn would have to get out and climb it on
her own soft-skinned feet. I rather hoped so; it would be edu-
cational for her. Looking back, I saw the line of porters
stretching behind us across the coralfield as far as the shore of
Vass, about a third of them burdened with offerings for the
Oracle, and fully half of them with Rinn's luggage. We were
to stay at the Sacellum for five days and nights as the honoured guests of the Divinatrix; Rinn had thought it necessary
to bring sixteen complete changes of costume. I was getting
very tired of Rinn.

She took three days to recover from the effects of the
masollar and another three to declare herself satisfied with the
arrangements for our expedition. At first she demanded the
use of the *Tasiil*'s smallboats, but the Frath refused to be cut
off from the *Tasiil* for even a few hours. Lillifer then offered
his own boat, but this was rejected by Rinn on the grounds
that it stank, which was true but tactless. For a while it looked
as though the expedition might founder; but at last the ever-
helpful Lillifer unearthed a Sherkin lady-litter from the crypts

of his great house and it required only a bit of regilding to be a suitable vehicle for a Miisheli princess. There were enough spikes and curlicues and useless ornamentations on it to satisfy even my lovely Rinn.

And so, I thought, there we were at last—headed for my tryst with Valsoria and whatever secrets the Lady said she held. Frankly, it surprised me that the Lady took this so-called Divinatrix seriously. Nothing in Coll's breathless stories suggested she was more than a skilled survivor, a manipulator of the people's superstitions, a very shrewd entrepreneuse. I had met her ilk a a score of times among the little cults in Gil.

Take care, Scion. Valsoria is both more and less than she seems.

I jerked and slipped. Growling, I picked myself up off the slimy stones. Chasco leapt to help me, but I waved him away.

Couldn't you warn me before you speak, madam? Clear your throat, scrape your feet, something?

I cannot. I have neither throat nor feet. I say again, beware of Valsoria.

This was too much.

By all the gods, Lady, coming here was your idea. What do you mean, beware of Valsoria? Couldn't you at least be consistent?

Silence; but also a prickling up my backbone, so poignant and surprising that I stopped short and whirled around, startling Chasco, who was walking behind me. Suddenly uneasy, I peered up at the white jumble of the Sacellum; the central building, horned with two towers, reared up forbiddingly against the sinister grey of the mountain slope. There were eyes up there, I thought, watching our procession as we neared the shore; perhaps searching for the toiling ant that was myself.

Villim differed from the town of Vass mainly in the precipitous slope of its ground. That is to say, Vass was a roughly horizontal maze, whereas Villim was a roughly vertical one, its ramshackle dwellings stepping up the mountainside on narrow terraces hacked out of the fertile volcanic soil and smothered in lush vegetation. A network of trails and precarious stairways wove these dwellings together, many of them branching off a slightly less narrow trail which Coll, with a straight face, referred to as the road.

This was the path we climbed, often with a foundation on one hand and a rooftop on the other; in some places, the roadway was cut across by stinking open drains, or overhung by cantilevered extensions that had to be stronger than they looked, since they didn't collapse on us when the mountain performed one of its frequent snake-dances. We collected the usual audience of children, but in Villim they did not trail us around as they did in Vass; they gawked at us from the undergrowth while we passed, then swarmed directly up the mountainside, to be waiting for us as we laboured up the next switchback of the road. They seemed to be especially entertained by Rinn's squawks and curses as the litter bounced from side to side. (I believe the bearers were doing it on purpose. Coll had translated some of Rinn's running commentary into Vassashin for their benefit.)

What I did not see was any trace of the ancient masterbuilders, but this was to be expected. When the great stone parabolas of Vass were raised, this mountain did not even exist. The Sherank, though, had left a monument: another caged corpse in the centre of the tiny plateau that served upper Villim as a marketplace. The Vassashin dutifully chucked some pebbles at it as we went by.

Gradually, as we climbed, the scatter of structures and terraces thinned and the jungle took over. The crowds of children began to melt away, although we were well above Villim by the time the last one abandoned us, and the air was already appreciably cooler. The road wound upwards between silent tangles of large-fronded trees, like ferns enormously swollen, many of them sprouting parasitically from the fallen trunks of their forebears, rooted in decay. It was all rather metaphorical, and I mused sadly on the cycles of history as we climbed—the fall of empires, the rise of new empires out of the rot of the old, and also the fact that running up and down the stairs in the Temple Palace had not prepared me for climbing a fullscale volcano. The higher we went, the less I thought about history and the more about the muscles in my calves.

At last the trees gave way to a continuous thicket of low aromatic bushes, and I could see the Sacellum was not far above us. The roadway at that point was hacked into the face of a narrow black escarpment like a vertical slash through the greenery, affording us our first unhampered view down the mountainside. I stopped with Shree, Coll and Chasco to gaze at the black shingle beach far below us, scalloped at the waterline with crescents of dazzling white sand. Perhaps a dozen fishing boats were pulled up on the shingle, surrounded by arrays of fish laid out to dry in the sun, looking from this height like a pavement of silver tiles. To the right, the beach was cut off from a small deserted cove by a broad black finger of rock that stretched far out into the water in line with the rockface we were standing on, possibly the relic of a rare lava flow that, not too many decades ago, had managed to reach the sea. Villim itself was invisible under the treetops.

At that moment there was a stir above us on the roadway. A small procession was coming downwards from the Sacellum. When they reached us, we stood aside to let them pass: three women swathed head to foot in flame-coloured silk robes, a tall youth in a white gold-belted gown, and a child of perhaps four or five wearing a white hooded cloak. They trailed past us without a glance, but the Vassashin in our party reacted dramatically to them. The bearers dropped the litter with a thump and everybody from the notables down to the lowest porter knelt on the roadway making reverent gestures with their hands.

Once they were past, Coll leaned to me and said in an awed whisper, "Gilman, that was the Kalkissann, the Great Saviour."

I gazed at the youth's white-robed figure as he disappeared around a bend in the road. "Really? He's no more than a boy. He looks too young to save anything."

Coll was shocked. "Oh, his time has not come. But the Divinatrix says someday he will save Vassashinay from a terrible peril; that is why he is called the Kalkissann."

Poor lad, I thought. I knew what it felt like, being expected to save a nation, but if Valsoria's prophetic powers were on the level I suspected, he had very little to worry about.

The bearers resumed their burdens—the quality of the silence inside the litter suggested that Rinn was too furious for speech—and we climbed the last few switchbacks of road to the scrubby open ground in front of the Sacellum. All my thoughts were on what was about to happen, none of them on the trivial encounter that had just taken place.

Later, I realized the Lady was playing a little game with me. In this instance, her joke consisted of keeping silent when there was a great deal she might have said.

The closed gates and twin towers of the Sacellum loomed over us. Lesser buildings straggled off to each side—a goat-byre with wide-open doors, a foundry, a long weather-beaten shed with laundry flapping on its roof, an open-fronted shelter stacked to the ceiling with racks of wide-bellied pots from the potter's yard beside it. Other buildings might have been factories or warehouses and one, higher than the rest, looked like a barracks. The place could have passed for the industrial quarter of a small town, not the outbuildings of a remote sacred retreat halfway up the side of a volcano. Only the Sacellum itself looked the part.

It was not very large—it could have been held comfortably inside the Gilgard's Hall of Harps, except for the twin towers that soared a good five hundred feet above us. The rest was a long plain rectangle running back into the mountainside, the free-standing portion being perhaps two storeys high; it was hard to judge because the few heavily grilled windows were staggered in level. The white plaster facing was fresher than on any of the outbuildings and shone a luminous blue-violet in the failing afternoon light. At sunrise, I thought, the Sacellum would be blinding. At the midpoint of the stark façade, three broad stone stairs led up to the solid wooden doors.

Shree turned to me and grinned through his beard. No one else was standing nearby. He said in a low voice, "I'm looking forward to this, Tig."

"To what?" I snorted rudely. "The possibility of seeing your old lady-friend again? I hope not. I've got used to having you around, even with that hair on your face. I wouldn't like to see you fed to the volcano."

He laughed. "What's my name again?"

"Selki. Lady's sake, man, fix it in your head! And stop scratching your beard, they'll know you're not used to it. And tuck the knife further back in your belt, so it doesn't show. What are you trying to do, draw attention to yourself?"

"Calm yourself, Tig. You'll be spitting on a nose-rag next to wash my face with. But if the lady-friend you're worried about is that Vassashin shint in Iklankish, chances are she went down along with the rest of them."

"That's mixed comfort," I said bitterly. I eyed a row of tall wooden posts driven into the ground to one side of the stairway. Another monument to Sher. By Coll's account, a number of Sherkin troopers had died rather slowly tied to those posts, with their eyelids sewn open so they could admire the expanse of empty ocean where the shoreline of Sher used to be. I was about to point this out to Shree—Selki—when the doors of the Sacellum began to swing open.

Two pillars of red silk stood in the open gateway, looking out at us through the veils that swathed their heads. Silently they turned their backs on us and moved out of sight. It seemed a cool kind of welcome to me, but the Vassashin notables, unsurprised, trooped silently through the doors, dipping their heads almost to the ground as they passed between the white-plastered brick jambs. I offered my arm to Rinn—she had at last decanted herself from the litter and was standing beside it with a thunderous face while her women fussed around her—and together we entered the Sacellum, hard on the heels of Shree and Chasco.

The two Daughters of Fire paced slowly ahead of us, leading us along a short dim corridor with plain white walls. At the end, we stepped out midway of a very long, narrow sunken courtyard, deeply shaded by the high walls of the building that enclosed it. The façade opposite was partly native stone, partly unfaced brick, slotted into the mountainside; the peak, with its plume of dark smoke, loomed sheer above us. The courtyard was empty at first except for some Daughters drawing water from a great rain-tun in one corner, but then a door opened directly opposite the portico where we stood and a small procession emerged and came towards us.

In the lead was the Divinatrix, distinctive by her tiny stature and flame-coloured robe. Flanking her were two taller Daughters in scarlet robes with scarlet silk surplices, carrying round-bottomed pottery jugs in their hands. Behind them came an even taller Daughter with a black surplice and an oil-jar and then about a dozen of the rank-and-file in their plain scarlet robes. Valsoria's shrewd little face was the only one not covered by a veil and she wore a look of dignified welcome.

The procession reached the centre of the courtyard. Reverently, one by one, the Vassashin notables approached the Divinatrix. Each received a quick blessing from her and a few drops of liquid on the head from the three women holding jugs, then stood aside with rapt looks on their faces. Some kind of purification, I reckoned—much the same as supplicants to the Priest-King and the Lady in Gil used to undergo, back in Gil's good old days. Coll followed, stumbling in his eagerness, after the Vassashin notables; then it was our turn.

Rinn, however, hung back, holding my arm. "No!" she hissed into my ear. "My hair will be ruined!"

I sighed. "It's just a few drops, Rinn. Come along and get it over with, or the fire-gods will have nothing to say to you. Don't you want to know about the crown of Miishel?"

She pouted, but allowed me to lead her forwards, making only a token gesture of dragging her feet. I looked up just as Shree received the Divinatrix's blessing—and then there was a shocking crash, so explosive that I thought for a moment the volcano had erupted; but I saw that the flagstones around Valsoria's feet were littered with pottery shards and glistening with oil, a pungent oil that I could smell from where I stood.

Behind Valsoria stood the tall Daughter with the black surplice, frozen, her hands poised in front of her as if they still held the fallen oil-jar, her veiled face tilted at Shree's. She took a hesitant step towards him, seemed to glance past him, froze again, then abruptly whirled and pushed her way through the lines of Daughters and vanished the way she had come.

26

SO MUCH FOR the scholar Selki.

It now seemed like a good idea to resort to our old back-to-back strategy for absenting ourselves from hostile culthouses. The timing was good—the Daughters were in disarray, the Vassashin were aghast at seeing a familiar ritual go wrong. If we could get down the mountain before the alarm did, there'd be plenty of fishing boats left unguarded on the beach and I was prepared to have the theft of one of them on my conscience. I hissed to Shree, but it was Valsoria who turned to me first, with an expression of profound satisfaction shining on her face. She did not even glance at Shree. When her eyes met mine, she smiled broadly.

"This is an omen of great power." She spoke in Miisheli, loudly enough to stop the whispering in the Daughters' ranks. She stooped to dabble her fingers in the spilled oil, stepped forward, reached up to trace some sort of rune on Rinn's forehead. Rinn drew herself up as if trying to decide whether to be offended at the presumption. The Divinatrix, however, rose on tiptoe to bring her lips close to Rinn's ear. Whatever she whispered brought a smile to Rinn's face.

Meantime, I was still trying to get that fool Shree's attention. I could feel Chasco hovering at my back, primed to follow my lead. Any moment, I expected a horde of ravening red-robed Daughters to pour through the far door and cut the best friend I ever had into bleeding Sherkin titbits for the firegods' delectation. I dared to hiss again at this potential blood sacrifice, and this time he condescended to notice me. He shrugged. His fingers flashed. *Too tall for my liking.*

I gritted my teeth. What did he mean, too tall for his liking? I signalled back: *bugger the aesthetic judgements. Head for the door.*

The pocketing idiot only grinned at me and went to stand smugly among the already-shriven. At that moment, I could cheerfully have dismembered him myself.

Later that evening, nearly midnight, we sat in a row on Chasco's pallet, with the moonlight striking through the slatted window of his cell. It was the first chance we'd had to talk freely since arriving in the Sacellum. Rinn and the others had gone to sleep at last, lulled by the Daughters' excellent dinner and large but not lethal doses of masollar. The Sacellum was silent except for the pacing of a Daughter on sentry duty in the courtyard below Chasco's window and a grumble now and then from the mountaintop. Shree heaved the third in a succession of patient sighs.

"It was not the same woman, Tig. I keep telling you, the shint in Iklankish was shorter."

"How can you be so sure? You can't even remember her face. How can you possibly remember how tall she was?"

"I know my own tastes. In those days, I would never have chosen such a tall shint. I always liked them short and fairly rounded, like Lissula. This one was at least your height."

"And thin," Chasco put in judiciously.

I glared at him with no effect, and turned back to Shree. "But she fled at the sight of you—"

"She wouldn't be the first."

"This is serious, Shree!"

He sighed again. "Not as serious as you make out. There are several possible explanations. She fumbled, the pot slipped, she was embarrassed. Maybe she was afraid she'd be punished for disrupting the welcoming ceremony—were you watching her at the time?"

"No," I confessed.

"Neither was I. How can we be certain it was the sight of me that startled her? What does the Lady say?"

"The Lady says nothing, and I wouldn't ask her."

We sat in awkward silence for a few moments, listening to the slow scrape of the sentry's feet in the courtyard.

"What was the Daughter's name again?" asked Chasco.

"Carrinay. Coll said she was also called the woman-from-over-the-sea, all run together, like a title, and another title in a language I couldn't identify. From over the sea, indeed! That's a strong-smelling bit of evidence, Shree. Iklankish was over the sea."

"Everywhere is over the sea from here," Shree replied serenely, "and the name Carrinay doesn't pluck a string in my memory."

I banged my fist on the pallet. "I still say we should get you out of here."

He chose not to hear that. "There's another thing. She may have been looking at me when she dropped the jar, but not when she turned and ran."

"What do you mean?"

"She was looking past me—maybe at you. You and your bride were in that direction."

"She was veiled, how could you possibly tell—" I began, with some heat.

Chasco laid a hand on my arm. He rose and glided to the window. "Hush," he whispered, "someone's come in."

We scrambled to join him. The moon was high, and flooded the courtyard with a strong silver light. A small group was crossing towards the processional door on the far side of the court, from the direction of the outer gate: three women in robes that looked black in the moonlight, a youth in a white gown carrying a white bundle in his arms. The processional door opened and two dark figures emerged without hurrying, one of them very short. They waited in the shadows by the door.

"It's the Kalkissann," I whispered, "home from Villim."

"Yes, and the Divinatrix to greet him. What's he carrying?" Chasco leaned past me to see better. "A child, it looks like."

"There was a child with them this afternoon."

"I'd forgotten. That's it, then." Chasco's whisper broke off as the two groups met and their voices rose clearly to us in the stillness.

The Divinatrix said in Vassashin, in a sharpish tone, "You're very late. I was about to send Lorosa down to look for you."

The youth transferred his burden into the arms of Valsoria's tall companion. "He wouldn't be dragged away—you know what he's like when madam his mother isn't there, with respect, madam. But we thought it would do no harm. You know how much these outings mean to him, being with the other sprogs and all."

Laying her hand on Valsoria's shoulder, the woman holding the child murmured something too softly for us to catch. She turned to the door, at the same time gently shifting the child so that he was clasped upright in her arms, with his head cushioned on her shoulder. His hair shone almost white in the moonlight against the dark gown. It caught strangely at my memory. As they disappeared through the door, the mountain underlined the moment with an almighty rumble.

I became aware then that the Lady was prickling insistently at the back of my skull. Even when I bit my hand to shut her up, I could still feel her, keeping her own counsel for the time being, but twanging with expectation. I looked down at the courtyard again, empty now; even the sentry had followed Valsoria through the door. Nothing there to justify the Lady's excitement. I shut my eyes, expecting to glimpse her, as I often did, shadowy indecipherable face, crackling clouds of hair, mist-wrapped, but the only inner vision was of a small head gleaming in the moonlight against a black silk shoulder.

Someone was shaking my arm.

"For the last time, Tig, what do you think?"

"About what?" I blinked at Shree.

"Haven't you been listening? What do you think of Chasco's plan?" When I continued to stare at him blankly, he groaned and pounded his fist on his forehead a couple of times, and said, "Listen carefully. If we try to leave now we'll have to steal a boat and load it with provisions, which we'll also have to steal, and there's a high risk that we'll be caught before we get off, and then we'll never have another chance, right? Because the Frath Major will lock you up from that moment until the very moment we land in Cansh Miishel—not to mention what that she-devil you're married to might do."

I shuddered at the thought. "So? What are we supposed to do instead? Buy a boat?"

"Why not? You've got that bag of palots your uncle gave you—two hundred palots should cover one of these miserable little fishing scows and enough stores to get us past Zaine."

"True. But if the Frath Major caught wind of it—"

"Why should he? Tell him, Chasco."

Chasco sat forward and spoke in a low voice. "My lord Tigrallef, there is a custom among the Zainoi for large ships sailing near the southern current to tow a smaller ship behind them—they call it the lorsk, which means the gift."

"Yes, I've heard of that. Then if the ship gets into trouble with the current, they cut the lorsk adrift as a sacrifice to the sea-gods, in hopes the ship itself will be set free. So?"

"So we buy a boat from the fishermen in Villim, telling them it's for a lorsk. And we get them to provision it, my lord, because a lorsk is always sent to the sea-gods loaded with goods, and sometimes slaves as well, or very junior members of the crew. And we tell them it's a gift for the Frath—"

"Wait. My honourable cousin-by-marriage is not stupid enough to swallow that."

"He won't hear about it. We tell them it's to be a surprise, my lord, and we give them enough palots to encourage them to keep their mouths shut. It should only be for a few days at the most. Say, until the last night we're to spend in the Sacellum."

They both looked at me eagerly while I thought it over. I did like this plan, except for one thing. Staying meant taking a chance on the woman Carrinay's continued silence; for however Shree judged her height, there was still a chance she was the shint from Iklankish, and that she had recognized his face. Why should we wait until the knives were at his vitals? But still . . . Chasco's was the better plan.

"All right," I said at last, "we'll buy ourselves a lorsk."

I felt dead in every bone when I got back to my own cell—separate from Rinn for a blessed change, since celibacy was enforced until the divinatory process was complete, and I must say that the thought of even a narrow pallet all to myself was delicious—but I couldn't sleep. This was the Lady's fault. She was still excited about something; she felt like a flock of moths whispering their wings in the back of my head and the damnedest part was that there were words in the whispers, just on the edge of being comprehensible, and it was impossible not to strain to understand. I lay grimly on my back, in britches I was too tired to shed, with my eyes open and my arms stiffly at my sides, while the moon-stripes spent an immensely long time in crossing the wall at the end of the pallet. At last I sat up and propped my chin on the windowsill and gazed sourly through the slats at the empty courtyard.

A quiet rasping across the way; the processional door opened and a tall figure stood silhouetted in the glowing yellow rectangle. I sat up straight, nerves coming alive. The figure moved as it drew the door shut behind it and was momentarily caught crosswise in the light—long enough for me to see the black silk overlying the scarlet, before the light thinned and vanished and the figure moved out on to the silver-washed pavement. Now she looked all black again, a pillar of darkness, but it was Carrinay, all right, unless there was more than one tallish Daughter who wore a black surplice. She walked almost soundlessly across the courtyard towards the outer gate.

I grabbed my boots and tunic, but didn't pause to pull them on. Barefoot, shirtless, I was out of the door of my cell in under two seconds, flying along the dim corridor, missing the stairway, casting back to find it, leaping down three risers at a time, stopping at the bottom with my back pressed against the wall. The hallway leading to the outer gate was just to my right; I poked my head around the corner, heard the gateway easing open, felt a draught on my face, heard the gate snick shut. The woman I presumed to be Carrinay had left the Sacellum.

I followed, with only the vaguest idea of what I'd do when I caught up with her. My knife was back in the cell, and even if I'd had it with me, the poor woman's blood was too high a price to pay for our safety. All I could think of was to hail her in some isolated place, to talk with her, to discover if she had indeed been Shree's shint in the warcourt; and, if so, to make her see that Shree was Selki now, a Gilman, a reformed character, an exemplar of virtue, anxious to apologize in person for the clouting he'd given her in Iklankish.

When I crept through the gate, Carrinay was just disappearing around the corner of the Sacellum, to my left. I stopped long enough to pull my boots and tunic on, then sidled along the wall and peered cautiously around the corner. Although she was not in sight, the only path she could have taken was a narrow alley between the Sacellum and the high wall of an adjacent warehouse; when I held my breath, I could even hear her footsteps.

I followed her by sound through the rising tangle of outbuildings that lay beside the Sacellum, and caught sight of her again when I paused in the ruins of a byre on the outskirts. She was already free of the settlement by then, climbing a steep slope into a field of pale boulders and scrubby dead bushes. I lost sight of her again almost at once, though I could hear her feet echoing hollowly on the naked rock.

I hurried to catch her up, depending on the clatter of my boots to announce me, intending to wave in a reassuring manner as soon as she was in sight again; but just as I reached the shadows among the boulders, the footsteps above me stopped. I looked up. She was not more than thirty feet diagonally above me, peering down from the brink, and I was deep in the shade where she couldn't see me. She called out in a low voice, in Vassashin, "Who is it? Who's there? Are you following me?"

I froze. The voice was familiar, but impossible.

"I know someone's there. Come out and show yourself."

Still I could not move—disbelief, mostly, also an atavistic chill that raised the hairs on the back of my neck. The dead are supposed to be beyond speaking.

"Who's there? Show yourself at once." Her voice was louder; a note of impatience had crept in.

I recognized that particular quality of impatience, too. At last I could move. I took a few paces forwards into a patch of moonlight and stared up at her with my jaw hanging slack.

She made a soft sound, something between a moan and a gasp. She stepped back and turned to run. I cried, "No!"—and leapt at the base of the cliff, and started doing my incompetent best to scrabble straight up the vertical face to reach her, managing by a miracle to get more than halfway there before crashing down again in a shower of pebbles. Above me, a cry. Panting on my belly among the stones, I heard rapid footsteps, and looked up to see that the clifftop was empty.

"No!" I bellowed, "come back!"

I raised myself as far as my hands and knees and took a ragged breath. There was a quantity of blood on the stones and I realized with no interest that it was mine. Head spinning, I staggered the rest of the way to my feet, took a few steps sideways, and lurched directly into a soft but solid object. After a confused moment, I flung my arms around it.

It said in Gillish: "There is a path, you know."

I jerked at the back of the veil until it pulled away from its fastenings and floated to the ground. Calm now and moon-pale, she stared back at me.

"It's you," I breathed. "Calla, it's you."

27

"You knew very well it was me," she said. "Are you hurt?" Stunned by the sheer wonder of finding her alive, I could not answer her at once, and I hardly noticed the tone of her voice and how stiffly she was standing in my arms. The golden mist that often signalled the Lady's interference in my affairs also began to gather inside my eyes and over the next few minutes the dry bushes around us budded and blossomed, but these minor matters did not bother me until later. I could entertain only one miracle at a time.

I wanted to sing; I wanted to hold Calla, touch her, pick her up and leap about with her, and then collapse with her on to the grass that had mysteriously begun to sprout out of the bare rock under our feet, and wipe out once and for all the grief of the last six years. She stepped back and I moved with her.

She struck my arms down and pushed me away.

"Stop this. Let me be."

Stunned, I peered at her through the golden mist. It had finally penetrated that she did not look all that happy to see me. Her chin was high, her eyes were narrow, her face was cool in the moonlight. She was, for all that, so beautiful in my eyes that I found it hard to breathe when I looked at her. For a moment it occurred to me that I might be dreaming, but I rejected that theory at once. This was no dream. In my dreams, Calla was friendlier.

"Calla, it's me. Don't you know me? It's Tigrallef."

"Of course I know who you are. I recognized you in the Sacellum."

"Then why—?"

"Why did you come after me?" she interrupted. "Why couldn't you leave me alone?"

Honesty took over. "I thought you were someone else."

"Someone else?"

"Oh, yes. I thought *you* were dead." Remembering my grief, I tottered towards her again, half-crazed with the need to touch her, but she took another step back.

"Better that you still thought so." She turned away.

"Calla!"

At the pain in my voice, she looked at me again, a long and thoughtful look, and her face softened—a little. "I'm sorry. I've had hours to think this over, but I suppose you haven't, not if you didn't know it was me. And you've already managed to hurt yourself! You're not one grain more sensible than you used to be." She raised her hand reprovingly towards my torn and bleeding chest.

I flinched away, not because her touch would hurt, but because I knew the damage under my bloodstained tunic was already healing with embarrassing speed, by grace of the Lady, and I did not want to trade shock for shock. I caught her hand in both of mine. It was softer than it used to be.

"Never mind about me, it's hardly even a scratch. But what's the matter with you? Look at me, Calla—stop treating me like a stranger."

She did not take her hand away, but it had about as much warmth in it as an empty glove. "I'm sorry, Scion. Of course it's good to see you." Her voice was polite and very formal. "I'm happy that we can meet again as friends."

I gaped at her.

"What?"

"I said, I am happy we can meet again as friends, after all this time."

"Friends?"

"I should hope so. To be quite honest, I didn't think you'd remember me so charitably—if you remembered me at all." Her mouth curved in a smile as thin and cool as a crack in a block of ice.

"What?" My own mouth was doing a kind of gasping-fish imitation. I stopped it, and gathered my breath. Suddenly I was outraged. "Charitably! Friends! What kind of pious rubbish is that?"

"Tigrallef—"

But I was well away. "Remember you!" I snorted at the sheer breathtaking immensity of the understatement. "Remember you! How could I forget you? I'll forget my own name before I forget yours. There wasn't a night in the last six years when I didn't dream about you. Not a day went by that I didn't grieve for you. Charitably! Friends!"

Her face hardened again. She snatched her hand back. "You must stop talking like this. You're making it harder for both of us."

"Making what harder?"

"Making it harder for us to part as friends," she snapped.

At that my anger froze into terrible dread, the dread of losing her a second time. The golden motes were thick in my eyes now—the mountain was rolling uneasily under our feet, the white blossoms whipping on the bushes in a vicious, short-lived blast of icy wind. Calla shivered and pushed her long windblown hair back over her shoulders in a way that pierced me with its familiarity.

"Listen to me," she said. "Six years is a long time. We're settled in different lives now, we're different people. I'm trying to be sensible about this."

I stared at her for several moments. At first glance she looked prepared to be very sensible indeed. No nonsense about this astonishingly resurrected Calla: firm forbidding red slash of mouth, firm high-held chin, arms crossed like a barrier, a genuine certified one-woman fortress with her gatehouse securely locked and barred. I went on staring, however. Something struck me as not quite convincing—the depth to which her nails were cutting into her palms, for example. I peered at her through the golden motes, frowning, until finally her eyes were the first to fall.

"Don't look at me like that."

"But I think you're lying to me."

"I am not! You assume too much. I'm leading my own life now, I'm happy in Vassashinay and I didn't ask you to come here. Go back to the Sacellum and never try to see me again." She pointed down the path with a theatrical gesture, not her style at all.

Now, if I had thought she was telling even a small selection of the truth, I would have swallowed my agony, patted her on the cheek and walked away; but I am an expert in knowing when I'm not wanted, having had much experience in that regard, and Calla showed none of the telltale signs. It seemed to me on the contrary that, behind the fortress façade, it was breaking her heart to send me away.

"I'll go if you truly want me to," I said slowly, "but at least talk to me for a little first. I have so many questions. How did you survive the shipwreck? How did you get to Vassashinay? Why didn't you return to Gil?"

She said nothing.

"Six years, Calla! Why did you let me go on grieving? Not so much as a word to let me know you were safe—"

She kept her eyes on the ground. "I couldn't know you'd be fool enough to grieve," she interrupted primly. "After all, I was the one who betrayed you to the Sherank."

"Odd, I hadn't thought about that in years. You weren't to blame, not really."

She glanced up. "You blamed me then, Scion. Anyway, I knew if I left you alone, you'd forget me in time, and find a woman you could be happy with. And you see? I was right." The voice and the face were rock-hard, but I saw a single tear take shape at the corner of one eye and spill on to her cheek. I was beginning to understand.

"You mean Rinn?"

Another tear formed. I do not think she noticed she was crying.

"Yes, of course. I saw her with you in the courtyard. She's very beautiful. I'm glad for you, Tig, I really am."

I reached out and wiped the tear off her cheek. "Yes, you look glad." I started to shake. A great ball of laughter was jammed in my throat.

"It's not funny. Stop laughing."

"I see it all now. You think I'm in love with that gilded she-monster. You think I married her by choice. You're trying to be dignified about it—oh, this is rich."

"Stop it!"

"I'll wager you spent all afternoon thinking it over and deciding what to do. You came out here because you were too miserable to sleep. You weren't going to acknowledge that you were here, were you? You were going to hide behind your veil until we went away."

"No!" A pause. "Yes." She was crying in earnest now. Suddenly she threw herself against me, weeping with great heaving shudders that shook both of us. I eased her down into the grass and lay with her in my arms, stroking her hair, staring up at the studded sky and at the white masses of blossom, which even at that interesting moment caused me a qualm of anxiety. Then Calla's sobs died away and she sat up shakily and looked down at me.

"You mean, you don't love that woman?"

"Never did," I said happily, reaching up to push her hair away from her face. "My marriage was a political arrangement, forced on me by the Primate of the Flamens. You never met him, did you? Lucky Calla. No, I don't love Rinn. I love you. Do you still love me?"

"You pocketing fool, why else would I have been so miserable?" she said—but tenderly. Then she started to sob again, which was confusing.

"What's wrong now? I thought we'd just sorted everything out. We've found each other again, we're both alive, I love you, you love me. What could be better?"

"But you'll be leaving Vassashinay soon."

"When I leave Vassashinay," I said firmly, "you'll go with me and Rinn won't. I'm not losing you again. Now do you feel better?"

She did not look exactly thrilled; she looked thoughtful. "It may not be that easy—I haven't told you everything yet."

I sat up and looked straight into her eyes. "Neither have I." I was thinking of the Lady, who, it now occurred to me, was conspicuous by her absence. It was not like her to be tactful. I breathed my first prayer of appreciation in a very long time and put the thought of her away. "Never mind, we can bare all our secrets to each other later. We're going to have plenty of time, Calla, all the time in the world."

"But it's important—"

I stopped her protest by the simple, effective and personally rewarding tactic of fastening my mouth on to hers. She carried on trying to talk for a moment, then her arms moved around me and she held me as closely as even I could have wished; and at that point, a fire that I had carefully banked down and buried and tried to forget about for six long loveless years burst gloriously into flame.

• • •

After the conflagration we lay together for a long time, head
to head, toe to toe, on the convenient grass under the massed
and uncalled-for blossoms, and only when dawn began to outline the grey edge of the Sherkin Sea did I say to Calla, tracing
my hand down the satin skin of her back: "What did you want
to say to me that was so important?"

"Oh," she said drowsily, "I was going to tell you about your
son."

28

THE SACELLUM GLEAMED like a bank of new snow in the
early morning sunlight. I paused by the main doorway to
allow a file of white-veiled apprentice Daughters to come out,
each with a pottery amphora slung on her shoulder. I stretched
and yawned and tried to look casual, just a man returning
from a brisk sunrise constitutional, but none of them seemed
interested. Calla had taken a quarter-hour headstart and used a
different entrance so there would be nothing to associate her
arrival with mine. Secrecy, she told me, was vital.

I knew that anyway, but I stupidly thought at first that it was
only on my account. What I had not yet realized was that
Calla and the child were as much prisoners in their own way
as I was in mine; and I had yet to recognize the single greatest
danger that faced us.

A few Daughters were in the courtyard, busy at little morning tasks. I turned casually into the staircase leading to our
quarters, then sprinted up the stairs three at a time. Nobody
was up yet; the corridor was deserted. Rinn had obtained the
Divinatrix's assurance that nothing would be needed from us
until an hour before noon, and it seemed that the whole party
was taking this opportunity to be indolent, including the Vassashin—masollar headaches in a few cases, I suspected. I
slipped into Shree's cell and found him fast asleep. With all
the abandon of sheer happiness, I poured about half a beaker

of cold water over his face. He spluttered murderously as he came awake and caught sight of me. I beamed at him.

"Someday," he growled, "I'm not going to realize in time who you are, and I'm going to split you from—"

"Calla's alive."

"—your chin to the nape of your neck, the long way round—what did you say?"

I grabbed a nose-rag from the shelf and tossed it to him. "Calla's alive. She's here, in the Sacellum."

Shree stared at me while he swabbed his face; then he closed his eyes. "Oh, yes."

"Really, it's true. She survived the shipwreck, and she's been here ever since. I spent most of the night with her—I left her not half an hour ago."

Eyes still closed, he clucked his tongue sadly. "I thought you said masollar didn't affect you."

"It's nothing to do with the masollar." I shook him; he responded by turning over and appearing to go back to sleep, so this time I used a whole beaker of cold water. Shree sat up so violently that he grazed my chin with his forehead.

"Tigrallef," he said dangerously, "you've had another one of your tupping dreams. You can tell me all about it later, but now I would like to sleep a little longer, if you don't mind."

I turned to his jug for another beakerful of water. The threat alone was enough to get his feet menacingly on the floor, so I set the beaker down.

"Listen to me," I said. "The woman in the courtyard yesterday, the one who dropped her jug of oil—I saw her leaving the Sacellum in the middle of the night and I followed her. I thought it was the shint from Iklankish, and that maybe I could talk to her and tell her what a gentle, sensitive person you'd become—yes, all right, perhaps I was going to stretch the truth a bit—but when I caught up with her, it was Calla. *Calla.*"

Shree's face was still sceptical. Then he noticed my torn tunic, still stained with a residuum of dried blood, and he nodded grimly.

"I see you managed to have an accident as soon as you were out of my sight. Tell me, did you hit your head when you got that?"

"No." Elated as I was, a certain irritation was setting in. Off to my right, something pinged. I looked over, startled, and saw a tiny cloud of smoke above the table where the beaker had been; as I watched, it gradually precipitated on to the table as a neat pile of terracotta-coloured dust. A moment later the water-jug did something similar, the water itself vanishing in a billow of steam. Shree and I stood there for some moments, looking at the table. Shree cleared his throat.

"Did you do that?"

I cleared my throat, too. "Not that I know of." Belatedly, however, I was beginning to see a pattern of sorts in all these unsolicited acts of the Lady, from the Primate's near-fatal encounter with a beaker of wine to the blossoms on a bank of dead bushes. Uneasily, with my eyes on the table in case it started acting up as well, I began to give Shree the bare bones of my story. At first his disbelief seemed to have vanished along with the water-jug, but when I got as far as Calla falling into my arms, he interrupted me.

"You're certain it was really Calla? In the flesh, I mean; the original flesh."

I was taken aback. "Of course it was Calla. How could I be mistaken about that?"

"It's not a trick of the Lady's—or your own wishful thinking?"

I squinted at him, not understanding.

"I've seen you and the Lady bring legends to life, Tig," he said gently. "What if this is—"

"It's not." From the corner of my eye, I saw the table tremble. When I frowned at it directly, it stopped and looked solid again, an innocent construction of wood and iron with two little heaps of dust on top and no intention of misbehaving. "I'm sure it's not," I said loudly, and then added, with a touch of smugness, "anyway, there are details in her story that even I couldn't have dreamed up."

"Tell me."

I moved to the window and pushed the slats aside. The courtyard was empty now except for a pair of Daughters drawing water from the well in the corner. The processional door was propped open and someone was dimly visible in the chamber inside, scrubbing the floor on hands and knees. A peaceful, domestic scene.

"Shree, the question you should be asking is how Calla survived and came to Vassashinay, not whether she's a product of the Lady plus my overheated imagination."

"All right." He came to stand beside me, followed my gaze dubiously to the open processional door. "Tell me," he repeated.

Deep breath. "To begin with, she recalls nothing about the wreck of the silver ship. I remember now—Lord Kekashr had her drugged just before she left the Gilgard, after that very decent chaos she created."

"I remember," said Shree sombrely.

"All *she* remembers is that she woke up in one of the silver ship's smallboats, all alone, bobbing around on an easy sea, in the middle of a mass of wreckage and drowned Sherkin sailors. She had no idea who put her there, or what had happened, or where she was, or why the smallboat hadn't been smashed to tinderwood along with the ship, and herself drowned along with the others. She was drenched, which means she must have been in the water at some point, but the boat did not have so much as a crack in the boards nor a drop of seawater in the bottom, and there was a cask of fresh water and a bag of rations under the thwarts—the kind your army used to take to battle, I suppose."

Shree frowned. "All smallboats were stocked in case the crews had to take to them in a hurry. And they were sturdy little boats as well, but I remember the violence of those waves, Tig, and I don't believe—"

"I'm coming to it," I said. The scrubber had finished inside the chamber now, and was busily stoning the step in front of the processional door. It would not be long now. "She drifted like that for several days; probably in the same current that caught the *Tasiil*, because she remembers passing an island that sounds like the Tooth of Raksh, and she said the sea for miles around it was covered with debris and floating bodies—"

I paused here. Now I could see it for myself, the flotsam of Sher: Calla's little boat bumped along the barnacled hull of a great ship, turtleways in the water like the back of a whale with a skin condition; nosed through great mats of greenery, roots and all, floating islands that spun slowly in the current and broke apart and formed themselves again on either side of her; and all around there were knots and clumps and crowds and whole concourses of the people of Sher, all silent, all bloated. A wooden chair, wondrously carved and satin-seated, kept pace with the smallboat for a long time before becoming entangled in one of those floating islands; a tapestry undulated gently on the surface of the waves nearby. Calla retrieved this one artifact and used it to shade herself from the sun, but how could I have known that? She had not mentioned it. The only sound in my ears was the sea-kites squabbling over the greatest abundance of carrion they would ever know . . .

"Go on," said Shree.

"What? Sorry. Where was I? Oh yes—she drifted for days, she said, until the food was gone and the water was almost gone, and by then she must have crossed the whole of Sher, because she was picked up by fishermen from Vassashinay who were combing the flotsam above Kishti on the south coast. She says half the houses in Vassashinay are furnished with Sher's leavings. Of course they saw the ruins of her dress and thought she was a Sherkint, and some of them were in favour of sacrificing her then and there to the seagods, but others thought she'd make a tastier morsel for the volcano—look there, Shree."

A young man in a white robe was crossing the courtyard. He stopped and exchanged a few words with the woman scrubbing the doorstone, and then laughed and stepped over her and vanished through the processional door. I felt my heart thudding like a pestle.

Shree said impatiently, "So? That's the Kalkissann, isn't it? We've seen him already."

"No. He's not the Kalkissann." I watched the doorway with fierce intensity, but it remained empty.

Shree sighed. "You're getting worse by the day. Raksh knows what you'll be like in your old age. Just get on with your story, I'm almost starting to believe you."

"They brought her to Vassashinay and gave her to the Sacellum," I said obediently, not ceasing to watch the doorway. "She told them she was a Gilwoman being borne off to

Iklankish—so the Divinatrix examined her and confirmed her story, and took her into the Sacellum as a Daughter, and here she is. Then—"

"Hold on a minute. What do you mean, confirmed her story? The Vassashin knew our customs as well as anyone, poor sods; she'd have to be a pregnant concubine for the governor of Gil to be sending her to Iklankish."

"Exactly."

"But Calla wasn't—"

I let my gaze leave the doorway long enough to give him my most dazzling smile. His jaw dropped.

"You don't mean—"

I nudged him to shut up. Action in the courtyard. The youth was just coming out of the processional door, carrying an archery target and a sack. The fair-headed child was right behind him. Shree looked from him to me and back again, and leaned on the windowsill murmuring a string of Sheranik oaths in a voice of pure wonder.

"That child," I said, "is the Kalkissann, the Great Saviour. But the name Calla calls him by is Verolef—the Scion's tag, notice. The Lady would have let her drown without a thought, except that she was carrying a Scion inside her. And so here they are—the two of them."

Behind us, the legs of the table and pallet began to tap on the stone-flagged floor. I swung around and glared at them both. "Stop that," I said. They stopped immediately. I turned back to the window, forgetting them at once, and lost myself in the spectacle of my son at his lessons.

The first thing I noticed, bless heaven, was that he looked more like Arkolef's child than mine. He was wearing a short brown shift that ended at his shapely brown knees, and there was no hood this time, so that his bowl of bright yellow hair shone in the sun. When he took the small willow-bow from his tutor, he moved like a natural athlete, sturdy and graceful, and his first shot struck the target not far from its centre.

Shree draped his arm around my shoulders as we watched. This was rare for him. He had stopped swearing, and made no comment when I had to turn around to reprove the furniture again. There was a broad smile on his face throughout.

After we'd watched for a while he said, "He's got promise, but that tutor's a three-fingered clown. When we're out of here, I'll teach the boy how to shoot and fight properly."

I smiled back. "And I'll make sure he knows how to reckon and read."

We watched for a long time, until Chasco came in and I had another welcome chance to tell Calla's story, while the sun smiled down like a promise on the Sacellum and, far above us, the mountaintop grumbled and spat fire.

29

AT THE APPOINTED time, an hour before the sun reached the zenith, a party of novices came to rout us out and ready us for the first rites of the divination. They carried buckets of warm water scented with herbs for us to wash ourselves in, plain white robes for us to put on after, and no solid food, only trays of a bitter broth in which I thought I detected a taste of masollar. When we were properly washed, dressed and dosed, the novices led us into the courtyard.

The archery target was gone and there was no sign of my son or his tutor, but Calla was there among many others; I recognized her by the black surplice and also by the greeting she flashed at me with her fingers while pretending to adjust her veil. Shree drew his breath in sharply and I knew he had seen the greeting as well. There was no sound from Chasco, but that was characteristic—he had accepted the news of her survival with well-bred restraint and a few matter-of-fact questions.

I saw at that time what I had been too dazed to realize before, that Calla was no ordinary Daughter of Fire. The black surplice set her apart, of course, but she was also one of only three standing directly behind the Divinatrix, well in front of the massed columns of red robes and veils. I felt a surge of pride in Calla, pride that she had risen to such high rank by her own qualities in this foreign place, and pride that my son

Verolef, the Kalkissann, was held in reverence by an entire nation. I was still not thinking very clearly.

Rinn was being quite tractable, for her. I could not help wondering how she looked in Calla's eyes. Her hair was a glittering rainbow flowing loose down her back, and the white robe gave her a virginal aspect that struck me as almost unbearably funny. She stood beside me, swaying slightly, possibly a little befuddled still by the masollar, while the Divinatrix raised her stubby arms in the long flame-coloured sleeves and began to speak.

Shree was on my other side, and I felt him stiffen a few seconds before I stiffened myself. What we were hearing could not be real—but the longer I listened, the surer I became that my ears were telling the truth. The nonsense syllables unwinding in a long string from Valsoria's mouth were familiar, and were not, strictly speaking, nonsense. She rolled them out with impressive power for such little lungs, and the Daughters responded with a strange melodic roar at the end of every line, something like this:

> *Elas aro aro tili*
> *Pilian aro elian*
> *Elas caro calos pili*
> *Aro aro elian*
> *Pili pilian varo eli*
> *Pilian aro elian*
> *Elian aro calos vili*
> *Aro aro elian . . .*

And so forth. Valsoria's dark eyes were fixed on my face as she intoned line after line, stanza after stanza, of a language that I had never understood, but which had been drummed into my head from earliest childhood, the lost language that Oballef had brought with him to Gil, the tongue in which the Wills and the Caveat were couched. Although the sequences and combinations were unfamiliar, there was no question about the words. Inside, I felt revulsion struggling with the excitement of being handed the key to a long-locked treasure-house.

Then the Lady addressed me directly, her words resonating

through Valsoria's chant. *Scion—I told you the Great Tree, the
Naar, was once rooted in this place.*

*So you did, so you did. Whatever the Naar is. But this—
Lords of Fathan, what a find this is! And tucked away all this
time, behind the back of nowhere—*

*Beware of Valsoria. She is more and less than she seems. I
guided you here to find that Other, and now that we have
found him, we must take him and go.*

*Yes, I fully intend to—but this is unbelievable! Why, maybe
she can translate the Caveat for me—*

*The Divinatrix is less than she seems. She speaks with the
tongue of the Naarhil, but she does not know all that it means.
She cannot help you. And she would not help you—she is
more than she seems. The Harashil was not intended for her
kind. Think of Itsant. Think of Myr. Think of Fathan. Think of
Gil . . .*

*Stop! I'm thinking, Lady, that even if Valsoria can't trans-
late the Caveat, she may have enough texts here to enable me
to decipher it myself. And maybe then I'll know how to get rid
of you.* (I had not intended that last to come out, but it is hard
to dissemble when you're talking to someone inside your own
head.)

The Lady answered: *the two are one, seed of the Excommunicant. And when you need to know what the Caveat means, I
shall tell you.*

What was that? What did you say?

Ask, and I shall tell you—in our own time.

Abrupt silence internally, while externally Valsoria's voice
rose in pitch and the ancient words continued to roll into the
hot noontime air. Damn the Lady! I was shaking with fury.
Maybe I had never asked her directly what the Caveat
meant—but she knew my mind, didn't she? She was right
inside it, by Fathan! She knew very well I'd be eager to understand the Caveat, quite apart from any scholarly obsession, so
that I could know the nature of the surpassing oddness that
had fallen on me and was deepening day by day. I railed at her
in my head, probably mouthing the words and grinding my
teeth too, because I sensed Rinn glancing sideways at me. I
grunted when Shree's elbow dug warningly into my other
side. Valsoria chanted on without losing her rhythm, but she

was watching me as an eagle watches a fox cub that has wandered from the den. Calla, behind her, was standing straight and still with her knuckles whitened over the handle of the oil-jar. I got the impression that she was watching me through her veil, and was worried by what she saw. I smoothed my face with some difficulty and pressed my lips together.

Lady in Gil—Harashil—whatever you are—why didn't you tell me this before?

Did you not know you could ask me? The two are one, twig of the Great Naar—yours the will, mine the hands, ours the power. Ask me anything.

I swallowed my rage. *All right, I'll do that: what is the Caveat? Tell me what the words mean?*

This is not our day, Scion.

I'd have gone for her throat then if she'd had one, but I was distracted at that point anyway by the first tremors of quite a respectable earthquake, which may or may not have been my doing; after all, we were standing on the flank of a restless volcano that was fully capable of shaking without my encouragement. Whoever was doing it, the fire-gods or me, it had the peculiar effect of calming me down, whereas Rinn shrieked with terror, the Divinatrix paused in her chanting and even the Daughters, who must have been accustomed to this sort of thing, showed signs of disquiet at the long duration of the tremors. When at last the ground stopped shaking, the Lady seemed to be gone, and no amount of mental bellowing could attract her attention.

At least the earthquake, if I could take credit for it, supported the theory that had been forming in my mind: that the Lady's magical activities took place mainly when my rational mind was being assaulted by some powerful emotion. I went over what incidents I could remember—it could be grief and anger, for example, that almost choked the Primate to death on a mouthful of wine, terror that sent the parth-asp packing, fury that shook the ground, joy that drew flowers out of dead bushes and grass out of bare rock, destroyed crockery and set the furniture dancing. The storm that blew the *Tasiil* off course could have arisen out of shock at realizing I had not destroyed the Lady, mixed with disgust at the jubilant

Miisheli preparations for spilling yet more barrels of blood. Admittedly, I was half-asleep for the grisly death of the Frath Minor, my would-be assassin, but that was not a counterproof: sleep could lower the barriers of my reason as effectively as emotion.

What bothered me most was that the effect seemed to be strengthening, as if, with every day that passed, the spark of my own soul came closer and closer to being swallowed by the flaming great bonfire that was the Lady; as if, despite my best efforts at resistance, the two were truly becoming One. And if this were the case, and I could find no way to stop the slow, insidious process of melding—who, or what, would that One be?

Shree prodded me from behind. Valsoria's chant was finished and she had already turned around and was pacing along an aisle opened for her through the congregation of Daughters, preceded by Calla and the two in scarlet surplices. Though nothing was said, it seemed to be taken for granted that we supplicants would follow them. Taking Rinn by the elbow, I paced slowly behind the Divinatrix towards the processional door.

We stepped through into the chamber I had glimpsed from the outside, a small bare room, longer than it was wide, with a heavy wooden door in each of the walls. Those on either side of us were small and plain, and I guessed they led to the Daughters' living quarters, but the doorway straight ahead of us was high and broad and double-leafed, with blackstone lintel and jambs that appeared featureless at first glance—only when I was passing through them did I see they were carved in intricate low relief with hundreds upon hundreds of minutely detailed hieroglyphs. I had a feeling that the doorframe was much older than the building it was now set into.

It led into a corridor broad enough for four to walk abreast, which after a few steps began to slope downwards, and then levelled out again after a few more. Ahead of us, far beyond the reach of the dim light from the foyer, a faint red glow silhouetted the figures of the Divinatrix and her three lieutenants. I counted my paces as we passed along the corridor, and calculated that it was nearly two hundred feet from end to end. We were moving deep into the mountain—I began to understand how the Sacellum, which looked so small from the outside, could house so many Daughters.

The air thickened and grew hotter as we advanced along the corridor towards the diffuse red glow. From behind us came the voices of the Daughters chanting as they followed, the music blurring and swelling in that confined space until it seemed that a thousand-strong choir was on our heels. All at once the silhouettes of the four figures ahead of us appeared to grow shorter and then to vanish into the floor; a few steps further, and I could see why.

Rinn and I were standing in a portal midway along the curved edge of a great cavern, a buried amphitheatre, its ceiling arching up into shadows, its floor sloping down and around like a fan-shaped section cut out of a funnel. Except for the wedge of smooth stone floor descending straight from the doorway, the sides of this funnel were terraced into twenty or more rows of curved stone benches, enough seating to accommodate all the Daughters I'd seen and still be half-empty.

The red glow was emanating from a large circular well at the point of the fan—at least eighteen feet across, I estimated as we walked down the stone ramp towards it, with a low stone parapet dividing it from the lowest tier of benches. It appeared to be bisected by a black stripe of darkness, which, as we got closer, turned into a narrow stone bridge spanning it from the foot of the ramp to a raised platform, like a stage, cutting further into the heart of the mountain; and on that stage, one Daughter in a plain scarlet robe was kneeling before a massive black altar. The floor was warm under our feet.

Valsoria continued alone across the bridge to join the solitary Daughter, while Calla and her two colleagues stopped to bar the way, the three of them standing shoulder to shoulder across the bridgehead. Out of curiosity, I moved around them to the parapet and peered down into the well. A blast of burning air hit my face; the well was a stone-lined pit floored with liquid fire that simmered and bubbled and cast up tortured vapour-shapes, only a few feet below me. Live lava, molten lava. One of the Daughters, not Calla, grasped my arm to pull me away; Calla herself motioned to me to sit in the lowest tier

of benches, closest to the well, with Rinn on one side of me
and Coll and Shree on the other. Chasco and the Vassashin
supplicants were in the same tier, on the far side of the ramp.

I looked across the pit of fire to the platform. The Divinatrix was standing with her face towards us, between the kneeling Daughter and the altar. Her eyes were closed, her hands
were on the girl's veiled head and she was chanting to herself.
The Daughters entered carrying lighted candles and spread
themselves, tier by tier, throughout the amphitheatre. Their
song echoed from wall to wall, and was the purest and most
intricate harmony I had ever heard. Every word that I could
pick out was in Oballef's forgotten language.

Shree nudged me and I looked quickly back at the platform.
Calla and her cohorts were just filing across the bridge—no
handrails, I noted, one false step and they'd be shrieking cinders within a second or two. Valsoria had her back to us now,
and her arms were raised over her head as she addressed
something invisible to me, deep in the shadows beyond the
altar. I wondered uneasily if the kneeling girl was going to
have something gruesome and final happen to her, like a quick
fling over the parapet into the bubbling flames; but I was
about to learn that human sacrifice can take many forms, and
not all of them are immediately fatal.

30

VALSORIA TOOK A took a long pole from behind the altar and
dipped one end of it into the well of lava. It came out flaming.
She waved it in the air, tracing arcs of fire against the darkness
as the chanting swelled, deepened, boomed off the walls until
it was almost painful to hear. Then she touched the fire to the
altar, which burst into a dazzling blaze, although it never did
appear to be diminished by the burning. Its flickering bright-
ness revealed a high pointed archway at the far end of the platform, closed with double doors that gleamed like polished
metal.

Calla and one of the red surplices paced to the doors and swung them open just far enough to allow a slim person to pass through. Valsoria and her other assistant removed the veil from the kneeling girl, raised her between them, drew her towards the archway, directed her gently through the doors. She drifted like someone in a trance. On the instant that the doors closed behind her, the chanting ceased and all the lights went out. The fire on the altar died as abruptly as if a black pall had been dropped over it and the Daughters must have snuffed their candles on the same cue, so that the only light was that odd, headache-inducing red glimmer from the lava well.

And then we waited. Gradually, as my eyes adjusted to the diffuse blood-coloured light, I could distinguish four motion-less figures on the platform by the blurred shadows they cast across the altar, three long, one very short. After a while I could even pick out Valsoria's face, a dim reddish circle with two black shadows where the eyes would be, and it seemed that those eyes were fixed unswervingly on me. I shifted on the bench with discomfort. The only sound was a subdued bubbling and gurgling from the depths of the pit.

The near-silence and the dimness dragged on, but other small sounds began to intrude. Rinn was swaying gently beside me; when I turned to look at her, I could see her eyes, wide and unblinking, picking up the red glow. The rustle of her robe had a multitude of whispered echoes. Faintly at first, then more distinctly, I began to pick up a pungency in the air that reminded me of the taste of masollar. That was just before I heard the first scream.

It sounded muffled and far away, a high shrill keening; nobody else seemed to notice it. When I turned to Shree, his eyes were as blank and unseeing as Rinn's, and I had to shake his shoulder to get his attention. He blinked at me in that hell-ish light as if just wakening from a not very pleasant dream. His body tensed as the screaming sounded again. He started to rise, and I pulled him back on to the stone bench.

At that moment, flames burst again from the altar, achingly bright after the long red darkness, bringing Rinn out of her trance with a little start. This time Calla and her colleagues moved very fast, virtually sprinting to the great arched doors to swing them open—they seemed stubbornly heavy now, resisting the women's efforts while the screams behind them rose in volume and intensity—and then they were open, and the unveiled Daughter burst through and was caught in Calla's arms before she could rush headlong into the fiery altar.

She stopped screaming and started to babble in a high, breathy voice. I could distinguish no words, neither Vassashin nor Sheranik, not even the Naarhil tongue of Oballef. The girl would have fallen if Calla and the other had not held her, but they hauled her between them to where the Divinatrix was standing beside the altar and let her drop to her knees at Valsoria's feet. So softly at first that it was almost below the level of my hearing, the Daughters around us recommenced their chanting. The girl's delirious rush of words rose to a shriek and then cut off as she collapsed twitching in front of the altar. At least the twitches indicated that the unfortunate girl was still alive. Then it was Valsoria's turn.

Rinn, wide-awake, clutched my arm. The fire-gods had spoken—we were about to have their words translated for us. I knew what Rinn wanted to hear, and was pretty certain that the Divinatrix knew as well; I suspected the servants who attended us in Vass, and the novice Daughters who tended us here, had good ears and some training in picking up whatever information the Oracle needed. Indeed, I had dropped a few false but harmless hints myself, just to see if they would show up in Valsoria's pronouncements.

But that day we were doomed to disappointment. Valsoria, talking softly but with a penetrating power, directed her remarks to one of the Vassashin worthies who had accompanied us from Vass. The message concerned an additional wife he was contemplating taking, and it appeared the fire-gods thought it was rather a good idea, assuming the prospective bridegroom made the proper sacrifices and dedicated a reasonable percentage of the bride's marriage portion to the use of the Sacellum. I lost interest altogether when she got into the financial details—it seemed a trivial sort of revelation to risk a young woman's life for.

And that was the end of the first day's divination.

• • •

Out in the open again, Rinn sulked visibly as she and I walked across the courtyard towards our quarters.

"I will have that witchwoman's skin for leather," she fumed. "Not a word to me—to me! Sitting all that time in that dark stinking hole, and for what? For nothing! I'll—"

"Rinn, my petal."

"What?" She rounded on me.

"Don't be angry with the Divinatrix. Remember, she only translates what the fire-gods say. We'll be here another three days—I'm sure the fire-gods will speak to you before we go back to Vass."

"But I am Rinn of Miishel! The fire-gods should speak to me first! I honour this miserable little hole just by being here!"

I improvised hastily. "No doubt they are aware of that honour, my lovely flower, and are simply disposing of the minor bits of business first. Or perhaps their message to you is of such power and magnitude and astonishing significance that they have to," I paused for a moment to grope for impressive words, and gave up, "they have to work up to it. Or something like that." My mind wasn't really on this. I had better things to think about, Calla, my son Verolef, the Naarhil texts I presumed to be in Valsoria's possession.

Rinn sniffed. "It was a dishonour to allow those stinking fish-merchants to come with us at all. Perhaps I should have them killed, yes, and then all the messages will be for me. Yes?"

I pretended to think it over. "Perhaps you'd better not; it's a bit extreme, my shining star. And you know you mustn't try to hurry the gods—even the little gods of a place like Vassashinay."

"*That* for the gods of Vassashinay—" she started, but her next words were drowned in a thundering boom from the mountaintop. It was not me this time, but I could not have timed it better myself. The ground shuddered. Rinn squealed and clutched my arm until the tremors subsided. Her pique had been shaken out of her.

"Careful what you say, petal," I said to reinforce the lesson. "Gods are gods, wherever you may find them. Come on, I'll take you back to your bedchamber, there's time for you to rest a while."

Later that afternoon, while I made up for the sleep I'd lost the night before and the sleep I dearly hoped to lose that night, Shree and Chasco went to Villim to do some shopping. Smug with success, they returned just as dusk was falling. I awoke suddenly with a faceful of water and saw Shree standing beside the pallet with a beaker in his hand and a broad grin on his face. Spluttering, I sat up.

"So how did you do?" I asked, mopping my face with the edge of the blanket. "Did you find a suitable lorsk?"

He sat down on the edge of the pallet. "We found one that Chasco's reasonably pleased with. It stinks to high heaven and it needs a new sail, but he says the hull is sound. It'll get us past Zaine, anyway."

"How about provisions?"

He ticked them off on his fingers. "Five barrels of fresh water, four bales of dried loaves, three kegs of cheese and one of wine, ten leathers of dried meat and fifteen of dried fruit, assorted, and one skin of oil. If we catch a few fish and ration the water, assuming four adults and one child, Chasco says we can go for two months without landfall."

"You've done very well," I said with genuine admiration. "When will it be ready?"

"We've promised the chandler five palots extra if it's ready and loaded by the next night but two—the night before we're scheduled to return to Vass. Here's the beauty of it: the *Tasiil*'s being beached tomorrow."

I lay back again with my arms crossed behind my head and grinned up at the ceiling. "The Frath won't be able to chase us for days."

Chasco came in just in time to hear this. He closed the door behind him and came to stand respectfully beside the pallet. "It won't do to be cocksure, Lord Tigrallef. The *Tasiil* isn't the only ship in Vassashinay. Some of those boats on the beach are built to be fast. If they decide to give chase, we'll need to have a good start on them."

"That's no problem," I said. "We'll sail as close to midnight as we can, and nobody will miss us until late in the morning.

I'll arrange things with Calla tonight, so she can have herself and Verolef ready when the time comes. What a plan, Chasco! Of course, there is one thing I'll regret."

"Rinn's golden body?"

I looked severely at Shree. "Valsoria's Naarhil texts. I doubt now if I'll have a chance to ask her about them."

"Never mind," said Shree. "Didn't the Lady tell you she'd translate the Caveat for you someday?"

"I don't trust the Lady."

"Does that mean you trust Valsoria?"

Did it indeed? I frowned and started to formulate a cautious positive reply, hedged about with several ifs and maybes, when a loud shout burst inside my head with a devastating explosion of white light and shattered all thought.

No! No! No!

I gasped for breath and held my ringing skull together with both hands. "I don't know yet," I said weakly.

Shree and Chasco weren't looking at me. They were examining a little pile of terracotta-coloured dust on the table where the jug had been standing a moment ago. Shree turned to me, shaking his head.

"You're going to have to stop doing that, Tig," he said. "What if we have to pay for these?"

I slipped out of the Sacellum that evening as soon as the court-yard was empty and made my way to the same rocky stretch of mountainside where Calla and I had met the night before. It was a peaceful night, windless, and the only clouds were a few wreaths high on the neck of the volcano. I stretched out on the smooth grass and lost myself so completely in golden images of the future that I did not hear Calla's footsteps until the Lady whispered: *she's coming.*

I sat up. *Good. Now perhaps you'd lose yourself for a little while?*

Scion, you cannot deny me for ever.

I can try, can't I? But we'll discuss that later. For now, just go.

There was no reply, but that was no guarantee of anything. I sighed, wondering if I would ever feel unwatched, normal and in full possession of my own self again—but at that moment Calla came around the corner of the path, pulling the veil from her face as she went, and my heart burst all over again with the miracle of finding her. Suddenly, it did not seem to matter whether the Lady was watching or not; I felt as if the entire population of the known world could be standing around, even cheering us on with ribald cries, and we would still have been the only two people under that jewelled southern sky.

31

CALLA HAD NOT come empty-handed; she had brought with her a small skin of wine, real wine, not masollar, a loaf of fresh bread, two beakers, and couple of strange, sweet, thick-skinned Vassashin fruit. These all lay forgotten for some time where she had dropped them on the edge of the clearing, until at last she untangled herself and went to retrieve the sack. The moon was considerably higher than when she had first arrived.

"Go on then," she said, pouring me out a beaker of wine, "tell me what this failproof plan of yours is."

I explained about the lorsk. Her face grew graver as she listened.

"When?"

"The third night from now. We're supposed to be returning to Vass the next evening, right after the final session with the Oracle—I suppose Rinn's message from the fire-gods is scheduled for that session?"

Calla grinned, a little shamefacedly. "Your princess is paying by the day—the Divinatrix wouldn't risk satisfying her too early, not our Valsoria."

I raised my beaker. "To Valsoria! Long may she rule. Though you might tell her to toss Rinn a few small prophecies in the next couple of sessions, just to keep her interest up."

"I believe Valsoria has planned something of the sort," Calla said drily. She passed me a chunk of bread.

"Are all the Sacellum's secrets open to you?" I asked, thinking of the Naarhil texts.

The moonlight was just strong enough to show that she was blushing. "I know how the Oracle works, if that's what you mean. There's not much to it."

"I'm not judging you, Calla. I'm sure Valsoria gives excellent value. That's more than can be said for most cults. And she seems fairly benign."

"More than that," Calla said. "She saved Vero's life, you know. I owe her for that. We both owe her for that."

I swallowed a mouthful of bread. "How did she save him?"

Calla leaned against me and nestled her head on my shoulder. "By naming him the Kalkissann at the moment of his birth. He'd have been thrown to the fire-gods otherwise, because the Vassashin thought he was the child of a Sherkin father. Even if I'd confessed the truth, he'd still have been killed for the quarter-measure of Sherkin blood he got from me."

"Did they tell you that?"

"They didn't have to, it was obvious. They were still killing the garrison when I arrived. There's a lot of bitterness behind those smiling faces."

"I've seen their idea of a war memorial. Did you try to escape?"

"I was never given the chance. I wasn't badly treated, but I know just how a sow must feel in a piglet farm. I was all set to denounce myself when he was born, so I could die with him— but Valsoria was there, and she put her hand over my mouth and hissed at me to shut up."

"And that's when she declared him the Kalkissann."

"That's right." Calla raised her beaker in another salute.

I didn't. "But up to then, you were sure he'd be killed at birth?"

"There was no reason to think anything else."

"So," I said thoughtfully, "Valsoria had a sudden change of heart."

"Perhaps."

I frowned at the moon. "But why? I wouldn't take her for the sentimental sort. Quite the reverse." I was thinking of Coll's bloodthirsty stories.

Calla shrugged. "I'm not sure of that. Mostly I think she

kept us alive out of true goodness of heart. She seems very fond of Vero, almost like a grandmother."

"Yet you say you're not sure."

She grimaced. "I don't know what she has in mind for him in the end. Saving Vassashinay? How? What does poor little Vero have to do? Or is it just something she dreamed up on the instant, to save his life? I wish I knew."

"You *don't* trust her, do you?" I turned Calla's face so that I could see her expression. She looked troubled.

She sighed. "For all her good intentions, Tig, the Divinatrix is really a kind of milcher. The whole Sacellum is based on a lie. There's no magic in the fire-mountain; there's a kind of poisonous air that comes up from the mountain's belly and fills the oracle chamber, and anyone who breathes it for too long chatters like a madwoman for a while. That's all there is to it. And masollar is just ordinary wine with that air bubbled into it."

"And the Divinatrix is free to make what she wants out of the chatter, is that correct?"

"She means well for her people, Tig."

"I'm sure she does. Actually, this method of divination isn't unique. The dreamflowers used by the Niltha cult outside Canzitar have an almost identical effect, also I seem to remember an obscure little sect on one of the Satheli islands—"

She laughed out loud, breaking the uneasy mood. "You haven't changed at all." She kissed me hard, possibly to shut me up or to change the subject, and examined me in the moonlight with a half-smile on her lips. "It's true, you know. You're just as you were six years ago—maybe a little thinner."

"You haven't changed either," I said hastily.

"Oh yes I have. There are lines on my forehead," she guided my hand to them, "and the skin is thickening under my chin, and I found my first white hair two years ago, on my twenty-eighth birthday. But you—"

You cannot feel the claw of time while I am in you. The two are one, Scion.

Shut up. Go away. To Calla I said, "You look just the same to me." I kissed her, and then sighed; it seemed that the night was passing too quickly, and we still had business to do.

"Calla, we haven't much time left. We need to talk about the lorsk. You'll have to find a way to take Verolef to the head of the road that night, so we can all go down to the harbour together. Can you do that?"

She had sobered as well. She heaved a sigh that was so deep it seemed to start at her toes. "Yes, yes. But I don't feel quite right about it."

"Why? Chasco says the lorsk is a solid little ship. He should know." An unwelcome thought struck me. "You do want to come with us, don't you?"

"Of course I do." She picked up one of the Vassashin fruit and began to peel it in an absent-minded, finger-busying sort of way. "It's only that Valsoria has been kind to us, no matter what her reasons were—and I don't know what will happen when the Vassashin find their Great Saviour has left them."

"I can tell you the worst that will happen," I said. "The Sacellum's income will drop."

Her profile was still troubled. "Doesn't it seem ungrateful, just to leave without a word? Perhaps . . ."

"Perhaps what?"

"Perhaps I've been wrong in doubting Valsoria. Milcher or not, there's more to her than shows on the surface. Perhaps we could trust her—we could ask her if you could take sanctuary in the Sacellum. Perhaps she'd let us stay together . . ."

I turned Calla to face me. "I have to leave."

"Why? We could be happy in Vassashinay."

I hushed her impatiently with a hand over her mouth. "You don't understand. Even if we could trust Valsoria, the Frath Major wouldn't respect the sanctuary of the Sacellum—if he had to, he'd slaughter the Vassashin in droves to get me back. And someday, if he does get me back in his hands, I believe something more terrible than you can imagine is bound to happen. No, I have to go."

She shook my hand away from her mouth. "Why?" Her brows were drawn together. "The Lady is broken and gone— the Scions of Oballef are just like other men now, so how can you be worth so much to the Miishelu? And if they wouldn't respect sanctuary, Valsoria might agree to hide you on one of the other islands until they're gone."

I hesitated. "The Lady can't be discounted so easily."

"What do you mean? You broke the thing, you told me so yourself."

I hesitated again. I half-expected the Lady to rise up and block me, to throw a golden screen between myself and my own words, but everything was dark and quiet inside my skull. In as few words as possible, I told Calla why, unhappily and against my will, I was still of absorbing interest to the powers that wanted to rule the known world. Her face set into bleaker and bleaker lines.

When I had finished, she reached up and broke off one of the hitherto-unmentioned blossoms from the bush over our heads, and moved her fingers from the lush petals to the dry dead stalk that held them.

"So the Scions are still cursed," she said softly.

"I'm very happy to hear you say that," I said, feeling both surprised and pleased. "I have trouble getting Shree and Chasco to see it as a curse."

"I'm thinking of Vero as well as you."

Her voice was dull, and I experienced a peculiar catching of the heart. That aspect of the matter had not occurred to me before. My son was also a Scion. Other dangers suddenly took shape, dark speculative structures built in my imagination out of the pieces of the truth I already held, but gaping here and there with great dark holes. Who else, I wondered uneasily, held pieces of the truth? The Bequiin Ardin, probably, and through him the Frath Major; the various assassins and ill-wishers who had inconvenienced me; perhaps the Divinatrix herself? After all, there was the possibility of the Naarhil texts . . .

"Calla," I said urgently, sitting up straight and putting my hands on her shoulders, "this is important. The history of the Sacellum, the words of the divination ritual—tell me everything you know."

She knew enough to fill only one page of my notebook when I returned to the Sacellum at dawn, but my speculations filled four pages more. I knew where we were now: one of Valsoria's many titles, rarely used and not widely known, was "the Heretrix of Vizzath." So this, I speculated, was the Vizzath of old, and the Lady had indeed been here before under a differ-

ent name, as had my ancestors; and the empire of Vizzath had
been mighty for a time, and then had fallen, as empires have a
curious habit of doing. I scribbled away excitedly, with a
strong feeling that the Lady was looking over my shoulder.

Calla knew of no books or scrolls in Valsoria's possession;
the incantatory songs of the Daughters were learned by rote as
novices, and it was forbidden to write them down, on pain of
penalties of a thought-provoking ferocity. However—and my
pen trembled as I recorded this—Valsoria had a sanctum into
which no other Daughter was ever permitted, where no
novices ever cleaned, and which no eyes but Valsoria's had
seen since Hassana, the previous Divinatrix, had died; and
Valsoria herself had first entered it on the eve of Hassana's
death. It had been kept a closely guarded secret from the
Sherank through all their centuries of brutal invasion and
occupation, perhaps the only chamber in all of Vassashinay
that had remained closed to them. Calla knew where it was
and had seen the door, deep in the mountain, but it was
locked, and only Valsoria held the key. There, I told myself,
was where the Naarhil texts would be found. If they existed.

Shree came in at some point, rubbing the sleep out of his
eyes. He yawned and flopped down on my still-unused pallet.

"Don't tell me. A love poem."

"I wish it were," I said, frowning. I blotted the page carefully and tossed the notebook over to him. "Look at the last
few pages."

Muscle by muscle, he became alert as he read, but he
turned over the last page as if expecting something more substantial. "Vizzath, eh? You've mentioned that name before.
Well, well, well." He tossed the notebook back. "This is fascinating, Tig, but I don't see why you're worried."

"Everything about the Lady and her history worries me. I
wish we could leave tonight."

"I'm sure we could, if you'd call on the Lady."

"We've been through that." Annoyed, I opened the notebook in front of me, picked up my pen again and started to
write, ignoring him.

"Forget I mentioned it." He got up. "We're just on our way
down to the harbour to see how the lorsk is getting on. Don't

fret, we'll be back in time for the Oracle. One thing: is there any way the Divinatrix can connect you with Calla? Or with the child?"

I relented and put the pen down. "No, thank the gods. Calla swears she's never mentioned me. The Vassashin still think Verolef was fathered by a Sherkin. There's nothing to connect us."

"What about Calla's reaction when she first saw us? How did she explain that?"

"She told them she'd suddenly felt ill."

"I hope they believed her."

I smiled wryly. "She spent much of the evening making herself throw up, just to add a certain colour to her story."

"Good for her." Shree nodded with appreciation. "My cousin always was a resourceful girl. I'm looking forward to meeting her again."

We heard Chasco and Coll talking in the corridor; Shree went to the door and stopped beside it. "Don't worry so much, Tig," he said, "as long as the Lady behaves herself for the next couple of days, I think we'll be safe." He waved and went out, and I heard the three of them clumping confidently down the corridor. I sighed, wishing I could be so sure of a happy outcome.

The next two days and nights passed uneventfully. The Lady kept pretty much to herself, although the crockery continued to suffer. I continued to spend my daylight hours alternately tickling and smoothing Rinn's feathers, filling pages and pages of my notebook with puzzled speculations, snatching what glimpses I could of Calla and my son, and worrying—above all, worrying. Something wrong was in the air, but I could not guess what—I could not even tell whether the Lady shared my sense of danger and foreboding. Nobody else did.

Rinn was happy. On the first of those afternoons, in the middle of a spate of rubbish about some property dispute on the outskirts of Vass, Valsoria produced a dramatic reference to snakes in my beloved's hair—not, one would think, the kind of prophecy to produce anything but disgust, but Rinn took the meaning that Valsoria intended her to take. As far as she was concerned, the viper crown was as good as on her

head. The next afternoon produced nothing relevant, but by
then she was content to wait for the main event. The fire-gods
had already proven their good sense.

The Divinatrix continued to pay me no obvious attention,
appearing only for the rites of the Oracle. I could think of no
way to get more information about the Naarhil texts, and
doubted that the attempt would be worthwhile anyway; I had
to balance my curiosity and the dim chance of learning something about the Caveat against the very real risk of endanger-
ing our escape. And I didn't need the Lady's oft-repeated
warnings, since I was already dubious about Valsoria and her
motives.

I will write no more about my meetings with Calla on the
moon-washed mountainside; I am only a memorian, not a
poet. But the tedious days and glory-filled nights passed
somehow, and at last it was the morning of the night on
which we were to make our quiet departure from Vassashinay; the morning on which everything began to go seriously
strange.

32

I DIDN'T BOTHER to undress that morning, just threw myself
on top of the bedclothes when I could no longer keep my eyes
open and fell instantly asleep. It had been very hard to part
from Calla at dawn. The formless anxiety that had weighed on
me for days felt heavier; our escape plan seemed transparent
and foolhardy, a child's scheme for playing a trick on its eld-
ers. However, since I could see no better alternative, I had
watched Calla walk away from me, followed her at the agreed
interval and contented myself with scribbling my fears into
my notebook as soon as I was back at my table in the Sacellum. When I fell asleep at last, a couple of hours after dawn,
my dreams were troubled.

What awoke me was an uproar in the courtyard below my
window—shouts, heavy boots, slamming doors—and feet

pattering urgently along the corridor outside my door. I lay still for a moment, trying to untangle the strands of my Iklankish dream from what my ears told me. My first clear thought was that the Sacellum was under attack, and this seemed to be confirmed when I was awake enough to stagger to the window. The courtyard was swarming with Miisheli uniforms, the red robes of the Daughters swirling through a mêlée of battleskins and flashing armour. A shock went through me that splintered to tinderwood every stick of furniture in the room.

Be calm, Scion.

At second glance, nobody was killing anybody. All the weapons in sight were safely in their scabbards or leg-sheaths. The Daughters were neither screaming nor defending themselves; most of them, indeed, were ducking through the mill of troopers with great armloads of bedlinen or crockery. The only confrontation in sight was between Han-Frath Zimin, standing with his back to me in a posture of stubborn insistence, and Lorosa, one of Valsoria's red-surpliced chief priestesses. I could not hear Lorosa's words over the other noise, but she was standing with her arms akimbo and her head back and every so often she would poke at Han-Frath Zimin's breastplate to emphasize a point. The Han-Frath was bravely standing his ground.

My second thought was just about as bad as my first: that the Frath Major had somehow caught wind of Rinn's designs on the viper crown and sent a small army of troopers to carry us all back to Vass in chains, and what price the lorsk then? But that didn't explain the bedlinen; I was puzzling over this when a hush fell on the courtyard and all faces turned to the entrance. The troopers in sight snapped to attention. A moment later, a small party of men moved into my field of view and towards the centre of the courtyard. At the same time, Valsoria herself emerged from the processional door and came to meet them. I counted seven Fraths Minor, the Satheli envoy, the Bequiin Ardin, Lillifer the Burgher of Vass—and the Frath Major.

Shree and Chasco burst into my room about then. They stopped short at the door, looking around at the wreckage of the furniture, then at each other, shaking their heads. Shree clucked his tongue as they picked their way over to the window.

"Raksh knows how we're going to explain this to the housemistress," he said. "The crockery was one thing—"

"Forget the housemistress," I snapped. "Have you seen who's here?"

"Your honourable cousin-by-marriage was coming up the road a few minutes ago. You mean him?"

"Look for yourself."

Lillifer and the Frath Major were bending over the Divinatrix a few feet away from the others, talking earnestly. The Frath straightened and beckoned to Han-Frath Zimin. A few soft words into the Han-Frath's ear, a few barked commands from the Han-Frath, and the milling troopers quietly formed themselves up and marched towards the main gate, leaving only a squad of a dozen or so at a short distance from the party of Fraths Minor. The conference continued.

"What's happening? Any idea?" Turning from the window, I noticed that Chasco had a small water-skin slung across his shoulder and both he and Shree were powdered with dust from the road.

Shree grimaced through the window. "We were going down to the harbour for a last check on the lorsk and met this lot coming up. There's trouble in Vass, Tig, bad trouble."

"What is it? Troopers out of control? Insurrection? What?"

He shook his head, still keeping an eye on the group in the courtyard. "Sickness. A plague."

I shut my eyes and had a momentary vision of people dancing in the dark square of Vass—or was it Gil? "What plague? What kind of sickness?"

"I don't know anything more about it," Shree said grimly, "but Han-Frath Zimin stopped us on the road and advised us not to go down the mountain. They're afraid it's going to break out in Villim next."

"What kind of plague?"

"I told you, I don't know!"

I went to sit down on the chair, remembered it wasn't there any more and instead began to hunt among the debris for my notebook, thinking furiously.

"What are we going to do, Tig?"

I found my notebook and blew the wood-dust and splinters off it. "I suppose we'll leave tonight, as we planned."

"By midday, there'll be a small army of Miisheli troopers camped outside the main gate," Shree reminded me.

"There is another gate—I don't know where, but Calla uses it when she comes back from meeting me."

"But—"

"Quiet, Shree, I'm trying to think." I paced up and down the room, kicking up clouds of sawdust that reminded me of something—what was it? It came to me at last: the billows of ooze that followed my footsteps on the drowned streets of Iklankish. I stood still and forced myself to concentrate.

"Tig?"

"I'm all right. Tonight will still be best, before this damned plague takes hold in Villim or spreads to the Sacellum. I'll get a message to Calla, arrange a place to meet her in the courtyard, and we'll all go down together, tonight. No, wait! Chasco."

"My lord Tigrallef?"

"You'll go down now; we'll find some way to cover for you here. If the Miishelu are still setting up camp, there should be enough confusion for you to slip through to the roadhead without being noticed. You were in the Web, you can get through if anyone can. Go down to Villim, take delivery of the lorsk—can you sail it by yourself?"

"Yes, my lord."

"Good. Move it out of Villim. I remember when we were looking down on the harbour, I saw a cove away from the main beach, around a point of black rock—do you know where I mean?"

"Yes, my lord."

"Anchor there and wait for us. We'll come. Tonight if we can, otherwise tomorrow night, or the night after that, but wait for us."

Chasco grinned and started to raise his hand in the formal parting salute of a Gillish officer-of-the-guard—but stopped himself, and answered in the Web's fingerspeech instead: *the Lady be with you.*

"She will, she will," I muttered. "Oh, and Chasco! Wait."

He stopped by the door and looked at me questioningly. I ran to the ruins of my clothes-box and poked around until I'd unearthed the satchel holding the few scrolls and books I'd brought with me, and the roll of pens. Shoving the notebook in on top, I thrust the satchel into his hands.

"Take this with you. How many palots are left?"

He caught his breath sharply. "Thirty-eight, my lord." He looked over at Shree, who dug the pouch out of his tunic. I took it and counted out five coins, and handed the rest over to Chasco.

"We'll keep some in case we need to pay a few bribes. You take the rest and see what herbs and physics are worth buying in the marketplace. Wortroot if you can get it, it's good for several kinds of plague, also calfgrass, melis powder and dried corm. Verlessence, if you see any. But Chasco—get out of the marketplace as quickly as you can. Keep your distance from anyone you talk to, and talk to as few people as possible. Do you understand?"

"I understand very well, my lord."

I clapped his shoulder and added a fervent blessing in the fingerspeech. When he was gone, Shree startled me by snapping his fingers in applause.

"Very decisive, Tig. You see, you can take charge when you need to. Myself, I'd forgotten I was carrying the palots. He wouldn't have got far trying to claim the lorsk without the chandler's bonus in his hand."

"If the chandler's there to take it," I said unhappily. "This plague worries me."

"This furniture worries me," said Shree, "and I wonder what the Frath Major will make of it."

"The Frath Major will be delighted, if we can't prevent him from seeing it, because it will confirm all his hopes about me. Come on." I was already brushing myself off and making for the door.

We intercepted the Frath Major and his faithful shadow, the Bequiin, at the foot of the stairs. I stopped dramatically and then rushed to embrace the Frath in the Miisheli fashion.

"Cousin!" I cried. "What a surprise!"

"Is it?" The Frath Major looked at me keenly. I reached past him to greet the Bequiin Ardin, but the Frath Major moved to

block me. The Bequiin stood with his head cast down and the
hood of his grey robe pulled forwards.

"Yes, my dear cousin," I said, "a great surprise. I didn't
expect to see you until tomorrow evening at the earliest, in
Vass. Did you come to have your fortune told as well?" I saw
the Bequiin glance up at this, and our eyes met for a broken
moment—his were beaten and hopeless.

"We came to escape the plague," the Frath said flatly.
"Have you not heard what is happening?"

"Not a word, cousin."

He eyed me suspiciously, as if he suspected me of starting
the plague myself. "These islands are cursed," he said bitterly
when he'd finished his scrutiny. "They have all gone mad in
Vass—they prance about in the streets with pus rolling down
their faces, faugh! Bodies lie about in the bushes since yesterday, and nobody thinks to move them or to burn them. Badly
managed! No organization! If Miishel had the running of
these islands, we would make a few changes."

"The Sherank tried that, I believe."

He bridled at my innocent tone. "Do not jest, Scion. I have
seen many plagues, but never a plague like this. When the
Tasiil is seaworthy—"

"When will that be?"

He frowned. "Perhaps tomorrow, perhaps the day after.
Alas, she was pulled up the rollers just before the plague
became known, and I have ordered her down again after the
most serious repairs have been finished. We—"

He stopped and whirled around as Coll approached with
one of the Daughters behind him. As she stepped past him to
greet the Frath Major, I caught sight of the black surplice.
Clever Calla, I thought with relief—there was another problem solved. She didn't turn her head in my direction, but it
was her hands I was watching anyway. They were held in
front of her, low down, out of the Frath's sight, and anyone
who saw them might have thought that she was twisting her
fingers out of pure nervousness.

*Tig, my dearest, this is our only chance to talk. What do you
want me to do?*

Meantime, she was beginning a long, respectful and complicated speech of welcome to the Frath Major—in fluent Vassashin, via Coll. It took Coll a good five minutes to translate this and add the fine oratorical flourishes which no native of Vass seemed able to resist, and all the while Calla's fingers and mine were flying. Yes: there was another way out of the Sacellum. Yes: she could still spirit Verolef out of his bedchamber that night. No: she had not told the child anything. No: Valsoria had voiced no suspicions. No: Calla knew nothing about the plague, this was the first she'd heard of it. And yes: she would meet us in the shadow of the rain-tun housing, in the corner of the courtyard, one hour before midnight, with Verolef, and good luck to us all then—we'd need it. By this point Coll was in the middle of some metaphors of his own devising, certainly well outside the original content of Calla's speech, so there was time for a few messages of a personal nature (Shree tactfully averted his eyes) before Coll finally dried up.

The Frath muttered a few obviously insincere words of gratitude, which gained hugely in Coll's translation; and after these courtesies had been duly dealt with, Calla came to the point, that is to say, the trivial and humdrum domestic details of bedchambers, mealtimes, ritual arrangements and the location of sanitary facilities for the visiting Fraths. Then she tacked on a few parting compliments and walked away while Coll was still rendering them into Miisheli. This translation, including embellishments, took so long that the Frath Major had turned an exciting shade of purple well before the end.

"These damned speechmongers," he muttered when Coll finally ran out of words and went away. "I tell you, any Miisheli governor running these islands will start by cutting out a few tongues."

I could not help sympathizing with the Frath's critical assessment, but I thought the Miisheli solution was typically extreme. The Bequiin Ardin refused to catch my eye.

Rinn and her women appeared in the doorway at that point. My bride's deportment was just what you'd expect from a veteran of many Miisheli court intrigues. She greeted the Frath Major with the same blend of deference and arrogance that she always gave him, no fear and no effusions, nothing to

indicate that she had anything to hide or that she was worried
by his arrival at the Sacellum. The news of the plague, of
course, interested her not at all. Plagues were for common
people. She was Rinn of Miishel.

33

I COULD NOT face breakfast because my gut had taken a
notion to behave like a butter churn. I could not go back to my
bed because I had destroyed it. Shree's temper was on a short
Sheranik tether, the heat was stifling, the forced inactivity was
torture. After the brief pleasure of seeing Calla in the courtyard, my anxieties returned in even larger sizes and darker
colours than before—what kind of risk was I asking her to
take? What kind of danger was I exposing my son to? Furthermore, even if we did manage to escape safely, was my son
going to like me? I found that last question preying more and
more on my mind as the long dismal morning wore on.

The long dismal morning was followed by a long dismal
midday meal. All the Fraths Minor were there, but the Frath
Major and the Bequiin were not. Rinn was very much there,
bored and querulous because she'd just heard that the rites of
the Oracle had been suspended until such time as the fire-gods
(bless and feed them) were ready to pronounce on the plague,
which left my bride without her regular entertainment for the
afternoon. This shifted the plague from being an inconven-
ience to being an actual affront, and Rinn was not one to suffer an affront in silence. I picked at my food and agreed with
everything she said, and at the earliest possible moment Shree
and I burped politely and took ourselves upstairs. We still had
a full ten hours to kill before we could make our move.

The corridor was deserted except for an old charring-
woman on her hands and knees scrubbing the floor-boards
outside Shree's cell. The door just before his was open, and I
glanced in as we passed, then stopped short and went back for
a better look. It opened on to a dark, narrow corridor with a

dim archway at the end, framing the bottom turn of a steep blackstone staircase. Shree and I looked at each other. What better way to pass the time than to explore? Provided, I reminded myself, that it was permitted—this was not a good day to go looking for unnecessary trouble or calling official attention to ourselves. I approached the charringwoman and asked her where the stairs led, trying to soften my Sheranik into a passable approximation of Vassashin.

She looked up at me as she wrung out her scrubbing cloth. "The south tower, pilgrim. But you do not want to go up there. It is not an easy climb." She slapped the cloth down hard on the floorstones and twitched her long greying plait back over her shoulder.

"What's up there?" I asked.

She stared at me, taken aback. "Nothing." Unspoken meaning: how ignorant can you offlanders be? She sounded very much like Coll.

"In that case," I remarked to Shree, "it will make the perfect diversion, not unlike reading a very bad book—no point to it, but it pushes the time along. Let's go."

"It is not very safe," the charring-woman said without looking up.

"All the better," said Shree. "I'm bored."

The charring-woman looked up at that, and rocked back on her heels to watch us go.

The stairs (one hundred and forty-seven of them by actual count, and built too badly to be the work of the Ancients) came up into a fair-sized chamber like the inside of a box with one open side, the side facing away from the mountain. A blackstone balustrade had been built across the open end, but it was sadly weathered and rather frail-looking, with a long vertical crack at one end.

We trod gingerly towards it, noting that the floorboards creaked and groaned under our feet. The charring-woman had been right in saying it was unsafe and a hard climb, wrong in saying there was nothing at the top. There was a view, a very large one. Most of it was taken up by the broad polished-silver mirror of the Sherkin Sea, but by leaning out far enough so that Shree hissed and grabbed the scruff of my tunic, I could see down to the patch of open ground in front of the Sacellum. I whistled softly.

"Look at this, Shree."

Muttering, he released me and leaned cautiously over the railing. "What is it, a festival?"

"I don't think so."

The stretch of barren ground now looked like something between a mass picnic and a used battlefield. The red and yellow banners of Miishel fluttered over a small enclave of order near the gate, a precise square of dark tents around an exquisitely tidy supply dump. Everywhere else was chaos: scatters of hasty lean-tos and ragged tents, large clumps of people gathered around excited speakers or makeshift food stalls, a great many straw mats laid out randomly as if marking small patches of private territory. I could see two separate brawls in progress, each with its own knot of interested spectators, and here and there the distinctive scarlet robe of a Daughter of Fire moved through the mob. On the road up from Villim, whatever short stretches of it were visible through the tree-cover, I could see a steady stream of people climbing towards the Sacellum.

"Refugees from the plague," remarked Shree.

"Supplicants," I amended, "asking the protection of the fire-gods. Of course, it might be the worst thing they could do. Everything I've ever read about plagues suggests that crowding together only helps to spread the contagion. These people should be dispersing, not congregating. Valsoria should be— what is it, Shree?"

He had stiffened. Now he growled, grabbed my arm for stability, and leaned out even further than I had dared to. He was not looking at the Vassashin mob below us, but down at the nearshore waters, at a point that I reckoned was roughly opposite the main fishing beach at Villim. I could see nothing there of any interest.

"What is it, Shree?"

"Keep watching—it's gone out of sight. No, there it is again! Through those trees, Tig—out on the water."

I saw it then: a dark moving boat-shape partly masked by the trees, vanishing for a few moments, appearing again, clear of the trees at last, a little two-masted windcatcher with all sails set. It seemed to be tacking out to sea.

"It's a boat."

"It's the lorsk. But where in the name of Raksh does that tupping fool think he's going?"

"The lorsk! Are you sure?"

He snarled, which I took as a yes. I craned to get a better view. "If that's Chasco, he's moving past the cove where I told him to meet us."

"I can see that."

"It looks like he's heading out to sea."

"It does."

"Leaving us behind."

"So it seems," said Shree through gritted teeth.

We watched for a few minutes, as long as the lorsk remained in sight, me in silence, Shree muttering vivid and poisonous phrases. At first I was just puzzled. I found myself almost hoping to see other boats in pursuit of ours, if only to explain why Chasco appeared to be leaving without us, but the lorsk was alone on the sea. Even so, I could not believe Chasco was betraying us—a former member of the Web, a fellow Gilman, a descendant of the great Clanseri poets. A friend. At any moment I expected him to tack around and run for the shoreline. I was still expecting it when the lorsk passed out of sight behind an outlying flank of the mountain, still apparently pointed in the direction of Zaine. Shree spat out a most impressive curse and smashed his fist down on the balustrade.

Shall I destroy him, seed of the Excommunicant? The two are one.

The words echoed and re-echoed inside my head. I played with the idea, finding to my surprise that I was furious now too, almost furious enough to agree. Without the Lady's two-are-one business, I might have done it. But her voice in my head was too eager—I formed a strong impression that the Lady was seeking her own advantage in this. Every outburst of power so far had been involuntary on my part, and, though I could not have said why exactly, it seemed important to keep things that way.

"No."

"What did you say, Tig?"

"I wasn't talking to you. But you're going to break the railing if you keep on beating it like that." And in my head, I repeated: *no*.

The Clanseri has betrayed you. He has stolen your ship of escape. Command me to destroy him and bring the vessel back to you.

I will not command you.

A charged silence. Then: *he has fled the plague. He has abandoned you, not caring if you die, and the other Scion with you. Command me to punish him.*

I will not.

Shree was shaking my shoulder. "Pay attention, Tig. He's gone. The bastard's gone and saved himself and left us behind, and there's nothing we can do about it." These were the first complete and repeatable sentences he had spoken for some minutes. I stared at him, distantly noting the fury in his eyes. Then I realized that my own anger was fading; I did not completely trust the appearance of things, I had enough faith left in Chasco to make me reserve my judgement. Most of all, I did not trust the Lady's burning eagerness to condemn and destroy him.

"There is something I could do, Shree, but I won't. We'll just have to steal a boat after all, and somehow we'll catch up with him, and when we do—"

"When we do, I'll make a noose for him out of his own traitorous guts."

"You'll do nothing of the sort. When we find him, we'll ask him why he left us behind. He might have a perfectly good reason."

Shree glared at me in disbelief. "What reason? What reason could be good enough?"

"We'll ask him anyway."

"But he's betrayed us!"

"We don't know that for sure."

After a few moments Shree let his hands drop to his sides in defeat. "All right, we'll question him. And *after* that we'll string him up by his own guts."

I didn't say anything more, having made my point. Any-

way, that good old Sheranik temper was well up and Shree
was in a dangerous state. I didn't want him to start pounding
the balustrade again, or starting on the walls—I was afraid he
would bring the whole tower crashing on to the heads of the
pilgrims below.

Halfway down the stairs, we met Coll coming up to find us.
He was breathless from the climb and the excitement of having a good story to retail. This was the story of the dragon-
ship, the fisherman, and the chest of golden palots.

If the dead choose to take their gold with them when they
sail to the afterworld east of Zaine, who would dare to rob
them? And those who would dare have only themselves to
blame if the dead decide, quite properly, to punish the crime.
That was the popular view of the origins of this plague. It had
already resulted in the slow sacrifice of several dozen of the
salvagers' close relations in the hope of appeasing the outraged dead—the salvagers themselves were beyond reach,
having been the first to dance themselves to death. And now,
since direct appeasement had failed, the people of Vassashinay were turning to their blessed fire-gods for protection.

Since early morning, by ones and twos and threes and
whole families, the faithful of Vassashinay had been toiling up
the mountain to gather on the field in front of the Sacellum.
Appalling tales were being passed around of conditions on
Korviss, the island immediately west of Vass; the fourth and
most remote island, Masslivan, where the dragon-ship had
been taken and the palots melted down, had fallen under a pall
of ominous silence. On the main island, Vass was the town
hardest hit, although the first horrors had started to break the
evening before in the villages of Alssorvan and Tinnas on the
island's south side. Villim had not been touched so far, but I
had a feeling it was only a matter of time.

Coll seemed excited rather than anxious. He had perfect
faith in the fire-gods' power to overcome the malign influence
of these deceased and vengeful outlanders. True, Valsoria had
just ordered the Sacellum gates to be sealed from the inside,
but that was for the protection of the populace camped outside, not those inside. Sometimes when the fire-gods were
roused to action, he kindly explained, they were a little unpre-

dictable at first—as when they rose up to drown the towers of Iklankish and happened to drown several hundred Vassashin at the same time. No, Coll proclaimed with confidence and great pride, the Divinatrix and the fire-gods would overcome those hellbound angry spirits from the west and send them and their damned disease screaming past Zaine with no more than a few flicks of her fingers. I asked when. He said, when she was ready. She knew how to cover herself, all right.

When Coll had finished his story and hurtled off to find somebody else to tell we repaired to Shree's cell, deep in thought. Not only did we appear to have lost our best means of departure, but the vast and swelling crowd encamped around us was not going to make it any easier to leave the Sacellum. And there was another thing—at that time I had no knowledge of the broad scale of this disaster, no idea that the rest of the known world was already stinking with death and thudding to the dull blows of a million dancing feet, but I could read the signs. The dragon-ship was clearly a Calloonic trader, and it was also the local wellspring of the plague, which made me wonder about what was going on in Calloon at that moment. Moreover, no Calloonic ship would sail as far east as Vassashinay without passing the Archipelago and Gil on its way, which in turn made me wonder what was going on in Sathelforn and Gil City. Somehow I could not believe that Vassashinay was being treated to a plague of its very own, compliments of a shipload of disgruntled corpses.

I sat tensely on one end of Shree's pallet while Shree sprawled restlessly across the other. "I'm wondering," he said after a while, "whether this plague has struck anywhere else."

"Like Calloon, Sathelforn, Gil? I was just wondering the same thing."

He looked at me gravely. "It may be just as well we're planning to bypass Zaine—if we can steal a boat, that is." His eyes hardened, and I thought he was probably brooding over Chasco and the lorsk again. I was wrong. "And it's just as well," he continued, "that we're leaving tonight. I don't imagine the Sacellum walls will keep the plague out for long, even if Valsoria has barred the gate."

"A little late for that anyway," I said with a somewhat

forced cheerfulness. "Between the Frath Major and his party, and the Burgher of Vass and his party, several dozen pilgrims have moved into the Sacellum since sun-up. Any one of them could have brought the plague with him."

At that moment there was a gentle rapping on the door, soft enough to be called furtive. Shree sat up on his end of the pallet and drew his knife, hiding it under a loose fold of the coverlet. He frowned at me fiercely, so after a moment I followed his example. Then he called out, in a not very welcoming voice, "Who is it?"

The door shot open a few inches; a slight grey figure burst through and closed the door again rapidly and silently and pressed one ear to the door-crack, breathing in short hard gasps.

I looked at Shree. He looked at me. This day was becoming really very interesting indeed.

"Welcome, honoured Bequiin," I said. "Do sit down."

Ardin replied by throwing himself across the cell towards me. I didn't know about his dagger until I felt it slide between my ribs.

34

I STARED DOWN at the haft sticking out of my chest. Apart from the pain, which was considerable, there were strange and unpleasant sensations, in places that weren't intended to have them; you're normally too dead to feel cold iron in your heart. Furthermore, my second-best tunic was ruined. I glowered at the Bequiin Ardin as I took hold of the haft with both hands and yanked the blade free.

He was a face-down heap of grey rags on the floor by that time, with Shree's knee in his back and Shree's knife on the upswing of a blow designed to be fatal. Shree was clearly upset; he looked like a Canzitrine berserker, the one warrior in the world more insanely bloodthirsty than a Sherkin. I threw myself at him, wincing at the waves of agony from my chest, and knocked his arm away on the downswing, barely in time. "Don't kill him," I said quickly, "we need to question him."

"You're not dead!" The astonishment that replaced the crazed grimace on Shree's face was enough to set me laughing, but the extra pain this caused sobered me up. If the Lady went so far as to make me unkillable, I thought bitterly, it would be nice of her to block the pain as well, though already the wound was starting to hurt less and itch more as the healing process raced ahead. There was very little blood.

Shree climbed off the old man and lifted him, not tenderly, on to the chamber's one chair. I pulled his grey hood back and saw a large plum-coloured bruise on his forehead, just above the left eye. His breathing was shallow and tormented and his hands clutched the arms of the chair so tightly that his blue-veined knuckles turned white. My extreme annoyance at being stabbed in the heart began to fade.

"Honoured Bequiin," I said, fairly gently, "why did you do that? I thought you liked me."

He peered up at me with despair. "Too late," he cried, "too late! Now you cannot be killed!"

"Let me ask him," Shree said tightly.

"No, thank you. I know where you learned interrogation techniques." I sat down on the pallet so that my eyes were on a level with the Bequiin's. My mind was beginning to clear as the pain diminished, and a number of previously puzzling items were starting to make sense. I stared at the old man in front of me, trying to match him with the shadow-figure glimpsed in a dark corridor of the *Tasiil*, and reached out after a moment of adding things up to put my hand on his knee. "Tell me the truth, Ardin. Have you tried to kill me before?"

He nodded tearfully, not looking at me.

"The parth-asp? The poison? The Frath Minor in the Gilgard?"

He wiped the tears from his face with the sleeve of his grey robe, seeming a little calmer. "Billiil's attempt was not my doing; he was ploughing his own field then; he knew nothing about you except the Frath Major thought you were important."

I accepted that. "But the other incidents?"

"Yes, I tried several times to arrange your death while still

you could die. And it would have been better for you,
Tigrallef, if one of my hirelings had found his mark, for now it
is too late." He began to weep again, feebly. "It has already
begun, Scion, has it not?"

I was confused. "What do you mean? The plague?"

"The prophecy, bedamn it! I looked for you first in your
own cell. I saw what was there."

"Ah," I said, "the furniture. I can explain."

A few tears coursed down his battered face. "No need. You
have declared the two are one, yes?"

I bit my lip, surprised. Those words again, the ones the
Lady had been irritating me with for some time. "So far," I
said cautiously, "I've avoided saying any such thing."

He regarded me openmouthed; disbelief, hope, relief,
chased each other across his face. "*Marrich!* I feared greatly
when I saw—but the prophecy has not been completed. *Marrich frath!*" And he closed his eyes and babbled grateful
prayers in Miisheli for a few moments, before he slipped off
the chair to kneel in front of me, looking piercingly up into
my face and breaking again into Gillish. "Scion, you must not
carry out the prophecy, you must not speak the words of affirmation, there may be no going back for you if you do. The
Great Nameless Last, Scion! Empires always fall, but this one
will not—"

I rather lost his thread at this point. Do not imagine that the
Lady was allowing me to listen without making her own
views very clear. There was a wind rising inside my skull,
freighted with words: *he is a blaspheming fool, he is not of the
Naar, he should not know these things, command me to
silence him for his arrogance and presumption, command me,
Scion, command me, the two are one, the two are one, command me, the two* . . . I bit my hand hard enough to draw
blood from the fleshy mount of the palm and forced myself to
concentrate on the pain. Then I could hear the Bequiin again.

His face was mottled with emotion. He was still babbling
about something called the Great Nameless Last—unknown
to me, but the words plucked at a string. I nodded to Shree,
who rose at once and lifted the old man back into the chair,
more gently this time, and poured him out some water from
the new jug on the table. The Bequiin broke off what he was

saying to stare at the beaker as if he had never seen one before, and I took advantage of the lull.

"Drink up, Ardin, you'll feel much better. And then you can explain to us what you're talking about, because I honestly don't understand."

His efforts to calm himself were both visible and painful. After a few moments he accepted the water from Shree and took a long drink, and gradually the hectic colour in his face subsided. Shree and I patiently watched him struggle for control. When he spoke again, it was with all the dignity and detachment of the great scholar I knew him to be.

"Tigrallef—how shall I begin?—you were correct to doubt Cor Cahn's treatise on the fall of Fathan. And also right to compare it with the Clerisy's lies about the fall of Sher."

I nodded after a moment, trusting this was not the complete switch of topic it sounded like. "All right. Lakshi Cor Cahn lied about the fall of Fathan. But what does that have to do with trying to kill me?"

He overrode me with a schoolmasterly kind of gesture. "Why did I defend Cor Cahn's truthfulness to you? Because at the time you wrote to me, there was no evidence to gainsay him. That came later. It is true, I had doubts like yours and for the same reasons, but even speculations must have some solid basis before they can be explored."

"I don't agree," I began, but he raised his hand again.

"I have not come to discuss the philosophy of knowledge," he said with a flash of spirit. "Listen to me. It was twenty years ago that I first proposed a certain expedition to seek out the knowledge of the Ancients—I will tell you in a moment where I thought it could be found. But that was at a time when Sher was threatening to break the treaty with the League of Free Nations, and the court had better things to think about than a quest for historical truths and such playthings, which are, as you probably know, of interest only to scholars and other fools. They told me to go back to my books and be thankful for the privilege, and so I did, and so the matter rested for nearly fifteen years."

"I know that feeling. Our book budget in Gil—but never mind." I shut up hastily at the look in his eyes.

He slumped back into the chair and folded his hands in his

lap. "Five years ago," he said softly with his eyes on the door, "a powerful prince and general named Liithis of Shiilk fought his way—no, Tigrallef, swam his way, through a sea of blood, to become the present Frath Major. He had been a pupil of mine many years ago, an intelligent and promising pupil, and I was pleased at first. I thought perhaps he would place more value on matters of scholarship than the illiterate barbarian who was Frath Major before him—and so he did, so he did."

I traded puzzled glances with Shree. "Not a good thing?" I guessed.

Ardin sighed. "No, Tigrallef. As it happened, not a good thing. He called me to him when he had been Frath Major for half a year—he had been looking through the records of the court, he said, and was very interested to find mention of the expedition I had proposed fifteen years before. What fools the court of the time had been, he said, to turn me down! Wisdom for the sake of wisdom, he said! Knowledge for the sake of knowledge! So much there was, he said, that we could learn from the Ancients! *Marrich frath!*"

Ardin's voice had risen, but he caught himself now and held his breath and listened. We listened with him, perforce— a comforting silence in the corridor. In my head, on the other hand, the Lady was murmuring sullenly to herself.

"It was a grand expedition," Ardin went on, almost in a whisper. "I was given everything I asked for. A thousand of the best animals, five hundred of the Frath's best troops, enough food and supplies for a year's quest, and the promise of more to come, as much as I could ever want. When we left Cansh Miishel, our caravan stretched for two hours' march along the road, and our encampments were the size of a town." He fell silent again, musing.

I reached out to touch his arm. "And did you find what you were looking for?"

Softly: "Yes, Scion."

"Where did you find it?"

Looking up sharply: "Can you not guess?"

I could, but Shree got there first. "Fathan," he said positively. "There were no ships on your list, and there are only two places a caravan can march to from Miishel—Grisot and Fathan. You went to Cansh Fathan."

Ardin looked at him thoughtfully. "Cansh Fathan. Yes."

Purposeful feet thudded down the corridor. Ardin half-rose, his face pale, his hands fisted in front of him, not breathing until they had passed Shree's door and continued down the corridor towards the stairway. Shree sighed and started to pare his fingernails with his knife.

I leaned forward. "Bequiin Ardin, what did you find in Cansh Fathan?"

Ardin sank back into the chair. His face was pale, but his eyes met mine steadily. "I found the imperial archives."

If he was intending a dramatic impact, he got one. I lost my breath; Shree dropped his knife. The imperial archives of Fathan! The long-lost written records of the most corrupt and cruel, the most gilded and glittering, the most heartless and gorgeous and barbaric and labyrinthine imperial court in the memory of the known world! I was dazzled by the sheer wonder of it—but for only a moment, until a few natural doubts set in.

"Ardin, I find this hard to believe. Fathan was completely destroyed by fire—all the historical traditions agree on that, from Storica to Zaine; and the few travellers who have dared to cross the boundaries of Fathan all describe—"

"A black and blasted land," Ardin cut in passionately, "where the soil was burnt to the bare rock, and the rock melted and flowed and froze again into vast stretches of hot black glass that burns even now to the touch, and nothing has grown since—yes, yes; it is true, Tigrallef, it is all true."

To avoid his eyes, I examined the inkstains on my fingers. "So how did the archives survive? If nothing else did, I mean." I looked up.

A dreamy smile came over the Bequiin's face. I recognized that quality of smile; I'd seen it on Angel and Shree, on the face of the First-Memorian-in-Exile, and felt it on my own face now and then: the smile of a scholar contemplating some personal victory of scholarship, great or small, some puzzle unravelled, some significant connection made, some truth uncovered.

"Twenty days," he said, "we crossed a land like the backside of a Storican hell. Flat plains of black glass, and endless ranges of black hills covered with rocks like cinders the size

of my fist, and forests of blackened stumps that stretched as
far as an eagle's eye could see, and nothing grew, and no
water flowed; but on the twenty-first day, Scion, we came to
the ruins of Cansh Fathan itself, which no traveller had seen
for better than a thousand years—and Tigrallef, this is the
wondrous part." His eyes sparkled into mine. "Tigrallef,
Cansh Fathan was *never burnt*."

There was a grunt from Shree's direction. "Oh," I said after
a moment.

"Never burnt!" he repeated. "Ruined, yes; tumbled and
overgrown, but not one mark of fire, not a charred stone, nor a
burnt timber, neither a speck of soot nor a streak of old
smoke! And this in the midst of a land like a great hearth built
by giants! Never burnt! Oh, I could tell you many other won-
ders of that place, and the strange and terrible things that happened while we were there—I arrived with half a thousand
men, and I left with fewer than two hundred—but I have not
the time now. I will say only that when I returned to Cansh
Miishel, I took with me thirty-two wainloads of the court
records of Imperial Fathan. Thirty-two wainloads, Tigrallef!"
He peered eagerly into my face.

"Astonishing, Bequiin. A treasure beyond any valuing.
Which brings me," I said carefully, "to my second question.
Why didn't you tell anyone? Why didn't any memorian out-
side Miishel hear even a whisper of this remarkable find?"

He looked suddenly ashamed. "Liithis—the Frath Major—
persuaded me."

"Persuaded? You mean, forced? Tortured?"

"No, no, if duress had been used, I should not despise
myself so miserably now." He rose painfully and came to sit
between us on the pallet. Even so, his voice dropped so low
that I had to strain to hear him over the Lady's mutters. "He
had vision, Liithis did, I will grant him that. Grisot was pressing hard again on our northern borders—these standoffs are
so costly, and that is all that our history has been since Fathan
fell, a thousand years of standoffs. Liithis persuaded me that
the ancient writings of Fathan might hold a secret that could
tip the balance in our favour, and help—" He stopped, blushing as only the old can blush, a fine network of veins redden-
ing under his papery cheek-skin.

"And help—?" Shree prompted.

"And help to restore the empire," Ardin whispered, looking down at his hands. "So blind can we become to the lessons of history."

"But did you find such a secret?" I asked.

He raised his hands and dropped them again; a Miisheli expression of resignation. "I found you, Tigrallef."

"Me?" I laughed out loud. "In Cansh Fathan?"

He caught my hands. "Not by name, no, of course not. But like this." He shut his eyes and began to chant in a soft monotone, word after liquid word: Oballef's tongue. An instant later the Lady howled, causing a burst of pure agony that I thought would crack my head wide open—I grabbed Ardin by the front of his cloak, frantic with the pain.

"What does it mean? Tell me what it means!"

It was Shree who stopped me from accidentally strangling the Bequiin; he broke my hold and shoved me back on the pallet, and transferred the gasping Bequiin back to his chair. Then he shook me. I was still half-mad from that explosion inside my skull, and Shree told me later that the mountain started to tremble violently and only stopped when I managed to uncross my eyes; but all I remember is the Bequiin leaning forwards again, unafraid, and speaking softly but firmly into the dead afternoon silence.

"The texts were fragmentary—in Fathidiic, and Old Miisheli and Old Grisotin, and also in Naarhil, the secret tongue of your ancestor Oballef." He smiled faintly at the shock on my face. "Yes, Scion, I have long known of your Secrets of the Ancients—but of these texts, I could read some, and some I could decipher, and some defeated me. And this is what I learned: that there was an ancient race called the Naar, and its talisman was called the Harashil, and together they shaped the rise and fall of many great nations. I could understand nothing of their beginning, but Tigrallef—I could read a part of their end."

"The prophecy?" I held my breath. The Bequiin brought his face very close to mine.

"The prophecy, yes: that one day a man descended from the Naar would free the Harashil from its material bonds, and accept its power, and the two would become one; and together

they would found a nation that would never fall until the
world itself came to an end—the Great Nameless Last." His
voice was hushed.

My head was an aching void suddenly, empty of whispers.
"Is that all of it?"

"No, there was more, perhaps much more, but the text was
too damaged for me to decipher."

"And what does it have to do with me?" This was said just
to be difficult, because I already knew the connection all too
well.

The Bequiin took my face between his hands, a look of pity
coming into his eyes. "Tigrallef. You are the man of the Naar;
the Lady in Gil is the Harashil. I understood this even before
the deciphering was done—the great misfortune is, the Frath
Major understood it as well. We knew the truth of what happened to Sher. Everyone knew. And when you shattered that
thing known as the Lady in Gil, you carried out the first part
of the prophecy."

I took his hands from my face and held them in mine.
"What about my ancestor Oballef? How did the Naar become
the Scions of Oballef?"

"Who knows? Fathan fell a century or more before Oballef
landed in Gil—who knows what happened in the meantime?
Perhaps he came to Gil from the ruins of Cansh Fathan; but
who knows? The texts end well before Fathan's destruction."

"Of course they would." I closed my eyes, trying to clarify
my thoughts, but the Bequiin began talking again.

"The Frath believes he can harness the Harashil through
you—he desires to make Miishel the heart of the Great Nameless Last, and rule it himself by ruling you. He hopes for
immortality and power. But he is a fool! He does not know the
nature of the power he meddles with, and the evil that would
come of it. An empire that would never fall! An empire that
would end only with the world's end! An empire that would
bring about the world's end . . . think of the lessons of the
past, Tigrallef, and then think of the future."

"You don't need to tell me," I said glumly. "I already
know."

The Bequiin lurched to his feet and paced unsteadily back
and forth between the pallet and the window. "Then you are

wiser than I—for by the time I saw the danger, I was already the Frath's creature and in the Frath's trap." He touched his fingertips to the dark swollen bruise on his forehead. "Forgive me, Tigrallef. I could not stop Liithis and so," his voice sank with shame, "I tried to stop you."

"Don't feel bad," I said, "part of me wishes you had done a better job of it. But Ardin, why do you blame yourself? You got the Frath Major involved, but that's all. You're not responsible for the prophecy; I broke the glass before you ever went to Fathan. Short of killing me, there's nothing you could have done to help me."

Apparently there was. He overhung me, his eyes burning into mine. He had started to sweat. "Listen carefully. The prophecy will not be complete until you declare yourself one with the Harashil—until you knowingly and willingly accept its power; that part of the text was very clear. And you have not done so."

"That's true, I haven't. She's tried to trick me into it a few times."

"Then you have felt her—it—the Harashil?"

"Yes," I said, with feeling. "Oh, yes."

The strength seemed to be draining out of him. He collapsed on to his chair and wiped a hand across his streaming forehead. When he spoke, his voice was weaker. "You cannot be killed, that is clear. But I believe there may be hope for you if you do these things: first, go from here. Take yourself as far from the Frath Major as you can. And second—resist the Harashil, break the chain that binds you to it, if you can find the way—"

"Can that be done?" I broke in.

He hesitated. "I will confess, I am not certain. There were intimations that it might be done, but the text was damaged at that point and I can tell you nothing more. Scion, I am tired and afraid. I have not long to live. Promise me you will do those things."

"Anything," I said. I sat still for a few moments, trying to decide on a course that would comfort him, and in those moments he began to cough, a tired sound like the hack of a horse sinking in its traces, and he slid deeper into his chair. I made up my mind.

"Bequiin Ardin, I will tell you something: we are escaping

from Vassashinay, tonight. Come with us." I ignored Shree's warning gesture and drew a long breath. "Come with us, Ardin. You can escape the Frath's trap as well."

He looked up and seemed to be considering it, but only for a few blinks of an eyelid. Standing heavily, he laid one hand on my head and the other on Shree's, as if blessing us in the old Gillish style, and I remembered distantly that the gesture had the same meaning in Miisheli.

"It is too late for me," he said. "I came here to kill you and stayed to warn you—some small payment for the evil I have been party to—and now that I am done, I must leave you. I hope I will not see you in the morning. Goodspeed, Scion of Oballef."

Shree looked thoughtful after the Bequiin left. "I don't quite understand," he said after a while, "why you and Ardin are so disturbed about this Great Nameless Last. It sounds all right to me. Isn't it the hope of every empire to last for ever?"

"Hopes have nothing to do with historical reality," I said tartly. "All the great empires on record seem to have started out well and then degenerated into cruelty and vice, and eventually ended in fire or flood. Not an impressive record for empires. And if I hear Ardin rightly, the Great Nameless Last will get caught indefinitely in the cruelty and vice stage, until such time as it brings the whole world down with it. I find that disturbing—don't you?"

He grimaced. "But there have been breaks in the pattern before. Sher wasn't raised by—the Harashil; Gil didn't go sour."

"Sher was *destroyed* by the Harashil. And Gil went soft instead of sour." I frowned. "But I agree, Gil doesn't quite fit the mould. I would like to know a great deal more about my ancestor Oballef and how he came by the Harashil." The words I was groping for came into my head: *Seed of the Excommunicant.* I shook off a chill. "The point is, Shree, that the Lady doesn't appear to come equipped with a moral sense. She was just as effective at killing the Sherkin millions as she was at making Gil a garden of culture and learning; she saved Calla, but only because a Scion, a child of the Naar, was in Calla's womb, and otherwise she would have let her drown."

"But—"

"No, let me finish. The Lady may have been the instrument for many wonderful things—but she's been the instrument for just as many evils and atrocities and, on the whole, I think the world would muddle along better without her. If I can break the cycle, I will."

"But *you* have a well-developed moral sense, Tig. Over-developed, if anything. Enough and to spare for both you and the Lady."

"Oh really? I wish I could believe that." Gloomily, I slumped against the wall. "But how long do you think I'd remain a moral being once the power became a habit? And you're forgetting something else."

"What?"

"Who it was that ordered the sinking of Sher."

A long silence. "Oh yes," he said at last.

He never defended the Lady again.

35

"SHE'S NOT COMING," I breathed.

"Keep your voice down. Of course she's coming."

"She's late."

"A few minutes. Don't be—hush!"

Three novices were crossing the courtyard from the direction of the main gate, heading directly towards our hiding place in the shadow of the great rain-tun. I froze every muscle and held my breath; but they were chirping away excitedly in Vassashin, not keeping their voices down, and they passed by on the other side of the tun's housing without noticing us. I peered around the curve of the housing in time to see the little side-door a few feet away close behind them. The courtyard was deserted again.

I began counting to pass the time. By the count of fifty, I assured myself, Calla would come, and she would have

Verolef with her, and I would never let either of them out of my sight again.

Forty-nine, fifty. No Calla. Although the Sacellum was quiet and only a few lights showed in the windows of the Daughters' quarters, a sound like distant surf floated over the walls from the faithful and distressed gathered outside.

One hundred.

They had stormed the Sacellum just after sunset, poor wretches; one man, said to be from Villim, had risen from his mat and started to dance, and the sight of the pustules swelling on his face as he danced had caused a stampede that crushed a dozen or more citizens against the locked gate of the Sacellum a few moments later. The gate itself held.

One hundred and fifty.

The Miisheli troopers, never ones to pass up a good fight, had surged quite happily out of their enclave by the gate to control the riot, and I wondered if they had doomed themselves by doing so. One of the red surplices had addressed the faithful from the window above the gate, urging calm, promising safety, guaranteeing that the fire-gods were even now taking the plague in hand—but this did not prevent the unfortunate lone dancer from being thrown alive into one of the great bonfires that dotted the encampment. This was something that the Miisheli troopers did not try to stop.

Two hundred.

Where was Calla? I felt as though we had been crouched for hours in that patch of shadow in the wash of the waning moon, but I knew, in fact, that it had been scant minutes. Perhaps she could not get away—perhaps, in this desperate time, she had been drafted into some ritual duty devised by Valsoria in the subterranean amphitheatre, perhaps she had been caught trying to take Verolef from under the noses of his guardians, perhaps—

The mountain rumbled and shook. Shree shot out his hand to clutch my shoulder. "Stop it. Calm down."

"It's not my doing. We're sitting on a volcano, damn it." In fact, the Lady was being eerily cooperative; either that, or she was sulking in silence. Thinking about it, I decided it was the latter. She had stopped even muttering when the Bequiin

Ardin left us, and I had neither heard nor felt her through the endless hours since. This should have worried me, of course, but at the time it was just a relief.

Three hundred.

Two more lights were extinguished in the Daughters' quarters; from the encampment, a high shriek pierced the night and was suddenly cut off.

Three hundred and fifty.

The processional door opened and two dim figures came out, the Divinatrix and another. I heard the low tones of Valsoria's voice, and caught a few words—smooth the waters—all the time we need—that arrogant idiot—and then they disappeared into the corridor leading to the main outer gate. I did not think, somehow, that it was to throw the door open to welcome the populace inside; more likely to survey the punters from the safety of the window above the gate.

Four hundred. Nothing.

Four hundred and fifty. Shree pulled at my sleeve—the shadow that hid us was shortening as the moon floated higher in the sky, and our feet were about to become embarrassingly visible. I started to follow Shree as he edged around the housing when a creak from the corner of the courtyard immobilized us both. I snapped my head around, but Shree was in my way and I could see nothing. A second later, he grabbed the scruff of my tunic and hauled me after him towards the sidedoor behind the housing, which was half-open. The door creaked shut behind us.

The air inside was dank and close and smelled of lampgrease, as if a lamp had recently been extinguished there, but the room seemed dark as pitch after the moonlight outside. A hand out of the darkness found my face.

"Tig? Shree?" It was Calla's voice. From a few feet away, Shree whispered a greeting. Weak with relief, I followed the hand to the arm, found the rest of the body, tried to wrap myself around it; there was an obstacle in the form of a small warm blanketed object in Calla's arms.

"Here, take him, he's getting heavy," and suddenly the blanketed thing was in my arms. Fine hair nestled against my neck, soft regular breathing fanned my collarbone, a thin soft arm draped itself across my shoulder and dangled down my back.

"I gave him something to keep him sleeping," Calla's whisper came out of the darkness. "This way—hurry!"

My eyes were adjusting to the dimness and I could just make out that we were in a narrow flagged corridor, seemingly quite long, with a faint glimmer of greyish light at the end. Clutching my burden, followed by Shree, I trod as lightly as I could after Calla. There was no lessening of tension, but at least half of my mind was centred on the bundle in my arms, while the odd tight feeling in my chest had nothing to do with fear. My son. I was holding my son.

Our feet scraped along the rough stone floor. The light at the end of the passage was feeble moonlight filtering through a square skylight in one of the chambers off the corridor, just bright enough to show racks of winejars standing in piers all across the room. Calla stopped at the door and listened, then crept noiselessly into the chamber, vanishing almost immediately behind a pier of wine-racks. Shree prodded me from behind.

Calla was waiting for us at a door on the far side of the room, with her finger on her lips. Silently, she eased the door open. There was a flickering light beyond, and the crackle of a fire, mixed with muffled voices. After a few moments Calla slipped through the door with us on her heels. We were in another passageway, with firelight spilling through an open door on our left and darkness stretching away indefinitely to our right. I felt Calla's hand on my shoulder, guiding me further into the darkness. Verolef shifted in my arms.

We glided along the passage until some sense other than sight told me that we had come to the end. A door creaked; Calla was outlined against the glow of another fire. I detected onions and fresh bread, vinegar, beans, fish, the ghosts of old cooking smells. The room we crept into was dark and empty, but beyond it, through a door at the far end, I could see an old woman standing by an open fireplace and prodding in a bored fashion at something in a stewpot.

"Wait here," Calla whispered. We watched as she stepped confidently into the next room and greeted the old pot-tender.

She disappeared for a moment, then reappeared by the cauldron with a long wooden spoon in her hand. She dipped the spoon into the pot and tasted the contents, while the old woman watched with her head on one side; then, strike me dead if I lie, the two of them plumped down on adjacent stools by the fire for what seemed to be a long and cosy little chat. Verolef started to feel very heavy, so I sat down on the floor where I could keep an eye on Calla, and draped him comfortably across my knees with his head pillowed on my arm.

"Beard of Raksh—what's she doing?" Shree breathed, crouching down beside me. He was tight as a coiled spring; I, on the other hand, felt oddly calm and unhurried.

Then I looked down at the sleeping child in the dim light, and caught my breath—how frail he looked, how innocent and small and entirely vulnerable. Not that I was labouring under any illusions, of course. From my observations over the past few days, I knew he was pretty much a righteous terror when awake; but seeing him asleep, with his lashes resting on his cheeks and his fine little lips parted, I was struck hard by the pitiful inadequacy of his skin as an armour against the world, the terrible ease with which he could be destroyed— and the lengths to which I personally would go to prevent any such thing happening. I suppose it was in that instant that I fell, fearfully, helplessly and incurably, into being Verolef's father and his slave.

This had the effect of speeding up time for me again. "Balls of Oballef," I hissed to Shree, "what's that fool woman doing? Reciting the Endless Diversions of Belforell? Swapping recipes? We've got to get going!"

As if on cue, Calla rose from her comfy stool and gave another leisurely poke at the stewpot with her wooden spoon. This time, she sniffed appraisingly and exchanged a few more sentences with her good old crony and long-time conversational partner, who took a taste from the pot and nodded sagely. A moment later the old woman vanished from our limited field of view.

Calla stood for a few seconds longer, watching the direction which the old woman had taken; at last, she looked towards us and beckoned fiercely.

We went through the door like two arrows loosed from the

same bow. Calla grabbed my arm and hustled me across the cavernous kitchen. "We have to hurry. This way!"

"Now we have to hurry?" I muttered.

"What did you want me to do, knock poor old Vianna on the head? I've sent her to the herb room to find something that isn't there, but we've only got a few minutes. Shree, help me."

There was a double wooden door in the shadows beyond the fireplace, secured with a hefty bar, which Shree and Calla lifted down and hid in the nearest dark corner—there was a good chance that Vianna would not notice immediately that the door had been unbarred. Calla pried open one of the heavy leaves and looked out. When she looked back at us, she was frowning.

"No guards."

"Is it usually guarded?" Shree asked in a hoarse whisper.

"No—but I thought it might be tonight, because of the plague—"

"Never mind," said Shree. We all froze as halting footsteps sounded in one of the passages leading to the kitchen. A second later we were outside and Shree was propping a stone against the leaf to hold it closed. We were in the kitchenyard, with a broad wain-rutted passageway running off to the right between the Sacellum and a pile of roughly thatched masonry that smelled like a stable. At the end of the passage, we could see moonlight moving on a field of low scrub.

In a strange way, I think all of us would have felt easier in our minds if the kitchenyard to the Sacellum had been guarded that night. I did not need Shree's Sheranik instincts, nor the seventh sense of a born daughter of the Web, like Calla, to know that. Creeping along the passageway felt like walking through a forest that was too silent, wondering why no birds sang and nothing rustled in the trees except the wind. We could have dealt quickly and efficiently with a few startled guards—it was much harder to deal with this feeling of being observed, anticipated, invisibly cut off.

Tense and suspicious, we reached the end of the passage and surveyed the scrubland between us and the road. Empty. If we crouched low, we could reasonably hope that the scrub would hide us from any casual eyes. Shree bent down and started to move out from the shelter of the wall, but Calla pulled him back.

"Just a moment," she said. She stood in the mouth of the passage, a rigid silhouette; a rustle of silk, and the silhouette changed to something more human and definitely more female—Calla had shed her Vassashin surplice, robe and veil for what I hoped would be the last time in her life. As far as I could tell, she was wearing britches and a tunic now, and the grey moonlight flashed off something that could only be a knife in one of her fists. I smiled to myself—she was still the same old fierce and resourceful Calla, and never mind the soft white hands.

She glanced back and must have caught that look on my face, because she grinned too—a strained, nervous grin. She put her arms around me, including Verolef, and kissed us both quickly, me on the mouth, Verolef on the top of his head. Then she grabbed Shree and kissed him too. "Good fortune to us all," she whispered. "I'm starting to think we're going to make it."

And even as she finished speaking, there was a resounding crash behind us—the kitchenyard door smashing open against the stone wall. Torches flared in the kitchenyard. A bull voice roared in Miisheli, "Stop where you are!"

Shree whirled, knife and sword already in his hands. "Keep going!" Calla grabbed my free arm and pulled me along—Verolef stirred and started to whimper in his sleep. Trammelled by his weight, I tried to grope around him to find my own knife as we ran, but I couldn't reach it. By then we were on the edge of the scrubland, and Shree, who was right on my heels, cursed mightily; a moment later, metal clanged off metal close behind me.

I glanced over my shoulder in time to see Shree bring his sword down on the neck of a hulking great scragger who promptly fell out of sight among the scrubby bushes, but already three or four others were closing in on Shree—and on Calla, who was intent on jerking her knife out of somebody's midriff and didn't seem to see them coming.

Desperately, I shifted Verolef in my arms until I could almost reach my own weapon, then gave up and laid him down in the shelter of a bush and leapt to my feet, drawing my knife; a foot came out of nowhere and kicked it out of my hand. The next kick found my shoulder, spinning me backwards, the third and fourth crunched into my ribs. There was probably an unnecessary fifth, but by that point I was beyond noticing where it landed. I collapsed beside Verolef, and had just enough breath left to pull myself half over him, in a feeble attempt to shield him with my body. I could taste blood in my mouth. When somebody yanked me to my feet, I managed to lock my arms around the child and bring him up with me. Staggering under his weight, I shook the sweat out of my eyes and looked about me.

It was already over. They were all around us. The silver cross-straps of the Frath's Guard gleamed in the moonlight from a dozen or more broad chests. Judging by their positions, some of the troopers must have been concealed in the scrub before we ever left the Sacellum. We had been neatly trapped.

Shree arrived, slung over a trooper's shoulder. I was afraid for a moment that he was dead, but when he was dumped on the ground, he rolled over groggily and sat up. His tunic was slashed clear across and he was bleeding from cuts over the eye and on his chest. A few seconds later, Calla was frog-marched over to us between two creditably damaged troopers. She managed to pull free of them and gently took Verolef from me. She seemed to be unhurt, but tears were rolling down her cheeks.

Seed of the Excommunicant. A small, cold voice in my head.

I groaned, though not with pain. The pain was already draining from my body; I could feel my cracked ribs busily knitting themselves together. The groan was purely on the Lady's account.

Scion. It does not need to be like this. Command me. Tell me the two are one. Command me to crush these vermin.

By Oballef, I was tempted! It was fortunate for the Frath's Guardsmen that they did not try to finish off Shree, or tear Verolef from his mother's hold, for I am sure they would have died messily in the next instant or so. As it was, I looked up to see thunderheads racing across the sky towards us, knowing that a word from me, or even a lessening of my will to resist, would call the lightning down. And for that short-term gain, everything might be lost.

Command me, man of the Naar. Affirm the two are one.

I hesitated—so close, so very close to saying it—then shouted out loud, startling the nearest Miisheli into dropping his sword on his own foot, "No! I will not command! I will not affirm! The prophecy remains unfulfilled!"

There was a long silence, while the Miishelu looked at me and then at each other, and snickered and tapped their helmets knowingly at my obvious madness, except for the one who was cursing me for his sore foot.

Then: *you will command me when the time comes. The two are one, Scion.*

And the Lady was silent again.

36

THE TROOPERS TIED my hands and Shree's behind our backs, but left Verolef in Calla's arms. We were led back through the kitchen, past a pale and frightened Vianna, and out to the courtyard, which was no longer empty. Han-Frath Zimin was there with another half-dozen of the Frath's Guard, the rest of those who had been allowed to remain in the Sacellum. The windows of the Daughters' and servants' dormitories were lined with curious faces. Zimin took custody of the four of us and marched us smartly upstairs to the Frath Major's quarters, the door of which was opened by the Frath Major himself.

He did not look angry; on the contrary, he looked vastly pleased. He was fully dressed despite the hour, including light ceremonial armour and a courtcap, and he greeted me with the kind of fervour usually reserved for a long-lost debtor. As I came through the door, he reached up and sprinkled a handful of green powder on my head, then stood back with a gloating expression on his face.

His was a proper chamber rather than a cell, with carpets on the floor and enough room at one end for a circle of velvet-seated chairs around a polished wooden table. The table held an ornate rock-crystal wine service which I recognized as the very cream of Crosthic artistry; the amphora in the corner bore the mark of the best of the Calloonic vineyards, and an exceptionally fine year.

"Come and sit down, Tigrallef, and you also, Lady Carrinay—that is your name, is it not? Perhaps you would like to lay the child down?" He ignored Shree, while all three of us ignored him. Calla tightened her arms around Verolef and stared coldly into the middle distance. The Frath Major sighed.

"I hope you will not be difficult, Tigrallef. I think you must know why you're here. Do not play at ignorance, or you will anger me."

"You know," I remarked to Calla and Shree, "this is really interesting. It's not the first time I've met someone who wants the world under his heel, and I'm starting to notice consistencies in the behaviour."

"Scion, Scion," the Frath chided me. He put on a friendly smile. "Perhaps you do not understand your position."

I decided to notice him. "Perhaps you don't." There was a minor ripple from the Lady at that point, and I had to bite my lip to control it, which the Frath Major saw with satisfaction and probably misinterpreted.

"Do not fear me, Tigrallef," he said gently. "You will come to no harm—you will come to share with me in the exercise of unbounded power. Can you not see how it will be?"

"Actually," I said, "I was thinking how generous of you to want to share."

His face darkened, but before he could answer, the door crashed wide open and Rinn swept in. She looked like she'd come directly from her bed—that is, she was gloriously dishevelled and stark naked under a thin linen robe. She stomped over to the Frath Major, livid with fury, and shrieked at him in Miisheli. She paid no attention to the rest of us.

"How dare you! How dare you! At this time of night—to have me rousted from my bed like a serving slut, to have me sent for—how dare you! Even you! How dare you summon me?"

The Frath Major dug his fingers into the multicoloured mass of curls on top of her head and shook her until she shut up. This process took some time and was not unlively. Finally, when she'd passed from fury through hysteria and into a less noisy state of shock, he pulled her head towards him until they were nose to nose.

He said, "Thank you for coming to see me, my dear cousin. I thought you would like to know that your bridegroom tried to flee Vassashinay tonight, without you."

Rinn's jaw dropped. Then it snapped shut again. I thought for a moment she was going to lunge forwards and bite the Frath on the nose but instead she swung her whole head, Frath's hand and all, to glare at me. Her cat's-eyes were enormous with rage. They shifted to Calla for a cold few seconds, dismissed her as unworthy even of contempt, in her unglamorous tunic with Verolef dribbling down her shoulder, and returned to me.

"You would have left me? Me?" Her voice started as a sort of animal screech, and rose rapidly from there. "I am Rinn of Miishel—no man leaves me. No man! How dare you? How—"

The Frath started shaking her again, which had the welcome effect of absorbing her attention. Then he marched her over to one of the chairs and set her firmly down into it. She glared up at him.

"You failed me, lovely cousin," he murmured. "That has displeased me. Now you must close your mouth and be very good and quiet, and I may decide not to have you killed. For a little while, anyway. I want you here to see what is going to happen, so that you may be the first to learn to fear me." He paused. "Do you think I did not know what you were plotting?"

She opened her mouth, then seemed to be thinking deeply and shut it again. Improbably, I felt sorry for her. It occurred to me that she had not chosen to be a monster.

The Frath Major hung over her for a few moments, perhaps savouring this foretaste of power. Then he turned back to me, and his eyes were very cold and bright. "Now, Tigrallef, good friend and cousin," he began—which was the moment when the next visitor chose to arrive. An imperious knocking sounded on the door. The Frath Major gritted his teeth and motioned to Zimin to answer it. The look he gave me was almost apologetic: *so sorry, cousin, such tiresome interruptions, but fear not, we shall come to our business soon enough.*

Valsoria entered, followed by the two red surplices and an elderly serving woman. The Divinatrix looked no happier than Rinn had, but her presence was much more dignified and impressive. She marched directly to confront the Frath Major, and despite the difference in their sizes, the confrontation looked fairly well balanced.

She spoke in clipped, angry Miisheli. "The Daughter Carrinay and the Kalkissann, her son, were not part of our bargain."

"Madam—"

"You will surrender them to me, now. The Gilman is no business of mine, but the woman and child belong to the service of the blessed fire-gods, may they be exalted. Give them to me."

She was a stern and resolute little figure, but I wouldn't have thought this had much bearing on the Frath's decision. I don't believe he knew anything about Calla and Verolef in the first place, hadn't reckoned on bagging them, and didn't quite know what to do with them now that he had them. He hesitated, then looked to me with a kindly smile.

"Tigrallef, what is this Carrinay to you?"

"A compatriot," I said without hesitation, not looking at Calla. "A Gilwoman by birth, who had a yearning to see her native shores again. I told her she could travel with us."

"And the child?"

"Her son. Surely you wouldn't expect her to leave her son behind, great Frath."

He broadened his smile and reached over to pat Verolef's sleeping head. "Quite so, quite so." Calla glared at him. I knew the Frath did not believe me, but for some reason he was very sure of himself—it seemed to me that whatever he had in mind could be done without resorting to Calla. Uneasily, I wondered what he knew, or had, that made him so damnably confident.

With a gesture of great respect, so great that it became a form of mockery, he bowed to the Divinatrix. "I recognize your claim to the woman and child, priestess; take them. Believe me, I had no intention of overstepping the bargain we made." He motioned to the troopers standing almost on Calla's heels, and they moved away from her at once.

Calla stood for a few moments as if unsure whether she

were free to go, smoothing the sleeping child's hair with trembling fingers. Talking fingers. *Tig? I can't leave you. I can't leave you.*

My hands were tied, but I tried to make my eyes speak for me, and repeated the words inside my head. *Yes you can. Think of Verolef. Go quickly, before the Frath changes his mind.*

Calla's face went grey; her fingers moved. *I'll go.*

That was all the time we were allowed before Valsoria took Calla protectively by the elbow and impelled her towards the door. "Go with Lorosa, Carrinay, my poor child. There is blood—are you injured? Praise to the blessed firegods, may they feed for ever, that the precious Kalkissann is unhurt! Oh, Carrinay, what madness possessed you? Lorosa, make sure you send for the poultices and enough hot water for Carrinay to bathe, and a fresh set of robes for her as well. Go now."

And so, apparently in the hands of friends, Calla was led away. I prayed she'd have the good sense not to look back at me, and she walked out without turning her head. When she was gone, I breathed a sigh of relief. Whatever was going to happen inside this room, she would not be part of it, and neither would Verolef, and for that I could have swept the little Divinatrix up in my arms and covered her with grateful kisses, except for two things. One, my hands were still tied behind me. Two, the small space in the back of my mind that was inhabited by the Lady in Gil, and yet was still a part of me, was throbbing with cold mistrust.

And with fear.

The mistrust may have been habitual, but I could not understand the fear. What could the Lady in Gil, all-knowing and all-too-powerful, possibly have to fear from Valsoria, that short milcher, Valsoria who had only just removed my woman and child from a position of terrible menace? I did not have time to ponder this, and anyway the next few minutes wiped my gratitude away.

As soon as the door closed behind Calla, the Divinatrix turned back to the Frath Major. Her face had gone cold again. "There is another matter."

The Frath was having trouble restraining his impatience. "What is it, priestess?"

She swung her icy gaze to Shree, tilting her head back to survey his face. Then she looked around for the elderly servant who had entered with her, finding the old woman cowering behind the remaining red surplice. "Come forward, Hava—quickly, my dear, nobody is going to harm you. Is this the man?" She pointed to Shree.

Hava ducked her head. Yes.

"Are you sure, Hava?"

Yes again.

Valsoria crossed her arms on her narrow chest. "Very good. You have done well, and I will not forget that. And now you may go back to your bed."

I traded puzzled glances with Shree while the old servant virtually galloped out of the room. Hava was the charringwoman we had talked to in the corridor the previous afternoon, the one who had answered our questions about the staircase and the tower, and I suddenly remembered the strange way her eyes had followed Shree as we were leaving her. But, I thought, Shree had done nothing to her! He had spoken a few words in her hearing, and that was all. With a sick feeling in my heart, I wondered if that was too much.

"Frath Major," the Divinatrix said firmly, "you must give me that man as well."

"Why?" The Frath had moved over to the table and was pouring out generous beakers of the Calloonic wine, one of which he held out to Valsoria.

She waved it away. "He is not a Gilman, Frath Major. He is a Sherkin warlord. Give him to me."

"A Sherkin warlord, indeed? And what makes you think that?" The Frath sipped from his beaker.

"I know it to be so. Hava was serving-woman to a Daughter who was carried across the sea to Sher some years ago, to go whoring in the warcourt. The Daughter never came home, alas, but Hava did, a year before the warcourt became a playground for the fishes, and she is ready to swear—indeed, she has already sworn in the presence of the blessed fire-gods, exalt and feed them—that she recognized this man Selki as one who was a highly placed warlord in the Upper Peerage of Iklankish. Give him to me."

Shree was standing stiffly at attention, watching me. He was obviously learning to recognize the change that came over my face when the golden mist began to form inside my eyes. He had seen it often enough, and he was seeing it now.

"No, Tigrallef," he said quietly. "Don't do it. Keep hold, Tig, keep hold."

At the Frath Major's sign, one of the troopers stationed near Shree stepped forwards and drove his mailed fist into Shree's midsection with sickening force. Shree managed to remain on his feet, though a fine sheen of sweat broke out of his upper lip. A stream of fresh blood welled out of the wound on his chest. The Frath Major moved his hand again and the trooper behind Shree shoved him hard enough to push him off balance. He fell on to one knee, then staggered stubbornly to his feet again. The trooper took him roughly by the crook of his elbow and pulled him forwards.

"He is yours, priestess," said the Frath Major graciously, "and also I abase myself with apologies. Believe me, did I have even the faintest idea that this man was a Sherkin, he would not have set his cursed and filthy foot upon my ship."

"Then it is just as well you did not know." Valsoria viewed Shree with a half-smile on her face. "The blessed fire-gods, praise them, will be glad of the fresh meat. They thank you and I thank you, and now I will leave you to your own business."

She turned to the door. The trooper followed, pushing Shree along ahead of him. I was choked with fear for him. The golden motes gathered; the floor, almost imperceptibly at first, began to vibrate. Valsoria paused with a dreamy look on her face as if savouring the tremor. On the table, the Crosthic crystal wine service crumbled into glittering dust. The air was suddenly heavy with the sharp fragrance of wine. Shree dug his heels in, slewed around and broke from his guard and managed to topple against me.

"No, Tig! Keep hold! *Keep hold!*"

He was still shouting as they dragged him through the door. As for me, my lip was bleeding where I had bitten it through.

No matter—I knew that it would be whole again in a few minutes.

Valsoria nodded curtly to the Frath Major and followed Shree out, trailed by her retainer. At a sign from the Frath, the remaining troopers also went out. This left only Rinn, Han-Frath Zimin, the Frath Major and myself in the room. Of the four of us, only the Frath Major looked happy.

"At last, Scion! I thought the old trollop would never leave. Now where were we?"

37

THE FRATH MAJOR walked all the way around me and surveyed me from every angle. He produced a little vial from his pocket and shook some more of that pungent green powder on to my head. He looked intolerably smug. I sneezed.

"You must know," said the Frath, "that you can still save the miserable life of that Sherkin *fliis* if you follow the rules I set down for you. And get back that Gilwoman if you prefer her to my charming cousin. Or you can have them both, and a thousand others, ten thousand—all the world will be slave to you."

"Except yourself, I imagine. You know, I went through something like this with the Sherank. And I won."

He dipped his finger in the vial and used it to draw something on my forehead. When he stepped back to admire the effect, I felt a cold watchful stirring in the Lady's nest. Han-Frath Zimin, possibly seeing a reflection of this in my eyes, came a pace closer and kept one hand on his sword. The Frath Major waved him back.

"No need, Zimin. Tigrallef, this dust is a small something that your colleague the Bequiin prepared for my use. Wake up, Ardin! The moment is at hand. You must pay attention."

From the corner of my eye, I saw motion in the corner where the Frath's pallet was placed and turned my head to look. At first I saw only a rumpled heap of bedlinen, as if the Frath had already used the pallet that night and had been roused from his sleep. Then there was a groan and the heap turned over; a scrawny arm came into view and was pulled back out of sight under the bedcover. The Frath Major strode to the pallet and jerked the blanket away.

"Wake up, my old friend. Think of posterity. Think of the scholars of the Great Nameless Last who will read the annals of this time and bless your name. Surely your fingers are itching for a pen."

Slowly, painfully, the old man on the pallet raised himself to a sitting position and swung his legs to the floor. It was indeed the Bequiin Ardin, and somebody had used him cruelly since I last saw him. The purple bruise over his eye had been spread all across his face, his nose was broken and bloodied, the grey robe was stiff with dried blood. He cried out weakly when the Frath Major grabbed his robe and hauled him to his feet.

"This moment . . . in history . . ." Ardin gasped, "would be better left . . . unrecorded."

The Frath grimaced and slammed him hard against the wall, then took hold of him again and dragged him to the table and threw him into the chair beside Rinn's. Rinn recoiled from the Bequiin's smell, which reached me a second later— a stink compounded of sweat, blood, vomit and fear. I watched him with pity and horror, but he refused to meet my gaze until the Frath Major took him by the chin and forced him to do so. I have never, neither before nor since, seen such sadness and defeat in a pair of human eyes.

"He has too much shame to look at you, Tigrallef. And he has too much fear to look at me. Ardin, you should not have tried to cross me—you know how I hate it when my creatures forget their master. Remember what became of Han-Frath Mollis? Transh of Siimin? Remember the Tower Fraternity last year, and the Ring-of-Blood Conspiracy the year before that? Do you remember what happened to them?"

Ardin nodded with difficulty, because the Frath was still gripping his chin. I waited, almost with resignation, for the Lady to react to my twin bursts of loathing for the Frath and compassion for the Bequiin—nothing happened but the whisper of a small, sullen voice trailing away into silence: *command me*. The Frath leaned menacingly over Ardin for a few seconds longer, then spat in his face and released him.

He said, "The Honoured Bequiin has disappointed me, Tigrallef—but I suppose I might let him live, for he has tried to make amends. It was he who told me what you planned for this night, and made it easy enough for me to stop you. And this," he lifted the glass vial so we could all enjoy the way the green powder sparkled in the lamplight, "is almost enough to make me forgive him. How do you feel, Scion?"

"Stubborn," I said.

The Frath threw back his head and laughed. "Old Ardin also was stubborn at first. But how do you feel?"

I could not quite figure out what he was driving at. Generally speaking, I felt awful—anxious, defeated, uncertain of the future, puzzled at what the Lady was or was not doing, and at a loss for what to do next myself—but the Frath could see all that without asking. "Could you be more specific?" I said.

The Frath Major was still laughing. "You tell him, Ardin. It will come better from you. Wait, let me first make the Scion more comfortable."

He motioned to Zimin to cut the ropes from my wrists. Zimin looked worried about this and I became very aware as I rubbed the blood back into my aching hands that Zimin's triple-curved sword was hovering in the neighbourhood of my kidneys. The Frath seemed to find this amusing as well.

"Zimin, Zimin, he is unarmed and no warrior anyway—and if there were aught to fear from him, your sword would be useless against it. As well you might sink the *Tasiil* with a kilt-pin as subdue the Harashil with such a toy. Sit you down, Tigrallef, and listen to what the future holds. Now, Ardin."

With one eye on the sword-happy Han-Frath, who did not look all that reassured by the Frath's mockery of my fighting skills, I pulled a chair close to the Bequiin's. Ardin shied away from me, hiding his face.

"*Now*, Ardin."

The ruin of the old scholar lifted his eyes piteously. "Scion, I am . . . so sorry. He had me watched . . . he knew I came to see you . . ."

"And then he beat the truth out of you." I put my hand on

Ardin's shoulder, which made him flinch. "Ardin, believe me, I don't blame you."

"Only a fool would be so forgiving," the Frath said smoothly. "Never mind, we shall have many years together, you and I, and there are many lessons that I shall teach you. Carry on, Ardin."

Ardin's voice was a faint croak. "There is more, Tigrallef. In the Naarhil texts from Cansh Fathan, I found . . ."

He paused. His chin sank on to his chest and his eyes regarded the floor pensively, wide open. I thought he had died in the middle of his sentence, until the Frath roused him with a smart cuff on the ear. Ignoring the Frath, I took Ardin's dry, burning hand in mine.

"What did you find in the Naarhil texts, Ardin?" I asked gently. "You may as well tell me, I promise I'm not angry with you."

He seemed to rally a little. "I found . . . mention of a way to control the power of the Harashil."

"The Wills? But I knew that already—"

"Not the Wills, Tigrallef. The Wills are only for the Naar. Another way."

I digested this in silence while the Frath chuckled again.

"A way," I asked at last, "that would enable, say, my esteemed cousin here, the Frath Major, to control the Harashil?"

He nodded.

"To control me?"

He nodded again; a few tears rolled down his bloody cheeks, turning a watery red by the time they dripped off his chin.

I patted his hand and dropped it gently into his lap, then sat back in my chair with my eyes closed. "Why didn't you tell me this yesterday, Ardin, when there was still time for me to jump off the tower?"

"I am quite sure," the Frath put in, "that the Harashil would have landed you as softly as a feather falling. At any rate, Scion, Ardin did not tell me of this either until a few hours ago, after I persuaded him."

"Is the green dust part of it?"

"The green dust, as you call it, is a potion that binds the Harashil until my control over it is accomplished."

"Is that what it is? It looked to me like crushed wortroot, with a measure of mica flakes thrown in for a bit of sparkle. Do you really think it'll work?"

"The Bequiin will answer to me if it does not," the Frath said softly. "He prepared it for me himself according to a protocol in the Cansh Fathidiic scrolls."

"Ah."

"The weakness you feel," the Frath Major continued, "is from the Naarhil dust, but you must not worry. When you are one with the Harashil and my power is established over you, the dust will no longer be necessary. Anyway, Tigrallef, it is my hope that you will come to relish your part in the Great Nameless Last—I hope that, in time, you and I will become friends as well as master and servant." Smiling benignly, but with cold eyes, he patted my shoulder and turned away. "Ardin! Now is the time."

His back was turned to Rinn, who had been huddled quietly in her chair, slowly regaining her colour, throughout these revelations. At this point, she exploded into action. She aimed a solid kick at the Frath Major with both legs, catching him on the back of his knees so that he buckled, swearing; then, in one fluid movement, she sprang out of her chair, picked it up, and swung it with a sort of vicious enthusiasm at the Frath Major's back. He toppled under it to the floor.

This shocked the rest of us stupid with surprise, but I was the first to recover. While Rinn was still struggling to raise the chair for another blow—after that first magnificent burst of strength she appeared unable to lift it again—I grabbed a handful of crystalline powder from the heap that used to be a matchless Crosthic decanter and threw it like a sparkling cloud into the Han-Frath's face, diving for his sword at the same time. Zimin was thrown off his guard, but he had good instincts and excellent reflexes; I felt the blade slash across my right palm before I caught his wrist with the other hand and wrested the sword from him. Zimin countered with a mighty kick, which missed me since he had been half-blinded by that eyeful of crystal dust and had tears streaming down his cheeks. I brought the sword down in a great swipe that would have disembowelled him if I hadn't missed entirely—and he fell back unhurt, wiping his eyes.

The Frath Major was still under the chair, being systematically kicked by Rinn. The Bequiin Ardin, on the other hand, had not moved; he was staring at the floor again, with that same intense thoughtfulness, looking even deader than before. Shifting the sword to my left hand because the right was slippery with blood, I put an arm around Ardin's shoulders and hoisted him out of the chair.

"Rinn, that's enough! If you're coming, come now!" She didn't even look up. I gathered that the joy and interest of kicking her cousin outweighed the dull prospect of trying to escape. I called her name again, appeared to catch her attention this time, got a firmer grip on the Bequiin's robe and headed for the door.

In the excitement, I hadn't even heard it open. I was now faced with an entire picket fence of shiny swords, a whole row of hostile faces under very unfriendly helmets—the Miisheli guards must have been listening through the key-hole. In my instant of hesitation, the swords flashed and gathered, with cruel wisdom, at the Bequiin Ardin's throat instead of mine. I groaned, and after a moment I tossed Zimin's sword on to the floor.

The Frath Major was a man who learned from his mistakes. Within a few minutes, I was tied securely to one chair and Rinn to another—sporting a large swelling lump above her eye where the Frath had relieved his indignation at being kicked. There was no need to tie Ardin down. I was sure the old scholar was dying. Around the room were ranged all but two of the Miisheli troopers, swords drawn, eyes watchful; the exceptions were on guard outside the door. The Frath Major, limping slightly and fingering tender places on his face, paced back and forth across the floor. He did not look as angry as one would expect.

He stopped in front of me for another sprinkling of the green dust. "By rights, Tigrallef," he said, "you should have been too weak to move—but perhaps Ardin did not make this in the correct strength, or perhaps I had not used enough. How do you feel now?"

I felt normal, if tired and hopeless. "Too weak to move," I said in a faded voice.

"Of course I would not take your word for that," the Frath answered sweetly, checking the knots behind the chair, "but I think we have you secure now. And I have reason to believe that the green dust is effective nonetheless. Did you notice that the Harashil took no part in that little fracas?"

I had noticed, and I was worried. There were no voices in my head at all—I pictured the Lady in a sort of drugged stasis, curled foetally in the corner of some dark room in the back of my mind, waiting for the words that would bring her under the command of this power-hungry lunatic, and me with her. Why hadn't Ardin warned me about this? It didn't quite fit with the prophecy, and for a moment I doubted—but then, with a sinking heart, I remembered how Ardin had placed great importance on me getting as far from the Frath as possible, and realized that he may have been warning me obliquely—but why, why, hadn't he told me more?

I looked at him. He had slipped sideways in his chair so that only the armrest prevented him from toppling to the floor. His eyes flickered open and came to rest on mine; they were serene, almost dreaming. Throughout the next few minutes, while the Frath marked the historic occasion with a formal little speech to the troopers privileged to be there, I found an odd reassurance in Ardin's untroubled gaze.

Suddenly, with a shock, I realized that the words now coming out of the Frath's mouth were words I had used myself, once and only once, and then forgotten, and hearing them again took me back—six years back. I closed my eyes: I was on the lonely sun-baked summit of the Gilgard, with a flat blue sea, silver-dotted at the horizon, stretching away to the east, and a terrible wind was rising in my ears. I turned to look for Shree, who should have been part of this picture, but all I saw was the Lady. She was not far away and her head was tilted critically, masked by lambent hair, as she listened to the measured words falling out of the sky around us.

The Greater Will.

I opened my eyes. Up until then, I hadn't felt the Frath's hands resting on my head, as if in blessing. He spoke the last words of the Greater Will and lifted his hands and moved back, watching me eagerly. For a moment there was complete silence.

Then Ardin moved. He rose from his chair and took a shuffling step towards the Frath Major. And another. He was *dancing*. His eyes were fixed thoughtfully on the floor, but there was a dreamy half-smile on his face, and he was *dancing*. He reached the Frath Major, who was rooted to the spot with horror, and flung his arms around the Frath's waist and pulled him close.

"I lied to you, Liithis," he said. He dropped his head on the Frath Major's chest and held on very tight.

The Frath opened his mouth, but his scream was lost in the rising fury of a great wind. The troopers were open-mouthed, darting wild glances around the room; swords clattered on the floor. The room shuddered—my chair rocked, the troopers were tossed about as if we were back on the *Tasiil* in the greatest stormbowl that ever raged on the face of the Great Known Sea, the crystal dust whirled from the tabletop and danced in the tortured air—but I kept my eyes on the Frath Major, who was as still and solid as a rock in the eye of the storm. Then I heard Rinn shrieking, and realized that the wind was already dying; the floor seemed to ripple a few times, and then became solid. The sudden stillness was a shock.

"*Marrich frath*." That was Zimin, rising from his knees, staring with wonder at the centre of the room. Rinn began to whimper. Ardin and the Frath Major were still locked in their deadly embrace, statue-like, their robes frozen in the act of whipping around them in a vanished wind. The Frath's face was barely recognizable—a mask of terror and agony, hideous, lips drawn back over gritted teeth, eyelids stretched, beads of sweat frozen in the pores. Ardin's face was at peace. I could see his eyes shining under the half-closed lids.

This tableau did not last long. Before I could shout to stop him, Zimin lunged forwards and grasped the Frath's shoulder. The explosion that followed was silent, but it flung Zimin, gasping, back against the wall. When the flash faded, the dust of the Frath Major and the Bequiin was mingled in one grey heap in the middle of the floor.

I gathered my wits, cleared my throat. "I would advise you, Han-Frath Zimin," I growled, "to release me now, before I do the same to you."

38

You lied, Scion.

Where were you? Never mind, I don't want to know.

But it was not you who destroyed this blasphemer, seed of the Excommunicant, it was I. He was trespassing on the preserve of the Naar—

I know, I know. Just keep out of this.

But the Heretrix of Vizzath—

Keep out! Let me concentrate.

The Lady subsided. Back in the outside world, Zimin was hovering halfway between me and the remains of Ardin and the Frath Major, perhaps trying to decide whether to free me or to gut me. I fixed my eyes on him and began to intone, in a low and dangerous voice, some complex mathematical formulae in Old Middle Zelfic. That made his mind up right away.

The Miisheli troopers were looking to Zimin for their cue, but I could feel the fear coming off them like heat off a fired griddle. When Zimin laid his sword at my feet and knelt down before me with his neck bent in submission, they all sighed with relief and hastened to follow his intelligent example. They were accustomed to all kinds and speeds of death, these men, from fast and bloody to slow and ingenious, but the Frath Major's peculiar ending had managed to shake them.

"The Princess Rinn too," I said, when Zimin had finished sawing through my bonds. He moved to Rinn, who was staring slack-jawed at the sad grey mound of dust on the floor. Even when her ropes fell away, she did not move.

"You did that, Tigrallef? *You* did that? You slew my cousin?"

"Sorry."

She looked at me with shining eyes. "You must do the Fraths Minor next, all but Raalis and Honn."

"What?"

"All right, then—Raalis too, I do not care."

"Rinn—"

"And this one as well!" she broke in, glaring at Zimin. "He dared lay hands on me! He bound me to the chair!"

"Rinn—"

"Indeed, all these stinking *fliis* must die—kill them now, Tigrallef, while I watch. And when we get to Cansh Miishel, I shall have prepared a list—"

"Rinn, listen to me. I'm not going to Cansh Miishel."

She stared at me without comprehension. "Of course you shall go to Cansh Miishel. The viper crown—"

"—will look very pretty on you, I'm sure," I finished for her. "Rinn, I will never forget that you tried to help me tonight." She looked confused; in fact, she had probably been trying to help herself, not me, but I was impressed and curiously touched anyway. "I'm going away," I continued, "but I will do everything I can to ensure your safety and that of the *Tasiil* before I go."

"Going away?" she said slowly. "What do you mean? Where would you go?"

"Away," I repeated.

Her eyes narrowed to ominous slits. "It is that woman, yes? The skinny hag with the brat on her shoulder—yes?"

"Please, Rinn, don't make this difficult."

"Difficult! I shall make it impossible. No man leaves me! No man!" She stooped and snatched Zimin's sword from the floor, swinging it up in a clumsy but effective arc that cut a deep swathe across my belly and sliced clean through a rib or two on its way out of my chest. Rinn threw the sword down in triumph.

"Ouch," I said.

Her mouth fell open.

"Han-Frath Zimin," I added, "please tie her up again."

And so, it seemed, I was suddenly in possession of a small private army. I knew exactly what I wanted to do with it. First,

retrieve Shree and Calla and Verolef from Valsoria's custody—without bloodshed, if possible. Second, command the
troopers to escort us and the rest of the Frath's party back to
Vass and outfit a fishing boat from the *Tasiil*'s stores. Third,
send the *Tasiil* in one direction while we sailed off in the
other. At that point, it all seemed so simple.

In small words, I explained Stage One of my wishes to
Zimin. It was gratifying to see, for once in my life, how readily everyone jumped to do my bidding. In moments Zimin
had the troopers formed up and ready to move, with one of
them detailed to sling Rinn over his shoulder and start at once
for the *Tasiil*. Rinn was not happy about this, but there was little she could say through the nose-rag tied around her mouth.
She kicked out at me with her bound feet as she was carried
past—my miracle of shrugging off a potentially fatal stomach
wound had not awed her into submission for very long. I
stopped the trooper carrying her and bent to kiss her cheek.

"Goodbye, darling Rinn," I said. "I wish you happiness,
good fortune and the viper crown as well, if it's what you
want." She made enraged noises and tried her best to bite me
through the gag. Sighing, I watched her carried through the
door; I rather liked her, if only for her spirit, and I knew I
would never see her again.

Zimin was waiting for me by the door, but there was one
tribute I wanted to pay before leaving. As the last troopers
filed out, I knelt and gazed sombrely at the mingled dust of
my enemy and my friend. I picked up a handful and let it run
through my fingers. I felt no grief for Ardin—he had died
well, in the act of atoning for his mistakes, and had brilliantly
avenged his own suffering and death at the same time. And he
had died quickly, with no more pain; I had drawn the obvious
conclusion about his macabre last dance with the Frath Major.

"That was cleverly done, Ardin," I whispered to his ashes.

Then I rose and followed Zimin through the door.

Looking back, I reckon I was in command of my small private army for something under seventeen minutes. As I
stepped into the dark hallway, a sweet-smelling cloth was
clapped over my nose and mouth. The last thing I remember
before the floor slammed into me was a gag-muffled shriek
from Rinn, abruptly cut off.

• • •

I awoke in heaven—memorians' heaven, a cosy lamplit room with scroll-racks to the ceiling on all sides, broken only by a small door at either end. And scrolls, hundreds of them, though I noticed right away that many were in sad condition, and the racks on the far wall were almost empty. I was lying on a threadbare carpet that must have been very grand and gorgeous at one time, perhaps centuries ago, judging by the state of the pile. The battered wooden table a foot away, if repaired and polished, would have done credit to a princely banqueting hall; the two tall-backed chairs were ornately carved with motifs that looked very old and teasingly familiar. As I sat up with a clear but aching head, I remembered the carvings on the doorway leading to the hidden amphitheatre of the Sacellum, and everything fell into place. I was looking at relics of the ancient empire of Vizzath, religiously, if rather ineptly, preserved.

The far door opened; I hoisted myself up with the help of the table and peered through the shadows. Valsoria herself, with a tray in her hands. I grunted with further realization. So this was the secret room, the forbidden sanctum of the Divinatrixes of Vassashinay, and I was surrounded by Naarhil texts of unthinkable antiquity, inherited from ancient Vizzath. Under other circumstances I'd have been hopping with joy and demanding a reading-lantern. These circumstances made me nervous; very, very nervous.

Nodding affably at me but keeping silent, the Divinatrix laid her tray on the table. It held a decanter of rare blue crystal and marvellous workmanship, badly chipped and lacking one of its handles. The two beakers were also beautiful and damaged, and matched neither each other nor the decanter. Stretching to reach the decanter, the Divinatrix poured a good measure of wine into each beaker, then turned and climbed like a small child into one of the high-backed chairs. She had still not uttered a sound. Politely, I passed her one of the beakers.

"You honour me greatly, Divinatrix," I said carefully in my approximated Vassashin.

"I think," she answered in Gillish, "that I am the one who is honoured. Sit down, Prince of Gil and Sathelforn and Miishel."

I stayed on my feet. "Not really of Miishel, Reverend Madam."

"Why not Miishel, my dear?" she said. The mesh of wrinkles that mapped her face moved in a smile of surprising charm. "Why not Miishel and the whole of the known world? Aye, well, and the unknown world also."

"I have no idea what you're talking about," I said primly.

"Have you not? I think you do. Sit down, Scion of Oballef. You and I have a few matters to discuss. And by the bye, there are a dozen armed guards outside the door who will ensure we are not disturbed."

I hesitated and then sat down with a beaker in my hand, reflecting that Valsoria was taking no chances on my good nature (not that I would dream of damaging a dear little old lady who was just over half my height), and also thinking how pleasant it would be if the things she wanted to talk about were the same things I wanted to talk about. The release of Calla and Verolef. Shree's safety. Why she had drugged me to bring me to this room, when all she had to do was invite me— I'd been panting to see it anyway. Valsoria, however, perching on the edge of the chair with her feet dangling just above the floor, had other ideas.

"I am told you are a great scholar of religious practices, Tigrallef. May I call you Tigrallef? Were you impressed with our Oracle, our humble little cult of the fire-gods, may they feed for ever?"

"Oh yes," I said. "Very impressed."

"You don't have to be tactful, child. You were not at all impressed, nor should you have been. You know there's no real magic in Vassashinay—except you."

"Me?"

"Oh yes. I know about the Harashil, my dear, perhaps more than you know." She regarded me quizzically, no doubt watching for signs of surprise or knowingness, so I was careful to look as blank as I could with such a pounding heart. She sighed and went on. "The Harashil, Tigrallef. I know it has been inside you since you broke the glass which your misguided ancestor renamed the Lady in Gil, and it is waiting for you to complete the prophecy."

"Oh, you mean the *Lady*. That's all rumours and folklore, madam," I said cheerfully. "I'm surprised that an experienced fleecer like yourself should take them seriously."

"An experienced fleecer like myself," she said, smiling over the rim of her beaker, "can tell very well when someone is lying. Look around you, Tigrallef."

"Thank you. I already have."

"Look again. The writings in this room have been passed down from Heretrix to Heretrix in an unbroken chain, from the time the Empire of Vizzath fell and the Naar departed these shores, until now. It is a long, long time that we have been waiting for your return, more than two thousand years."

"How very patient of you," I said politely. "I suppose you can read the texts?"

She looked gently wounded. "I can read them."

I stood up and walked over to the nearest scroll-rack and chose a scroll at random. It was thickly covered with dust; as soon as I picked it up, it crumbled away into a multitude of dirty yellow flakes.

The Divinatrix sighed. "Some of them have not been read for many centuries."

"Apparently not." I returned the fragments to the rack and shook the dust from my fingers, clucking my tongue. "There has been something lacking in your order's stewardship of this treasure, madam. Not that I'm complaining—this is nothing to do with me."

"Tigrallef, it is everything to do with you." Again, that charming smile.

I refused to be charmed. My dismay was growing at how much she knew—this priestess was no ordinary provincial milcher. How could I have underestimated her so badly? How could I have shut my ears to the Lady's warnings? I saw suddenly that Valsoria was a dangerous woman, a devious and powerful woman with her own dark magic, rooted in Vassashinay's dark past, and it made her more dangerous than the Frath Major could ever have dreamed of being. A ruthless woman, as well. I thought of the fates she'd ordered for the

Sherkin garrison—I thought of Shree and sensed time dribbling away like the sands of the Pleasure, feeling a terrible
coldness settling in my belly. It was pointless to continue
feigning ignorance; time to take the offensive. I pushed the
coldness away and pulled myself together and looked down at
the Divinatrix severely.

"This is fascinating, Divinatrix, but I'm more interested in
other matters—and if you know about the Harashil, you also
know that it's unwise to displease me and that your weapons
cannot harm me. I demand that you return my people to me at
once and give us safe passage to the harbour."

"Your people?"

"My wife the Princess Rinn, the Miisheli delegation and
their guards, the Satheli envoy and his aides," my throat dried
suddenly, "plus my colleague, the memorian Selki of Gil, and
that Gilwoman who wanted to leave with us. Oh, and her
child." I finished my wine in a gulp and set the beaker down
with a determined click.

Valsoria's small monkey face wrinkled amiably. "You don't
need to worry about your wife and the others from the
Miisheli ship. I sent them down the mountain hours ago; the
ship is afloat again, and they should be on board already,
preparing to set sail, and if they haven't picked up the plague,
they should be quite safe. Your wife was not happy about leaving you behind."

So Rinn was out of my life. I silently wished her well and
forgot her. "And the others?"

"The Sherkin warlord, Carrinay and her child?" Valsoria
furrowed her brow as if she were trying to remember something that would be helpful to me. "Verolef, you mean? Your
child?"

I tried to cover my startlement at the cost of a little dignity,
by stumbling on the edge of the carpet.

She twirled the shaft of the crystal beaker between her
palms. "Your son, the Kalkissann, also called the Scion
Verolef," she went on. "A lovely strong child, you must be
proud of him."

At least an equal nonchalance was called for. I refilled Valsoria's beaker, then my own, and sipped in the style of a wine-

assessor in a tax year. Then I said, "What makes you think he's mine?"

"Why, would you disown him? Tigrallef, how could you?" She looked genuinely shocked. "I'm sure, when you and I have come to an arrangement and you get to know the child, you'll be happy I didn't feed him to the blessed fire-gods."

"What," I repeated through tight teeth, "makes you think he's my son?"

"You drink your wine, my dear, it's not the local fruitpiss, it's imported. And I know Verolef is your son because I was midwife to Carrinay when he was born."

"So?"

"Well—it was not an easy birth. It was hours and hours, and I truly thought poor Carrinay would die before it was done— you men don't know what suffering is, great overgrown children that you are—and when Carrinay was weak and wandering in her mind from the agony, there was one name she called upon, over and over. Yours, Tigrallef."

"Mine?" I sat down, to disguise how weak my knees had gone. "She called for me?"

Valsoria grinned. "Sometimes she called for you, some-times she wept for you, and sometimes she cursed your name—which proved to me that you were the child's father, for I've been midwife at many births through the years, and the father is often reviled at some point as the true cause of all the suffering. Quite right, too. And so, when I heard your name on Carrinay's lips—a name I had already heard in con-nection with the drowning of Sher, and the breakage of a cer-tain piece of antique glass—I knew that this baby was a Scion, a twig of the Naar, the son of the prophesied one; and that someday the Harashil would bring you here to seek its own. And that, Scion, is why I preserved his precious little life."

"Instead of feeding him to the fire-gods."

"Quite."

"To lure me to Vassashinay."

"Absolutely. And here you are."

"And now I'm here," I said, "what do you propose to do about it?"

"We'll have a little talk about that." Valsoria beamed and settled herself comfortably in the oversized chair. "Pour yourself some more wine, Tigrallef. And some more for me, if you'd be so kind."

Valsoria talked for a long time in a pleasant and motherly manner. I heard her out. When she was finished, I said: "No."

She looked pained. "You cannot deny the Harashil in the end. My dear, it's been prophesied."

"Prophecies," I said firmly, trying to sound as if I were quoting some ancient authority, "are made to be broken."

"Not this one."

"Especially this one, And anyway," I could feel myself becoming heated, "do you know what happened to the Frath Major of Miishel when he tried to play the same sort of game? Go take a look in his chamber—that miserable pile of dust *is* the Frath Major."

"I know, child, I was watching through the wall. I didn't give him that room just because it had carpets on the floor."

"And knowing that, you'd still be foolish enough to—"

"Tigrallef," she interrupted gently. "Tell me something. Is the Harashil speaking to you now?"

With a start, I realized that the Lady had been so quiet since I'd wakened in this room that I'd temporarily forgotten she was there. "Yes, she is," I said.

"It, not she. Is that how you see it in your mind? As a woman? I suppose old Oballef's responsible for that. It was a shining serpent to the Naarlings of Vizzath, you know, and a fiery skull in Fathan—and I have good reason, Tigrallef, to think it will take your form next, when the two of you become one. And no, it is not speaking to you now. It is losing patience. You won't hear much more from the Harashil until you're willing to complete the affirmation, and the two indeed become one."

"What makes you think that?"

She tried to look modest, with only middling success. "You see, child, the Frath Major was badly advised by his tame scholar, whereas I—I am the Heretrix of Vizzath. And unlike the Frath Major, I know what I'm doing."

"You'll make a very small pile of dust, Divinatrix."

"Not at all, my dear. I wouldn't dare try to summon or control the Harashil—yet. It cannot be controlled—yet. But to a certain extent, it can be distracted."

I caught my breath. I was starting to think that Valsoria could do precisely what she claimed: that she could force me to meld with the Harashil, and then she could use the resulting entity for her own purposes, which were roughly the same purposes envisioned by the unfortunate Frath Major, except she was better informed. Who could tell what arcane powers, fiendish protocols, potent spells, were laid out in the hundreds of crumbling scrolls around us? If Valsoria could keep the Lady quiet for as long as she had, then she obviously knew a thing or two I didn't.

"You seem very confident," I said.

"I should be, dear child. I spent the last five years seeking out and mastering the necessary texts."

"But how can you be sure you're understanding them correctly? Or that they're not corrupt? The scrolls must be over two thousand years old."

This was said just to needle her, but I could swear a shadow of uncertainty crossed her face. She was still for a moment, then sat forwards abruptly and dribbled a few drops of wine on the floor. "That's for the fire-gods, may they feed for ever—if they exist. Now, we've talked long enough, many people are waiting for us. What is it to be? Will you command the Harashil of your own free will, or do I need to persuade you?"

I sighed, suddenly weary. What, I asked myself, was so attractive about ultimate power, that had these people queuing up to get it? "You can try to persuade me, Divinatrix, but it won't work. No matter what you do to me, I will not complete this prophecy."

"I think you're forgetting the Caveat."

My interest sharpened for a moment. "No, I'm not forgetting it, though I'd appreciate knowing what it warns against. Breaking the glass, perhaps?"

"No, my dear." She slid from her chair and started to patter across the floor, beckoning for me to follow. "It warns against not completing the prophecy."

39

A TEPID DAWN was just breaking when Valsoria and I emerged from the processional door. As we stepped into the courtyard, we were hit by a veritable tide of sound, the roar of a large crowd in an extremity of fear and despair, and I was reminded of my dreams of the drowning of Iklankish. Valsoria and I stopped to listen, Valsoria because she chose to, me because the two large Vassashin scraggers I was fettered between also stopped. Several veiled Daughters were standing nearby.

"Listen to that," said Valsoria, pleased. "I should think they're nearly ready."

The roar faded, dwindling to one faint, clear voice that seemed to be repeating a single phrase over and over again; I strained my ears to catch it, but the crowd quickly picked it up and the massing of so many voices obscured the words.

Valsoria suddenly seemed to be in a hurry. She beckoned to one of the Daughters, who came closer and knelt in front of her. "Is everything in order, child?"

The woman nodded.

"Good. Ten minutes more," said Valsoria, "and then get started. But tell Lorosa she must be firm, there must be no panic."

The Daughter hurried across the courtyard towards the main gate. Valsoria smiled up into my face.

"I must leave you now, Tigrallef, but these two will take care of you. I will see you presently."

She vanished through the processional door. My minders waited for a few moments and then followed, not stopping in the little foyer but pressing directly on through the carven doorway with its burden of ancient glyphs, and down the long hot corridor to the buried amphitheatre. Even before we reached the arched inner portal, I could detect the pungency of masollar in the air.

The amphitheatre, empty of people, was full of an uneasy,

flickering light. Oil-lamps had been placed all around the edges and down the ramps, defining the segments of the fan, dimming the crimson glow from the lava well. Only the plat-form beyond the bridge was still in darkness, as if the light did not dare to penetrate the deeper mysteries of the Sacellum.

The minders, big silent men whose clothing smelled of fish, marched me to the bottom of the ramp and pulled me down between them on to the first tier of benches. We were barely seated when the floor began to shake and a deep rumble rever-berated through the amphitheatre. All three of us were tum-bled to the floor, my head glancing off the stone parapet of the lava well on the way. Through the whirling stars and flashes of coloured light, I could see motes of gold sparking and shift-ing, just starting to coalesce into shimmering clots of a deeper, richer gold. "Are you there?" I whispered. Silence. A moment later, I felt myself being hauled back on to the bench, and the lights faded further into my head.

The mountainquake had loosened my minders' tongues. They sat nervously on either side of me, talking across me in a form of Vassashin so colloquial that I had trouble following it, picking up only the gist of what was said: six dancers in the camp since sundown—Tiv thrown alive into the fire—served him right, the great fat fleecer, for trying to corner the market in greasefish last year—astonishing omens from the fire-gods—clouds of smoke like giants in battle—voices from the vents up the mountain—voices of the blessed dead—Boran's great-aunt Dava, no doubt about it—salvation coming closer—but the outlander who escaped?—never fear, the sea-gods would get him if Sanvil's crew didn't—the Divinatrix—the Kalkissann—

They were interrupted there, which was irritating. My ears had pricked up at the talk of the outlander (Chasco?) and were gaping at the mention of my son, but chanting voices and shuffling feet were becoming audible at the entrance to the amphitheatre. My minders shut their mouths and sat up very stiffly.

I looked behind us and saw red-robed Daughters coming through the portal in double file, singing as they walked; but instead of taking places on the benches, they turned to file along the edges of the amphitheatre until they lined the whole arc of it from one side to the other. After them came a mob of the common people of Vass, who hesitated fearfully on the threshold of this holy place and then spilled down the ramps to fill the benches. I saw Coll take a place two tiers behind me, and behind him Lillifer, the Burgher of Vass, and a few of the worthies who had come to the Sacellum with Rinn's party, but there were far more incomers than could ever have been quartered in the Sacellum. I realized that the gates must have been thrown open to admit the refugees camped outside. Valsoria was wagering everything on one throw of the sticks.

Last of all, when the people, more than a thousand at a rough estimate, were packed into the benches as tightly as the seeds in a pomegranate, three more Daughters came through the portal. The first two, side by side, wore red surplices; the third—my heart thudded to see her—wore a black surplice. Calla! I jumped to my feet and shouted to her over the echoing din of the crowd, but my minders jerked me back and held me down in my seat until I stopped struggling. When the three Daughters came to the bridge, a few feet away, I peered desperately at Calla's hands for any message—but her hands were clasped against her chest, and she averted her veiled face.

They filed across the narrow bridge and vanished into the shadows of the platform. A near-silence fell across the amphitheatre. A few feet shuffled, a few shell ornaments clicked, a sibilant whisper several rows back was instantly hushed. Nothing else, beyond the constant bubbling murmur from the lava pit. The moments stretched; the growing tension of the tight-packed multitude began to express itself as a sweaty stench of fear that almost overwhelmed the insidious masollar. I found myself counting the seconds—if Valsoria was the showwoman I took her for, she'd recognize the proper moment when it came, and it was coming up fast. *Now*, I said to myself, and a broken second later the altar burst into flame.

I nearly applauded. Behind me, a vast chorus of breaths was indrawn with wonder. Valsoria seemed to be floating above the altar, enveloped in a golden cloak and ringed by flickering tongues of fire; she towered above the three dark silhouettes of the surpliced Daughters who were stationed in front of the altar. In her clear, powerful voice, she began to chant in the Naarhil tongue, causing a movement in the back of my brain like something uncoiling from an uneasy sleep. The rhythms of Valsoria's chant were soothing and compelling, almost hypnotic, and I was so preoccupied with those curious uncoilings in my skull, that I almost didn't notice when she broke into Vassashin.

"The evil has lingered," she cried in that oddly penetrating voice. "The towers of the warcourt lie fathoms deep in salt water, and seawrack grows in the gardens of Iklankish, and fishes travel the desert in shoals like the caravans of old, but still the evil lingers. Did you think, Vassashinay, that the weight of so many years could be thrown off so lightly? Did you think that Raksh and his minions could be quenched by the mere waters of the sea? No!"

"No! No! No!" The chorus began to swell behind me, a few voices here and there; a few more; many more.

'Water!' Valsoria cried scornfully. "Water! Such an ancient evil cannot be washed away by water. For how many centuries did the barbed heel of Iklankish grind the face of Vassashinay? For how many centuries did we suffer? How long, how long? And now the evil gods of Sher have returned from the deep with this filthy sickness, to murder us in our own country, to cause us to suffer again—how long, my children, how long?"

She paused and took a deep breath, necessary because she shrieked the next words at the top of her voice.

"Blood, my children! The fire-gods of Vassashinay demand blood! A tide of blood! A tide of blood to sweep Raksh and his plague-demons away on its crest and drown them in the darkest reaches of the furthest hell! Blood! Blood! Blood!"

And so forth. She went on for some time along these lines, apparently blaming the plague on some unexorcised spirits of Iklankish, while I reflected that a great deal of blood had been spilled already, including much Sherkin blood, and where was she going to get enough suitable blood for a tide of the magnitude she described? There weren't that many Sherank left alive in the entire known world, and certainly not in Vassashinay.

Then I felt as if a cold hand had slid its fingers around my heart. She had Calla—half-Sherkint. Shree—half-Sherkin. Verolef—fourth-Sherkin. The blood in their three bodies would hardly fill a decent beer cask, but it was a start. But there was Calla, safe on the platform in performance of her normal duties; and Verolef, surely Verolef was safe, he was the Kalkissann, the Great Saviour, and deeply revered by the Vassashin for some peculiar reason. That left Shree. Did Valsoria have the rhetorical skill to talk one bodyful of blood into a sweeping tide? Of course she did, but that was beside the point. She *wanted* me to save him. And I certainly couldn't save him without calling on the Harashil. Clever Valsoria.

By Fathan, that woman could talk! It took her about ten minutes to get the crowd stirred up into a frenzy of fear, vengefulness and bloodlust—Sherkin blood by preference, of course, but she gave a strong impression once she got going that any old blood would do, so long as it was still warm and spilled in the name of the fire-gods, may they never go hungry. I began to wonder if she had a bit of Vassashin blood in mind, and if she intended to warm the crowd up for the main event by sacrificing a few of its members. There was still no sign of Shree.

I sat quietly between my two minders, letting the hateful clamour of the mob wash over me. I was listening for something else, and finally it came: a small voice, thin and distant but very clear: *command me.*

No.

I saw Valsoria glance down at me, frowning as if she'd overheard and was disappointed, but not really surprised; she looked towards one side of the platform and nodded.

Then the Lady spoke again, and the amphitheatre faded as a picture began to build in front of my eyes: in the distance were the towers of a great white-and-gold city, rising in a broad verdant valley; below me was an expanse of golden cornfields cut by a wide straight road, which flowed like a river with high-piled wagons, fat herds of sheep and cattle, glittering battalions of troopers who sang as they marched. The golden sails of a great fleet shone at the entrance to the city's white, high-moled harbour.

The Great Nameless Last. Command me, man of the Naar, and this is what we shall build.

I sighed. *Very pretty, Harashil. But watch.*

This picture was under my control, and was not so pretty. The white walls and towers of the city darkened to sombre grey. In the cornfields, stubble rotted around a forest of metal spikes; I descended slowly, slowly, so that their glittering points rose to meet me, and I saw that on each spike a sun-blackened body writhed. On the road marched a grim army in black and silver armour, not singing, and the lowering sky was supported on a thousand pillars of smoke. I moved without effort over the blasted fields and across the grim ramparts of the city to the highest of the dark looming towers, into a dark room where a young-old man sat brooding on a high dark throne. He had my face.

This is how it would end, Harashil. I will not command you, because that would give it a beginning.

No answer, and the picture vanished. I was back in the amphitheatre, slightly dazed, trying to focus on a dozen or so Vassashin scraggers as they hustled two vigorously resisting figures out from the side to the centre of the platform. The crowd, which was noisy enough already, exploded with outrage. When my eyes started working well enough again, I understood why.

Sherkin and Sherkint. Clever, clever Valsoria. She'd saved up a complete suit of high-quality Sherkin armour, boots to helmet, and it gleamed as if its wearer were on full-dress parade in front of the Princes of Iklankish and the entire imperial warcourt of Sher. The woman's garb was not quite so grand, but it was very much in the tasteless, overdecorated and lethal Sherkint style, including tier upon tier of metal-sprung flounces and a long-fringed headdress that must have been half the height of the unfortunate female underneath it.

The Sherkin's gauntleted hands were bound behind him, but he managed to shake off the helmet and glare around at the mob, snarling his defiance. Through the blood and bruises on his face, I recognized Shree. His eyes widened as he recognized me in turn; he lunged for the bridge and was pushed back and surrounded by a wall of his captors. "Keep hold,

Tig! Keep hold!" He only stopped shouting when somebody shoved a rag into his mouth. It took four of them to hold him.

Command me.

I shut my eyes, but the pictures I saw there were so fearful that I decided on the whole I preferred the amphitheatre, and opened my eyes again. The Sherkint's headdress was now being removed; the black-surpliced Daughter (whom I silently congratulated on her sudden and very recent promotion) was working away at the system of buckles and straps that held the horrible object on, while the Sherkint—while Calla, that is—held her head high and disdained to struggle; but when the thing was off, Calla struck like a snake to wrench it from the Daughter's hands and raised it high over her head and flung it straight into the lava well—although I'll wager she'd intended it to go further and damage a few heads in the crowd.

Command me.

The mist was gathering; I was powerless to stop it. Frantic, I leapt to my feet and plunged towards the bridge—or the lava well; I forgot I was chained between two heavy and immovable Vassashin until the fetters on my wrists jerked me to a halt. Like a fish on a line, I was hauled back to the bench.

You can save them. Command me.

The Divinatrix was watching me expectantly, Calla was watching me without expression, and Shree was not watching anything at all, because he was sagging in the arms of his captors with a fresh stream of blood pouring down his face. The mountain began to shudder. One after another, the pottery lamps ranged along the edge of the lava well flickered and went out, and then exploded into clouds of dust.

Command me. Affirm the two are one.

The crowd was beginning to notice that the floor was shaking; shrieks of hatred turned to shrieks of terror.

Command me.

For some reason the Lady was now speaking with Valsoria's voice. I raised my eyes wearily to check whether Valsoria was still bodily where she had been before, whatever the evidence of my innermost ears, and saw that Calla had now been pushed forward to the very lip of the lava well. The two Vassashin who were steadying her by her shoulders looked quite capable of pushing her over the brink instead. Her face was contorted with rage and when she caught my eye, she began to shout.

"No, Tig! Give her nothing she wants! Let me die first!"

I groaned and bit my lip, hard, until I felt something wet and warm coursing down my chin. Even so, with a sound like a crack of lightning, the great stone altar split down the middle and collapsed into a heap of smoking rubble. Valsoria teetered and tumbled, arms whirling, through the flames to the floor—landing unhurt but furious beside the ruins of the tall black-painted stool she had been perched upon.

Command me.

"Tig! Keep hold! Don't give in!"

Command me. Affirm the two are one. Command me, Scion, command me—

"No!"

I shouted it, and then I shouted it again, and again, inside my head, outside my head, until the mountain was still and the golden haze had vanished and the Harashil's voice had receded to a distant whisper. I kept on shouting it until one of my guards, at a signal from Valsoria, clouted me on the side of the head. Then, also at Valsoria's beckoning, the two of them hauled me to my feet and dragged me across the bridge to the platform, where Valsoria was waiting with a face like thunder. Shree was nowhere to be seen; Calla, looking straight at me with a proud smile on her lips, was being dragged into the shadows behind the ruined altar. For me, it was too soon to think of smiling—this wasn't over yet. What if they resorted to torturing Shree in front of my eyes? What if they dangled Calla over the edge of the lava well? How could I resist?

The knowledge came to me then, aching and cold: whatever happened, I had to resist. Even if it meant losing Calla; even if it meant losing Shree. Most especially if it meant my own destruction.

The Divinatrix, who was indeed furious and had a minor nosebleed from her fall, seemed to realize this as well. "I had hoped these two would be enough," she hissed, "but you leave me no choice, Tigrallef. I *will* have the Harashil. Over there with him—keep him quiet!"

I was pulled to one edge of the platform, which afforded a far better view of the amphitheatre than I really wanted. The mob was a surging sea of wild eyes and brandished fists, lit like a crowd-scene from a Lucian hell by the surviving oil-lamps. They wanted blood—and I rather hoped that Valsoria would offer them mine, which shows how I was still underestimating her.

Somehow, simply by lifting her arms and starting to talk in a soft persuasive voice, she achieved the impossible—as efficiently as she had whipped the mob into frenzy, she soothed it into silence. And when the only sounds were the incessant bubbling of the lava well and a few muffled sobs from the benches, she threw her arms wide as if to embrace the whole congregation.

"The time has come," she shouted, "for the blessed fire-gods to reclaim the talisman they sent us! Here, my children, is the salvation of Vassashinay! Here is the blood that will drown the demons of Sher!"

I saw them then for the first time, in an alcove on the far edge of the platform, hidden from the crowd: two white-gowned figures, one large, one small. The tall one was bent over the other and seemed to be embracing it; then he seemed to be urging it forwards, out of the alcove. Valsoria beckoned.

My heart froze.

Looking puzzled, but rather interested in these queer adult proceedings, Verolef strolled onto the platform and faced the mob. The sudden tumult appeared to surprise him, but he showed no sign of being afraid. Trustingly, he crossed to Valsoria and took the hand she held out to him.

"Behold the Kalkissann!" Valsoria cried. "Behold the salvation of Vassashinay!"

The mob howled. Verolef watched them calmly, a small frown starting to crease his forehead; but Valsoria turned her head to watch me, and she was grinning.

Command me.

I bowed my head. I had no answer for this.

40

COMMAND ME.

They were holding me flat against the wall, so that I was unable to move or to turn my head. I tried to close my mind, but I could not even force my eyes closed.

Command me.

Dimly, I heard Calla scream—once. Verolef heard her too. I saw his head snap around as he searched for her; he pulled his hand out of Valsoria's. Valsoria smoothed his hair fondly (my teeth ground together) and took his hand again.

I heard him say in Vassashin, "Where's my mother?"

She answered kindly, "Never mind for now. Go with Lorosa, Verolef. You must be a brave little man for me now."

No fool, my son. He looked at her with suspicion. "But where's my mother? Why was she crying? Is someone hurting her?"

"Of course not, darling. We'll find her later. Don't you want to help your dear granna now, my pet?"

"No," he said, with admirable directness. "I want my mother."

"Now, Vero—"

"Let me go! I want my mother!"

He was fighting her grip now. He managed to pull free and made to run around the rubble of the altar, where Calla's scream had come from; Valsoria snapped a command and four scraggers dived for him. He neatly dodged the first, went through the legs of the second, bit the hairy hand of the third as it came within range—his mother's child; but the fourth scragger scooped him up and pinioned the little body tightly in his great hairy arms. The mob hooted with excitement.

Valsoria glanced at me over her shoulder, as if to say: *you can stop this happening, any moment you choose*. Out loud, she said, "Bring the brat to me. And hold him." And when Verolef was set on his feet beside her, with the scragger's arm still locked around his little chest, Valsoria smiled and said in a gentle voice, too low to carry to the crowd on the other side of the lava pit, "You were right, Vero, someone is hurting your mother. And we will have to hurt you too, unless that man over there" (she pointed at me) "does what I tell him to do."

Vero's first look at his own natural father was dark with reproof. "Why won't he?"

"Because he's wicked and stubborn and he doesn't care about you," she answered evenly, "and it will be his fault if anything bad happens to you or your mother. Do you understand, Vero?"

He looked dubious. I could feel my control snapping, string by string, like a harp in the dry air of some scorching desert.

"She's lying, Verolef," I said quietly.

"I know that."

That surprised Valsoria as much as it surprised me. She raised her open hand as if to strike him on the cheek—and checked herself when the mountain started to tremble again, an ominous thunder heard through the soles of our feet, and started back sharply when a dusting of golden light began to flicker into existence in the air around us. This was a sight I was accustomed to having all to myself, so it was a shock to realize that, this time, others were seeing it too. Verolef watched it with wonder, his lips apart. The Vassashin on the platform were unnerved by it, and murmured fearfully, but gasps and ooohs of appreciation came from beyond the lava pit, where the crowd seemed to be under the impression that this was another of Valsoria's famous effects, or even an actual effulgence of the blessed fire-gods, may they for ever go hungry and be not in the least exalted.

Valsoria surveyed me anxiously for a broken moment, as if she and I had taken a wrong turning in the dark labyrinth of events we were treading together. Then she pulled her shoulders up and became urgent and brisk and businesslike again, summoning the red-surpliced Daughters to her side with a quick gesture.

"Hurry now—take the child—and the Sherkin warlord, and that ungrateful traitress Carrinay. Quickly! Quickly!"

One of the women lifted Verolef and carried him past the smoking wreck of the altar, followed by the other. The child went with them peaceably, watching the gathering golden mist with rapt eyes over the Daughter's red-surpliced shoulder, glancing once at me with not much interest.

The great doors opened. I saw Shree and Calla, both of them limp and bleeding, tossed like sacks into the darkness. I saw Verolef pushed inside, gently but firmly, a lonely little figure in white with his back to us; but as the doors swung shut, he turned and looked straight at me. His mouth was turned down with what looked like disapproval. Then the doors hid him.

Meantime, the Divinatrix had flung her arms wide and was again addressing her congregation. Blood. Sacrifice. Deliverance. The words punched their way through the thickening mist and the mindless bloodlusting roar of the crowd.

I bellowed at them myself, trying to drown out Valsoria's notable voice. "She's using you, you idiots! She doesn't give a snap of the fingers for you, or for the plague! She won't care if you all dance yourselves to death, if only she can get what she wants. Murdering the Kalkissann is not going to save you. Don't listen to her . . ."

I stopped when it became apparent no one was listening to me. Valsoria came closer and laughed up at me. "It won't work, Scion, there's only one way you can save the child and the others, if they're still alive, and you know what that way is."

"And if I refuse?"

"Then your son will suffocate along with his mother, in torment and terror. But don't imagine it will end there, for you'll still be in my hands—and, you know, Tigrallef, this plague really is a tremendous stroke of luck. It seems to me that just now I could order any number of sacrifices to the fire-gods and the people wouldn't think of protesting."

I glared down at her, repelled, wondering how many murders she was prepared to commit in order to shape my will to hers. And this was the woman who wanted to rule the Great Nameless Last, to have the power of life and death over all the known world! I closed my eyes to shut out the hateful sight of her face, while my rage and fear swelled and the mountain trembled. I expected to see the Harashil. Instead, I saw Verolef.

Although he was groping about in what was utter darkness

to him, I could see him as clearly as if daylight had pierced the solid flank of the mountainside. There were tears on his cheeks, but I think they were as much from outraged feelings as from fear. He was already coughing. He stumbled on the edge of Calla's now-tattered Sherkint finery, followed it to her body, groped along her body until he found her face, flung himself down on his knees beside her.

"Mother?"

He shook her shoulder pleadingly, then broke off for a fit of coughing so severe I thought his chest would fly apart.

"Mother?"

Calla didn't move, and I wondered with a sorrowing detachment if she were already dead, and Shree also. I could see Verolef was starting to feel the effects of the poisonous vapours; he paused to brush at something invisible on his face, batted at the air, focused on nothingness in the darkness across the chamber and uttered a short sharp cry of defiance. "Go away! Make it go away! Mother!" He threw himself down beside her on the floor and burrowed against her, trembling. His next fit of coughing shook them both.

Command me.

I opened my eyes. There was still that odious confident smile on Valsoria's lips, but I saw shadows moving in the depths of her eyes. Shadows of fear, phantoms of doubt. "Do it now, Scion, before the child dies. Affirm the two are one. The prophecy—"

"The prophecy," I interrupted, in a voice that was strange and sonorous even to myself, "goes beyond anything your mind could encompass, Divinatrix."

"Indeed?" She drew herself up, still smiling, and hurled a few words at me in the old Naarhil tongue, with an air of doing something decisive and unanswerable. I cocked my head, listening; these words meant nothing to me. They glanced off my ears like a hail of spent arrows.

"Divinatrix, is something supposed to happen?"

Valsoria's smile faltered. Shrilly, she cried out the Naarhil phrases again, varying the emphasis. I shook my head at her. Whatever key she was holding, she was trying it in the wrong lock.

"Perhaps," I said to her, "you should have taken better care of those scrolls of yours. Or maybe you should have read the surviving portions more cautiously. What do you think?"

She stared up into my eyes—I have no idea what she saw there, that leached the colour from her face. The next moment she screeched and seized a knife from the scragger beside her, driving it towards my belly. It shivered in her hands into a small cloud of metallic dust.

Command me.

A man's voice now, rather familiar, but I couldn't quite place it until I saw him standing just behind Valsoria. A slightly built young man with a plain pleasant face, mine as it happened, and a scholarly curve to his back and shoulders, as if he spent too much of his time curled around a book or bent over a writing table; the odd part was, he was at least twelve feet tall, and he shone. He stepped forwards as Valsoria backed away from me, her hands in front of her like a shield—for a moment I saw her body outlined within his, and then she was behind him, though I could still see her, as if he were an image reflected on a sheet of crystal glass. Nobody else seemed to notice him.

"We've gone that far already, have we?" I said out loud.

The Harashil nodded and spread its hands in one of my own most characteristic gestures. *Command me. The two are one.*

"Almost," I said. "Almost. Wait."

Think of the physically impossible: a paper-thin surface of black ice, smooth, level, featureless, scumming the top of a bubbling, surging, seething cauldron of boiling water. That was myself. And the ice was melting.

From behind the great double doors, a thin wailing rose and fell, rose again and held for a moment; faded away. That was Verolef. And he was suffering.

I suppose, in the end, Verolef was the raindrop that burst the dam. There was more to it than that, however, much more. I felt at that moment, as never before, the crushing, numbing, tragic, soul-blasting inevitability of it all—as the Harashil had once said, deep on the drowned streets of Iklankish, if you fulfilled a prophecy then willy-nilly you had to live with the consequences; and so, I gathered, did the rest of the world. I took a shallow breath and began.

"The two—"

Another wail from the oracle chamber, the pitiful cry of a child who is discovering that monsters are both real and present. The mob echoed him lustily. There was even some laughter.

"—are—"

Valsoria was still doggedly trying to get me killed. Her voice was shrill, her servants were backing away from me, except for the two who were pinning me to the wall. The mountain was still: primed, suspended, waiting. Verolef wept again.

"—one."

We were confounded at first by this double vision: a dizzying view down a long black spangled sweep of space, no beginning, no centre, no end, and at the same time a narrow cone of sight through holes in a box of bone, with a familiar but oddly limited feel to it, not unpleasant, decidedly small.

Then we began to swell with new sensation—on the one hand with blood surgings and breath takings and the smooth push-pull of muscles and the many but not numberless beatings of a heart, on the other hand with a surfeit of days, years, centuries, millennia, backwards and forwards, no beginning, no centre, no end. And then all we wanted to do was to sit down quietly somewhere and put our head in our hands and get used to it all; but when we remembered to look, we saw we were not alone.

Such paltry creatures.

Swarming and screaming, slopping back and forth like maggots in muddy water in a shallow dirty bowl we were tilting in our hand. Bleating meaningless noises, bleeding meaningless blood, thinking meaningless thoughts that scattered in the air like ashes whipped by the wind, ephemeral, trivial, nothing. They were nothing.

Except one.

Yes, we thought, yes, there was something here that was important, some duty we had to carry out. We rubbed our hand against our forehead, trying to remember through all this spinning welter of newness. Among these paltry creatures there was one who had to be saved, for a very good reason which we could not quite recall at this confusing moment, except it had to do with the terms and settlements of that long, ages-long, contract between the Harashil and the race of the Naar, though we were neither Naar nor Harashil now, but something more, and something much stranger.

We remembered. A child of the Naar lineage was in danger, dying—he was behind that eggshell of a stone wall. Very easy. *Very* easy. We found a fist at the end of an arm—ours, presumably, though we half-thought we might be seeing it from this angle for the very first time—and smashed it through the eggshell wall and the doors as insubstantial as mothwings, and plucked out the Naarling child, who felt warm, which pleased us, because we seemed to remember that this was a satisfactory state of body.

Our own body was becoming easier to use now. We flexed our fingers and brushed the tips of them lightly over the Naarling child's face. He stirred in our arms, which was also good. We had protected our own. We could leave now—there was so much to do, an empire to build, a prophecy to fulfill, a destiny to consummate. But first—

We looked around in distaste. Noisy, smelly not-Naar vermin infested this place; we remembered these vermin had dared to threaten a child of the Naar, had cried out for his blood and exulted in his terror, and thereby had become fully deserving of what we were about to do to them. We held up our hand. Deep within the earth, far beneath the roots of the mountain, many new rivers of liquid fire began to meander towards the surface.

A stream of not-Naar creatures was struggling to escape this bubble in the rock; we could have dammed it, but we let it flow out through the archway unhindered, except by its own panic. Inside the mountain, outside the mountain, it made no difference. The liquid fires would shortly boil up through vents in the rock and rain from the sky; there would be no escape for these creatures, not for any of them. The Naarling child's distress would be paid for in kind.

There was one who was not trying to escape. Valsoria—the name sprang into our mind surrounded by an aura of special distaste. *She had hurt the Naarling child*. She was cowering across the platform, trying to press herself into the solid stone, her mouth still gabbling words that were almost right but completely and offensively wrong, words that scratched without effect at the smooth glassy carapace of our will.

We stretched out a hand as far as necessary and encircled her waist with our fingers and brought her close to our face. She fell silent for a moment, staring up at us; and then she began to speak again, slowly and clearly. Correctly.

We felt unease. This was not a Will—she was no longer trying to command us. She was trying to save herself. We knew these words well, though we had never heard them spoken. They were our banishment, our death, our annihilation, wrapped up in five short Naarhil quatrains.

She befouled these words by speaking them with her unclean not-Naar mouth, but their power still fell about our shoulders like loops of finespun steel, constraining us, tightening around us; our rising fear of her pushed us to our knees.

She tasted our dread. Her voice grew stronger.

The words spun around us—spun a net, burnished gold, blinding silver, ice-blue steel. Slowly, relentlessly, it settled over us. The second quatrain. The third. The end was approaching, the substance bleeding from us; she began the fourth quatrain—the fifth would finish us. We bellowed with rage and fear.

Triumphantly, at the top of her voice, Valsoria began the fifth quatrain.

And in one corner of the net, a break appeared in the whirling metallic pattern of the colours; we watched it grow. Muddy brown, lichenous green: soft rotten strands that drooped and tore and parted under their own sodden weight— Valsoria had not yet noticed her mistake. The contagion spread from strand to strand, nexus to nexus. The net rotted away. We lifted our head.

Valsoria faltered into silence.

"Almost," we said, and our voice shook the mountain. "Almost, but not quite." Then we squeezed; and when she was empty, we took the loathsome shreds of her and tossed them into the convenient cauldron of boiling rock that separated us from the seething main herd of not-Naar creatures, and watched her fizzle into smoke and steam.

Thus ended the long, patient and somewhat dangerous lineage of the Divinatrixes of Vassashinay. We forgot her at once.

We had an empire to build.

41

THE PLATFORM WAS empty now except for us and the child; across the cauldron, the nearest tiers of benches were also empty. Screeching masses of the not-Naar were piling up against the far portal, clawing and trampling, fighting each other to get out. Only one head moved against the tide. We focused on that one, out of curiosity and to pass the time until our molten rivers arrived to wash these vermin away. We saw him reach the edge of the seething mass around the portal and push his way into the open, and half-run, half-tumble down the ramp to the foot of the slim stone arch that spanned the boiling cauldron. He was shouting, but our curiosity was not so great yet that we troubled ourself to understand.

He began to cross the bridge, hands and knees clinging to the narrow stone span as the mountain tossed back and forth. We watched with idle interest to see if he would make it across, and once it seemed he wouldn't, lurching sideways until half of him overhung the hungry lava as it extended its hot fingers up to him—but he scrabbled himself back into balance and slid along the bridge on his belly until he collapsed safely on the floor of the platform, almost at our feet.

"Tigrallef, stop it! Stop it! Remember who you are!" He staggered to his feet and grabbed our shoulders and shook us; he shouted into our face.

We were more than a little surprised. How odd this behaviour was! Odd enough so that we thought we'd refrain from pulping him where he stood, for a few moments anyway. He was no danger to us and we wanted to see what he'd do next.

He seemed to grow weary of shouting. He glanced around

wildly and stumbled to the hole we'd made in the eggshell wall, the ruin we'd made of the double doors and disappeared into the darkness. A moment later he reappeared dragging something—another of the not-Naar creatures, this one a woman with a bluish face, possibly dead. Then another, a man. The madman from across the bridge shifted frantically from one to the other, slapping their faces and breathing into their mouths, pausing now and then to shout at me some more.

Me?

"Tigrallef! Remember who you are! Try to remember! Tigrallef, help me."

Strange stirrings of familiarity. His name was Chasco, and I—we—knew him from somewhere. The name Tigrallef plucked a string in our memory as well, and though part of us sternly disapproved, the other part insisted on turning the sound over and over, examining its worn edges and its many nicks and scratches until we—I—began to remember. Tigrallef was our name. No. Tigrallef was *my* name.

The other man's name was Shree. The woman was called Calla.

We crossed the platform in a stride. The three figures sprawled there seemed at the same time to be seen from close up and from a point far above the floor, as if we couldn't quite decide how tall we were. We watched them tumble sideways as the mountain shuddered. Our streams of vengeance were very close now, we could sense the heat of them building up under the stone floor, feel the mountain's agony as it strove to accommodate a dozen raging torrents in a few narrow fumaroles. We felt a surprising twinge of regret that these three would die with the others, but they were not-Naar, and we could see no reason to protect them, even if we did know their names.

"My lord Tigrallef—stop! Remember Sher! Remember Sher!"

Sher? Of course we remembered Sher. Clearly. We had destroyed Sher by water, as we had destroyed Itsant and Baul; whereas Fathan we had destroyed by fire, and Khamanthana, and Myr, and Nkalvi, and Vizzath once before, as we would now destroy this upstart shadow of Vizzath by fire. Why should we remember Sher in particular?

But part of us was trying very hard to remember. Part of us had stumbled on to a hard little kernel of guilt and revulsion, and was encouraging it to grow. The anguished not-Naar screaming echoed off the high shadowed ceiling of the amphitheatre, and also off a great green slab of water that overhung a terrified city; the sea boiled over Iklankish. We remembered.

So many deaths.

Not-Naar deaths.

But so many.

Yes indeed. And more blood today.

Perhaps . . .

A great white-hot gout of magma spewed from the pit, splashed the ceiling, pattered down again as a lethal shower of rain. The bridge was gone. Chasco glanced at the disappearance of this escape route and shrugged. He went back to breathing into Shree's mouth and was rewarded suddenly by a cough and a feeble stirring. Shree tried to sit up but fell back again, gasping, staring at Chasco. Then he reached up and grabbed Chasco's throat. He didn't seem to notice us, nor the rumbling of the ground.

"Bastard," he croaked. "Tig and I saw you sail off without us?"

Chasco easily brushed his hand away. "I ran into trouble—too many people wanted that boat. There was a mob waiting for me on the beach in Tig's cove, so I found a safer mooring, and came back to fetch you."

We continued to watch and listen, finding this exchange curiously gripping.

Shree stared at Chasco a little longer, then collapsed again with his eyes closed. His skin was pale, like parchment. "Of course you came back, because here you are. I thought—never mind what I thought. But Tig had more faith. I was ready to kill you." He paused, still with his eyes closed. "Where is Tig?"

Chasco shot a desperate glance over his shoulder at us—me—and said nothing. We said nothing either. Shree groaned and put his arm over his eyes, and after a moment he said, "What about Calla?"

"I was too late for her. I think she's dead."

Dead, dead, dead. The word drummed against the walls. At

that point, we lost interest in Shree and Chasco's conversation. We were distressed.

I was distressed.

No!

But she is not-Naar.

No!

She means nothing.

No!

Dead, dead, dead. So many deaths.

"No," I whispered.

Yes. Sher by water, Vizzath by fire. More blood today, and tomorrow we begin the Great Nameless Last.

"No! No! No more!"

Suddenly the first massive surge of molten rock tested the roots of the mountain; in the dire agitation of the ground, a score or more of the mob that still clamoured around the archway lost their footing and tumbled down the ramps, some almost to the lip of the lava pit. One unfortunate woman hit the parapet hard enough to be bounced over it and dropped shrieking towards the liquid fire. Without thinking I shot my hand out, a long long way, and caught her well above the bubbling surface; and lifted her back over the parapet, and gently deposited her, still breathing, midway up the ramp.

We protested: *Not-Naar.* But our chief sensation was glad surprise—it seemed the power and the will could war with each other, and the will had at least an even chance of winning if it took the power by surprise. Struck by this, and ignoring many internal impulses, we dropped to our knees and laid the Naarling child tenderly on the floor beside his mother.

Again that double vision. We hung right over Calla, a few inches above her, and saw her still as a small crumpled figure far below us. With an effort, I forced the nearer vision. It was damnably difficult to maintain. I heard Shree's exclamation, felt Chasco's hand on my shoulder.

"Tigrallef?"

"For the moment. I don't know for how long."

I raised Calla in my arms and was flooded with relief. She looked dead, but my acute new senses told me she was still alive, barely, her heart just remembering to beat and her breath hardly stirring the flakes of dried blood that clung to her lips. Certainly she was beyond human help. I breathed an old, old word into her mouth—she stirred and opened her eyes, which was good, but that exercise of power shifted the balance, and suddenly we were confused and immensely tall again, groping for a name to hold on to.

"Tig?" she whispered.

I cradled her in my arms. She sat up and threw her arms around my neck, and just as suddenly pushed me away.

"Vero—where's Vero?"

"He's safe. He's beside you."

Indeed, Verolef crawled into Calla's lap at that moment and nestled between us. I rocked them both, keeping my eyes open—when I closed them, the name was harder to cling to.

"My lord, we can't stay here." Chasco was helping Shree to his feet. I pulled my eyes away from Calla and Verolef and looked around the cavern.

The walls were strange—vibrating, blurred like a hummingbird's wings, so intense were the forces building up beneath the mountain. I knew what Chasco didn't know: that Verolef and I, Naarlings both, were immune to any danger unleashed by the ancient entity who encompassed me. Further, I could protect whomsoever I pleased. All five of us could safely watch the destruction of Vassashinay from this excellent vantage point, watch the people flame like torches and the mountain melt around us and run hissing into the sea. This was our vengeance. We were in command. (The floor began to fall away.) We were the prophesied union of Harashil and the ancient race of the Naar; we could do anything we willed. We—

"Tig?" whispered Calla.

I held her closer. Deep within me, from that kernel of guilt and revulsion that clung to its own name, a small voice spoke. My voice. *Remember the Caveat.* This was not a threat, nor was it a warning. It was a rope thrown to the drowning.

Remember the Caveat.
Remember Valsoria.

That was all I needed to know.

I, Tigrallef, pushed Calla and Verolef gently off my lap and stood up—to my usual height.

My skull was a battleground; the movement of any muscle, a skirmish; the raising of my hands, a victory after bitter fighting. And that was even before the Harashil answered my challenge.

We faced each other across a narrow strip of ground on the summit of the Gilgard, with the sun baking the sparse grass under our feet and glaring into our eyes off the hard silver wastes of the sea. Then again, the seawrack rose around us on the streets of Iklankish, and the half-built omphaloi of old Vizzath, the grim iron ramparts of Fathan, the domes of Baul, the truncated pyramids of Khamanthana and the glass-lined pits of Myr, broken by ten thousand circular portals. The Great Nameless First was only a shadow, a shadow I did not dare to penetrate.

"We cannot do this," the Harashil said.

"Watch us," I said.

"But the two are one. We are one."

"That could well be true. But *I* am Tigrallef."

It winced, and I repeated the name like a spell. For a moment the Harashil seemed to be shrinking, and I was suspicious at the ease of my victory—rightly so.

Suddenly, the Harashil drew itself up to twice my height. Command radiated from it and washed over me, an inexorable will that demanded I submerge myself in it again, become one again, this time for ever. It held its hands out to me and I felt myself helplessly mirroring the gesture—but just before our fingertips touched irretrievably, I clenched my fists and slowly, with terrible pain, pulled them back to my side. The Harashil's face darkened with fury and bafflement.

It said: "We shall carry out that which was ordained. We have no choice."

"There must be a choice—or why would the Oldest Ones have written a Caveat? If there was never any chance of defying the prophecy, why set a penalty for doing so? I'm right, aren't I?"

It answered reluctantly. "In part."

"We do have a choice?"

Even more grudgingly, as if it were extracting its own fingernails at my request: "Yes."

"Then tell me. You said when our day came, you would tell me about the Caveat. This feels like our day."

It hesitated. "There is no advantage for you in this. You can delay, yes. You can even dominate. You can bend my power to your will, against my will—for a time. But during that time, you shall suffer."

"That's nothing new. I can live with that."

It moved closer. Our faces were on a level now, and its eyes, ringed by copies of my own rather short eyelashes, were dark and fathomless chasms.

"You shall suffer from *me*, Scion. I shall not leave you, not ever. I shall goad you and torment you. I shall be the stone in your shoe and the sand in your bread—"

"The lump in my mattress? The bit of gristle between my teeth?"

"—the taste of ashes in your mouth, the black dreams that haunt you in every hour of darkness," it finished sourly, ignoring the interruption. "You shall strive with me, Seed of the Excommunicant, in every moment of every day, waking and sleeping, and in the end you shall go mad—you shall become all things in the world that you most loathe and fear, a cruel god. Vicious. Heartless. Mad. All these things you shall become, and worse."

My mouth became very dry. The sun beat down on my head, the ooze drifted around my feet.

"And then?"

"And then we shall still build the Great Nameless Last, you and I, and someday bring the world to its ordained end; but there shall be no age of glory first, no shining city set for a time in green fields—the Great Nameless Last shall be built out of your madness, and shall be terrible beyond any imagining. Consider that well, Seed of the Excommunicant."

Duly, I considered it well. This was not the kind of threat for which I was prepared. This was far more disturbing.

"Surely it is better," the Harashil added, more kindly, "to give the world a few centuries in the light before we bring the great darkness down. Build with me now."

It moved closer. It smiled at me, a shape that sat strangely on those copies of my own lips, since I never smiled in that way myself.

I smiled back. *Remember the Caveat. Remember Valsoria.* The end did not have to happen as the Harashil said. The game was *not* over. I still had a stick tucked up my sleeve, ready to throw on the pile.

"You know," I said casually, "it occurs to me that Valsoria nearly succeeded in banishing us."

The Harashil recoiled.

"I can delay, you say. That's good, that's very good—if I can stay sane long enough, I can still defeat you and the prophecy, not to mention the tupping Oldest Ones."

Even as I spoke, the Harashil began to swell. The golden mist welled out from the pores of its skin, and it reached for me again, urging me with grim desperation to lift my hands to meet its hands. The pull was strong and terrible. Its eyes expanded into great golden wells . . .

And I *wanted* to fold myself into it again, to lose myself in the grandeur and rightness of being prophesied and powerful, the ripener and the builder and the destroyer, the trunk of the great tree. I *wanted* to build my empire. Why risk madness and horror if the outcome would be the same in the end—except worse? Better to yield now, to merge and to build, to rule in the light for a time and then accept the descent into darkness as the specified way of things . . .

"No."

Biting my lip, fighting, remembering Sher, using guilt and revulsion and sheer stupid obstinacy as the only strengths left to me, I managed to keep my fists at my sides. The Harashil roared and I willed it to be silent, and somewhat to my surprise, it did. Then it lunged at me and I willed it to pull back, and it did that too. Then it tilted its great shining head on one side and waited for me to speak. I had the words all ready.

"Listen to me," I said. "I will find the spell of banishment. I know it exists, because Valsoria had a corrupt version of it. I know it can work, because I felt your fear. And I will find it. Even if the road leads me through every pit you ever dug in the last ten thousand years, and takes a hundred lifetimes to follow to its end, I will find that spell. And when I find it, I will finish you."

It loomed over me. "At the risk of destroying yourself?"

"Yes, if that's how it happens. Someday we'll see."

The Harashil nodded. "Then you have made our choice—for now. So be it—for now."

It bowed its head, waiting. The battle was over—for now. The war was another matter. I lifted my hands and stretched them out. With an air of resignation, the Harashil mirrored my action. Its hands fell to meet mine. Our fingers touched.

I awoke to screams and thunder and searing heat. A hideous tiredness dragged at every muscle. It was as much as I could do to lift my head and instruct the mountain, in whispers, to behave itself; to order the magma to freeze in the fumaroles and the fiery rivers to cease flowing and the ground to be still. As an afterthought, I suppose to make amends, I banished the plague from Vassashinay. After that I swore to myself, on the head of Verolef my son, that I would never use the power of the Harashil again; and then I fell asleep on my feet for a while, or I think I did, because the screams and thunder grew instead of diminishing, and revolting shadows stalked me just beyond the edges of my eyes.

I have no memory of the dark backway that linked the platform with secret chambers of the Sacellum, nor the maze of corridors that brought us to the open air, nor the treacherous overgrown path that led us down to the cove where Chasco had moored the lorsk. Calla told me later that I carried her most of the way, but I don't recall that either. When I opened my eyes again, we were already sprawled on warm deckboards under real sunshine, and the only visible remnants of the doom that almost befell Vassashinay were a few tatters of black cloud drifting above the mountaintop and dispersing in the wind off the sea. I groaned and sat up, holding my head.

Calla was curled up beside me. Shree was lying against the deckhouse nearby with his eyes closed, pale and bloody but breathing well, and beside him Verolef was apparently attempting to fall over the gunwale headfirst. I reached over and grabbed the seat of Vero's robe and hauled him back to safety.

"I saw some fishes," he announced. "I'm going to catch some."

"Good," I said, "but I think you'd better do it from inside the boat."

He considered this and nodded. Then he was up and off like a small dust-devil to midships to help, or hamper, Chasco in hauling the foresail up the mast. A few moments later I heard the clatter of little feet down the companionway to the cabin below.

"It's all new to him," Calla said weakly. She struggled to sit up. I helped her over to the gunwale and propped her against it, and sat down beside her with my arm around her shoulders. Something crashed below deck. "He'll settle down," Calla added.

"I hope so," I said dubiously. "I think I can manage the Harashil, but I'm not so sure about Verolef."

"Don't worry. Just be grateful he seems to have forgotten already—what happened to him in the Sacellum." She pivoted her head on my shoulder, to frown up at me. "What did happen in the Sacellum? What's the Harashil? And what about the Lady? How did you—?"

I put my hand over her mouth. "I'll tell you everything, but not just yet. I have to think of the right words first."

I found myself staring at my hand. It was still made of flesh and bone, but it was numinous with power now, and I thought with foreboding of the years of labour ahead of me: labour to keep that hand its proper shape and size, to limit its actions to fleshly ones, to keep the Harashil subdued while I sought out the means to banish it for ever. I could feel the Harashil now, patiently inside my skin, as much a part of me as my heart and lungs and that hand of flesh and bone.

"Calla? I need something from you."

"Anything."

"I need you," I said, "to keep me sane."

She nodded soberly. In that instant, she guessed everything there was to know.

We sat there quietly together for a few moments longer, hand in hand; and then I left her tending to Shree while I helped Chasco to raise the heavy mainsail and headed the lorsk out to sea.